CHRISTOPHER MORLOCK's

STRIKING OUT

THE CHRONICLE OF CALVIN CONNOR.
Striking Out (2016)
Foul Territory (2024)

STRIKING OUT

THE CHRONICLE OF CALVIN CONNOR,
VOL. 1.

CHRISTOPHER MORLOCK

The Foul Territory Publishing Co.
Pennsylvania, United States of America
www.foulterritory.com

Colophon

NOTICE: do not attempt any stunts or activities portrayed in this novel. The author and publisher are not responsible for your actions or any resultant consequences of your actions.

Tip of the Whalers cap to G.V.B. Jr.
Sorry, Mr. Bachner didn't make the final cut!

7 8 9 10 11 12 13 14
Second Foul Territory Publishing edition, February 2024.
ISBN-10: 0997180803
ISBN-13: 978-0997180800
e-book ISBN-10: 0997180811
e-book ISBN-13: 978-0997180817
Also available as an audiobook narrated by B.J. Harrison.

For Rob.

Contents

No A.I. was used in the creation of this novel.
It is, in its entirety, the product of a human being.

Dramatis Personae

TROOP 666
AXSUBEEN, PENNSYLVANIA.

Oldroyd/Dick'll—Troopmaster Richard Oldroyd, 38.
Mr. Maguire—Assistant Troopmaster Paul Maguire, 40.
Inky—Junior Troopmaster Konrad Schultz IV, 16.
Father—Junior Chaplain Matthew Duffy, 17.

THE BEAVER SQUAD
Art—Captain Arthur Maguire, 14 (Mr. Maguire's son).
Sandy—Lieutenant Anthony Sandmiller Jr., 15.
Spazz—Billy Watson, 15.
Chicken—Cuauhtémoc Ysderrhi, 15.
Denny—Dennis Sandmiller, 13.

THE HAWK SQUAD
Zedz—Captain Sammy Dzedzy, 15.
Calvin—Lieutenant Calvin Connor III, 14.
Jon—Jonathan Oldroyd, 15 (Oldroyd's son).
Ryan—Ryan Phillips, 14.
Gus—Augustus Jacoby, 13.
Crowe—Shawn Crowe, 12.

CAMP SOUVIENS RESERVATION
GROTON, CONNECTICUT.

Mr. Grant—Camp Ranger Richard Grant, 59.
Kermit/Murph—Camp Director Jake Murphy, 43.
Satan—Deputy Camp Director Horace Lyons, 36.
She of No Fixed Name—Camp Dishwasher, 15.

Chapter 1

CALVIN TAKES THE HILL.
SUNDAY, JULY 26, 1987.

THE CHRONICLE OPENS with Calvin Connor—yes, *that* Calvin Connor—about to go to summer camp. He has just finished eighth grade, is fourteen years old, and couldn't possibly be hornier.

An enormous areola and nipple, surrounded by a bulging bulb of peach flesh, bobbed in front of his face. The stale brick rowhomes and crumbled sidewalks of Calvin's unfortunate mountain-bound home-town barely reached his eyes in favor of the massive imaginary mammary. The kid tripped along Main Street in a mirthful trance.

The knocker in question was a mental freeze-frame from a porno tape watched in his friend Sandy's basement. Even this early in Calvin's life, he'd encountered *real* boobs, but none so large. None like this epitome of tit, this holy grail of gazongas.

Calvin—a large kid for his age, in the final throes of his last major growth spurt—bumbled along until he reached Axsubeen Borough Fire Station. Trudging down the gravel entranceway, Calvin skirted the station itself and made for a wooden shed-like building skulking next door. The boy's beefy hand settled on the barn door handle.

For a moment, Calvin beheld the big bezume bafflingly boogieing before his beak. Did such behemoth baloombahs even exist in real life? When would he get to feel some? *When?!*

Sighing, Calvin yanked the door aside and traded the titanic tit and bright summer morning for a stuffy, dark, and needless to say tit-free Troop Hall. Instead of finding his fellow teenaged boys ready to go, he found his Troopmaster, Oldroyd by name, and the man's belligerent prick of a son, Jon, seated at the puny lacquered table. The black cowboy hat, as always, rested atop Oldroyd's skull. The lit cigarette, as always, poked out his narrow mouth. Nothing about the man was anywhere even remotely as awesome as tits.

Oldroyd was just a dumb grown-up.

Calvin checked his Swatch, the kind with see-through band, hands, and face. It was 7:02. "So where is everybody?"

"Late," the Troopmaster said. "What the hell else is new."

"Well, *that's* new," Calvin pointed out with a laugh. "No one was ever late when General Schultz was—"

"The 'General' ain't in charge no more," Oldroyd spat through a blue blast of Marlboro smoke. "Or weren't ya here when he took his ball and went home a couple weeks back?"

Jon—a boy about the same age as Calvin, though smaller, blonder, and more plagued by acne—gave a nasty grin. "The General ain't the only one not comin'! That retard Zedz called first thing. Turns out his family vacation is *this* week."

"What a pudgeball puddin'-head." Oldroyd stamped out his smoke. "Makes you Acting Squad Captain again, Connor."

"Jaysus," Calvin breathed. As was automatic after a blasphemy, the kid's right hand crept up to cross himself.

"Yep, God help us," Oldroyd nodded.

"Can't be any worse than last time, sir," Calvin said, recovering his pride. Other kids would've whined, or begged off the promotion. Not Calvin. Though it *was* a disaster. He'd gone from ecstasy (jumbo jug) to horror (Acting Captain) in less than a minute. And it got worse immediately: young Jon lobbied to be appointed Acting Lieutenant for the week.

And the morning sun gave way to rain.

Calvin rarely hid his judgment of Jon as a privileged brat. "Fat chance," he snapped. "The Squad's gotta vote on it."

Jon rarely hid his haughtiness towards what he perceived as Calvin's jealousy. "No biggie. We just rig the vote," he said … with his father, the Troopmaster no less, sitting right there.

"We'll do it fair and square with a show of hands."

"Should do a show of fists. I'm gonna win either way, Connor. But if you wanna be a douchebag, then it's your funeral."

"It won't kill me," Calvin smirked, "even if you *do* win fair."

"Now that's my son y'all sassin' off to, Irish," Oldroyd snorted. "Startin' off just like *last* time you was Squad Captain!"

That "last time" was at a Troop meeting a couple months back, and had already reached legendary status. But the meeting had only been two hours, and everyone got to go home when it'd ended. This time, Calvin would be running the Hawk Squad for a whole summer camp—seven days far from home, deep in the woods, without any proper mattresses, modern toilets, conditioned air, or even any tits to speak of.

This was gonna suck. Majorly.

"I call quartermaster," Calvin said.

"Ah shit," Jon said, "I totally forgot to—"

"How many times I gotta say 'This Troop's got a PG-13 rating,' son?" Oldroyd said. He turned to Calvin. "You got the job, Connor. We'll start haulin' our shit out the second the other kids show up."

The next arrival wasn't for another five minutes, but (thankfully) it was a friend and ally, Ryan Phillips. Then they trickled in: the wild-child Spazz at 7:13, the rookie Crowe at 7:17, the fat-assed blob Gus at 7:22. Around 7:49—when a plurality of the Troop was present—the young men and their two adult chaperones began a glorious ritual of loading all the camping gear (backpacks, rucksacks, hatchets, first aid kits, ropes, and other outdoor-survival detritus) into the Troopmasters' trucks. Calvin, being the first kid of rank to arrive, had scored the primo job of managing Troop materiel from inside the Hall. All the others were stuck outside, in the rain, in the muddy gravel, trying desperately to get the truck loaded without killing one another.*

It quickly became evident that all their crap wouldn't fit inside the capped bed of Oldroyd's Chevy C-10 Silverado half-ton. Arguments on how to proceed ensued, and the operation halted. Occasionally one of the lads joined Calvin inside Troop Hall, but never to collect the remainder of the gear. Oh no. Just to whine: the rain, the pack-up, Dick'll's an idiot, Maguire ain't much better, we need the General back.

The baby-seal-shaped Gus burst in. "I'm spose'sta get the pots

---

* While appearing to be an erratum (n.b. at first it was *trucks,* plural; and then *truck,* singular), this deliberate discrepancy is a relevant clue as to the competence level of the Troop's two adult leaders.

and pans!" he woofed, with a fat red face that was all buckteeth and bulging eyes.

"Right there." Calvin pointed his pale beefy hand at the supply shelves. Gus dutifully collected the Troop's caked-black cooking pots and pans. "And send the rest of 'em in when you're back out there," Calvin added.

"'Kay," Gus nodded, scurrying out the door.

Calvin expected his order to go unheeded. Wasn't he surprised when all those present and accounted for rushed into the Hall, happily escaping the rain. "None of that," Calvin tsk-tsked, already using his new authority to supplement his direct personality. "Grab the rest of it and go!" Grumpily, the lads fetched every last stitch of portable Troop gear and hauled it outside. The last kid to exit, Jon Oldroyd, made a quick comment over his shoulder on why Calvin should stop being an asshole and just rig the vote for his lieutenancy already.

This great game of ineptitude, shuffling camping gear into and out of a pickup truck like a dim-witted street urchin trying to hide a nutshell under one of three peas, suddenly didn't need Calvin anymore. The kid watched through the open barn doorway as Troopmaster Oldroyd and his Assistant Mr. Maguire attempted, for the sixth time, in a driving rain, to get all the gear to fit into the capped bed of one full-size pickup truck. Since this operation had failed the five previous attempts this morning, and now *everything* was outside, *and* the gear was only getting heavier with absorbed rain, *and* apparently nobody could remember how the hell they'd managed to do it last time, Calvin held the fort. He refused to volunteer for this preposterous square-peg/round-hole venture.

Calvin flopped into a folding chair in the "office" corner of the Hall and shut his eyes. Darkness flung over him—a pure black image free of anything camping related. He pulled up the freeze-frame of the areola and nipple, surrounded by that dangling dirigible of delicious derma, and let it list playfully in the air like a mobile above an infant's crib. Calvin wondered what this mouthwatering melon might feel like. The two sets of *real* breasts with which the post-infant Calvin had made physical acquaintance had both been attached to girls his own age, and therefore had barely been breasts at all. This padded porno pillow would've put them pubescent puppies to shame. This dense devil's dumpling! Oh-so-malleable. Squeeze it, feel it reverberate. Let go, and watch the hand imprints slowly fade.

A shadow fell on young Calvin's whimsy. He opened his eyes and found Troopmaster Oldroyd standing over him.

A lit Marlboro sizzled under the man's salt-and-pepper mustache. He raised a skinny hand to pull the cigarette away; a bead of rain rolled off the right cuff of his pea-soup green long-sleeved uniform and plopped onto Calvin's dry lap.

"Maguire's under this stupid impression that *I'm* foulin' things up," he growled. "I've been sent to my room."

Oldroyd grabbed a chair and parked himself in it. Giving the open doorway a stern glance, he said, "I'm a-give that muskrat five minutes."

Calvin checked his Swatch. 8:22. When would this end?

An idea jumped into Calvin's brain's driver's seat. The lad looked at the puny lacquered table in front of him and riffled through the items cluttering it, ferreting out an old road map, a no. 2 pencil, and a slip of scratch paper. He took thumbnail measurements. He calculated with a grimace (he hated math). He bit the eraser thoughtfully, something he'd seen done in the Peanuts comic strip but had never actually tried himself.

Turned out, pencil erasers tasted like shit.

Oldroyd's grim eyes narrowed. "The hell're ya doin'?"

Calvin circled his answer and slammed down the pencil. "Mr. Oldroyd, if you wanna get to Connecticut by one o'clock, you're in *real* trouble!"

Fourteen-year-old Calvin Connor was brutally honest. Not a cheerful jokester like his best friend Sandy, nor a cynical know-it-all like his new friend Art; just a straight shooter. While he had quite a grown-up personality, he often rankled actual grown-ups—the lad came off as an arrogant bulldozer, not mature enough to know what he was talking about (or when to pick his spots when he did).

So the look on his Troopmaster's mustachioed face wasn't annoyance, chagrin, or bemusement ... but rage; a rage heated up by this morning's nonstop misery. *"Who's* in trouble, Irish?!" Oldroyd said, biting into the filter of his Marlboro.

"We are—we *all* are. I'll show you," Calvin said, maintaining his voice's strength (only just). "Axsubeen's not on the map, obviously, so I started at Altoona: there to New London is like three hundred fifty miles by the highways. If we go fifty-five miles per hour the whole way, it'll take six hours, twenty-one minutes, and thirty-six seconds."

Oldroyd's rage went limp so he could flap a cavalier hand. "That's it? Just the six and a half hours?"

Was he serious or sarcastic? Calvin wasn't sure. Sarcasm required a level of wit, and Oldroyd's level was no greater than –1. "Six and a half hours from now is three o'clock, sir."

"But openin' ceremonies is at 1 p.m. sharp." Oldroyd's rage bubbled back up. "We'll miss it by two goddamn hours?!"

"Only if," Calvin noted, "we leave this very second."

"Then that's exactly what we're gonna do!" The man rose from his chair, flicked his exhausted butt into the thronged ashtray, and stomped outside with a fresh "Okay girls, enough dickin' around! Let's pack this puppy!"

Just as the insanity began anew outside, a stocky, black-haired teenager wandered into Troop Hall. He was a fresh arrival but his face and gait were quite rotten. His pea-soup-colored uniform was shy the odd button and only partially tucked into his tan shorts. It looked like he'd slept in these clothes (probably the case; this kid's idea of saving time). His wobbly journey indoors started with a collision into the barn door's frame and ended with a stiff fall to the muddy floor.

Calvin helped the poor kid sit up. "Sandy!"

"Hmmm?"

"SANDY!" Calvin said—or found himself screaming—over the din of portly Gus racing in and tripping over Sandy's leg. The blob fell to Troop Hall's concrete floor, flinging wide on impact the half-dozen pots and pans he'd been lugging. Gus sprawled about in a limp attempt to catch even one pan … but alas, when the clanging stopped, the kid lay splayed empty-handed, surrounded by cookware.

Calvin's gray eyes flared at Gus, and the nincompoop sighed a defeated sigh. He collected the pans quietly. Inexplicably, he stepped over Sandy's leg and scurried back *outside.*

"Was that the dinner bell?" gargled Sandy with a laugh.

"If *only* it was dinner! Then we'd be done with all this insane bollocks!"

"Wait, there's gonads going on? *Insane* gonads?"

Calvin didn't fall for it.* "Get up, we're taking a walk."

"Speakin' of insane gonads—it's rainin' outside!"

"Exactly," Calvin said, "I'm not letting you sleep through this." He got Sandy to his feet and pointed him at the open doorway. Sandy veered straight into the doorframe again. With a cry of "You're fuckin' hopeless," Calvin actually took hold of Sandy's hand and led him out.

In the muddy gravel parking lot which the shed-like Troop Hall shared with the Axsubeen Borough Fire Station, Oldroyd's green Chevy pickup sat framed by three disheveled piles of camping gear and backpacks. Messrs. Oldroyd and Maguire sprinted around these piles in tight figure-eights, shouting out either a different, brilliant new plan for stowing the gear in the truck, or a different, brilliant new way of saying *"he's* an idiot; listen to me!" The boys of the Troop, virtually all present and accounted for at this late stage, occasionally participated in the show, but during this latest in a series of interminable "In-A-Gadda-Da-Vida"-esque adults-only solos, the lads sat Indian style in the mud, cracking jokes and catching smokes. It had been the kids' lot to do the actual loading during the morning's six hilariously unsuccessful attempts. As the two grown-ups feuded over how to go about attempt seven, they insisted it would be the last, and therefore most successful, attempt.

Calvin shook his head. "Actually, *this* is fuckin' hopeless."

"Oh is it now," Sandy laughed, mimicking Calvin's accent.

None too kindly, Calvin tugged at Sandy's hand, pulling his friend towards Main Street proper. Once on the sidewalk, both lads took a moment to kick the mud off their white Reebok high-tops. They slogged a ways to the bicycle shop at 9 South Main Street, in front of which sat

---

* Young Calvin, as you damn well know, was born in the Republic of Ireland and moved to America at age ten. Those close to him knew what he meant when he referenced *bollocks.* It was rarely gonads.

the royal blue Ford Bronco belonging to Mr. Maguire, regarded by the boys as the Troop's one remaining passably intelligent leader.

(Mr. Maguire, see, not the Bronco).

But only *passably* intelligent—had Mr. Maguire's Bronco been parked in the fire station lot alongside Oldroyd's Silverado, as it should've been, the Troop would've found the packing-up job so much easier. But the Bronco was not parked there. Ergo, not enough room for all the gear.

Yep, shrugs the chronicler, *it's as simple as that.*

That's Troop 666!

Mr. Maguire's son Art napped in the Bronco, his face plastered against the passenger seat's window, fogging it up with snores.

Calvin and Sandy looked at the dozing, dry Art. Abruptly Sandy broke from his woozy stupor, yanking his hand from Calvin's. "Leggo of me, ya faggot!"*

Sandy climbed up to sit on the Bronco's hood and churned over his butter-ish brain. Calvin took a moment for hair-care. He wore an '80s haircut: the sides and lower back were buzzed close to the skin while the wavy top was long enough to cover his face. He liked it pushed back from his forehead and held there with Aqua Net, but the rain made an icky mess of it.

"Do a ponytail like Boy George." Sandy laughed through his nose. "It'll look *completely* gay then!"

"Go and shite!" Calvin snapped once he could see again. "I got a real problem now: Zedz's vacation is *this* week!"

Sandy lay back on the Bronco's hood, moaning like pain. *"This* week? So no Zedz?"

"No Zedz."

"Meanin', you got promoted to Captain again?"

"I did."

"Kill me now." Sandy appeared to mean it. He curled into a wet ball on the Bronco's hood with all the intention of dying.

---

* You'll see a lot of this talk in the chronicle's early volumes, especially from the kids; political correctness wasn't a thing in 1987. (If that bothers you, go fuck yourself.) Also, we called Broncos *trucks* back in the '80s. *Sport utility vehicle,* the acronym *SUV,* and all opinions pertaining thereto were likewise some years away.

Calvin felt like shoving the kid off the truck and into Main Street. Part of Pennsylvania's State Rte. 666, Main Street was alive this Sunday morning with roaring station wagons and pickups. Sandy would surely be killed, as requested.

"Remember back in English class?" Calvin mused. "Shakespeare used rain as a symbol of death."

"Of death—yeah, I remember," said Sandy. "Did ya really just bring up English class right before I'm about to die?"

Calvin gave Main Street another glance. He debated throwing himself into it. "Tell Art to keep the Beaver Squad as far away from us as possible, or we'll *all* be dead now. Jon wants to be my lieutenant even!"

Sandy stayed on the line until Calvin said *lef-tenant*, then hung up: "Think I'm gonna use rain as a symbol for a blanket."

Again, he meant it. "Thanks a bunch, Sandy."

"No biggie, dude."

Calvin stomped off. "My best friend, ladies and gentlemen," he crooned, "Mr. Anthony Sandmiller! Big hand, please!"

Sandy made a crowd noise, then let it fade away.

The morning's deluge waned into a cool drizzle. Sandy's curly black locks—a normal haircut, the kind also seen outside the '80s—directed water to his ears and along his neck. Drops went *dink!-dink!-dink!* killing themselves on the Bronco.

Then he felt a *thunk!* reverberate through his back; shockwaves jarred the puddle of rainwater on his chest down to his tan shorts, where it soaked through to his Hanes and shrank his scrotum. After that, a sudden sense of gravity swallowed all his senses.

During his slow descent off the hood, Sandy watched Calvin ram Gus's dopey noodle into the side of the Bronco again. Then Sandy crashed onto the sidewalk, and saw nought else.

Gus lay like a beached whale on the sidewalk, or indeed, a sidewalked whale. His thirteen-year-old body, a considerable slab of retained water and misspent carbohydrates, looked rather a prize catch, something to be hoisted up on a tether and photographed for the record, surrounded by the brave, drunken men who'd removed it from the sea. The older, stockier Sandy, lying next to Gus, seemed a minnow by comparison.

Calvin felt anything but victorious. Again he gave menacing Main Street/State Rte. 666 a good look. Cars ripped by at forty-five miles an hour, despite the 25 m.p.h. limit. Look at that lumber rig ripping along! Being smooshed by a rig going that speed—would you even feel it before death took you?

Of course you would. It'd be the last, and certainly worst, thing you ever felt.

He looked again. If he could *cross* Main Street, he could bolt for home. It was only half a mile away. Screw this camping trip. It would only get worse, right?

And as he looked, the air along Main Street rent aside with the boisterous popping noises of a million tiny gas stations exploding sequentially. The Harley—a sweet, glossy black '82 FLT Tour Glide—swept past the Bronco, hove to, then disappeared down the entranceway to the fire station's parking lot.

Well, Inky was here now.

The popping stopped and the shouting started. "What the hell!" was the first yell, and it echoed up and down Main Street's line of three-story brick rowhomes and shops.

A meeting of the Troop's leadership corps was inevitable, and the Squad Captains, Calvin Connor and Art Maguire, would need to attend. Calvin ended Art's forty winks, face against the glass, by yanking open the Bronco's passenger-side door.

For a moment, it appeared Art too would fall asleep on the cracked sidewalk—three fish caught—but the rainwater soaking into his uniform made the kid spring to his feet with a high-pitched scream. He slapped his long gangly hands down his uniform to try to wipe off the wet smear.

Seeing Calvin there smiling, Art added two and two and sucker-punched the big kid right in the gut. "Calvin, you fuck!"

Doubling over from the blow, Calvin nonetheless got his witty retort in: "Only on the weekends."

Art jerked when he caught sight of the two inert lads nearby. "Yo, what's goin' on here?!"

"Let me worry about Gus. Sandy's *your* problem!"

Art ran a hand, sweetly cinereous in color and shiny from the moisture, through his perfect half-inch flattop. "Hungover again?" he sighed, slapping Sandy's face; the stocky kid moaned in delight and rolled over. "Or still shitfaced!"

Standing, Art jutted a thumb at Gus. "What about wide-ass?"

Calvin spun the yarn: "Gus was in charge of the pots and pans. The grown-ups told him to put 'em back in the Hall, since the camp's got a cafeteria so we won't even need them."

"Logical. Are you sure the grown-ups told him that?"

"Maybe it was your da. Anyway, Gus comes bumbling in and drops all the pots on the floor. I give him a dirty look, like 'smooth move, Ex-Lax!' So he picks them up and goes back out, then—cuz he don't want anyone else to yell at him—he dumps them by the railway out back."

"*On* the tracks?"

"*On* the tracks."

"Next stop, Derailment City!" Art made a train horn sound.

"Exactly. So after I got him to gather up that shite and put it away proper, I made a Squad Captain decision." Calvin puffed his chest. "I told Gus to watch over Sandy with me. When we got here, I threw him into your da's truck."

"Wait a minute—how are you Captain?"

"Cuz Zedz is so thick. His Florida holiday is *this* week."

Art sighed. "Only dipshit Zedz could screw up readin' a calendar." He looked down at Sandy and Gus again. "So I see it's gonna be like last time you were Captain? You're already beatin' up the guys. You and Jon buttin' heads too?"

"Fuck Jon. And I *had* to wallop Gus. I'm just—" Calvin searched for the words. "—asserting my authority!"

Art's know-it-all snort, a common conversation tool, hissed out. "You don't have the 'authority' to beat up the guys!"

"Oh I don't now? *I* was beat up plenty of times when—"

"That don't matter, Calvin! Beating people up ain't the Squad

Captainy thing to do!"

"Like I know what the fucking 'Squad Captainy thing to do' is!" Calvin roared. His tall frame grew taller with his wroth. "I am totally not looking forward to dealing with Gus, or Jon, or the dumb rookie—or Inky, or Oldroyd—or myself!"

"Better get used to it now," Art snapped, not cowed despite being dwarfed by his friend's size. "Ya can't be all full-steam-ahead like normal, Irish. Us Captains gotta think a little. I mean, what ya gonna do when Gus wakes up and tells on ya?"

"He knows I'd beat his arse. Gus ain't that dumb."

"Oh, he's *not?!* He'll probably go straight to Dick'll, and Dick'll take away your Lieutenant badge and give it to Jon. Which'd make *Jon* the Captain this week. How's that sound?"

Calvin's face went dead. "Eh," he said.

Art slapped his arm over Calvin's shoulders. "The best Squad Captainy thing to do is think. And I mean think *first.*"

"Okay," Calvin said, getting a grip on his emotions. "Let's think. Imagine you're a Captain."

Art gave his bright beam. "I am!"

"You are. And you just knocked out one of your guys."

"I wouldn't of."

"But suppose you did. What would you do?"

"Easy: subliminal suggestion."

Calvin's left eyebrow rose Spock-like.

"We plant the idea in Gus's head that he did it to himself." Art's big brain was in high gear, and he had a devious twinkle in his cold blue eyes. "Like an accident. Yeah. He was walkin' by, concentrating on openin' his Snickers or some shit, and oops!—slammed into the Bronco."

"Go and shite!" Calvin said, rolling his eyes.

"Yo, trust me. And *now's* the time, before he starts dreaming. If we tell Gus what 'really' happened, he'll dream about it."

Inky's shouting from the fire station parking lot stopped. Wouldn't be long now. So Calvin gave up. "Brilliant. Let's do it."

They each took an ear and knelt by it.

"Gus ..."   "Listen to us ..."

"You had a Snickers."   "You didn't see the Bronco."

"You hit your head."   "You didn't get pushed—"

(Calvin recoiled as Art punched him.)

"You hit your head."   "It was an accident, Gus."

"An accident ..."   "Snickers bar ..."

"... Bronco door ..."   "... hit your head ..."

"... accident ..."   "... Snickers ..."

"... Bronco ..."   "... head ..."

They stood up. "Pleasant dreams," hushed Calvin, but Art added, "fat-ass." The teenagers laughed diabolically.

Dick Oldroyd bellowed from down the block: let it be known, hear ye hear ye, that a Troop meeting is about to commence, and all those with a rank before their name had better get their asses in Troop Hall. Right now.

Art checked the time on his calculator watch; his eyes bulged at how late they already were. "Inky's gonna kill us all."

Chapter 2
MEETING ON THE MOUND.

FIVE OF THE six leaders squeezed around Troop Hall's puny lacquered table and commenced bickering. Troopmaster Dick Oldroyd, Assistant Troopmaster Paul Maguire, Junior Chaplain Matthew "Father" Duffy, Hawk Squad Captain (Acting) Calvin Connor III, and Beaver Squad Captain Art Maguire bandied about salvos of disavowal and recalcitrance. Every second sentence started with, "It is *not* my fault!"

Oldroyd put out his smoke in an ashtray heaped with butts. Last week, upon ascension to the title of Big Cheese, Oldroyd stationed a small glass ashtray on this puny table as his first act. This morning, his first act was gluing a second ashtray to the table's lacquered top so it wouldn't be thieves' booty like the first one. It'd only occurred to the man just now that emptying this ashtray would be an arduous task!*

Oldroyd picked up the tin coffee pot (freshly brewed on the Troop's as-yet-unpacked portable propane stove), found a mug not full of cigarette butts, and quietly poured himself a cup. The leadership corps raged on. Oldroyd's strategy, from his experience as a father, (ex-)husband, and business owner, was to let the others whine until the point of exhaustion ... then apply a death grip on their weakened throats. And Oldroyd was a master at getting each hole in a leaky ship plugged with a timely finger.

There was an additional hole this time around: Calvin. Two

---

* Oldroyd carried over his predecessor's rule prohibiting smoking in the Hall, with an exception for himself. And, after he thought about it, everyone else. In the graceless barbarity of the pre-indoor-smoking-ban world, ashtrays were everywhere: hotel corridors, hospital waiting rooms, even bolted to Pac-Man machines.

Yes, by 1987, we all knew smoking was unhealthy. But it'd be a few more years before we actually gave two shits.

months ago, Hawk Squad Captain Sammy "Zedz" Dzedzy missed the weekly Troop meeting because his mommy feared his sniffle would get worse. Lieutenant Connor ascended to the throne, and the forceful lad became an instant tyrant. The kids under his charge balked at his orders. Faced with rebellion, Calvin affected passive persuasion; faced with abuse, he affected apathy; faced with total havoc, he affected pugilism.

At the next meeting, then-Troopmaster Konrad Schultz III had a banner made and hoisted to the ceiling, bearing the number 731 (the total punitive push-ups the Hawk Squad had earned over the course of two hours) and a list of the guilty kids' names, marking the event for all time as a cautionary tale.

Oldroyd moved his eyes to the ceiling. Nestled amongst the many banners and standards, the new-ish 731 felt flapped incongruously, like a mug shot in a family photo album. The faded emblems surrounding it spoke of pride, tradition, and good standing:

Troop 666, winners of the Klondike Derby orienteering race, 1987. Troop 666, 1st Prize in the Canadian Jubilee's Campfire Contest, 1985. Troop 666, Blair County award for community service during the Vietnam War, 1972. Troop 666's golden anniversary, 1916–66. Troop 666's china anniversary, 1916–36 (if china had indeed been given, none lasted to this day). Troop 6's Meritorious Service Award, 1925.*

Craning his neck, Oldroyd spied at the far end of the Hall the first ever banner, marking Troop 6's 1916 inception, with a list of the ten founding members. Seeing the names of nine long-dead boys and their even longer-dead Troopmaster, who collectively stood guilty for setting into motion an eye-popping chain of events spanning many decades and leading to this week's awful camping trip, was the antithesis of the pride

---

* Main Street out front was but part of a path whose termini lay thirteen miles to the north in downtown Altoona and forty-two miles to the south in Orbisonia. When this contiguous stretch of road received the designation "Penna. Rte. 666" in 1928 (during Pennsylvania's controversial commonwealth-wide roadway route numbering debacle), then-Troopmaster Smokey Malone applied for—and received!—permission to re-number Axsubeen's Troop from its arbitrarily given 6 to a more form-fitting 666. Axsubeen, a fiercely Christian community about two-thirds Irish Catholic and one-third German Lutheran, nearly revolted. To this day, the devout *never* refer to the state route or the Troop as "six-six-six," but instead like so: "six-*sixty*-six."

and tradition Oldroyd sought from the celebratory banners.

A fine mess y'all assholes started! he thought instead.

Oldroyd's eyes shifted from Troop Hall's rafters to the rotted wooden walls. The Troop's standard, a large flag with block letters decrying **TROOP 666, AXSUBEEN, PENNA,** hung on the near wall. He wondered why this hadn't been packed up: they'd need it for the camp's opening ceremony parade!

Oh. Right. Never mind.

Along this wall ran a series of small banners, similarly sized and inscribed, one for each Troopmaster in the history of Troop 6/666, with the years of his reign stitched beneath. The series began with a dilapidated felt for one Seamus "Smoky" Malone, who led from 1916 until his death in 1931—the longest reign on record (a miraculous one in Oldroyd's eyes). A dozen more felts followed, immortalizing men like B.C. Halloran, Kurt Hundhausen, Dennison "Thump" Clancy, and Axsubeen's most notorious living inhabitant, Toby Stuart (who, in 1959, had been summarily removed from the Troopmaster position [as well as his position as manager of Axsubeen High School's varsity baseball team {and his position as deputy chief of the borough fire company (and his job down at Schultz's Lumber [not to mention his status as shop steward at said business])}]) for a very, very stupid offense.

At the end of the line hung a freshly updated banner: *KONRAD SCHULTZ III, 1983–1987.* Mr. Schultz was the township's richest man and supreme monarch of the Schultz family empire. He personally owned Blair County's largest lumber concern and Axsubeen township's largest farm; relations of his ran political arenas such as the borough's mayoralty, the position of township supervisor, and the office of Sheriff. Mr. Schultz had been a tyrannical Troopmaster, to the point of being called "General" behind his back; he held every kid accountable for all words, deeds, even thoughts. He'd demanded the best. But those days were over: Mr. Schultz had unexpectedly resigned the post two weeks ago with a grim grunt of "Fuck this." He gave no reason. His son had no comment.

His senior assistant, Dick Oldroyd, took over.

Oh yeah, and now Oldroyd had his *own* banner:

DICK OLDROYD, 1987–

It looked like a tombstone. The man actually laughed at the thought. *There'll be some graves dug this mornin', all right!*

With a screech, the barn door slid open. Inky stomped inside, briefly blocking the gray light of the outside world. The bickerers inside Troop Hall fell silent. Even the morning spritz shut itself off in respect. Konrad "Inky" Schultz IV, son of the former Troopmaster, set down his black skid-lid and took his seat at the puny lacquered table. His black cycling leather crackled ten-hut! The only other colors about him were the pale white of his German-American face and the tight wave of red hair on his scalp. He looked like a walking black Bic lighter.

A massive Bic. Calvin Connor at fourteen was a big kid, standing just over 6' 0 " and weighing a good 180. Inky, two years Calvin's senior, was 6' 6 " (at least) and 250 (at leaster).

All eyes fell on him. Inky's eyes fell on them—and Inky's could duplicate the effect of the Death Star weapon. "Bullshit!" he seethed through clenched teeth. He panned his eyes across the table, causing considerable fright. "Can't I take a squirt out back without you god-damn idiots starting to argue again?!"

A polite "Ahem" from Father, the teenage Junior Chaplain.

"What's wrong with taking God's name in vain?" Inky said to him. "You guys are two hours late."

Father smiled quaintly. "But is Our Lord to blame?"

Inky ignored the whole digression, instead leveling an accusatory look at Oldroyd. "What the hell's keeping us here?"

There was no reply. This would be Oldroyd and Inky's first confrontation without Inky's father around, and everyone present knew it. Mr. Maguire nervously filled the gap: "You're keeping us here," he said with a thin laugh.

Teeth gnashed in Inky's mouth. "What kept you here before I got here?"

Mr. Maguire sighed. "We can't pack up all the gear."

"I've taken dumps that're smarter than you people," announced Inky. "Get your Bronco in the parking lot, Mr. Maguire—things will suddenly get a whole lot easier. Going camping ain't Einstein material!"

Inky's blocky face reverberated, taking sudden ill-note that Calvin was in Zedz's spot. He enunciated, for his own benefit, "Zedz is not present or accounted for?"

Father added, for all (or none) of their benefits, "Not present, but accounted for: he's in Orlando."

The news made the room hotter. "Calvin," Inky growled, "please tell me you didn't let Zedz leave for Florida without getting his Connecticut road map."

Calvin lowered his eyebrows, declaring terrible open war against an obviously tougher opponent. Truth to power, even if it meant suicide: that was teenage Calvin. "How could I 'let Zedz leave' if Zedz was never here? I was the first one here—on time, I might add!" Dumbly pressing his luck, Calvin held up his sheet of calculations. "I even worked out how late we'll be!"

Inky snatched the sheet. The black-clad ogre glanced over the computations, nearly burning the magnesium off the page. "Six and a half hours?" One Death Star eye cocked at Calvin. "How did you work this out without a map of Connecticut?"

Calvin pointed to the shabby East Coast map on the table.

"That old thing? We can add a half hour more at least, cuz we gotta stop and get a real Connecticut road map. Not to mention gas, and five-minute breaks ... "

Waving Calvin's calculations, the Junior Troopmaster continued in a crescendo-ing voice: " ... and while you were working this out, the Hawk Squad was outside sinking in the mud. That's my point—we should be long gone, not still here bitching about how late we are!" He crumpled up the paper and chucked it at the Hall's trash bin, where it stuck to a week-old slather of tar which ran down the bin's south-facing side.

Troop 666's leadership corps sat tense and quiet. None wished to join the eviscerated Calvin on the butcher's rack.

Except one, who felt it was high time to get it on.

"We ain't gonna need no Connecticut map," Oldroyd said, his country twang piercing the silence. He leaned forward for full effect, and his prized cowboy hat left the shadows and entered the spotlight. Black as night, adorned with gray and light blue feathers from a jay, garnished with a chrome buckle ... and the hat was dry, despite the morning's rain.

The thing infuriated Inky to no end. It was gaudy, anachronistic (Troopmasters usually wore official ballcaps or a dark brown campaign style hat, sometimes known by the illicit nickname "shit-nipple"), and symbolic of what Oldroyd was: a fiercely proud redneck. The sort who, if he discovered his personality pissed someone off, made his accent thicker and his attitude more ignorant.

Worse still, Oldroyd was a rich redneck—his son, the Hawk Squad's haughty prick Jon, went to the exclusive Larsen Academy for Affluent Boys up in Altoona—so the man fancied his backwoods ways as those of an eccentric, worthy of legend and statues, to be cherished by lowly Axsubeen's peons.

Young Inky, while also from a wealthy family (the township's wealthiest, even), found Oldroyd's hick tendencies abhorrent—especially the man's dismissive attitude regarding the poor, the non-American, and/or the non-white. (God help you if you were all three.) Working class white men always got a pass since Oldroyd dealt with them all day at his heating oil business. Everyone else, though, was a worthless piece of shit from the start. Oldroyd was so cocksure in this regard that he'd use epithets right to the faces of destitute kids like Spazz, foreign types like Calvin, or black folk like the Maguires.

Paul Maguire had a white mother and mahogany skin; when Oldroyd tossed around slurs, Maguire usually let it go, chalking it up to Oldroyd's character (or lack thereof). Young Art also had a white mother and skin as pale as silvery ash, but wasn't so forgiving a soul (he would "sass off"). Inky Schultz—despite being of German descent and therefore as white as people came—shared his kingly father's view that hicks like Oldroyd gave quaint woodland towns like Axsubeen a bad name. The Oldroyds of the world were why society saw farmers and lumberjacks as retarded inbreds. If Oldroyd committed a crime of arrogance around Inky, an argument followed.

Without fail.

Troopmaster Schultz (the General) had never stopped these wars, but his mere presence had forced Oldroyd to fight fair. On three occasions, an Oldroyd/Inky argument turned into a shouting match in the parking lot, and once had even ended in blows—or rather, a blow, one that knocked Oldroyd's cowboy hat clean off his balding dome.

But the General had split; never coming back. So this was Oldroyd's hour: the new Troopmaster sat at the leadership table and looked on Troop 666 as his Troop. Across the table, Inky glowered at him, thinking it was his hour. His Troop. "You know every street in Connecticut, do you?" he quipped.

Oldroyd flippantly tilted his hat. "The state ain't that big, son. How far can anything be from I-95?"

"You're right. Let's just roll across the border and ask for directions. That's being prepared."

"Versus wastin' five bucks on some map? Damn right!" Oldroyd clucked his teeth. "Talk is free, and any gas station attendant can give ya directions! Use your head, son."

Young Inky's face scrunched up tighter at that. "I'm not your son," he noted.

"And I'm not your pop. But I am the Troopmaster, so looks like I hafta take over for him as the one real man in your life."

Breathing stopped. The Hall had never been so silent. Art Maguire's nerves tingled with fear and he wished to be elsewhere; conversely, his friend Calvin Connor actually leaned closer so he wouldn't miss a moment. Mr. Maguire and Father swapped anxious looks. They wouldn't have been surprised if Inky and Oldroyd had leapt over the table and traded cuffs.

"The only 'real man' here," Inky growled, "is me."

Oldroyd blew out a snort that ruffled his mustache.

"You doubt me?" Inky went on, locking Death Star eyes on each leader in turn. "Art talks like he knows it all. Calvin acts like he knows it all. Father prays to who he thinks knows it all. Mr. Maguire at least knows that he doesn't know it all." The Death Star eyes stopped on Oldroyd. "What do you know?"

"I know I'm twice the man you'll ever be," Oldroyd said. His eyes shone with determined fire. "After all, I'm a grown-up. I can drive after midnight. I can have whiskey at the bar. And I know what pussy tastes like. Do you know what pussy tastes like, son?"

"Like you," Inky said. Lamely. Oldroyd's last shots seemed to do some damage. "Just a guess, though."

Oldroyd smiled at his successful manipulation of the moment.

This was his Troop, after all. "So, gettin' back to the important shit here, the route we oughta take is 666 to 99 North to 80 East, then—"

"You mean the route we oughta take?" Inky scoffed, pronouncing route to rhyme with scout. Oldroyd had said it as one would say root.

"Route!" Oldroyd exclaimed, his way.

"Route!" Inky exclaimed, his way.

"ROUTE!" Oldroyd cried, his way, standing to his full height of 6'1".

"ROUTE!" Inky cried, his way, standing to his full height of 6'6".

"ROUTE!" Oldroyd screamed, his way, pounding the puny table with his fist, and in doing so knocking over a coffee mug that released a gray-brown ooze full of cigarette butts over the pencils, then the scratch paper, then the old map, then off the table, where the thick sludge splashed onto Troop Hall's concrete floor. Art Maguire had to scoot his chair back to prevent the mess from dropping into his lap.

"ROUTE!" Inky screamed, his way, pounding the puny table with his fist, successfully putting his hand all the way through it, tipping the thing like a see-saw. Inky plucked his fist from the hole he'd created just in time for the map, the pencils, the papers, the coffee mugs, the cigarette butts, the gruel mixed from ash and coffee, and the coffee pot itself to come to a crashing halt at the tabletop's edge, where they teetered but did not plummet.

Mr. Maguire stood up, pudgy legs rocketing his folding chair behind him. "STOP IT!" The glass in the Hall's two windows sang. The empty aluminum storage shelving rang. Out in the parking lot, the mud-caked boys stopped whatever they were doing, unsure if they were the ones getting yelled at.

"Enough bullshit!" Maguire glared at Oldroyd and Inky. "From this moment on, call it a 'planned way,' not a 'route!'"

"Route," Oldroyd and Inky said, their own ways, in unison. They gave each other cold looks.

Mr. Maguire unsheathed a dark finger which swung back and forth between them. "We're here to learn about maturity and survival, and you two ain't gonna survive me kickin' both your asses if you don't get mature—stat!"

Paul Maguire meant the words. He'd been to 'Nam, had personally and deliberately slain people, and was known in his youth not to take shit. But he was soft and flabby now, bereft of reasons to use his guns, weighed down by years of excess hamburgers and cigarettes. Were this to actually develop into a brawl, Mr. Maguire had no chance of taking on the more fit and far younger Inky, and Oldroyd seemed the type to fight dirty if he couldn't win fair.

Still, Mr. Maguire's outburst had had a calming effect. After some slight cowboy hat adjusting, Oldroyd continued as if nothing had happened. "So anyways, the 'planned way' that I'd take to Camp Souviens is—"

The chronicler's description of the action to follow requires a page of backstory:

Last Christmas, General Schultz decided that Troop 666 was not going to Lucid Pond Reservation for summer camp.

Troop 666 went to Lucid Pond for summer camp every summer. And the chronicler means every summer. Not to mention every winter for the Klondike Derby orienteering race. Lucid Pond's only redeeming factor was its proximity: fifty miles north-northeast up I-99, deeper still than Axsubeen within Pennsylvania's portion of the Appalachians.

"Hell with that," the General said, "time for something new!" He asked his boys to vote on a new destination for the coming 1987 summer camp. Trouble was, the only places the boys had ever gone besides Lucid Pond were Lewis & Clark Campgrounds near Gettysburg (for the annual camporee and dance bringing together the boys' and girls' organizations) and an exchange trip to Canada. The General held the vote anyway and the boys used their imaginations. The tally: three votes for staying home in Axsubeen, two votes for Three Rivers Stadium to see the Pirates, and one each for Timbuktu, East Jabip, Iceland, Uranus, Hell, and Your Mom's Bedroom.

Disgruntled but not yet defeated, the General dug up a list of camp reservations licensed by the Trooping International Tribunal and taped it to the wall. The two older ranked kids (Inky and Father) and the two

Squad Captains (Art and Zedz) threw darts, and lo, Inky and Art both nailed Camp Souviens Reservation in Connecticut. Father had hit La Fils' Acres in Eastern Pennsylvania, and Zedz had coincidentally hit Swamp Hollow outside Orlando. So Souviens it was. The boys went around telling friends and family they were going to Camp "SUE'·veenz" for summer camp.

"Dick'll do the busy work," the General noted, and Assistant Troopmaster Oldroyd did indeed do the busy work of filling out and mailing in Troop 666's bid for a campsite. Two weeks later the camp called to confirm, and Oldroyd discovered they'd been butchering the name: it was pronounced soo·VEE'·en. According to the impossibly sepulchral voice of the Camp's Deputy Director, the word was French, derived from a popular French-Canadian slogan; but after he hung up, Oldroyd forgot which one.

At the next meeting, Oldroyd told the gang it was pronounced soo·VEE'·en but added, "I don't give two shits what them frogs call it— it's spelled 'SUE'·veenz,' so that's how I'm a-gonna say it!"

Despite several double standards the boys pointed out—like why Oldroyd referred to his new C-10 Silverado as a SHEV'·roe·LAY instead of the spelt SHEV'·roe·LET—he was steadfast in his mispronunciation. Instantly it became a joke to call out "soo·VEE'·en!" anytime Oldroyd butchered it, and the General made no move to stop the boys from making fun of a grown-up.

Oldroyd reacted to these calls with anger. And, as the reader will see now (and in later events involving both the man and his son Jon), no Oldroyd vented his anger properly.

"So anyways, the 'planned way' that I'd take to Camp Souviens is—"

Mr. Maguire, Inky, Father, Art, and Calvin said, "soo·VEE'·en!" in perfect unison; one of those rare times when many sound waves gelled into a uniform chord.

Oldroyd waited for the resultant laughter to end. Once it became clear the laughter would never end, the man stood. Bent with rage, he marched out the door and screamed so loudly at the kids loafing in the parking lot that they made the most efficient stab at packing-up the day had yet seen, and within ninety seconds, every damn thing not mud or alive had been crammed into the capped cargo bed or chucked in the cab of Oldroyd's Silverado.

The truck groaned under the additional weight of its driver, then roared to life. Flooring it—sending gravelly mud everywhere—Troopmaster Oldroyd pulled out onto Rte. 666 without looking.

Chapter 3

COLLISION AT THE PLATE.

CALVIN CONNOR'S PLEASANT nap-time dream, in which his kisser careened off porn stars' coconuts, ended with a close-up of Gus Jacoby's flying saucer eyes. "Get offa me, Gus!" Calvin yelped.

The blob wobbled in fear. "They said they're gonna make me sleep in the latrine! I ain't no rookie no more! How come's I gotta watch my back every campin' trip, Calvin?"

"You *won't* have to sleep in the latrine! You're so gullible!"

Gus's eyes bugged some more. He showed the look to everyone in the Bronco: to the backs of Mr. Maguire and Anthony "Sandy" Sandmiller; to Ryan Phillips, quietly sitting on Calvin's other side here on the Bronco's bench seat; then to Shawn Crowe and Jon Oldroyd, the two kids flopping around in the cramped cargo area.

Jon's red acne flared at Gus for being a tattletale. Quickly Gus faced front and his normal, stupefied expression returned.

Calvin took a minute to recover from such a close-quarter encounter with his most malodorous charge. He then performed a damage-control check: fingers rubbed over hair, forehead, eyebrows, eyelids, nose, cheeks, chin, lips, neck. Calvin brought down his hands to check, but saw no evidence of laughingly planted shaving cream, toothpaste, makeup, etc. So the Hawk Squad hadn't gone after their acting Captain as he napped. They hadn't gone after him at all.

Yet.

Calvin glanced over Ryan's shoulder out the window. It was 2:54 in the afternoon and they were still on the highway. Since Oldroyd split without taking any of the boys with him, young Father, the Troop's seventeen-year-old Junior Chaplain, had to ride bitch on Inky's Harley back to his house on the outskirts of town to get his banged-up 1975

Chevrolet Vega station wagon. Most of the Beaver Squad (Art, Spazz, Chicken, and Denny) rode with Father, while Sandy volunteered to accompany his pal Calvin and keep an eye on the novice Captain (731 push-ups, remember). Inky followed on his bike. Had Mr. Maguire's Bronco been in Troop Hall's parking lot from the start, or had Father and his Vega been included in the pack-up and people-moving plan from the start, virtually none of the previous 25 pages of bullshit would have happened.

The chronicler shrugs again: that's Troop 666.

In any event, the Troop had left at nine sharp—precisely two hours late—and proceeded on their boring trip eastward, along vista-free* highways and smoke-choked New York City toll bridges, towards Camp Souviens in the hilariously named town of Groton, Connecticut.

Almost at once, the vehicles driven by Mr. Maguire, Inky, and Father got separated. No songs were sung in the Bronco. The game of Punch-Bug, begun as they traversed the George Washington Bridge, had run out of steam. It was such a long ride that even *ironically* saying "Are we there yet?" got old. The lads just sat silent, immersed in the stank of still-damp-and-muddy class A uniforms. Meanwhile, miles and miles away, an opening ceremony had occurred, and in said ceremony there'd been a thirty-foot gap in the parade that Troop 666 ought to have filled.

Calvin quietly asked Mr. Maguire if they'd reached Connecticut while he'd been dozing.

The man's encouraging response? "We passed New Haven a while back. That's in Connecticut, right?"

From his spot in the front passenger seat, Sandy pointed. "Look— 'New London, next four exits.' That's close, isn't it?"

"Is it?" Chagrin oozed from Mr. Maguire's dark face. "If we hadn't gotten separated, at least we'd be lost together!" He reached up to his sun visor and ferreted out a sheet of paper. "See what you can make out of this."

Sandy took the paper—a copy of Inky's version of a "planned way" to Camp Souviens—and scratched his head in wonder. Sandy was

---

* If you see a mountain or a valley out of every window of your house, seeing them out your car window does not count as a *vista*.

no longer hungover or shitfaced, but he was damned if he could figure out this abstract thing. He tried holding his pocket flashlight up to it, as if literally "shedding some light on it" would help in metaphorically doing so. He twisted it 'round and around, turned it over and examined the back, held it up to his pocket mirror, then folded the ends together like the posters on the back cover of *Mad* magazine that present an image of a mushroom cloud but when the ends are folded together produce a rude picture of Ronald Reagan.

Quite spookily, when folded in this manner the "planned way" produced an excessively rude picture of Ronald Reagan. This bonus feature did little to enhance the "planned way's" actual purpose, nor did it justify the further ten minutes of late-time it had taken Inky to craft it … ten minutes spent by the rest of Troop 666 worrying a) if they would ever see Oldroyd again, and b) if not, where they'd acquire clean underwear for the rest of the week.

Inky had made two quick copies of his "planned way" and dished them to Mr. Maguire and Father. This copy brought forth no set of directions that would lead them anywhere (i.e., somewhere important; viz. their destination; n.b. Camp Souviens in Connecticut) and in the end Sandy grumpily proclaimed that he couldn't make head or tail of it.

"Give us that now," Calvin muttered, sticking out his hand, "there's a good lad." Sandy passed the paper back and Calvin had a good hard go. He determined that the mysterious double-squiggle on one edge was the inscription *Atlantic Ocean,* and that at least prompted which way the paper ought to be held. Still, it was little more than a series of wiry lines with glyphs that might've been route numbers.

Calvin passed the "planned way" on to Ryan Phillips, and in turn every kid had a look. It reached Jon Oldroyd last; he wanted to know who Ronald Reagan was. When bluntly reminded that Mr. Reagan is *only* the President of the United States of friggin' America, Jon said, "Oh, I knew that," and then, to show 'em all, he shoved the "planned way" down his pants.

Calvin couldn't resist: "You're not gonna get many votes doing that."

"I'm gonna get 'em all," explained Jon, making a bodily movement somewhere between a shrug and a middle finger. "Then I'll piss on this paper later. Everyone'll love it."

"Gonna take it out of your shorts first?"

"What? Shut up, boner-face!"

The only hope in preventing an official declaration of "we're lost" had just found its way down Jon's shorts and was now ineffectively trying to negotiate a retreat from the kid's naughty bits. Mr. Maguire, already sweating, bucked when a light on the Bronco's dashboard came on—it read, FIND A GAS STATION IN THE NEXT FIVE MINUTES, OR ELSE FUCK YOU.

"Shit shit shit," he hissed. An exit ramp approached, and Maguire took it. "Okay boys, find me a gas station—stat!"

Sandy called land ho: "Dude! Dead ahead!"

All looked. A gas station sat just past the end of the ramp. The boys erupted in riotous cheering. And look who was pulling *out* of said gas station—Father's Vega station wagon!

"Hooray!" Mr. Maguire yelled, and therefore didn't hear the engine gurgle and die. He hit the brake with normal force, which did little, then stood on it, which did little better.

If the day ended in a Y, it was a good day for Connecticut State Police Sergeant Robert D. White to get violent with the citizens. He had tried to be one of those even-keel cops, the kind who never let anything bother them. He really did try. But the goddamned citizenry he was sworn to protect—some days, they practically *begged* to get tapped with the nightstick.

It always started the same way, with stupid civilians being stupid about something stupid, and always ended the same way: with an ass-chewing from this Captain, that Commander, or the other Commish; and/or a threat about badges, guns, and retirement benefits, and the prospect of losing one, two, or (most common) all three. But White had never been suspended or fired; that simply didn't happen to cops unless the media made a thing out of it. And so Sergeant White puttered along Connecticut's roads on his cop bike, grim expression hidden behind a white helmet and mirror shades, ticking like the time bomb he was.

Today, he fixed his grim gaze on the accident scene at Old Joe's Texaco & Mini-Mart in New London. In the parking lot, ten or so young men engaged in a painful ritual with a pigskin football: anyone who caught it was immediately pounced, beat up, and forced to pass it again. The process repeated. Sergeant White recalled a similar game—called Smear the Queer—that he played in his teenaged years. Back when his name was Bobby White, back when he *was* rather an even-keel person, back when he had emotions other than grimness.

Sighing, the cop refocused on the "accident." Another pointless dinger. No limbless corpses. A lack of flaming debris. Totally bereft of automobiles vulgarly interconnected, smashed into one mass, as if they were a couple of huge, fierce, desperately horny machines who'd had a go at some real rough fucking and only failed since they'd bashed heads and fallen unconscious while slamming about trying to find the right spot to stick it in.

There was none of that. Just a full-size utility truck and a butt-ugly green wagon parked in a close V at the edge of Old Joe's lot. And a lot of teenage boys tackling each other.

Sergeant White told the drivers to move their vehicles back from the roadway. When the older, more rotund, and altogether blacker of the two drivers eased his royal blue Ford Bronco back, it exposed the full extent of the damage: a two-inch fold in the Bronco's front fender and a two-inch dent in the left front wheel wing of the young white kid's crappy Vega. New London's most disreputable body shop couldn't squeeze more than five hundred bucks total outta this! No one even banged their head on the dashboard or anything! Sergeant White turned and cursed. And cursed, and cursed a bit more. Even Old Joe, the gas station's proprietor, got an earful for immediately calling the cops about something so ridiculously minor.

White took down notes on the damaged vehicles' makes and plates until he felt a tug on his sleeve. He turned to find a kid about sixteen years old standing behind him, hands in pockets: the driver of the Vega, dressed in a once green, now muddy class A uniform shirt. A patch on the kid's shoulder bore a white crucifix and the words JUNIOR CHAPLAIN.

"Hello, sir," the kid said. "I wanted to apologize for our accident here. I've only been driving a year now, and Mr. Maguire ran out of gas and couldn't stop as he came down the ramp ... well, I for one am sorry."

"You can say that again," White growled.

"Yes, sir. Uh, could I bother you for directions? We're actually lost. Can you tell us how to get to Camp Souviens?"

The sergeant's grim eyes went bright white.

Camp Souviens.

"No, I—excuse me." With a jerk, Sergeant White stomped over to Old Joe's Mini-Mart and threw open the door.

The crash-happy Assistant Troopmaster and Old Joe chatted at the counter. Three boys stood by the soft drink refrigerator units: one had black curly locks, one had a long semi-flop of wavy brown hair, and one had a perfect military-short afro flattop. At Sergeant White's jarring entrance, all present turned to face him.

"What the hell are you all looking at?!" the cop screamed.

All present ducked as if shot at.

Across the inside of Sergeant White's mirror shades, overtop the darkened image of a gas station mini-mart interior, the words "Camp Souviens" flashed in frightful red letters.

The sergeant whirled, knocking over a snack cake stand. The three boys reacted wildly: Curly Hair broke for the door, Flattop dove to the floor and covered his head, while Long Hair merely took a position out of White's range.

Proprietor Joe, meanwhile, fell flat behind the cashier's counter. The portly black Troopmaster put up cautionary hands. "Easy there," he oozed. "There's no need for trouble."

The image of a pudgy, buzz-cut, lock-jawed kid in a pea-soup-colored Troop uniform appeared on both lenses of White's shades. The pudgy kid was large for his age, squint-eyed, dirty, and downcast. Unseen parties taunted him.

Look at that fat shit!

How much you weigh, two hundred ... tons?

The pudgy kid trembled with fear, cornered. Rude hands appeared and rubbed foreign substances into his hair.

A voice from White's left said, *Call this a buzz-cut?*

A voice from his right said, *Think yer in the Army?*

A voice, behind: *Why do all you faggots got buzzes?*

A voice, in front: *Let's wash his hair with battery acid!*

Above: *Imagine sharin' a tent with this fat son of a bitch!*

Below: *Grab them baked beans! Give this homo a new look!*

"SHUT UP!" the sergeant shrieked, swinging around 360° and sending askew a magazine rack on the counter. Old Joe found himself immersed in five dozen of the latest copies of *Weekly World News, National Enquirer,* and *Soap Opera Digest.* Mr. Maguire took a hurried step back; atop his head, the brown "shit-nipple" campaign hat wobbled in a silly way.

The ghostly hands attacking the pudgy kid suddenly recoiled. Drenched in blood. Limp and aslant. Echoes of crying.

Who said you could take the law into your own hands? called a voice from the other side of the mini-mart. This voice conjured odd, disjointed images: a chin-strap beard floated in mid-air, and an ostentatious watch whirled back and forth, as if the invisible wrist it was attached to flailed about.

The off-screen voice continued: *Cry, you goddamn baby! Cry for the blood you've shed! Cry for the blood you will shed!*

Sergeant White sprinted to the other side of the mini-mart and drew his nightstick. "SHUT THE FUCK UP!" he shouted at the villain cowering there: a rack of potato chip sacks.

The pudgy kid in the shades fell to his knees, wiping tears from blackened eyes. He glared up at the disembodied beard and watch, and spoke for the first time:

I'll get you, he said in a strong voice. *You wait and see.*

And with that, the kid in the shades ...

... disappeared.

Sergeant White spent several moments gaping at a normal, shades-darkened view of many sacks of Doritos. Slowly he became aware that the nightmare was over. He turned. A real kid in a Troop uniform lay sprawled on the floor by the fridges. Another, the long-haired one, stood nearby with a curious look on his smug mug. The gas station owner, old bearded Joe, peeked up from behind the counter. The portly Troop-master stood by the door with his hands still up.

Joe raised his eyebrows. "Y'okay, Bob?"

Sergeant White snapped his stick back into its belt-slot. "Yes," he said, wiping his brow with a sleeve. "Just, er, releasing the tension." With a sigh, he stomped out of the mini-mart.

Joe got to his feet, bearded face seething with rage. "Now look what ya's done t'him!" he growled.

"Me?!" returned Mr. Maguire, aghast.

"Y'all come in here lookin' fer Camp Souviens, 'Howja get to Camp Souviens!' Don't ya know that poor cop got his brain damaged at Camp Souviens?! Y'all brought it all back!"

Maguire gagged. "He got his brain—*what?!*"

Joe fussed about his pockets for a home-rolled smoke with hands nervous enough to tell that he needed one. "Was 'bout fifteen years ago. Bob was in the local Troop. They-all went to Souviens fer summer camp, when this guy there went and ... "

Inhaled. Trailed off. Exhaled.

"And?" prompted Mr. Maguire.

Joe's eyes sank back. "... and ... " After another drag, he floated around the counter to his office and shut the door.

"Let's scram, stat," Mr. Maguire belched, heading out the door. "We wanna get there before *closing* ceremonies, right?"

Neither Calvin Connor nor Art Maguire moved. The white lad just stood there breathing heavily, having witnessed a major event. With all due dread, the black kid got to his feet. "Holy shit," he said, "that was totally—"

The door opened and the maniac cop re-entered. Back down to the floor with Art. Calvin faced him. "Oh hello, officer."

Without a word to him, the cop stomped to the back and entered the office. "I should apologize for that ugly display," Calvin heard the cop say before the office door shut again.

"... whatever," Calvin said to himself.

The office door flung open. Art braced his hands over his head as the cop bellowed, "Where'd that moron go?"

"Which moron?" asked Calvin.

"The black guy! Your Troopmaster!"

"He went out the front, officer."

The cop kicked the mini-mart's front door open. Art heard the door's glass ring with dissatisfaction. The cop grunted, "I'm a *sergeant*, not an *officer!*" The door calmly shut itself.

"Then fuck off, *sergeant!*" Calvin hissed. He let out a bleak sigh. After a long moment, he asked Art, "You want a Coke?"

Art peeked up from the floor. "Sure."

Calvin opened the door to the soft drinks fridge and stood there a moment. "It'd be 'the Squad Captainy thing to do,'" he said, "if I bought one for all the Hawk Squad. Right?"

"Yes," Art said, slowly making it to his feet. "Wow, did you just think that up? All on your own? Like an *actual* Squad Captain?"

Calvin didn't respond. He fetched a six-pack of New Coke in cans and held the glass fridge door open for Art. When Art reached his hand in, Calvin slammed the door shut on his arm. "I'm not fucking retarded," he said tartly. "Should we leave money on the counter or just steal them?"

Once Art finished making *Ow!* noises, he scoped the vacant mini-mart with narrow eyes. "Looks like it's Freebies Day!"

Chapter 4
Handing in the lineup card.

Sergeant White allayed Troop 666's fear that he wanted to kill them. Well, he allayed their fear that he *would* kill them—there was no question he wanted to. The cop apologized for his behavior and gave succinct directions to the camp. "Back on 95 East," he said, pointing, "and take the exit for Rte. 117. Make a left, then very next left. It's up the reservoir, you can't miss it."

And they went east on I-95, and exited at Rte. 117, and made two lefts. This narrow road took them away from civilization and into a wooded quiet spot with a large reservoir of blue-green water peeking through the trees on their right. Soon they came upon a sign: two blackwashed telephone pole sections held aloft the Souviens mascot, a burly lumberjack in a red checked shirt and coonskin hat. His right hand was positioned above his brow, glassy eyes scanning leftward for some nice spruces to chop down. He had a small mustache with waxed upward points. JE ME SOUVIENS appeared on his coonskin hat in that awkward, diagonal, chiseled-out-of-wood script that always adorned anything camp-like.

According to the Beaver Squad's Billy "Spazz" Watson, "Je me souviens" meant "I'm Mr. Souviens." Spazz justified the translation thusly: "I took French! *And* French-kissin' your mama!"

A blackwashed board hung below the lumberjack:

WELCOME TO
CAMP SOUVIENS RESERVATION
RATED NO.1 IN NEW ENGLAND

Matthew "Father" Duffy put his turn signal on. The boys wiped salty moisture from their eyes. "Oh Lord," Father whispered, "we thank You for Your guidance during this trip. In the name of the Father, the Son, and the Holy Ghost, amen."

"Amen," the kids breathed in unison.

Father hit the gas and the Vega lurched onto Camp Souviens Road. There was applause and high-fiving and leaning out the windows to bellow "Amen!" into the forest.

They passed a nice ranch home with a modern addition marked "Ranger's Office." Later on they reached a fork: the right road (the Red Trail) grew narrow and vanished into the trees; the left opened into a stone parking lot, full of vans, trucks, and even an old school bus. Father cut a sharp left.

Mr. Maguire's Bronco followed. They parked at the far end of the lot, as they were ruinously late and the closest spots had long ago been taken. The Bronco's passengers got out dancing to a Bob Seger song in which he arrested his listeners. Even Mr. Maguire twisted his hips in giddy excitement. "We did it!"

Troop 666 rejoiced.

When some shitty Whitney ditty came on the Bronco's radio, the excitement wore off. The boys collected the trash from under their seats and set out on the long walk to camp. Twenty feet in, Jon Oldroyd started complaining. Denny Sandmiller complained about Jon complaining. Cuauhtémoc "Chicken" Ysderrhi complained about Denny complaining about Jon complaining. Calvin Connor complained about how complaints rarely get answered with anything other than more complaints, so why don't you all shut your gobs. Gus Jacoby complained that he didn't know what "gob" meant.

The boys reached the fork in the main road and trudged their aching bones down the packed-dirt Red Trail. Sandy wondered aloud where Oldroyd and Inky might have gotten to. No one had seen a brand-new forest green Chevrolet Silverado in the parking lot. Nor a black Harley softail.

"Probably got lost like us," offered Calvin.

"Guess they took the wrong route," Art deadpanned.

Troop 666 arrived at Centre des Trois, the heart of Camp Souviens, and marveled at the large cafeteria building. The ground floor was a mostly open-air affair with dozens of wooden picnic style tables. Concrete support stanchions ran along the building's perimeter, supporting the second floor's offices. These offices and the ground floor's kitchen area were shrouded in flat brown wooden siding with only the occasional glass window. Given the kids' previous camp cafeteria experience (viz. the rotting feed wagon at Lucid Pond back in PA), the Centre des Trois caf came off like Camelot.

The Troop rested their bones on the comfortable benches within the caf. They could smell the cool water from the nearby reservoir. After taking a moment to look around blankly, Mr. Maguire plodded to the giant stairwell at the far end of the building, next to the enclosed kitchen facilities. He disappeared upstairs, leaving Troop 666 to its own devices.

It was 3:53 p.m., and he was still Acting Captain, but Calvin Connor chose not to digress. He crossed himself to thank Jesus and soaked in the joy of having made it. Alive. Able to walk.

Then roly-poly Gus asked him what "Je me souviens" meant.

"It's French," Calvin said, "for 'I remember.'"

"Nut-uh!" Spazz hollered from the next table. "It means 'I'm Mr. Souviens!'"

Calvin returned the holler: "How the hell do you get 'I'm Mr. Souviens' from that? 'Monsieur' isn't even in it!"

Spazz was recalcitrant. "Don't talk back to me, Lé Calvan de Douchebag! I took French in school!"

"Oh did you now? How many years?"

"One. Well, I flunked out." Spazz ribbed his partner Denny Sandmiller and turned the embarrassment into a joke. "Fooled all you suckers! I was gonna say it meant 'give me ten bucks' but only the rookie woulda been dumb enough to fall for that shit!"

Ignoring the roars of laughter, Calvin turned back to Gus. "I start French 2 next year. It means 'I remember.'"

"I don't get it. That's two words. 'Je me souviens' is three."

"French is weird that way. You ever heard of a souvenir? Something to *remember* your time on holiday?"

The young blob worked this over and released his conclusion on an unsuspecting world: "This is Camp Remember."

"Pretty much."

"Well, what does KEN'·trey des·TROYS' mean?"

Calvin spent a minute explaining that, when pronounced SENT'·day·TWAH, this was French for "Center of the Three," obviously referring to the three trails that converged here at the cafeteria. Gus seemed to grasp that there were three trails, and that the caf was at their intersection, and that the Troop had come in on the Red Trail, and that there were two other trails called Yellow and Green, but he claimed he didn't get it.

"What specifically don't you get?" Calvin huffed.

"Um," Gus said, "what's 'spiffically' mean?"

"That's English! I do French only!"

"What? I don't get it."

"Art! Calvin!" came a bellow. "Come up here—stat!"

Calvin exchanged a *Fuck it, let's go!* look for Art's *What'd we do now?* look. They got up from the dining tables and dragged their frames to the stairwell.

At the top of the stairs, they found a dark, stuffy hallway with doorways on both sides. "In here," came Maguire's voice.

"Yo," Art responded, ducking into the second room on the left, marked RECORDS. Calvin followed. The room was pitifully small, crammed to the ceiling with papers and logbooks and binders and a gunmetal desk. A tall, gaunt white man with a comically round, heart-shaped face perched behind the desk. He wore khaki shorts, a green polo shirt, and an ill-fitting baseball cap; both the cap and the polo shirt had Camp Souviens's French Canadian lumberjack on them, forever searching for something somewhere to the left. (For this reason, the staff had nicknamed the mascot Lefty.) The gaunt man took off his cap and wiped a hand over his balding head. With a hundred-watt bulb directly overhead cooking a windowless, unvented room on the second floor (in late July), the gaunt man was practically a slice of bacon, sizzling quietly in a skillet.

He indicated a logbook on the desk. "Sign in your Squads, boys," he said—easily the deepest voice ever heard by Calvin or Art, nearly of too low a register for human ears!

Art took the proffered pen and scribbled in the book. He handed the pen to Calvin and backed to the doorway nervously. The setting, and the voice, had made it feel as if he'd signed the Beaver Squad's souls over to Satan.

"Now you," Satan rumbled, pointing a long finger at the next column over. Calvin jotted down the names of the Hawk Squad and handed Satan his pen. "Thank you," Satan smiled.

Art was too spooked by this. Even with his father present, the kid decided it was time to leave, and scampered out.

Satan went through his pockets and produced a brass key on a nylon cord lanyard. "I'll bet you boys are thirsty," he said to the much braver Calvin. "Here you go, son."

Calvin put his hand out. "Thank you, Mister …"

"… Lyons. Deputy Camp Director Horace Lyons."

"Mr. Lyons, sir." Calvin took the key. "What's it for now?"

"The yellow fridge in the kitchen. Go through the back door to the dishroom and you'll see the fridge. There's enough pop for your whole Troop, so help yourselves." Satan gave a wink. "Then leave the key with the Camp Dishwasher."

"Thank you, sir," said Calvin, inching out of the room.

"Now, Mr. Maguire," he heard Satan say, "we've put you in Campsite Quatre …"

Calvin reached the foot of the steps and found Art shuddering. "That was spooky," the kid gasped.

"You can say that again," Calvin nodded.

"Okay." Art cleared his throat. "That was sp—"

Calvin kicked him.

"—asshole! Remember this morning? I told ya you don't have the authority to beat up the guys!"

"Ha ha, African, you're not one of *my* guys!"

"Ha ha up your ass, Irish! I didn't say they had to be *your* guys!" Art jutted a petulant finger under Calvin's nose. *"Burnt!* Call him 'Melba,' cuz he's toast!"

Beaten verbally, then beaten down verbally. Crankily, Calvin punched Art in the gut and marched out, heading for the back of the building. He disappeared around the corner.

Art scrambled up and tore after him. He caught up just as Calvin stepped around a large stack of empty milk crates near the kitchen's back door. Art leapt him, sending them headlong onto the dusty packed-earth. The lanyard with the key flew from Calvin's big hand.

"You're such a dick!" Art shouted, grabbing a fistful of the dry road dirt and flinging it at Calvin's face. Art got to his feet and positioned himself out of range of a blindly thrown fist.

Calvin wiped his eyes clean. Pulling his large frame upright, he made fists. He'd been in his share of scrapes and was quite poised. Art, by contrast, was a jittery, dancing novice.

"Finally found your balls, did you?" Calvin spat. "I've known you for six months, and you've finally found your—"

"I found 'em in your sister's mouth!" Art squealed.

"Your balls in her mouth?!" Calvin laughed. "Did she even notice your tiny cock tickling her nose?"

Art opened his mouth to fire another salvo; however, drowning in adrenaline and frustration, he flung himself straight at his opponent, spearing Calvin in the chest with the crown of his head. Art wrapped his arms around Calvin to body-slam him on the tough dirt.

Confident he'd won, Art pushed himself to his feet. Gasping for air and thirsty for revenge, Calvin reached up and used the flats of his palms to slap Art over both ears. The move sent Art flailing, his usual weak-kneed scream trailing after.

Two small boys from another Troop, younger than the battlers and passing by on business of their own, came jogging up and propped Calvin and Art to sitting positions. "Are you okay?" the kids cried in unison. "Do you need an ambulance?"

Art vented a hollow laugh—these words were verbatim first aid procedure straight out of the *Handbook,* obviously being employed for the first time. "I'm cool," he said, though his face scrunched up with pain.

Calvin rolled over to all fours. "I think you broke a rib!"

"Oh gosh!" one of the kids whooped. "I'll get a doctor!"

"Don't even, you cunt!" Calvin urged, grabbing the kid's arm with his meaty hand and nearly wrenching it loose.

"Ow, leggo of me!"

"Only if you listen now: just get where you were headed, and not a word to anyone."

The kid nodded desperately. Calvin released him.

"It was an accident," Art reiterated. "Don't tell nobody."

"Are you sure?" the other kid pipped.

"We're sure," Calvin and Art groaned.

The interlopers stood, looked at each other, and beat feet.

Art wailed softly. "It's over, right? A tie?"

Calvin laughed, a comic laugh from after a joke. "Looks that way. Stay away from my sister's mouth—you don't know who else's bits have been in it." He fetched the key. "Let's get a move on before those boyos find a grown-up."

Art slapped the dust off his wrinkled class A uniform. "What's that key for?"

"A gift from Lyons. The man in the room."

"You mean Satan?"

"*Satan!* 'Sign in your Squads, boys!' That name fits!"

"Yo, not even *close* to how deep his voice really was!"

Calvin turned to the caf. In between a mammoth carbon dioxide canister and the stacked milk crates sat a wooden door. It was painted flat brown to match the rest of the building, and had a screen window. The sound of Madonna floated out from it. "The key fits in there somewhere. After you, African."

"Thanks, Irish."

Madonna accused you of possessing the unlocking utensil.

Art heard what Madonna had to say, saw someone into whom he might like to insert his own key, and mindlessly let the screen door slip from his hand.

It slapped Calvin's face quite sharply. "Fucking cunt!" he yelped, bursting inside with a hand cupped over his nose. They were in the kitchen's dishroom, a greasy little place lit by flickering fluorescents and made noisy by a gray plastic boom box. He went to an empty sink in a triple-sink unit and pulled away his hand. A shot's worth of blood dripped down onto the shiny stainless steel, pooling up by the drain.

There was a second piercing yelp. Calvin jumped, noticing for the first time the girl standing two sinks down. "Oh sorry, love," he said, grotesquely pinching a thimbleful of blood out of his nose, flicking it in his sink, then snorting up the rest.

The young lady, dressed in lime green shorts and a grease-spotted T-shirt, a dirty apron and a Hartford Whalers cap, raised a suds-coated hand to her face in horror. She was around their age and had a boy's haircut, rather like Calvin's. The sides and back were buzzed close; the long tresses poking from under her kelly green cap were dyed bright red.

She turned around to spare herself the sight of blood.

"Er," Calvin stammered.

"That's a record," Art joked. "Only took like four seconds for her to never want to see you again!"

"Fuck off," Calvin hissed. Still, her reaction wasn't a total loss; now that she faced away from them, they got a gander at her ass. Icing, baby—smooth icing. Delicately dabbed onto the cake. Calvin hadn't seen a girl's ass in two days. He drank it in.

He needed a cleaner face. He fumbled with the tap and stuck his hand under the jet of water. "Jaysus on wheat toast!" he howled. "Don't you have any *cold* water?"

"It's busted," the girl said over her shoulder. "Can you, like, bleed somewhere else?!"

"Give us a moment." Calvin grabbed a cloth dishtowel from a rack above the sinks and held it under the tap.

The girl whirled around to face him. Her eyebrows, glaringly black, lurched towards him. Even her acne seemed pissed off. "Hurry it up, buster, I got dishes to wash."

"Calvin's my name," he said, gingerly patting the towel over his sore nose. The boy trained his gray eyes on the girl's brown and didn't budge them, in spite of her scrumptious curves (and grinding teeth). "You can call me 'Asshole' if it makes you feel better," he offered.

"Okay, Asshole: what'cha gonna do with that rag now that you spread yer blood all over it?"

Art guffawed from behind them. Calvin sheepishly tossed the towel in the sink. He killed the tap and pulled the steaming towel out with a thumb and forefinger. Still had bloodstains on it. "Good question," he admitted. He looked to Art for help.

"Oh no," Art said, with the smuggest of smug looks on his gray face. "You're on your own, Irish." He nodded at the girl, saying, "Feel free to *completely* destroy him."

Calvin bit back the urge to say "fuck" again—he'd used it twice now and that was probably once too many in the first few minutes around a new girl. Instead, he twisted that energy into his best grin, what his brother Robbie called the "shite-eating grin." It never failed to disarm even the chilliest girls.

"I'm good at destroying boys," she said, aiming the words directly at Calvin's grin.

This girl *was* something like amazing, especially considering her competition in this setting (viz. none). That endearing round face, that wholesome frame bookended by a frostingly yummy fanny and ample boobs. Her air of earthiness: this girl could wash dishes in a camp-grounds for boys without going completely apeshit! Awesome.

But right now, she *did* seem precariously close to a status involving the fecal matter of man's ancestors.

"The towel?" she growled. "You're doing what about it?"

Calvin looked at the bloody towel. "I can … pay for this? It's obviously no good to you now, what with my blood on—"

The girl rolled her eyes and peered into the sink Calvin had used. She took some Comet off the shelf and poured a handful in. "Scrub that out first. And sure—five bucks."

Calvin cursed himself for the awkward offer to pay. Her acceptance was equally awkward. He wrung out the towel, draped it over his left shoulder, then dug out his wallet. The lad carried a man's wallet; not a Velcro thing with Ewoks on it, but a man's leather wallet. He handed over a fiver. "There you are. A fair price considering the emotional damage we caused."

"Oh what-fucking-ever, Mr. Wordsmith!" She stuffed the cash in her lime green shorts' ass-pocket. "Next time, go see Doc George—the First Aid Shack's down the Yellow Trail."

"Thanks for the tip, love."

"STOP THAT!"

Calvin backed up a step. A droplet of blood fell from his nose to his chin, but he dared not wipe it off.

"*Stop* calling me love!" she said. "It's *sooo* irritating!"

Art's snorty, choking laughter filled the dishroom.

Calvin quietly started scrubbing up his mess. The girl put her hands back into her sink. Pretending to be alone, she washed a three-gallon pot. Calvin's peripheral vision told him she was deliberately not looking their—his—way. He risked further dialogue: "So we came in cuz we were given a key. Mr. Lyons said we could—"

"What a dickhead," the girl spat, clearly referring to Satan and not Calvin. She pointed a sudsy hand at the far wall. "Yellow fridge is right there. Lay off the Dr. Pepper, that's mine!"

Calvin flicked the key over to Art; it was a perfect throw, swift and accurate, nailing the kid in the nuts. "Shithead," Art snapped. He fiddled with the Master Lock holding a latch across the yellow fridge's door.

"Spic and span," Calvin announced, beaming at his cleaned sink, "or at least Cometized. Sorry for the trouble, miss."

"Don't call me that, either!"

"What *can* I call you?"

"You can call me one really pissed off dishwasher!" The girl launched out her hardest look yet, all manner of combustion hurtling from her face.

For a dangerous moment, their eyes locked.

Calvin turned away and helped Art gather cans of New Coke in his folded arms. After re-locking the fridge, he handed the key to the girl. "Thank you," he smiled, "Miss Ever-Persevering in the Face of Stupid Boys." They went through the door to the kitchen and left her alone again.

Art released his interlocked arms and thirteen chilled cans of New Coke thundered down on the dining table. A few rolled away, sliding across the concrete floor of the caf.

Sandy looked up from his hardcover of Stephen King's *IT,* which he'd asked for at Christmas simply to see if he could finish it before he died. He was on page 13 (of 1,138). He'd been on page 13 for two weeks now, and this latest interruption pissed him off to no end. "You can't just hand 'em to us, dude?"

Art plucked one of the red cans off the table and aimed it at him. In self-defense, Sandy chucked the book and wielded a can of his own.

One ... two ...

"Three!" Calvin said, popping the tab of *his* can, spraying a beige stream of foam over them both. And the cola-war began!

Spazz snatched up a can and used it on Sandy. Sandy rolled under the table and gripped a can that lay there. He wetted Art and Calvin's shoes. Art knelt down and popped a can open right in Sandy's face. As Sandy opened his mouth to try to orally absorb the salvo, Calvin slammed himself into the table, kicking blindly under it. Sandy took a kick in the face and responded with more soda on Calvin's precious Reeboks.

And so on, until all thirteen cans of New Coke had been sprayed about and just about every kid in Troop 666 was wet. Calvin and Art stood in the center of the battlefield, dripping.

"Strike last!" roared Art.

"Strike fast!" roared Calvin.

"Get bent!" said Sandy, worming out from under the table.

Calvin called out, "If anyone wants to help clean this up, follow me." He turned on a soggy heel and marched to the kitchen. He didn't expect anyone to follow. However, Art grabbed Sandy's shoulder and whispered in his sticky ear. Sandy crashed through the kitchen door, his wet curly black locks trailing behind him. "Dude, where's the babe?!"

Calvin paused at the dishroom door. "She's mine, Sandy."

"Dibs don't count with babes."

They went in.

Whatever blessed place towards which Bon Jovi had headed, they were at the midway point.

Calvin smiled at the girl, who'd turned around at the door's creaking. "So guess what, Miss Ever-Persevering in the Face of Stupid Boys," he said, wiping back a sticky clump of hair. "There's been another accident."

"We're all set," Mr. Maguire said cheerfully as he stepped up to the Troop. He found the boys swabbing the caf's concrete floor with mops, spraying window cleaner on the dining tables, and soaking up soda-covered benches with paper towels.

Maguire blasted a look at Father, charged with maintaining order as Acting Junior Troopmaster in Inky's absence. Young Father sat at a table twenty feet away, his head buried in a legal pad and open copies of the Bible and *Mere Christianity*. Staticky snoring blared from Father's open mouth. As he breathed in, top page of the legal pad flapped intermittently against his lips.*

"What the hell happened here?" Mr. Maguire bellowed.

Art shook his head. "I think New Coke has more fizz, Dad."

Rather than deal with this bullshit properly, Maguire just let it go. "We're registered and ready to camp our brains out. Campsite Quatre.

---

* Father, born Matthew Adam Duffy, had gotten his nickname from the Catholic members of Troop 666—a considerable majority. As Junior Chaplain for a Troop which had no official adult Chaplain, Father fulfilled all the Troop's religious needs. The boys ballyhooed his fun version of Mass, a staple on the Sunday morning of a weekend camping trip. Since this particular trip had *started* on a Sunday morning, even the most devout kid hadn't gone to the real Mass at Saint Brigid Cathedral on the corner of Main Street and Bald Eagle Pike (one of the very few non-brick buildings in "downtown" Axsubeen).

Here in the Camp Souviens cafeteria, Father had been preparing a late Mass to be held just before bed tonight. Events yet to be chronicled will further force Father's Mass to be the loosest ever on record: the Lord's Prayer, no hymns, and a thirty-second tale from Luke 19 about Zacchaeus the sudden repentant sinner, all done as the boys passed 'round a rain-soaked hoagie roll and quart tin of Welch's, making the Eucharist self-administered to save time.

Amen.

That's Frog for 'four.' Let's go say hi to Inky."

Sandy blinked. "Inky's here?"

"Came in 'bout an hour ago. Apparently he wasn't happy."

"Is my dad here?" Jon Oldroyd chirped.

"No. I'm sure that's *why* Inky wasn't happy."

Chapter 5

THE OFFICE OF THE COMMISSIONER.

A PAIR OF thin slits stared out the office's window. This office was at the geometric center of Camp Souviens, at exactly the point where the Red, Yellow, and Green Trails intersected; the very heart of the camp. Though if you use the word *heart* to describe the office's occupant, go ahead and tack on a *-less*.

The slits watched as a Troop came into view down below. A flabby, bearded adult "leader," whose skin was a shade not often seen in this setting, barked, "Fall in!" The boys executed a dizzying series of unsynchronized wobbly maneuvers, like a dozen Foster Brooks impersonators all vying for the same mic.

The "leader" barked, "The left!" Almost predictably, half of the Troop stamped their right feet down.

The "leader" barked, "Forward march!" The slits had, at this point, closed up. After a painful pair of seconds they reopened to find five (five!)* boys marching backwards.

The "leader" "led" his Troop as they marched down the Green Trail. Of course, *marched* wasn't really the word for it. *Trudged,* perhaps. *Slogged.* Maybe with *clumsily* before it.

So, more properly: a late-arriving Troop clumsily slogged down to the Green Trail in search of their campsite.

"Bad," a mouth below the slits said. *They're going to show their act to everyone.* "Very bad," the mouth said, going dry.

There was a knock at the door, and in slinked Deputy Director Lyons carrying Camp Souviens's Summer 1987 registration book and a yellow carbon copy flimsy. "Hiya, Murph," he said in his sepulchral voice, tossing the items on the office's massive oaken desk. "What'cha

---

* *FIVE!*

looking at?"

"The end."

Lyons parked his gaunt frame in a chair. "Of what?"

"Of Camp Souviens." The owner of the slits turned.

Camp Director Jake Murphy was a short, thin man whose very fabric had been woven out of pure histrionicity. He wore closely cropped hair and an immaculately pruned chin-strap beard. His spotless white polo shirt was tucked neatly into wrinkle-free designer khaki shorts. He wore knee-high woolen socks and that sort of shoe Nike had just started marketing which looked like a hiking boot but wasn't really capable of hiking or booting. Murphy's hairy arms led either to a gargantuan bejeweled Trooping International Tribunal ring or a watch of such stupendous ostentation that time-telling was obviously a secondary function—if it bothered with it at all.

Murphy's slits burrowed into Lyons's face. Thick brown brows above those slits curled together like performance artists showing the value of world peace whilest entwining naked in front of a horny group of white-haired "art appreciators."

Lyons lowered his already low voice to what could only be described as Darth Vader wheezing. "What now? Hair too long? Uniform patches misaligned?"

Murphy's slits grew tighter. "I mean it this time."

"You mean it every time," Lyons snorted.

"I *really* mean it this time."

"You *really* mean it every—"

"Knock it off, Lyons."

"So what's this latest scourge's big crime?"

"Need I pick just one?" Murphy turned to the window. Although the Troop was long gone, he called up a replay from memory and paused it on a shot of the boys walking backwards into each other. "Look at their uniforms," he said, fogging up the glass. "Look at their haircuts," he said, wiping the fog off with his hand. "Or total lack thereof!" he went on, fogging up the glass again.

He spun back to Lyons. "Filthy … unruly … smelly …"

"'Smelly?' How can you tell *that* from up here?"

Murphy handed Lyons another set of slits from his vast collection.

"It's a very visible stench."

Lyons laughed. He couldn't help it.

Murphy stared at him. "Clearly you don't appreciate—"

"—the gravity of the situation," Lyons finished. "I've heard this speech before, Murph. I just met their Assistant Troopmaster and the Squad Captains, and you and I both met the Junior Troopmaster earlier. All normal folks."

Murphy flopped into his stately leather-bound chair. "I'd term that Junior Troopmaster a thug of the most barbarous order. I mean, black motorbiking leather? Who's their Troop's sponsor—the Hell's Angels?!"

Lyons let breaths out his nose in lieu of another laugh.

Murphy fumbled with the carbon copy flimsy Lyons had brought in. "Let's see from where these putrid shitheads hail." The flimsy was the camp's copy of an application for a campsite, mailed in some months ago. It was, puzzlingly, crumpled and a bit sticky. Murphy flattened it with his palm and squinted at Oldroyd's chicken-scratch.

Lyons grabbed the registration book and searched for the relevant page. "It's some one-horse town in Western Pennsylvania. In the mountains near Altoona, I gathered. A farm town."

"'Axzubean?' Dreadful penmanship!"

"Here," Lyons said, slapping the book down on the desk. "As long as you *insist* on calling them a rogue's gallery."

Murphy picked up the book. "Troop 666?!" he bleated. "Are you kidding? Who'd actually use *that* Troop number?!"

Grinning: "Perhaps the Hell's Angels *are* their sponsors."

Murphy was not amused. He read off names from the book: "Dick Oldroyd, Troopmaster. Paul Maguire, Assistant. Konrad Schultz IV, Junior Tr—Konrad! With a K, no less!"

Continuing: "Matthew Duffy, Junior Chaplain. Beaver Squad: Captain Art, Sandy, Spazz, Chicken, and Denny. Hawk Squad: Calvin Ciarán Connor III, Captain (Acting); Jon the jerk, Gus the fat slob, Crowe the rookie, Ryan the silent."

Murphy slammed the book shut. His eyes met Lyons's, turning to slits again. "Spazz," he droned. "Gus the fat slob," he droned. "Ryan the silent," he droned. "Clearly Satan's spawn."

"Then just burn them at the stake!" flapped Lyons.

The bits of Murphy's face uncovered by well-shellacked hair adopted a red glow. "I'm only thinking of the integrity of this reservation. We have a glorious history of serving the tee-eye-tee *and* generating big bucks in the process, and I won't jeopardize that for some shitheads from Axzubean or whatever goddamn rock they crawled out from!"

Lyons stood up and put a gaunt hand on Murphy's shoulder. "You're getting worked up over nothing."

"You saw them! If this isn't the 'scourge,' who is?"

"Okay, fine—they're a scourge! But a minor scourge, at best!" Lyons went into calming mode: "This camp made it through the Bobby White thing in '74, and no situation since has been more dire. We'll make it through this." His heart-shaped face now bore a reassuring grin. "I'll do all the dealing-with-them that we need to do, if that'll relieve your anxiety."

Murphy's face entered a photo booth. At three second intervals he looked taken aback, widening his eyes. After four goes at this expression, he faced Lyons. "Sounds acceptable."

Lyons nodded. "A week from now, you'll sit in this office and have completely forgotten that Troop 666 was ever here." With that, he popped out to return to work.

Murphy rewound the tape in his head to have a second look at his only personal encounter with someone from Troop 666. It'd gone like so: Murphy had emceed the opening ceremony up at Lacroix Memorial Field next to the parking lot and attended the special luncheon get-together here at the Centre des Trois caf. Once free of welcoming and glad-handing duties, he went upstairs to his office to start the camp's food order.

He jolted in alarm: his office door stood ajar.

Murphy tiptoed to the doorway and peeked in. An ogre sat in the better of the two guest chairs—and *sitting down* he was taller than Murphy! The guy had a pair of I-beam arms with ferricrete hands;

ICBM legs, heaved into silo-sized black leather pants; and a head of hair so red the air around it was hazy from heat. It may have been a Troopmaster, or a Troop-member himself—or neither. He wasn't wearing a uniform; just black biking leather.

Murphy drew a stabilizing breath. "Can I help you?" he said, striding purposefully into his office.

"Yes," the ogre said, not turning. "I'm arriving for camp."

Murphy went behind his desk, then leapt up at the sight of the ogre's face. It was curled down, snarling, viciously rotten! "Well, *I* can check you in," Murphy stammered, importantly shuffling papers. Once he'd found a very official-looking piece of paper and his Mont Blanc: "Which Troop are you from?"

"I'm the first to arrive," the ogre growled, lowering his eyes to meet Murphy's. "The others are late. Very late. Didn't you notice our absence during opening ceremonies?" The guy cracked his knuckles (a noise like trees snapping). "When they finally arrive, I'll kill them for their incompetence."

Murphy tried to disbelieve that remark. "You can wait for them at your campsite. I can tell you which one that is, if you tell me which Troop you're from."

"All they had to do was follow me on 80 East." The ogre flexed his colossal hands. "Just following me was too much for them. They are the dumbest people on Earth. If I were you, I'd tell them they ain't welcome. Or just kill them."

"Son, could you please stop using the word 'kill?' I won't lie to you, it's making me nervous." Arguing with this ... young man was not an option. Murphy made a note along these lines on the paper. "If I could ask again which Troop you're from."

The ogre dipped his shoulders, a maneuver which made the muscles in his neck spread like a tanker truck blowing up in *The Terminator.* On that note, Murphy jotted down, the ogre did look like Arnold Schwarzenegger. Or an amalgamation of *two* Arnold Schwarzeneggers.

The Two Arnold Schwarzeneggers said, "Troop—"

"Hey Murph," came a call from the hallway.

Murphy jumped at the interruption. Lyons popped his head

through the door, but Murphy ignored him. "I'm sorry," he said to the Two Arnold Schwarzeneggers, "repeat that?"

The Two Arnold Schwarzeneggers groaned. "I *said,* Tr—"

Lyons, thinking *he* was being addressed, said at the same time, "Hey Murph?"

Murphy shut his eyes—this encounter had drained his mental stamina, and he'd yet to even castigate the Two Arnold Schwarzeneggers for breaking into his office! All he needed was a Troop number so he could focus his anger properly. "I'm sorry, er," he said, fumbling at the Two Arnold Schwarzeneggers's real name—had he even gotten it? "This is Deputy Director Lyons. Normally he handles Troop arrivals."

"My Troop *hasn't arrived!*" the Two Arnold Schwarzeneggers countered. He stood, and his very shadow flopped down on Murphy like a heavy woolen blanket. "I thought I'd made that point pretty clear."

"That's okay," said Lyons, stepping up to the Two Arnold Schwarzeneggers and offering a hand. Lyons was a tall man but he paled next to the Two Arnold Schwarzeneggers. It was like asking Woody Allen to guard Kareem Abdul-Jabbar. "I'll get you squared away while you wait. You a Troopmaster?"

The Two Arnolds ground his teeth, creating the ungodly noise of two trains colliding. "*Junior* Troopmaster."

"Tall for your age," Lyons smiled, ushering himself and the Two Arnolds out the office. "Follow me."

Here ended the replay. Some sixty or so minutes later, after Murphy had learned the number of the Troop and seen their act and argued with Lyons about it, the irritation built into something physical. Like the warm pressure in one's chest just before vomiting.

Okay, so Murph had yet to hear of any malfeasance these shitheads might have committed. They had, after all, only just arrived. But he would hear of it soon. Tonight perhaps. By breakfast tomorrow, assuredly.

So he called a meeting of his kitchen staff.

Murphy struck a callous pose, letting the strong pre-dinnertime sun drift through the windows and caress his hairy features. In front of his majestic oak desk, the nicer of the two chairs teetered under the nervous direction of its occupant, a bug-eyed, hippie-bearded, maladroit stutterer filling the role of Camp Chef. The not as nicer of the two chairs swayed arrogantly through its occupant, an irascible teenage girl playing Camp Dishwasher.

The girl whined about how silly this meeting was, especially with dinner imminent and there being work to do; Murphy could only react with a Golden Globe-winning sigh.

"Today witnessed the arrival of the 'scourge.' Troop 666—seriously—of some pisspot in Pennsylvania called Axzubean. The boys of the Devil's Troop are the seediest collection of juvenile delinquents ever assembled. We are having this conference because you two *will* come into contact with them. It'll take no later than one day's time before someone knocks on my door to report miscreant-ish behavior from Troop 666, resulting in additions to the Kitchen Patrol. When that happens, and I'm confident it shall, and I'm advising you two ahead of time to make absolutely clear on this point ... er. What was I saying? Oh yes, when they report for K.P. duty, you *will not fraternize.* Assign duties and follow up on their work and the like, but I will not have anybody from my staff seen cordially conversing with these shitheads; least of all, anyone responsible for food preparation. Am I clear?"

The dishwasher arrogantly tipped her chair back on two legs. "Whatever. I just talked to a couple of 'em an hour ago."

Murphy's eyebrows spiraled up. "And ... why would you have occasion to?" he asked (accused).

"Cuz ... they came in my dishroom?" she replied (mocked).

He took his right hand and cupped it around his watch. The watch's hands were made of crystal, making very arduous the actual telling-of-the-time part of the watch's time-telling function. "And why was your K.P. crew *still* washing up from lunch 'an hour ago,' which was quarter of four?!"

"Nooo!" came the caustic reply. The dishwasher girl tilted her head forward, expressing a lack of patience with the man allegedly

responsible for every aspect of the camp.

Murphy fired right back with the slits—an expression which came in some six hundred and eighty-seven varieties, listed in order of abominability. These relatively mild slits (#335, "don't you talk back to me, young lady!") were still quite slim, and afforded Murphy a tightly letterboxed view of the girl's head: her brown eyes, her black eyebrows, and clumps of her fake-red hair poking from under a kelly green Hartford Whalers cap. The colors in this shot were dim since the slits restricted light to the iris, so Murphy's brain, equipped with a special effects department to make Industrial Light and Magic look like a flaming paper plate floating over a papier-mâché New York by means of fishing line in an Ed Wood production, got to work and intensified the colors. The red in the girl's hair suddenly stepped up in hue to the *Little House on the Prairie* barn-side red Murphy was used to ... and irked by.

"The week just *started* a couple hours ago," the girl testily said, requiring the camera operator in Murphy's head to turn the *y*-axis crank and tilt the shot down to her zit-covered nose, cheeks, and chin. "There *ain't* no K.P. crew yet!"

Murphy slung down his chin, forming slightly more menacing slits (#210, the "you're skating on thin ice!" variety).

"Who gets in trouble at the opening ceremonies?" the girl said. "No one—that's who!"

"Your attitude is not appreciated, young lady."

"My attitude doesn't work here. My hands do."

"They are hands juggling grenades," he zinged, winking at the chuckling studio audience between his ears.

"Just hope I don't throw one your way, Mr. Murphy."

The studio audience did one of those *Happy Days* "Oooo" noises heard whenever somebody at Al's accidentally spilt a soda on Fonzie's jacket. "Get on with your story," Murphy said.

"I was washing some cooking pots when the back door opens and in comes these two guys," the girl explained. "The patches on their sleeves said '666'—I noticed that right away. One of them was bleeding all over the place."

Murphy arched a mild eyebrow (#583, "There's more to this than what you're telling me ...").

"The bleeding guy was, like, annoyingly charming. His name's Calvin. He's got the coolest accent, like Irish or something. The other one, I don't know his name. He was kind of a wise-ass. He just stood there, totally eyeing me up."

Murphy wore a frozen face. If working with this young lady for the last six weeks had taught the man anything, it was that females should not work at a camping reservation for boys. She, being teen-aged and curvy, constantly complained of bad behavior from boys who should be off tying knots or helping old ladies cross the street. Murphy was disinclined to believe any boy would be interested in a recalcitrant brat sporting fluorescent red hair (curves or no). One time, Murphy had said as much; her reaction had been explosive.

"Aside from the blood, they're okay," she continued. "Even when I was rude, that Calvin was a gentleman. More of the bastards should be like him. I even made five bucks off him."

"Selling yourself," Murphy began, automatically, to say: he got as far as the N in *Selling* before he caught himself. "Selling what?"

"The bloody rag."

Like I said. Half a malicious grin crawled on Murphy's face.

"I hope you break your neck falling off your high horse!" the girl barked. "I will *cordially fraternize* with anyone I want. If you don't like it, wash the goddamn pots yourself." She got up and stomped out, slamming the door behind her.

Murphy held the slits' tight letterboxed view at the now-empty space above her chair. After a spell he snapped his eyes wide to return to full-screen vision; continuing the motif, he performed the terrible automated pan-and-scan that adds to the hilarity of watching 1970s kung fu movies—scrolling rigidly from the empty chair over to the one with the hippie Camp Chef shifting nervously in it. "Anything to add, Jim?"

Chef Jim's worrisome bug-eyes splashed all over Murphy's face. "Su-su-supper's coming up. Got th-th-things to do," he said. He limped out of the office with one hand gripping his long beard like it was a walking stick.

🔥

In just sixty minutes, Troop 666 had turned Murphy's sacred ground into a trespasser's paradise and gotten his staff shaking their heads at the boss. Wouldn't get better with time. Only worse. A fatigue sank into Murphy's shoulders. He took a time-out, letting his head gracefully drop like an Olympic diver in a slo-mo replay. *Thunk!* went his noodle as it hit the desk.

He studied the green desk blotter while letting out a sigh. This was no way for the Big Cheese to behave, alone or not, and doing so only gave Troop 666 another victory. With renewed determination, he sucked in a breath and—

—a sheet of yellow carbon copy flimsy, vacuumed up by his inhaling, stuck to his face. Murphy jerked back his head and the yellow flimsy flittered down to land on one of three neat stacks of the things sitting equidistant to one another on his desk blotter.

"What the ...?" he whispered.

The whole scene had props and dressing that had not been there a moment ago. Two metal hand-stampers sat nearby; the sideboard on his desk was out, an appointment book and pencil resting neatly on it. The Camp Director jolted to find himself decked in snow pants and an insulated red-checked shirt. Lyons was here with a sudden beard on his chin.

Early February, then: Murphy and Lyons were in the midst of processing bids from Troops wishing to stay at Camp Souviens during the eleven-week summer season. While not July by any definition, February *was* several months in the past (or future), long before the irritation of Troop 666 would emerge (or long after it had finally gone away).

Was this time-traipse something Murphy could control? Was it an out-of-body experience or flashback? Or a warning he was going mad? Or part of "his life flashing before his eyes," which alarmingly indicated he was very shortly about to die?

He studied the three stacks of yellow flimsies. The left stack, the tallest, were bids to be considered. The middle ones had been stamped APPROVED and the right ones, REJECTED.

"Goddamn, it's cold in here," he griped, rubbing his arms. The chill did not subside, as if it were from goosebumps. "Tell Kevin to get my kerosene heater up here!"

Lyons turned the legal pad in his lap around. "I've taken note of it—all *ten* times you've said it today."

Murphy squinted at Lyons's pad, pock-marked with notations like *get Kevin to bring heater* and *kerosene heater — tell Kev.* "See that Kevin gets all ten messages. I want that fat bastard to realize he's got work to do."

"Noted," Lyons said, who dutifully noted it (*fat bastard's got work to do*). "If you don't mind, I'd like to finish up before my beard grows another inch."

"Agreed." Murphy snatched up a flimsy from the left stack. "Troop 43 from Wyoming, Rhode Island." He said to the flimsy, "How can you be from both?!"

Lyons laughed. "Wyoming's a town in Rhode Island. Troop 43's been here before. Walt Meadows is the Troopmaster."

"Ah yes, Meadows, good people. Week of July 19th to 25th." He consulted the appointment book. Seeing an open campsite, he penciled Troop 43 in, *choo-chinked!* an APPROVED on the flimsy, and slid it into the middle pile.

On to the next one. "Troop 116, Derry, New Hampshire."

"Good people."

"Very good. Nice kids. Well-groomed. June 21st to 27th ... good." Scribble. *Choo-chink!* "We're tearing through this job this year, eh Lyons?"

"This is the third day we've worked on it, Murph."

"Yep, breezing right through it." Murphy fetched the next flimsy. "Troop 666—*Troop 666?!* Are you kidding me?"

Lyons sat up. "Is that really their number?"

"That *could* be a zero—606. What dreadful penmanship! From Axzubean, Pennsylvania, wherever the hell that ... "

Murphy scratched a neatly trimmed nail through the neatly trimmed swath of hair on his chin. "Listen to this, Lyons: 'Our Troop is seventy-one years old. Every summer we go to Lucid Pond Reservation nearby, we also go to Lucid Pond winters for the Klondike Derby. We're fed up with the place. We heard good things about Camp Souviens so we want to give you a shot. [Signed,] Dick Oldroyd, Assistant Troopmaster.'"

"Sounds okay to me," said Lyons. "Standard rhetoric."

"Is it? They're 'fed up' with Lucid Pond—what gives them the right to be? And they 'want to give [us] a shot.' And see if we measure up, in other words?!"

"Murph, just book them. They sound like good people."

"My ass they do! Bad comma splice in that sentence. And what kind of name is 'Oldroyd' anyway?"

"Sounds like something Chewbacca would have in his attic," Lyons laughed.

Ignoring him, Murphy fumbled for the REJECTED stamp.

The laughter died. "You can't reject them."

Murphy gave Lyons a particularly nasty brand of slits (#50, "Don't tell me what to do, slave!").

Lyons was not deterred. "You know the rules. Rejection only if we're booked full that week."

"Or if I veto them based on instinct. And their number says it all—this is the Devil's Troop."

"You've used both your vetoes already."

"I've done no such thing," Murphy snorted, though his face spoke of doubt. "Only the pot-heads of Troop 551 in Hartford."

"Yesterday you vetoed Troop 9 from New York City. Those black kids who did a rap at closing ceremonies last year."

"Ah yes." Murphy took a second to compose a new strategy. Hoisting the REJECTED stamp, he proclaimed, "What a shame, we're booked that week."

"You didn't even check, Murph!"

Murphy testily turned to the sideboard and leafed through the appointment book. "Sorry, we really *are* booked that w—"

"You don't even know *what* week!" Lyons leaned over the desk and snapped the flimsy from Murphy's hand. "Week of July 26th to August 1st!" he shouted at the Director's defiant glare. "Check it!"

Murphy did so. Adrenaline coursed through his arteries, making his finger shake slightly. "Only two campsites open."

Lyons's gaunt eyeballs nearly popped. "So give them one!"

"Suppose one of our better customers wants one?"

"Tough. First come, first served."

"Some of these bid forms aren't dated, Lyons! How—"

"Because I check the postmarks when the bids come in, and I keep the flimsies in such order, to prevent this very—"

Murphy swept his right hand about two inches above the surface of his desk, creating enough wind to ensnare the thin sheets of yellow flimsy in a maelstrom. "There!" he said in triumph as dozens of flimsies rained about the office. "Now *none* of them are 'in such order,' you bureaucratic Nazi!"

"You get like this every fucking year!" Lyons waggled Troop 666's flimsy at Murphy's slits. "These boys are next!"

Murphy dropped the appointment book, snatched the flimsy from Lyons, crumpled it into a ball, and shoved it in his mouth. "Noh hif Hi *heat* her hid!" he gargled, dribbling spittle down to his thin beard. "Hen herr'll bhe hoe hevidhens!"

Lyons swept up the appointment book and the pencil. "Bon appétit! I'm giving them Campsite Quatre!"

The tall Lyons stood, then held the book up where the short Murphy could not reach. "Hive he hat!" Murphy burped, swatting up at Lyons's elbows. "Hat's hmy bhook!"

Lyons planted the book on the ceiling and scribbled. Then he let down his arms and handed the book to Murphy. "Better spit out that form, Murph. Aren't carbon-copies poisonous?"

Murphy emitted a sullen growl. Balefully he spat out the bid, and watched it land in what was left of the ACCEPTED pile.

"How poignant," Lyons said, digging out his Winstons. "I'm taking a smoke break. You should take five yourself." The gaunt man took his leave.

Murphy crashed into his leather throne, ruefully watching his expensive oaken desk tremble. He went for the pencil, intending to erase the Troop 666 entry. Frustratingly, the pencil was gone. That damn Lyons probably took it with him, just in case! Murphy searched his desk for another pencil, and found one, but it was a mechanical pencil and had no eraser. "Shit!"

He placated his annoyed mind: it *was* early February, after all; he had ages to locate another pencil.

With a nasty knock Murphy's vision swelled on him, reverberating. The man blinked to find a dimmed, all-too-close view of the green desk blotter before his eyes.

He yanked back his head and took survey of his person and surroundings: it was July again. He swept through the drawers of his desk and came up with the appointment book. Week of July 26th to August 1st. Campsite Quatre: Troop 666, Axsubeen, PA. The penmanship was sloppy, since it had been done upside down. And—*and!*—it was still there.

Murphy had never gotten around to erasing it.

Another small victory for the scourge.

Chapter 6

REUNITED AT LAST.

INKY'S BOWIE KNIFE chopped down on the long maple branch in his hand with a satisfying crunch. He delivered the killing blow by snapping the branch over his knee. With a grim smirk, he chucked the two bits onto a five-foot-high stack of wood he'd piled up. At the sounds of slogging behind him, the Junior Troopmaster turned around. "About time," he gnashed.

Father put up a glad hand. "Hello, Inky! You managed to beat us here!"

"Like that's an achievement," Inky said. He looked over at Mr. Maguire. "So where's Oldroyd?"

Mr. Maguire did not respond.

"You're joking. He had a half hour lead on us!"

No one dared comment.

"Excuse me." Inky marched away from Troop 666. "I need to take a shit. And plan someone's funeral."

The harried boys watched the teenage ogre trample ferns and pine cones like a Japanese actor in a Godzilla suit waltzing over a cardboard Tokyo. Inky entered a wooden shack tucked into the woods and slammed shut the door. A spring from the door twanged grievously and could be heard bouncing off the concrete foundation.

Mr. Maguire raised his doughy arms and announced, "Troop 666, meet Campsite Quatre. Let's have a look around."

The Troop clumsily slogged down the by-way from the Green Trail to the campsite's fire circle—a clearing of naked dirt about twenty feet in radius with a small circle of rocks in the center, designating (for intellectually challenged Troops, a not-unheard-of subspecies) where a campfire really ought to be built. Remember what Smoky says! Inky's meticulous stack of timber all but buried the rock circle. The stack loomed over the shorter kids; even Inky's unlit campfires reeked of his menace.

Medium to dense forest surrounded the fire circle, save the by-way back to the Green Trail and two goat-paths: one snaking to the north, another to the west.

The north goat-path went about seven yards to the shack into which Inky had vanished. This was the latrine shitter, and a decent one as far as such things went: blackwashed wooden walls, tiled roof, and an outside wash basin and pump crank covered by an overhang; all of which sat comfortably on a slab of cracked concrete. Strange gurgling noises came from Inky inside (or maybe from inside Inky).

Troop 666 ventured down the westward goat-path, which split at a fork into north and south tributaries. They chose north. The foliage got thicker and the rocks lining the trail increasingly greener with moss. The path meandered this way and that, going on for quite some ways ("This is one big-time campsite!" Art declared). Eventually the kids came upon a clearing with a large eight-man tent in the center, elevated by an ingenious foot-high wooden floor foundation (or "deck"). Nylon rope hitched the tent to wooden pillars positioned along the deck. The thick canvas flaps on the tent's front and rear had been rolled up and tied neatly with yellow cord, exposing four double-bunks, lined two per side, with a comfortable aisle down the middle. Thin mattresses of a wan color like dried sweat lay on the bunks. Six-foot wooden support poles bisected the tent's front and rear openings.

The goat-path snaked south for about twenty yards, revealing a second tent same as the first; then, a ways on, a third tent. Sandy and Calvin popped inside this one, noting its appropriate height of six feet, and stepped out the rear. Calvin spotted a part in the ferns behind the tent; they followed it through a wooded copse to the shore of the reservoir.

The boys stopped in their tracks. A long wooden jetty thrust into the reservoir before them. Floating green splotches of algae peppered the dark water, as well as the crazy rings of crash-landing dragonflies. The late afternoon sun skipped up and off the water, shining wobbly rays into their eyes. Geese honked in the distance.

Calvin reeled giddily. "We made it."

Sandy's throat was parched. "Yeah. We're here, dude."

This was the stuff of future memories, and the teenaged boys knew it. Goosebumps paraded over their arms. Checking their breath, they nearly wept at this spell of wonderment.

"Hey, you assholes coming?" shouted Jon Oldroyd.

Troop 666 clumsily slogged off east, where the goat-path snaked on; it made a wide loop and turned out to be the southward tributary of the original fork. Mr. Maguire counted off the tents, proclaiming homes: "First one's the leadership corps and grown-ups; second, Beaver Squad; last one, Hawk Squad." He sighed. "Nap time."

"Rise and shine," said a familiar hick voice.

Calvin pried open his eyes. A Caucasian figure with a gray mustache and a black Stetson stood framed by the tent's front support pole and parted flap. "Mr. Oldroyd!"

"Connor." Oldroyd's cowboy hat smiled.

The others in the Hawk Squad stirred at this noise. "Hey guys!" cried Jon. "My dad's here!"

Oldroyd put up a thin hand. "I'm here. A li'l late, but y'all weren't a buncha spring-chickens yerselves."

"Didja get lost like us?" yelped Jon.

"Not really. Had a little trouble with my Chevy."

"Did Inky let you have it?" laughed the rookie, Crowe.

Oldroyd ignored that. In fact, he changed the subject entirely. "Mr. Maguire says we gotta stick around Sentrey dess Troys after supper to sign up for merit badges. After that, we'll slope up the Red Trail to my pickup and get our gear."

The Troopmaster gave Calvin an even look. "How you doin', Connor? How's bein' a Captain again workin' for ya?"

Calvin returned the even look. "So far so good. Right?"

"Not ne'ssarily. You pick a lieutenant yet?"

Calvin's look was less than even now. "They get *elected*, Mr. Oldroyd, not picked. And not yet."

"Don't dick around—get it done. Welp, lemme go talk to the Beaver Squad." And with that, Oldroyd left.

"I thought *you* were the lieutenant," Crowe peeped.

Calvin climbed out of his bunk. "I'm the *acting* Captain this week. So I'm gonna need my own lieutenant."

"*Lef*—you mean *loo*-tenant?!" said Crowe, laughing again.

"Micks like him put an F where it don't belong," Jon said.

"I'll put an F in your ma if you don't stop calling me that now," Calvin said, more angrily than jokingly.

Jon simply rolled his eyes.

Calvin took a breath and had a good, long look at his mates in the Hawk Squad.

Augustus "Gus" Jacoby tried to sit up in his bunk, drink from a canteen, and position an *Amazing Spider-Man* comic in his lap to read. Predictably, he failed at all three tasks, and even fell out of his bunk in the process.

Having Gus around required patience. Lots of it. It was like calmly telling a clumsy toddler to use both hands; then, a second later, reminding him with a sigh; then, a second after that, slapping him upside the head while fetching the broom to sweep up the broken plate. Then, repeating the process. And repeating it again. And again. *And again.*

Gus presented no deliberate threat to Calvin's authority; the feckless clod actually looked up to the Irish kid. But Gus's natural idiocy would be a source of constant headache. He was an unlikely candidate for the Squad Lieutenant (Acting) post.

Ryan Phillips lay in his bunk across the aisle. Ryan was abnormally strong for a fourteen-year-old, with defined biceps and dense calves. His sharp facial features and naturally blond hair made him the cutest kid in Troop 666. But he was awfully quiet, and often distant—"private" was the word.

What went on in Ryan's mind? No one knew. There were whispers of Satanism and the occult, mostly on account of his Book: a handmade journal about the size of a small bible. It had a few dozen rough leaves, like watercolor paper, bound with stitching and covered by worn, black leather. No words adorned the cover or spine. Anything said of the Book was hearsay, since no one had ever managed to read it. Only one boy had gotten more than a fleeting glance at a page.*

Ryan never read the Book where others could peer over his shoulder (hence, the kid's bunk at the front of the tent; Ryan sat with his back against the canvas, facing the aisle). Since it fit most pants' pockets, Ryan kept the Book on his person at all times. Even, it's worth noting, while sleeping.

Given such ambiguity, plus Ryan's indigenous silence and the boundless imaginations of teenage boys, the Book instantly became legend. It wasn't just a book. It was "the Book."

Calvin considered Ryan a friend. They were the same age, lived on the same street, and had known each other since Calvin moved to the United States three-plus years ago. They'd hung out at each other's houses, gotten along well, and shared some interests (those Ryan had allowed to be known, such as pornography). Ryan also made a great listener since he seldom interrupted. And how can anyone *not* want a strange guy like Ryan to be a friend? Better that than an enemy!

Ryan might be reluctant to accept a leadership rank. It's tough to hold rank *and* privately sit at the back.

Jon Oldroyd stood near the rear bunks with an anxious look on his zitty mug. He was a gainsayer and a brat. Calvin detested dealing with Jon and made that fact known. Jon was only mildly annoyed by Calvin's sound and fury; he actually believed his station to be above Calvin's (and all the other kids, these sons of farmers and plumbers). Any punishment detail Jon didn't like usually got pardoned by his father, the once Assistant Troopmaster, and now the Big Cheese.

Jon had narrowly lost the vote to Calvin some months ago to become Captain Sammy "Zedz" Dzedzy's lieutenant. Now, Jon practically drooled at the idea of scoring even a temporary leadership rank.

Lastly, the rookie Shawn Crowe stood next to Calvin near the tent's front entrance. This kid was barely twelve and toiling in just his fourth week with Troop 666. Hitherto, Crowe had been quite shy; now

---

* And that was Art Maguire, during the kid's first meeting with the Troop six months ago. He'd refused to reveal what he'd seen beyond saying it was a frightening illustration. The only reason Art's hair hadn't stood up on end was because it'd been forever entombed in that position anyway.

that he was away from Zedz's gruff anti-rookie attitude, Crowe was more outgoing, unafraid of being taunted. Did he really just make a crack to Oldroyd's face about Inky kicking his butt? Wow, that was fearless. Or stupid!

Being so green, the boy had no chance of being elected. Still, Calvin made it a goal to win Crowe over. That's what Squad Captains do, right?

After another deep breath, Calvin got on his soapbox. "You heard the Troopmaster now. We need to vote for an acting Lieutenant. I'll only cast a vote if it's a draw. I'll point at each of you, like you're the candidate, then it's a show of hands."

He pointed towards Gus Jacoby just as the bulbous doofus asked, "A show of what?"

"A show of *hands*," Calvin sighed, "meaning you raise your hand to vote." He put his left hand in the air to demonstrate, keeping his right index finger pointed at Gus.

Gus stuck his dense arm straight up. "I vote for me!"

"Okay," Calvin said, settling his limbs and pointing next at Jon Oldroyd. The Troopmaster's son rocketed both his arms in the air, then bucked when no one else voted for him. "C'mon, guys!" Jon wailed. "My dad's the Troopmaster! We got a total free pass outta punishment if *I* got a rank!"

The desperate words died against the thick tent canvas.

"Next," Calvin said, pointing at Shawn Crowe. The boy was a little startled that he was even a candidate. As predicted, no one voted for him, not even Crowe himself.

"Last," Calvin said, pointing at Ryan Phillips. Crowe raised his hand. Ryan, though, hadn't voted yet for anyone.

"You don't wanna cast a vote?" Calvin asked him.

The blond enigma gave a slight shake of the head.

"I won't force you to," Calvin shrugged. "So: one vote for Gus, one for Jon, one for Ryan. It's a three-way tie, and I get to cast the deciding—"

"Nut-uh," said Crowe, "you voted for Gus!"

"Go and shite."

"Your hand was up!"

"Yeah," yelped Gus. "It was, 'member? You put it up!"

"Bullshit!" bugged Jon. "He was just showin' the dumb-ass what 'show of hands' meant!"

A tense pause. Then Ryan cleared his throat and said, in his full, dark, rarely heard voice: "Your hand *was* up, Calvin. And it breaks the tie."

Calvin smirked, then loosed a full-on guffaw. "Then that's that— Gus, you're the Hawk Squad's acting Lieutenant."

Jon stomped his foot three times, steaming mad. "Holy shit, what a friggin' gyp!" The others laughed at him. Jon turned a snarling face to Calvin. "You totally screwed that up, Connor. Don't think I'll forget about it!"

"Eh, forget you," Calvin said, checking his Swatch. "Supper's on at five so let's get ready."

Chapter 7
PLAYING THE PERCENTAGES.

AFTER EATING A nice turkey supper at the Centre des Trois caf and standing in line to sign up for merit badges, Troop 666 hiked the Red Trail to the parking lot and finally retrieved their gear from Oldroyd's overstuffed Silverado. Breaking up into their usual small cliques, the boys made their way back to Campsite Quatre at their leisure. Even then, Calvin Connor, Art Maguire, and "Sandy" Sandmiller took their damn time.

Calvin suddenly dropped his newly reacquired rucksack on the edge of the Red Trail, then dropped his butt next to it. "I can't believe I signed up for Bowmanship!" he said, leaning back against a tree and waving his schedule of merit badges.

Sandy took leave of his legs also, his backpack falling atop Calvin's. "Better than Earth Science. It's gonna suck majorly!"

"Yo momma sucks majorly!" Art teased. His backpack joined the pile. The Red Trail cut through a long expanse of forest largely devoid of man-made structures (and man himself). For a main thoroughfare, it was quite private!

"Whatever, dude," Sandy said. "I just hate my merit badge situation. It's like, I *know* it's coming. What's the word, Calvin?"

"Premonition. When you *know* it's coming!" Calvin ran hands through his long hair, icky with rained-on Aqua Net and dried soda from the wild New Coke war. "I'm having one myself—Squad Captain my arse! And Gus is my lieutenant! That cop at the gas station shoulda just shot me and gotten it over."

"You laugh, but we almost bought it that time!" Art said. "Why'd you run away, Sandy? You missed the whole thing!"

Sandy did a double-take. "That's a question that answers itself, dude. Why the hell'd you guys stay inside?!"

"Black men can't turn their backs on cops," Art asserted.

"Guess that goes for Irishmen too," Calvin shrugged.

"You guys are such losers," Sandy muttered. "I just got good reflexes! Why was that guy so pissed off, anyway?"

Art explained it: "The old man told my dad the cop got his brain damaged here when he was a kid."

"Holy shit, *that's* a bad premonition!"

After a laugh, the three friends sat in silence for a spell.

"Dude," Sandy said, lowering his voice despite their being alone, "wha'ja guys think of that dishwasher chick?"

"She's hot," Calvin said. "I won't lie now, I want to see her some more. Good to have some tits and arse to look at, isn't it?"

Art boiled with envy. "Says the dickhead with the girlfriend already. Speakin' of, you finally pork Jenny yet?"

"Still stuck at third."*

"Hope yer stranded at third forever," Art spat, making Sandy laugh. "How'd *you* end up with Jenny MacDonald?"

Calvin's sharp, pale face looked snobbish. "You mean, how come I have a girlfriend and you don't?"

Art's gangly, cinereous face looked insulted. "That ain't what I meant at all!"

"If you say so. We've only known each other since Christmas, African. All this time you go on about being the total ladykiller back in Washington, but I ain't seeing it."

"Leave him alone," Sandy warned.

---

* Ah, the first baseball reference to leave Calvin's lips!

Wonder why the Chronicle of Calvin Connor, Vol. 1, doesn't include baseball? The answer is, Calvin's *life* didn't include baseball in 1987. *At all.* He knows nothing of the game, and would be shocked (to say the least!) to learn his destiny lay in professional sports stardom. There could've been a foreshadowing passage as the Bronco crossed the G.W. Bridge into Manhattan, but talk about shoehorning!

Okay, he just used a baseball reference. But the whole first base (kissing) second base (tits) third base (fingering) home plate (fucking) metaphor is just that, a metaphor. It's so venerable and transcendent from the game of baseball that it hardly counts.

"I'll have my say now," Calvin told Sandy. "Ain't the first time he's brought this up." To Art: "You're just jealous. Not only cuz I have Jenny, but cuz other chicks like me too."

Art scoffed at these thoughts. "Jealous?! Of an Irish porker with a freak's haircut? Bullshit! And that dishwasher girl *totally* don't like you. She practically punched ya in the face!"

"That's *how* I know she likes me. We *interacted!* You just did your comedy routine—she never even looked at ya!"

Sandy tried to soften things: "Some girls get off bein' played. The stupid ones. They like being won over by guys."

"I don't buy that one iota," Art said.

"Cuz you use nerdy big words like 'iota,'" Calvin noted.

Art fired off a condescending laugh. "Oh, you stupid retard! 'Big words like iota'—did you really just say that?"

"Eat me, African! What's more important—using the Queen's English, or me having more pussy than I got time for?"

"Screw you, Irish! You think you're the only one who gets pussy? *I* got some just last week!"

This brought everything to a stop. Calvin and Sandy had long suspected Art's tales of girls were total bollocks. Sandy scored some (third base), Calvin scored some (likewise), and Art talked about scoring ... but it wasn't the same. It was clinical talk, like a reporter relating things he'd heard witnesses say. *Not* the confident patter of the guy who'd *done* the deed.

Making matters worse, when Art first met Calvin and Sandy, he turned out to be one of those unfortunate early teenage lads who hadn't known all the dirty words yet. It's hard to take someone's bragging about sex seriously when they later ask you what you mean by "cumming."

Calvin and Sandy went back as friends since the very day in March of 1983 when the Connors moved to Axsubeen. The boys had shared many adventures and late-night discussions and rarely got sore at each other. They'd immediately liked Art, who first stumbled into their homeroom a week before this last Christmas. Art was quick-witted but sarcastic and abrasive, and he *did* get sore. It wasn't the same anything-goes friendship: mention a taboo subject with Art, expect a fistfight.

The others had failed to confront Art's obvious lies about girls the first few times, and now it was a de facto rule to let him brag about alleged old scores back on the West Coast. But Art just said "last week," so Calvin wasn't going to let it go; he wanted the truth. "Oh did you now?" he teased.

Art didn't take the bait. The kid was actually glad that Calvin asked in a dickheaded manner; it gave him an excuse to act pensive and pique their curiosity. "She said, 'Keep it a secret.'"

Sandy and Calvin made sarcastic noises. "Who cares what *she* wants," Sandy yapped. "*We* want to hear the story!"

Art perked up. "All right: it was at Sean Corgan's party last Friday. Or the one before—whatever. Remember it?"

Sandy nodded but said, "No. I got *really* drunk that time."

Calvin shook his head. "Jenny was such a pain. 'It's too smoky in here,' and 'This beer tastes like shit.' We left early."

"You didn't miss much," Art said, "except Corgan's sister ran around in her bra. But later on, Jill Pedersen showed up."

Sandy punched Calvin's shoulder. "Good old Jill!"

Art cocked his head to one side. "What's that mean?"

"Nothing," Sandy said, sounding genuinely innocent.

"Get on with it," Calvin ordered.

Clearly unconvinced but not willing to relinquish the floor in order to argue, Art pressed on. "Jill shows up wearin' this purple shirt cut way the fuck down to here. Might as well been a vest! Anyway, she comes over to the stove where the booze was. I was makin' a drink and she asks can I make her one too. And I show her my bartendin' skills. We talk for like an hour. She's all questions: what's it like in Washington State, and is there a bigger mall there than the one here. Totally into me. Totally. The party gets kinda noisy, so I says we should go to that tool shed behind Corgan's house where we can talk better. I was playing it cool, ultra-Lando Calrissian shit. Even gave her my wink." He demonstrated. "Always makes the panties wet!"

Sandy and Calvin gave Art the laugh he was looking for.

"So we sneak out. She's laughing, like a lot. She's got her arm around me. We start makin' out … and then I go for the gold. I get a good handful of titty, *under* the shirt, when outta nowhere Zedz shows up and pukes on the tool shed."

"Fucking Zedz?" Calvin whooped.

"What a douche," Sandy agreed. "He ruins everything!"

"Yo, it was the worst," Art went on. "I don't know what the hell he ate before the party but it must've been old boots or something. Fuckin' *rotten* ralphing. Jill fuckin' freaks the hell out. She books back inside and passes out on top of Karen McGillicutty. That was great— Corgan took a Polaroid."

They tittered. They took a breath to recover. "So," Calvin said, "not to be a dick, but the story had the title *I Just Got Some Pussy Last Week*... and there wasn't pussy in it."

"Eat shit," barked Art, a real bark this time, exposing the end of his patience. "I got screwed by bad luck! I woulda got pussy if Pukemaster Zedz hadn't fuckin' come by!"

"That's bad luck," Calvin said, and his delivery showed that he meant it. "But Art, let me pontificate for a minute."

This was not the first time he'd used the phrase. It was Calvin's way of saying, *I'm about to win this with a final blast of mega-logic.* Art— who'd already won, lost, and drawn his share of debates with Calvin— had just enough fumes left in his tolerance tank to hear it: "Shoot," he prompted.

"Zedz's barfing gave Jill the excuse she needed to get outta there before it went too far," Calvin explained. "Listen, Jill fancies a guy to pass the summer with. But just for fun. We've seen it before," he said, looking to Sandy for confirmation.

"Maybe you're the one this year, Art," Sandy nodded.

"Even if that's the case," Art retorted, "it don't mean she was automatically 'getting outta there before it went too far.' Yo, we made out! *And* I had titty under the shirt!"

"It's a long way from that to pussy," Calvin said. "Tits are nothing to some girls. I got Jenny's tits on the *first date!* It's almost boring that I get them practically every day now."

"Yes," Art said flatly, "must really suck."

"How *do* you keep the spice in your relationship?" cracked Sandy in a Charles Nelson Reilly voice, getting a big laugh.

"Fuck off," Calvin giggled. "My point is, pussy can be, like, sacred to chicks. It's only one step from there to actual your-willy-inside-her-body. That's a major thing. And I hate to, like, keep saying this, but you're just summertime fun for her."

Art turned to Sandy. "Why does he keep saying that?"

"I dunno," Sandy burped. "Way too fuckin' deep for me."

Art aimed an abject hand at Calvin. "Are you saying Jill's playing me for a sucker?"

"That's not it." Calvin frowned at having made too successful an argument. "Like I said, we seen this before with her."

"Oh yeah?" Art said sourly. He spent a minute absorbing it all. "So why'd she let me try? We were all alone out by the shed—I coulda forced the issue and she'd've been totally fucked."

"You'd never 'force the issue,' and Jill knew it. She's never as drunk as you think she is!" Calvin gave a knowing laugh.

"Guess not." Something snapped into place in Art's mind. He flung himself at Calvin, punching him on the chin. The two boys went rolling into the forest.

"Dude!" yelled Sandy, springing to his feet and locking Art in a wrestling hold. "What the hell was that for?"

"Ouch," was all Calvin could say. A beefy hand tenderly caressed his reverberating chin. "Ouch," he repeated.

Art was furious. "You've 'seen it before,' all right!"

Sandy pinned the gangly Art down on the packed earth of the Red Trail. "Take a chill pill, Art! What's wrong with you?"

Calvin sat up, wiping blood from his lip to the right leg of his tan Trooping shorts. "Let him go, Sandy."

Sandy turned with crazy surprise in his eyes; Calvin merely nodded. "It's yer funeral, dude," Sandy whispered.

Art, free of the hold, scrambled to his feet. Calvin got to his as well. They faced off at the edge of the Red Trail. The tall trees of the forest seemed to lean closer to get a better view.

"How far?" Art gnashed.

"One step further than you," Calvin admitted.

"You touched her pussy?"

"I *ate* her pussy."

"Gross," Sandy said under his breath.

"When? Last summer? Were you the guy she 'passed the summer' with last year?"

"Last summer," Sandy nodded.

Art stood utterly stone-faced at this news.

Calvin played it down: "Last summer, Jill and I went on a couple dates. Held her hand. Went to Sock Hop Saturday at the park and slow danced. I *hate* Journey. Oh, and Boyertown USA. We did the Toboggan but not the Leaps-the-Dips."

Calvin rather enjoyed Art's new face: befuddlement mixed with jealousy. Sandy saved the poor kid: "They're the rollercoasters up in Altoona. Leaps-the-Dips is, like, condemned."

"Oh yeah," Art said, though he clearly had no idea. Nor did he care. "So Jill ended it after the summer?"

"I ended it. We had the talk about being official, but she got snippy about my clothes and how her boyfriend could never wear what I wear. I told her to fuck off."

"So, no humping," Art clarified.

Calvin sighed at Art's incessant curiosity. "Nobody gets laid in seventh grade. *Nobody.*"

Sandy looked at Art. "She told *you* to keep it a secret."

"Yeah," Art said, a little ashamed to be reminded of that. Of the fact that he told them that, too.

"But she didn't tell *Calvin* to keep it a secret," Sandy said.

"Well," Art sighed, "I, uh … I left something out. When me and her were talking by the stove, Corgan yelled from the dining room, like, 'Art, throw me a beer!' So I got one out of the fridge and threw it to him. He caught it and said, 'Thanks Art! For half-of-a-half-a-nigger, you ain't half-bad.'"

"Har-de-har," Calvin said dryly, "that Corgan wit."

"The thing is, Jill didn't know I'm black," Art said. "Honestly, I thought everyone knew. Ain't like I keep it a secret, especially if you've met my dad. But suddenly, it was all she wanted to talk about." Art looked at the hand he'd punched Calvin with. "She kept touching my hand, like trying to wipe off the white and see the black underneath. 'And you have blue eyes too!' she says. And when I told her Corgan actually had the math right—a half of a half is one-quarter—she practically dragged me outside."

"Good! She totally had the hots for you!" Calvin chuckled.

"Uh-huh," Art said. "I had the hots right back."

"Hold on," Sandy said. "The point is, she still told *you* to keep it a secret."

"Well, of course," Art said with an eye roll. "No white chick wants to be known as a nigger-lover."

"So how come niggers don't worry about being called white-chick-lovers?" Sandy laughed.

"We worry about *not* bein' called that!" Art smiled. "I admit it, I'm all over the white chicks!" He turned his eyes back to Calvin and found himself grinding his teeth into glass. "So that pussy-lickin'-action you got ... that was recently, not last summer. Ya practically admitted that shit cuz you said 'she ain't ever as drunk as you think.' You weren't drinking at no Sock Hop Saturday, or on the Dips-the-Shits or whatever the fuck that rollercoaster is called!"

Calvin was surprisingly calm. "Good job, Sherlock. It was in Old Man Mueller's field like a month ago."

"Holy shit!" bleated Sandy. *"Last* month?! You mean you *cheated* on Jenny MacDonald?!"

Calvin spread his hands. "You wanna hit me too now?"

"I ain't mad," Sandy said. "Just ... amazed."

Art ran a hand through his perfect half-inch flattop and shook his body like a wet dog drying itself. "Forget it," he said, changing his mind about starting a second fight. "I'm sorry."

Calvin stuck a hand out. "Me too." They shook. Slumping to the ground, Calvin wiped his lip off. "Got me good. Again."

Art looked dejectedly at his merit badge schedule, folding it to give his fingers something to do. Sandy, satisfied that peace reigned, sat Indian style between them.

When two youngbuck kids ambled by, excitedly on their way to Centre des Trois, they saw three fourteen-or-so-year-olds sitting in a loose circle on the Red Trail. All three looked like they'd just lost an argument. One was bleeding.

The instant the young snots were gone, Sandy swapped gazes with Calvin. "What's it taste like?"

"You mean pussy?" Calvin thought of a witty answer. "Jill's pussy is so rich, it's got its own Swiss bank account."

"Ya mean, like, anyone can make a deposit and no one would know who?"

Calvin fell on his back in hysterics, booming belly-laughs at the trees until his cheeks smarted. "Gimme five," he said, holding up a hand. "That was a classic."

Sandy fived him with a proud laugh.

Even Art snickered. "Y'know, maybe she ain't the one for me. She's hot and all, but kinda flaky. How did you guys end up in Old Man Mueller's field?"

Calvin spun the tale: "I was at the mall with my brother and bumped into her at the bookstore. Robbie left us alone, and we got to chatting. I brought up our first date, back during the summer before: I'd gone over for supper at her house, and when her parents had finally stopped hanging around, we snuck out back into Old Man Mueller's field and watched the sun set. We didn't have time to do anything cuz her fuckin' ma almost called the cops thinking I kidnapped her.

"Anyway, back at the mall, we laughed at the, y'know, good feelings we got just by talking about those old times. She said I should call her later that night to talk some more. I said, let's meet up instead. So we both snuck out of the house around midnight and met in crazy Mueller's field. I put some of my ma's Dew in a Coke bottle for us to sip on. And that's that."

"Why'd ya put Mountain Dew in a Coke bottle?" Art asked.

"*Tullamore* Dew," Calvin said. "Irish whiskey."

"Huh. So ... no penetration," Art made clear.

"Jaysus Fuckin' Christ, we fuckin' went over this already!"

"Just answer the question, goddamnit!"

Calvin agitatedly crossed himself a number of times at all the blasphemes. "A finger and my tongue. Not my cock!"

Sandy blinked. "Jill *does* know yer going out with Jenny."

"She didn't care. Jenny's name never even came up."

"But what if she tells Jenny about it later?"

"So what?" Calvin dismissed. "Jenny hates Jill. It'd sound like total shite coming from some crazy girl."

"Jesus, you're really sure of yourself. That sounds like something a crazy girl would actually *do*. I don't think I could ever cheat on someone and get away with it; I'd be too afraid."

"I'm sure of myself, Sandy. There's no proof anywhere."

"You got it made with chicks," Art admitted. "And now that dishwasher girl likes you too. Give it enough time and you'll be—" Art put up a V-sign and stuck his tongue in and out of it, slurpy noises included. Sandy burst out laughing.

Calvin opened his mouth to go on, then made all the swift motions of someone trying to look nonchalant and totally not guilty of whatever it was you just saw him doing.

The others made the same motions, trusting Calvin had done so for a reason. They checked the Red Trail behind them for villains ... and found two men approaching. One was the Deputy Camp Director, a tall, gaunt man with a bald head and a heart-shaped face, looking like a teenage girl's lowercase "i" in real life. His name was Lyons, but Art had called him Satan.

The other man was an unidentified yuppie in designer Camp Souviens duds. Satan took slow steps with his long legs to match pace with the yuppie, a much shorter guy who seemed unsettled by his Nike hiking boots. "Hello boys," called Satan, deep voice chirpy. "You look lost."

"We just signed up for merit badges, Mr. Lyons," replied Calvin, standing up, still innocent as all hell. He flashed his schedule to Satan. He looked at the yuppie and bucked at the man's cheerless, brooding expression—like a vulture who couldn't find dead meat—or a Jewish vulture surrounded by non-kosher meat. The vulture's tight slits glared at the block numerals on Calvin's uniform sleeve.

666.

Sandy and Art, seeing the vulture's face, reflexively scrambled up and took flanking positions aside Calvin.

Satan slapped the vulture on the back. "Young men, say hello to Camp Director Murphy. He runs this whole she-bang."

Chest out, face up, Sandy bravely extended a hand. "Hello sir: Anthony Sandmiller, Troop 666, Axsubeen, Pennsylvania."

The vulture took careful note how Sandy had said the number

("six-sixty-six"), then shook Sandy's hand perfunctorily. A word like "Erg" left his mouth.

Art went next. "Art Maguire, Beaver Squad Captain." He shook the vulture's uncomfortably static hand ... claw!

"Rhm," responded the vulture.

"Calvin Connor, Hawk Squad Captain." Calvin went to shake the claw—

—except the vulture suddenly tilted back his head to give Calvin a wholly different set of slits. *"Ahhh,"* he trilled, the after-trail of recognition in his voice. "More accurately, 'Calvin *Ciarán* Connor *the Third*—Captain (Acting).'"

Calvin turned a bit red. With a devilish snarl that came from having the upper hand, the vulture trilled on. "So Mr. Connor, what's the rest of the Hawk Squad up to? Where pray tell is Gus the fat slob? Or Ryan the silent?"

Heat roared to Calvin's face. Not only would he have to explain this later to his mates, but he would, right now, have to respond to the vulture's nasty words. "Not here," he reported; taking a risk, he joked, "Gus is off doing calisthenics."

The vulture's face was frigid. "You're bleeding," he said.

"I am," agreed Calvin. "I do that a lot," he added lamely.

Satan broke the tension: "Never mind ol' Murph, boys. The Big Cheese must've had too much turkey at supper!"

The lads from Troop 666 nervously chuckled.

"It'll be getting dark soon," Satan said. "You oughta get a move-on back to your campsite."

"Krl," the vulture grunted, by way of *goodbye*. He walked away. Satan took a gaunt step to catch up.

Art, Sandy, and Calvin remained still until their ears could no longer pick up the flop of the vulture's Nikes. Only then did Sandy say it: "Fuckin' A, that was like meeting Darth Vader!"

The comment was electric, an observation with recoil. "You know," said Art, "Satan's not Satan—the other guy is!"

"We already gave 'Satan' to Mr. Lyons," Calvin pointed out. "But we need a good nickname for Murphy."

Art: "The Almighty Asshole."

Calvin: "The Vulture."

Sandy: "Kermit."

The others squinted. "He don't look like a frog," Art said.

"No," confessed Sandy, "but don't he look like he's wearing a hockey helmet, with that hair and chin-strap beard?"

"Hey, I like it!" Art said. "Frogs, like French-Canadians!"

"It'll do," Calvin shrugged.

Chapter 8
Horseplay in the dugout.

By the time the malingering Calvin, Sandy, and Art returned to Campsite Quatre, night had fallen. At the fire circle, Inky, Father, and Troop 666's two grown-ups had lit the tall campfire for a sing-along. Art elected to join in; Calvin and Sandy declined and headed down the goat-path to the tents.

They heard laughing from the south. All the flaps on the Hawk Squad tent had been unfurled; only a sliver of light peeked through a gap in the front flaps. Calvin and Sandy popped in to find the kid they called Chicken lying on the wooden deck, pretending to bang Gus's backpack.

Chicken, born Cuauhtémoc Ysderrhi, had an intense personality. He spoke the truth as he saw it and peppered his astringent words with random TV catchphrases (in a heavily accented voice). However, these comments came between long periods of awkward silence spent aiming his baleful black eyes at those around him. He earned his nickname from his love of all things *gallus*. Chicken's nose resembled a beak, he clucked a lot, and he had a queer fondness for down pillows. "It like restin' your head in a bag of chicken pussy," he'd say, and then be promptly told to shut up.

Calvin was not amused at finding one of the deranged kids from the other squad dry-humping a backpack. The aggrieved party here (Gus) was asleep, but if he woke and found out …

The others—Jon, Crowe, and Ryan—were having a ball. Jon said, "C'mon, Connor! It's Truth or Dare!"

Calvin acted out his role as stuffy Squad Captain. "Stop that, Chicken, you're embarrassing yourself."

"What would Foghorn Leghorn say?" Sandy cracked.

Chicken got up and wiped his brow. "He probably give hell to me, like to the chickenhawk. I gave hell to this backpack! She tired now." He heaved Gus's pack in an unoccupied bunk.

Calvin adjusted the Coleman propane lantern hanging via hemp rope from the tent's ceiling. "Dark in here," he said, focusing on the sweating Chicken. "It's your turn now?"

"Yes ma'am. Calvin, truth or dare?"

"Truth."

Chicken smirked. "Have you mooned someone ever?"

"I've never done that. Challenge me to a dare next time."

Any laughter got cut off by this: "Never fear, the Spazzmanian Devil's here!" The front flaps slapped open, presenting the Beaver Squad's Billy "Spazz" Watson and Denny Sandmiller.

These two had finally swapped their muddy class A uniforms for more natural skins: thin blue jeans and black Iron Maiden T-shirts. Denny, who was Sandy's little brother and Spazz's lifelong sidekick, ran the most casual hand known to mankind through his long dark locks, barely touching them. Spazz, the alpha male of this pair (and how), played some air-guitar while banging his head. *"Spazz is the one! / Your mama is done! / Come on and see! / I'm takin' a pee!"*

"Why're all you Beavers here in my tent?" moaned Calvin.

"Can't have enough beaver around," Denny laughed.

Calvin stood in front of Spazz, large arms folded. Spazz made himself still and threw his right hand out.

It hung there for a moment.

Then it hurtled back into Spazz's pocket and hurtled out with a pack of Marlboros. Using practiced fingers Spazz flicked open the lid: one cigarette poked its filter out exactly one inch. "Smoke from the poke, Calvinitwit?" He didn't bother waiting for an answer, jerking his hand away. A lit Marlboro dangled from his lips in short measure.

"There's no smoking inside a tent, Spazz."

"No smokin' inside yer mama!" A hand went to his temple and Spazz did his silly ESP routine: "I can see the future, Con-nerdo! And it's got Noxzema and Colgate written all over it!"

He reached into his jeans, ostensibly to grab his crotch but actually to pull out a tiny can of shaving cream. Denny fumbled about in his pockets, producing a tiny tube of toothpaste.

Calvin waved smoke from his face. "What are those for?"

"To slop up that there blob o' shit!" Spazz's outstretched middle finger aimed at Gus's spot in a rear bunk. The slobulous boob, heretofore blowing silent Z's, rolled over and started broadcasting his outrageous napalm-detonations. "We ain't havin' no circle-jerk! We're playin' Truth or Dare and it's in the rules: I gotta do what I wuz dared! *Time for a Spazzmattack!*"

Spazz made for Gus but ran into Calvin's outstretched arm. "C'mon, Connor," Denny said, clamping a hand on Calvin's obstructive arm. "We were having fun 'til you came back."

Sandy mashed his teeth at his dopey brother and clamped his *own* hand on Denny's arm.

Calvin told them, "My tent; my rules. You are *not* slopping up my lieutenant now."

"Your *lef*-tenant?!" Spazz burped. "Is there such a thing as a *right*-tenant? You're such a *cock*-tenant, Connor!"

"Your ma's my cock-tenant."

The others, hitherto silent, made gleeful *"Oooo"* noises. Spazz's face sprouted a frown: "Wha'ja just say, potato-boy?"

"You heard me," Calvin said. "She's late on the rent, too."

Spazz lowered his chin to match Calvin's smug expression. "My dick's itching," he whinnied, "and when that happens ... "

"... someone gets pregnant," Denny warned. It was the duo's catchphrase, usually recited just before fisticuffs.

Calvin shouted "OUT!" He threw his body at Spazz, then found Denny's body thrown at his when Sandy threw his own body on the pile. A confusion of arms and shoving and curses and tent flaps flapping, and all four lads ended up outside.

The dust cleared. Spazz and Denny were gone; Sandy and Calvin came back in the tent and closed the flaps victoriously. They showed everyone the spoils: a tin of Noxzema, a tube of Colgate, and a (now crumpled) pack of Marlboros.

"Wowsers!" Chicken clucked.

"Bitchin'!" Jon yelped.

"Neat-o," Crowe said.

"…," Ryan added, turning the page in his Book.

"*Zzzz,*" invited Gus.

"Sandy," Calvin said, giving his pal a grin, "truth or dare?"

"Dare."

Calvin pocketed the Marlboros and held out the Noxzema and Colgate. "Dare you."

"Thought you'd never ask, dude." Sandy took the items and knelt at Gus's bunk. Popping open the toothpaste, he spread a length of the stuff onto the sleeping blob's buzz-cut. Sandy looked over his shoulder at the others. "Jon—truth or dare?"

Jon, lying in his top bunk across the aisle, said, "Truth."

"Does masturbation give you full satisfaction?"

Without any introspection, Jon said, "Nope."

"Bollocks!" Calvin shouted. Gus reacted to this noise by rolling over and flattening the sloppy side of his head onto his pillow. Sandy frowned: plopping gunk on him to embarrass his ass was one thing; watching said gunk get ground into his pillow, which Gus would need to use for another six nights, was completely another.

Calvin went on: "You're such a ball-bag, Jon!"

"Them too," Jon said. "I play with my balls. Ain't ashamed."

"It's all the action you ever get."

"I get tons of girls, loser."

"You get tons of nothing," Calvin dismissed. "If you want satisfaction, you gotta place your hand between those legs and let your fingers do the walking for ten minutes."

The others thought this was a riot. The boisterous laughter woke Gus again, and this time he opened his eyes.

Jon sighed impatiently. "Okay, if you say so…"

Gus blinked. He saw Sandy kneeling in front of his bunk. Just as Gus was going to ask what's up, he caught sight of the white cream and green paste on Sandy's palm. Frantically, Gus shot a hand to his head and found that slop covered half of it.

Gus flashed his saucer dish eyes on Sandy, finally noticing that the guy had his curly-locked head turned to watch Jon play with himself. With a silent whimper, Gus laid his head back down on the pillow and pretended to be asleep.

Jon dug up his flashlight. Its beam shone through the kid's white briefs, giving the others a funky, if unique, angle on the proceedings. Calvin admitted defeat at the introduction of X-rated silhouettes: "Stop that wanking!"

Then Ryan Phillips shouted, *"Brace for impact!"*

Something smashed into the north side of the tent, followed by the splat and splash of disgorged liquid. The canvas snapped inward from the blow, then snapped outward in equal but opposite reaction. With a loud *flop!* the tent took a second direct hit. Gus was forced to show his alertness now, sitting up with a surprised yelp. The Coleman lantern jingled, swinging from the rope, and Calvin used a hand to steady it. They heard a third volley fall short, and laughter in the distance.

The chaos faded abruptly. The tent steadied itself.

"They're done," Ryan noted matter-of-factly. He stood and tucked his Book in his shorts' pocket. Riffling through his rucksack, Ryan drew out a one-piece ninja outfit. Originally a Halloween costume, it had proved useful on camping trips and he never failed to pack it.

Calvin pleaded to the kid's back. "Ryan, you can't go half-cocked. That's revenge and the Troopmasters'll go off." The words fell on deaf ears. "Retaliation is not the answer!"

"Reconnoiter," Ryan said. "Not retaliation." He zipped up the ninja outfit, pulled the cowl over his cute face, and left.

Jon slapped himself one. "Calvin, ya big wimp! If that'a been me, you'da stopped him—not let him waltz outta here!"

"I didn't let him *waltz* outta here!"

"You pussied out, too afraid of my dad. We all heard ya say it! At least admit it!"

Calvin balled up a fist. "Shut your hole!"

Jon and Calvin made cold eye contact. Neither blinked.

"I'm gonna have to talk this week," Jon stated plainly.

Calvin turned away, steaming mad. He saw the others' long faces. "We'll pay them back *after* Ryan gets us a report."

"But you just begged him not to retaliate!" Jon whooped.

"Did you even *hear* what Ryan said?"

Not a rhetorical question. Jon needed a second to realize that. "He said 'reconnoiter,' whatever the hell that means."

"Spy on them!" Calvin said. "We know who did it—everyone in the Troop is right here, except Art, Spazz, and Denny. And which of *them* sounds guilty? But maybe this is a trap, to flush us all out for a big attack—"

The rookie Crowe snapped, "Talk talk talk! We coulda kicked headbanger butt by now!"

Chicken, who was not a Hawk Squad member but was always up for a fight, *cock-a-doodle-do*'ed his concurrence.

"It's just cuz you stole his smokes," Sandy offered. "Give them back, and it'll all be over."

"Jaysus jam on toast! If we hit back, Spazz'll hit us harder. And on and on. It'll never end—and half you lot gotta sleep in the same tent as him!" Calvin pointed a hand at his chest. "Me, I flat-out refuse to spend this entire week looking over my shoulder to see if Spazz's got a condom aimed for my head."

Crowe choked on a laugh. "A *what?*"

"We use 'em like grenades," Gus told him helpfully.

"Stupid rookie," Jon spat. "We fill 'em with water and bombs away. What do ya think just hit our tent? Now shut up."

Crowe flapped his lips.

The steam to charge out for revenge cooled. Calvin looked them over again. "We can't start a war here."

Sandy shrugged. "Yer the boss."

"I'm just a lieutenant who got screwed by Zedz's holiday."

"*Loo*-tenant," Crowe said pedantically, laughing again.

"Jesus, shut the F up, rookie!" Jon said with some heat.

"Steady on," Calvin told Jon.

"Yeah!" bleated Gus. The blob popped out of his bunk, his rolls undulating under his too-tight T-shirt. "That ain't right, Jon. You leave the rookie alone!"

Jon bucked with laughter. Gus came over to Jon's spot in the top bunk, aiming a stern finger up at him. "I mean it, Jon! I'm the Hawk Squad Lieutenant now, and *I'm* tellin' you to stop!" Jon pointed at Gus's head, which still had green/white goop on it. Chicken and Crowe joined Jon in the laughs.

Calvin muttered, "Sandy, take him to get his hair washed."

"Sure. Time to hit the showers, Gus!"

"Be on the lookout now," Calvin added.

Sandy ushered Gus out. This left Calvin alone with Jon, Crowe, and the still-lingering Chicken.

Jon climbed down to his feet and wiped away a tear. *"Totally* hilarious, dude! He didn't know the shit was in his hair!"

"Oh didn't he now?" Calvin smirked. "Gus didn't ask you what you were pointing at. And he didn't wonder why I told Sandy to get his hair washed. Why is that, Einstein?"

"Oh my God—he knew!" Jon's eyes grew moist from so much laughter. *"And* he's going to the latrine with the guy that did it to him! I hope Gus kicks his fucking ass!"

"Give me ten, Jon. You can't use that word."

Jon sobered up. Fast. "What?"

"Ten push-ups. Troop 666 is rated PG-13, you know that."

Jon stepped up to Calvin. "Oh yeah?"

"Oh yeah. That's your da's rule, not mine."

"Fuck rules," Jon said, moving closer. They were toe to toe.

"Make it twenty." Like many Irish (and boys in general), Calvin was not uncomfortable swinging some fists. But he still had a surprise up his sleeve. "I don't see you doing push-ups!"

"Goddamn right," Jon said, sneering in such a way that the zits on his face got smooshed together. "Who's gonna make me do 'em? Sandy and Ryan ain't here to back yer ass up."

"Who needs 'em? Hey, Chicken?"

Chicken clucked. "Yeah?"

"Did you hear what Jon said," Calvin uttered out the corner of his mouth, his eyes not leaving Jon's, "about your ma?"

Chicken's body snapped to attention. "What!"

Calvin knew if this didn't work, he'd have *two* fistfights to deal with. He pressed on nonetheless. "He said it on the way up, in Mr. Maguire's Bronco."

Jon's eyebrows sank. He glanced at the crazy kid Chicken and saw rage on the boil. Calvin actually read the deductive reasoning on Jon's panicking face: the only painless conclusion was to diligently do his twenty push-ups. And so, Jon did.

Calvin's internal sigh was nearly audible. And the next Calvin/Jon confrontation was likely to be a bloody one.

Chicken growled, "So what he say?"

"That she is a very nice lady," answered Calvin.

The Fire of Inky. Truly, the miracle of Troop 666. The kid they call Father had given it its name four years ago on his first camping trip. Father had been asked what he'd thought of Inky's creation. "Like something out of the Old Testament," he'd said, mouth agape. "The Fire of Inky!"

The name stuck.

Five feet tall if it was an inch. Five more in diameter. Huge red flames licking off the top. Hot orange embers along the edges. Bright yellow logs gathered inside. Intense white atoms fusing to pure energy at the core. The scorching heat would certainly do a Michael Jackson to anyone's hair at three feet away—the chorus sitting around it now was no closer than seven feet. After an hour or two, the fire will have burned to three feet tall, with another three feet of crackling ashes surrounding. In four hours total, the fire would be out; only a flat circle of cold black soot would remain. Inky took pride in his work. In Troop 666, he alone made campfires.

At this particular moment, though, Inky wasn't feeling very proud. His meaty paws pulverized the stick he'd been whittling into seven cigarette-sized fragments. "Let me get this straight," he grunted. "You took 95 through New York City. After that you turned *north* and broke down in Hartford."

"That's right," said an unashamed Oldroyd. Idle fingers massaged his Martin guitar's strings.

Inky's face got as tight as possible, one notch before implosion. "And what exactly went wrong?"

"Gasket trouble."

"Your rich man's brand-new Silverado half-ton's got *gasket trouble.*" A pause. "That still don't explain you goin' north outta New York! We're practically on the coast here, like a mile from 95! You're the worst leader in history, Oldroyd. I'm glad we didn't end up relying on *your* knowledge of 'the territory.'"

Oldroyd's tune changed. "Well, I took a wrong turn is all."

Inky cast a vote for lunacy: "That much is certain. Serves you right, showing up late and being the butt of our jokes. You just hadda run off in a tiff, no time to find the proper route—"

"That's 'route,' son."

Assistant Troopmaster Paul Maguire stood up and threw his coffee on the fire. The liquid didn't even dent it. "We're not starting that shit again!" The others hanging out the campfire (Father and Art) found this quite humorous.

"The Big Cheese agrees," Oldroyd snapped. He fiddled with his guitar's tuning. "So what song we doin' next?"

"No more country," Art said. "Ain't no tears in my beer."

Father piped in with, "How about the Lucid Pond theme?" (and then grimaced at the collective groan).

"Please," Inky huffed. "Don't remind us how much *easier* this year's summer camp could've been."

Mr. Maguire actually lobbed his empty tin coffee mug; Inky merely deflected it with a hubcap-sized palm.

Their attention shifted as Sandy and Gus trudged from the goat-path into the fire circle, heading for the latrine. Gus's head was mired in a green/white slop. "What *now?*" Inky yelled.

"It's cool," Sandy said. "Just an accident."

Inky dismissed them with a snort. "Don't fall in the pit."

Art forewent the campfire chorus and hustled to catch up with Sandy at the latrine.

Gus tucked his head awkwardly under the wash basin's tap. Sandy worked the pump crank until water spewed out.

"Holy crap!" Gus cried. "So cold! *Brrr!*"

"Ignore it! Scrub it out, dude!"

Art smiled at Sandy. "Yo, what happened?"

"Long story. That's enough," he said to Gus. "Now rinse!" He gave the pump another good yank and let it go.

Gus wiped his head, then shook it like a dog, jetting water everywhere. "Thanks," he said, standing erect. His buzz-cut, or at least what passed for a buzz-cut, or at least what he called a buzz-cut, or at the very least what he called a buzz-cut when it was just slightly unlike a buzz-cut, or in any event Gus's haircut, period, did not react favorably to getting wet.

"Truth or Dare back at the Hawk tent," Sandy told Art. "Some jerk got him with Crest and Noxzema. I didn't see who."

"That's okay," yipped Gus. "I *know* who did it."

"Oh?" Sandy said, in his best innocent tone.

"Yeah. It was Jon."

"Oh ... kay? What's yer proof?"

"I saw 'im!"

Gus was so obviously lying. The kid was about as subtle as a blowjob. If anything was the truth, Gus probably saw Sandy himself do the dirty deed. "Well, what're ya gonna do about it?"

"I dunno. I'm lieutenant now, so maybe give 'im a million push-ups. Or maybe a zillion!"

"I got a better technique," Art said. "The Slimy Dung."

Sandy bristled. "Not the mud in a Ziploc thing?"

"Yes sir!" Art explained it: "You take some mud and stick it in a baggie and zip it. Then wet the outside and slip it in the target's sleeping bag. When he goes to bed that night, there's something all slimy and gushy there and it grosses him out."

"Cool!" barked Gus. "But I don't got a Ziploc bag."

"I got one in my pack with my toothbrush in it."

Art made to leave, but Sandy grabbed his arm. "Maybe later, dude." Sandy turned to Gus. "I wanna talk to Art about the bombing. You should head back, and be Calvin's backup."

"Yes sir," said Gus, and he trundled off.

Art fetched Sandy's flashlight, lying on the ground by the pump. "What bombing?" he asked.

"On the Hawk tent," Sandy said.

Art sighed. "Spazz, right? We at DEFCON 1 or what?"

"No dude, more like DEFCON 3."

Chapter 9

CHIN MUSIC.

GUS STUMBLED INTO the Hawk tent ready for anything. Calvin, Jon, and Crowe all chilled quietly in their bunks; Chicken had evidently split. Gus sighed in relief that it was so quiet here.

Calvin waved Gus close. "Listen: with Spazz acting up, things are gonna get ugly. Go to the sing-along at the campfire. Whatever you hear going on, you stay clear of here."

"No!" peeped Gus. "I'm your lieutenant, and I wanna stay and be your backup!"

"I know you do. But less of us is less targets."

"But what about ... " Gus did an overdone version of a subtle nod towards Jon Oldroyd.

"I'll be fine," Calvin said warmly.

Gus made a thankful look. "'Kay," he said, stumbling out.

"Way to save the fat-ass, fat-ass," Jon hissed.

"It's called teamwork, Jon. Look it up."

A ninja burst through the front flaps. He took off his cowl, revealing Ryan Phillips's striking features and blond hair. He launched right into his brief: "Father, Inky, Art, and the grown-ups are at the campfire. Beaver tent and Leaders tent are totally empty. Thought I saw someone in the woods behind the Leaders tent, but couldn't make out who, and he was really tall, whoever it was. Maybe it was someone from another—"

The flaps parted once more and Sandy and Art came in. "Just heard about the attack," Art said with a sigh. "You know I ain't part of it. I don't run my Squad that way."

"I know," said Calvin. "What're we gonna *do* about it?"

"Beats me. Sandy said you're waiting for Ryan's report."

The new arrivals turned to Ryan, who drew in a breath, preparing to recite his brief again.

The flaps opened once more: Spazz, popping in with both middle fingers in the air. "Just came by to say, fuck y'all! I had enough bullshittin' and bellyachin'. Me and Denny and Chicken are now the Weasel Squad!"

This week was full of new ones ... and it was only the first night! *"Ssssay again?"* was all Calvin could manage.

But Spazz didn't linger. Having said his piece and given his fuck-yous, the kid bolted back into the night. Hyper hyena-laughs boomed off the campsite's many trees.

"This is mutiny," a wild-eyed Ryan said.

"Nut-uh!" cried Sandy. "That ain't happenin' in my Troop!"

"Chill out, guys!" urged Art. "It's only World War III if you let him start a war!"

A voice behind them shouted, "Let's start it!"

All turned.

Jon Oldroyd pulled a dark sweater over his head. "What a great idea Spazz's got," he said, retrieving a long Mag-Lite from his backpack and tossing its heavy weight from hand to hand. "A civil war against asshole Squad Captains."

Calvin pushed Ryan and Art out of the way and stepped up to Jon. "If you try joinin' Spazz's mutiny, you'll—"

"I'll what?" Jon challenged. "I'll get what I deserve? Yeah, Spazz'll probably make me his lieutenant! *That* I deserve!"

"You deserve a kick in the teeth!"

Jon thrust the butt-end of his flashlight's metal shaft into Calvin's gut. As the Irish kid doubled over from the blow, Jon used two hands to bring the Mag-Lite up. The impact on Calvin's skull sent him into the air, bowling over his comrades.

Frothing with fury, Sandy leapt over Art, Ryan, and Calvin to get to Jon, but Jon made for the rear flaps. Sandy put all he had into a swing of his own: the lunchbox flashlight caught nothing of Jon, connecting instead with the Hawk tent's rear support pole.

This was a Reggie Jackson swing, so the wooden pole burst outward. The entire eight-man tent wobbled like a crippled zeppelin.

Sandy jettisoned his flashlight and grabbed the wounded pole, desperate to stop the tent collapsing on them.

The rookie Crowe got up in a panic. "I'm outta here!"

"Fucking prick!" wailed Calvin. His head flipped up, scattering dense crimson in a sickly parabola. The blood streamed down Calvin's face from a point above his left eyebrow.

After a remorseful pause, Crowe ducked around Sandy and out the back.

Sandy yanked the support pole inward. It cracked as he straightened it. He let go and covered his head; to his joy the tent did not cave in. Though a seasoned camper, this was his (and most of Troop 666's) first experience with eight-man tents. Sandy knew all the devices holding up a regular two-man tent (stakes, poles, pegs, ropes) work in conjunction—removing a pole usually just meant droop. But on a tent this huge, it was *serious* droop.

For now they were out of danger, so he checked his pals. Calvin pushed himself to his knees; Art stood over him, waiting for permission to help; Ryan tucked his head outside the front flaps. There were two puddles of blood on the deck—the original landing spot, and the one Calvin now hunkered over. Thin rivers connected these pools, the gross evidence of his recent movement. The lad's heavy breaths through his mouth sent drops of blood on new courses.

Suddenly he slapped a hand to his forehead. "Jesus Christ," he sighed, crossing himself with his other hand, "save me!" His long hair slumped down the sides of his face and gladly soaked up the blood. A third puddle formed.

Sandy gagged at the sight. "Holy shit, dude!"

"Don't move," Art said. He dug through the personal effects and gear piled on the Hawk Squad's junk bunk and found their official Trooping International Tribunal first aid kit.

The tent jerked with a noise like a whip cracking. Sandy grabbed the wounded support pole, which was rupturing before his eyes. "Ryan! Get something to rig this with!"

Art turned the first aid kit over, spilling its contents out onto the bunk. He fished for a gauze pad. "Come here," he said, then sighed and pulled the blinded Calvin towards him.

Calvin's head fell over the junk bunk and proceeded to drip blood on the thin mattress. There was blood everywhere on the lad. "Fix me up, Art," he said weakly.

"You're gushing, Calvin! This shit ain't gonna do the trick."

"Please—do what you can."

Art grabbed a nearby towel and wiped the excess blood from Calvin's face. Gripping Calvin's left wrist, he pulled the hand away, slapped the gauze pad over the huge slit above the lad's eyebrow, then shoved Calvin's hand back into place.

"I got good news and bad news," Art moaned. "The good news is, the blood ain't flyin' out in a big stream, so Jon didn't cut open an artery or anything—if he did, we'd be haulin' yer ass to the hospital right now." Art wiped off his hands with the towel, frowned at how quickly it'd gotten covered, and tossed it on the biggest puddle on the deck. He rummaged the medical junk, saying, "The bad news is, I don't think there *are* arteries on the front of your skull, so you got a busted capillary."

Calvin listed at this news, gripping the bunk with his free hand to avoid falling. "Tell me that's something minor!"

"Compared to arteries." Art tore open more gauze pads.

"How come you know so much about anatomy?"

"Helps with my Frankenstein experiments."

Calvin did not laugh. Still, the failed humor had a place here; it signified a lack of panic.

Ryan poked his blond head through the back flaps, showing Sandy a branch. "That'll do," Sandy nodded. "Get some rope and let's splint that shit on!" Ryan ferreted about and settled for the shirt Jon had torn off his body when he'd donned the dark sweater. Ryan tore the shirt into two strips (his biceps barely flexing). They began the difficult teamwork of tying the thick branch to the cracked support pole.

Art eased back Calvin's hand and tossed two new gauze pads over the original, now completely saturated, one. "Freeze!" Art pulled open the tab on a Bactine bottle with his teeth. He spat onto the deck (Bactine tasted like shit) and squirted a good measure of the fluid. Thin pink broth tumbled down Calvin's face. "Get that gauze roll," Art said, and together, they slowly wound it very tightly 'round Calvin's head, over the pads, and back around.

"That really burns," Calvin wept, spitting out the mucus that came with the tears. Unconcernedly, he gripped the front end of his class A uniform shirt, peeled it up to his nipples, and wiped the fluids off his face. "It fucking burns, Art."

Art ripped the cover gauze. "If we were in *my* tent, I could get the hydrogen super-peroxide outta my portable lab—*then* you'd feel a burn!" He sighed as he struggled with the impossible first aid tape. "The Bactine stings cuz it's killing germs."

"What germs?"

"Yo, we got germs everywhere." Art finally found the end on the spool. "Bacteria from your hair, and dirt on Jon's flashlight, and oil and shit from your skin. Hold still." As the tape wrapped around his head, Calvin licked the blood mustache off and spat it out. Art tore off a few supplemental strips and fixed them directly over the pads. "There." Art smiled. "Like the General always said: 'first aid pays in many ways.'"

Calvin wiped his face with his uniform again. He undid the buttons, chucking the bloodied shirt under his bunk. Art knelt down and tried soaking up the puddles of blood and splats of spat fluids with the towel. When the thing ceased absorbing and began dripping, Calvin said, "Good, it belongs to that cunt Jon, so fuck it now." He grabbed it from Art's gray hand and chucked it out the front flaps.

Calvin then fetched his own towel and wiped himself up. "Still got some here on your neck," Art said, pointing.

Ryan and Sandy pulled tighter on the strips of Jon's shirt and finished off the knot at the bottom of the pole. They eased back their hands. The pole tried to break but the splinted branch said no. "All those knots the General made us tie," Sandy panted, "are payin' in many ways too." He wiped his forehead and offered Ryan five. "Good job, man."

Ryan returned the five. "Hey, you okay?" he asked Calvin.

"Far from it." Calvin looked at his towel, the only one he had for the whole week. It was a useless gory rag now. He mopped the bits of blood off his body that he couldn't see (with the others' help), then soaked up what remained of the puddles on the deck, then filed the towel under his bunk to join his bloodied uniform shirt.

He threw his arms 'round Art and Ryan and cleared his throat. Sandy joined in to make the circle complete. "Look here, lads," Calvin said, eyeing at them in turn. "I'm gonna kill that fucking prick. No matter how many times we tell him to shut up—me, or Zedz before me, or Inky before Zedz—the result's the same: 'Fuck you, my da is a Troopmaster and I'll be a dick if I wanna.' Let's put an end to his shite. I'm not spilling that much blood—" (Calvin pointed to the deck) "—without revenge." He put a hand into the circle. "Who's with me?"

Art slapped his hand over Calvin's. "I am. Fuck Spazz too, for starting this shit. I want my Squad back."

Sandy put his hand on Art's. "I'm in. Lemme at Jon and I'll revenge your blood!"

Ryan gripped their hands in his: "All for one."

Chapter 10
CLOSE CALL IN THE SHITTER.

THE TWO OLDER teens (Father and Inky), the dim-witted chunkster
Gus, and Messrs. Oldroyd and Maguire were at the fire circle singing a
boisterous rendition of some cowboy song in which the protagonist no
longer wishes to remain employed, and in fact vigorously offers to hand
the position back to his boss. The campfire chorus didn't notice Art and
a shirtless Calvin go by (or Ryan, slithering along in his black ninja
outfit.)

The kids waited in the cramped latrine for Sandy, out taking a
quick sweep of the campsite first. Calvin asked the others to excuse him
so he might use the one-room latrine for its true purpose. Art and Ryan
bowed out and took up scouting positions in the nearby woods. Sighing
grievously, Calvin plopped his bottom on the left-hand of the bench
seat's two holes. Immediately he heard an owl toot—Art's all-purpose
warning call. With wide eyes Calvin scanned for an escape.

He had none. He was taking a crap, after all!

The latrine door burst open, revealing the gargantuan frame of
Inky Schultz surrounded by the strong glow of the distant campfire that
bore his name. Calvin quickly swept his hands up to his face. As the
door shut and darkness returned, Calvin pulled his long, icky hair down
to discreetly cover the gauze wrapping on his head.

Inky dropped trou and sat on the right-hand hole. There was no
physical privacy divider. Inky made short grunts; the sounds of projectiles dropping into the cesspool below, squishing with previously shat
excrement and congealed urine, made Calvin uneasy. When Inky decided to talk, Calvin nearly wept. "So, Connor, how you holding up?"

Calvin licked dry lips. He came from the school of Chatting-And-

Scatting-Are-Not-Acts-To-Be-Commingled.* The underlying subterfuge only made the situation more deplorable. "I'm okay," he said. He didn't turn, but not making eye contact in a latrine was an accepted move. "Been Captain all day with no push-ups to show for it. Beats my last go."

"Got that right," the ogre spat with some emphasis, for it was he who'd handed out most of the push-ups on that notorious 731 night in May. Suddenly the guy stood, having finished his business. Inky was notorious for his frequent but swift deposits—he *catshat,* Art had called it, after *catnap.* Calvin thought, *Where's the humor in that phrase now?* Inky let loose a chuckle and unashamedly used the T.P. "This week'll be a real test for you, Connor. It'll show if you got the stuff—" (he poignantly tossed the used toilet paper in the cesspool) "—or if you're no good. And you know what my prediction is."

Calvin snorted. If he was gonna go down, he'd go down swinging. "Wanna bet? Dollar says you're wrong … sir."

Inky hitched up his black denim shorts. "You're on, Irish." And with that, he was out the door.

Calvin wiped his butt and fixed up his tan shorts. He wasn't done, but there was no way he could concentrate on the job now. The door creaked open and Art and Ryan slinked in. "Yo, that was a close call!" Art wheezed. "If he'da caught all us in here, we'da been dead! Does he know something's up?"

"No," Calvin rasped, still rattled at the encounter, "he came in to take a dump. And tell me I'm not a good Squad Captain."

"At least he didn't come right out and say you suck."

The door opened and Sandy popped in, juggling his lunchbox flashlight nervously. The Weasels were nowhere to be found. Wide expanses of dense woods separated the tents, and indeed the campsites. Where were they?

The lads pondered a bit. The Weasels wouldn't hide forever. They'd hang out for a bit, talking shit and smoking cancer sticks, then come back and hit some target. But what …?

Ah. It was obvious what. Well, what to do?

---

* Everyone knows an asshole from the other school.

One idea, from Art of course, appealed to them. It'd work. But it meant he'd have to borrow his dad's keys and take a long detour to the parking lot. And then all the way back again.

"Fuck it, let's go," snarled Sandy.

Thunder rumbled off in the distance.

Chapter 11

Tentgate — YOU are there!

SPAZZ RAISED HIS fist into the air. Light drops of rain surrounded it. One finger. A brief flash of lightning embraced it. Then two. A rumble of thunder rolled across it. Then three.

The rookie Crowe tore out of the woods and jumped in the tent. Chicken vaulted the fallen tree the Weasels used as cover and strafed his buck knife across the nylon tie-downs on the north side. Denny and Spazz ambled out, taking hold of the front and rear entrance support poles respectively, their bodies leaning back. Jon took the point as lookout.

When Chicken finished with the north ropes, he looped around. Half the tent drooped. Inside, Crowe dumped backpacks and giggled at contents. It didn't take long to cut the south side's ropes: with all the tension on them, they snapped easily once stressed by a blade. The tent fabric sagged sadly, hugging the bunk beds within like a dust cover. Spazz made a soft bird whistle. Crowe tumbled out, his foot snagging on a bunk; this was the loudest noise of the operation. Spazz and Denny counted 1, 2, 3 ... then yanked away the support poles.

Jon heard something. He made an urgent noise through his teeth, and all the Weasels froze.

But the only sounds were the *tappity-tap* of rain hitting leaves, the indigestion of the sky, and the distant, out-of-pitch campfire crooners butchering some country song in which this guy was, once more, traveling his ass off. Jon swept his eyes full circle: neither the goat-paths nor the woods in between offered anything.

Jon was about to call his warning off when a lightning burst illuminated a limber Calvin Connor thundering up the near path, shirtless and juggling half a dozen condoms filled with water to the point of bursting. The Weasels then whirled to the far path as Ryan Phillips marched in, presenting two fists. All whirled 180 or some degrees between when, from a bush behind the wrecked Leaders tent, there sprang Anthony "Sandy" Sandmiller. The kid also wore no shirt across his fireplug frame. "Hiya, faggots," he scowled.

Spazz opened his mouth to yell "Scram!" but

POP POP POP!

he suddenly coiled back, gripping his chest. He collapsed in a limp heap.

Art shifted his aim. "EAT ME!" he wailed, strafing fire in an erratic arc. The rookie Crowe didn't know where the attacks came from so he dove for cover behind the tent; Art's trigger finger did not yield, and the tent canvas got pelted.

Calvin lobbed all six water-condoms at Jon's face. Jon brought up his hands to deflect them: half ruptured on impact, showering cold reservoir water over Jon's face and neck; the others tumbled aside uselessly. Calvin wrapped his arms firmly 'round Jon's waist and used his momentum to hurl both their bodies into the prickly underarms of a large pine. Their pale skin scraped across the abrasive bark. The water on Jon acted like a magnet for loose dirt and prickly needles—he found himself tarred and feathered.

Sandy socked his brother in the face. It was a battle which had occurred many times at the Sandmiller home; the results were no different. Denny was younger, smaller, and a pussy.

Ryan merely stared Chicken down, holding him in place with a ferocious glare.

Crowe waited for Art to stop firing. The instant that happened, the rookie scampered towards the tree in which Art sat, snatching up a small rock and hurling it upward. Panicking at having been spotted, Art brought the rifle barrel downward, loosing shots which struck the ground near Crowe's feet. A second rock connected sharply with Art's left arm; he lost his grip, then his balance, and plummeted fifteen feet to Earth.

Sandy flipped Denny over and planted an elbow into his spine. Calvin and Jon found themselves more wrapped up in the painful branches of the pine than they were in each other. Ryan and Chicken remained static.

Art, dazed by the fall and the awkward landing on his hip, fumbled for his rifle and pumped off three rounds in Crowe's general location. The rookie caught one square in the throat at practically point-blank range. A flash of lightning exposed Art's frightened face. In the darkness that followed, he heard Crowe's slight body fall with a wicked choke.

Then, gasping with desperation, Spazz sat up.

The wild-child craned his head, eating all the oxygen he could. His hands tore at the Iron Maiden T-shirt and peeled it off, rending a split in the collar. He inspected his sore chest. "Son of a bitch," he sighed, marveling at his continued existence. Springing to his feet, he took a quick survey of the various standoffs; saw Art struggling to his feet near the splayed corpse of Crowe; and broke into a mad run.

Spazz dove head first on top of Art and jabbed him in the back. Art bleated in pain and rolled away. As Spazz pushed to his knees for another attack, Art slammed the kid in the head with his rifle's shoulder rest. Spazz answered by crushing Art's nuts with a right hook.

Chicken and Ryan continued their stare.

Jon Oldroyd broke free, finally. A face of great rage and acne bellowed, "You asshole!" as two Adidas-shod feet punted blindly. Calvin covered his wounded face and took the blows on his torso and arms.

Sandy, satisfied that he'd fully whipped Denny's ass, made for the pine. He hollered to Ryan, "I got Calvin—you get Art!"

Ryan moved his eyes off Chicken to glance at Sandy. Chicken leapt on the distraction and took a quick step forward—and fielded a brutal punch in the face. The blow knocked Chicken clean off his feet, tumbling him over the ruined Leaders tent. A pencil-thin stream of blood fed out of Chicken's beak, following him through his descent like a pesticide mist trail spitting out the back of a biplane. Of the many fights Chicken had taken part in—all more two-sided than this—he had *never* taken such a shot!

After several swift bounds, Sandy leapt and cradled Jon's legs. The brat crashed to the ground, a felled house of cards.

Spazz pried the gun loose from Art's weakened grip. The seconds Spazz needed to search across the black rifle (in the dark) for the trigger were all the time Art needed to grab the insect-repellant squirt bottle taped to his right forearm. Art depressed the cap-trigger and a thin stream of liquid squirted into Spazz's face. *"AAAAUGH!"* the head-banger wailed, a wail to do Bruce Dickinson proud. Spazz dropped the gun to bring both hands up to his burning face. Art slammed him aside, fetched his rifle, and used it to get to his feet.

Ryan arrived and steadied Art—his right hip was wobbly. "Yo, let's jet!" Art said. Ryan maneuvered them to the path for a hasty retreat to the Beaver Squad tent.

Calvin flopped to the path on all fours. Sandy dumped Jon to the ground. Another lightning burst showed a new audience, that of Troop-master Oldroyd, Mr. Maguire, Father, Inky, and Gus, who'd bounded up to see what all the noise was about.

"WHAT THE HELL IS GOING ON!" Inky screamed, and all creatures alive within half a mile started sweating.

Spazz slowly drew himself to his feet. His body shook, fighting off Art's homemade Mace. And the fear of Inky's rage.

And ...

... and the fact that he was being watched.

Fear gripped the young metalhead's mind: his watery eyes could pick out movement in the dark before him. Not Art; not Ryan; those two had moved off in the other direction—so—so!—*who was it?!*

Mr. Maguire swept his flashlight across the wet battlefield; the beam presented Spazz with a tall shape, eight feet away. The shape did not move.

The light was too brief to give any more details (since Mr. Maguire had found a lot of damage to point at). Spazz could've waited for another lightning flash, but panic found him and nearly choked him— this shape was not familiar, and something about it (looming? silent? lurking?!) made his blood cells shrink. The shape was not from his

Troop.

Spazz realized the shape could probably make *him* out—him, an open target, this far away from the others.

From the shape's direction, something went *cheep!*

Spazz shat in his pants and danced over to the milling crowd. He saw Calvin lying on the path and he focused his jumbled energy into a chuckle. Calvin had a bandage on his head—or had *had* one there and it had just come off—and the guy's head oozed blood. Spazz didn't really find this funny, but laughing at it was a suitable alternative to bugging over the shape ... stalking in the dark ... lying in wait ...

... *for Spazz to*

be alone again.

He huddled closer to the guys.

"Not funny," Calvin snapped at the laughter. He pushed back his hair; blood slicked it like viscous red pomade. Spazz—and some of the others—nearly threw up.

"Christ!" Mr. Maguire yelped, kneeling over Calvin.

Father began chasing his damp clothes as they whipped away in the wind. His purring-mad whisper wondered how the devil his clothes had gotten out of his pack, which had been dumped out of his tent, which itself had been torn apart and covered in red paint. "Jesus, give me strength," he sighed.

Jon Oldroyd, still lying at Sandy's feet, broke the awkward quiet—shattered it, more like—with an hysterical laugh. Sandy nudged him urgently with his shoe but Jon kept on laughing. *"They* did it!" the prick yelled, struggling to his feet. He wiped his nose and pointed a hemoglobin-dripping finger at Art, then Ryan, then Sandy, then Calvin.

Art and Ryan were near the wrecked tent, and their separation from the crowd made them easy targets for Inky's frenzied glare. They didn't dare refute anything, but Art sheepishly tried to hide the paint-ball rifle.

"What total shite!" Calvin yelled. Gross slurpy slime, nuggets of blood/snot, slithered from his bottom lip to his chin then to the wet earth below.

"All of 'em!" whooped Jon, nodding at his dad. *"They* did it! All four of—"

Sandy, still swept up by the emotion of the battle and a personal dislike for kids who ratted to fathers, sucker-punched Jon square on the chin and watched him fall to the ground.

Oldroyd menacingly brought up his own fist. Young Father interceded. "Easy, Mr. Oldroyd! Control yourself!" Though barely restrained physically, the words stopped Oldroyd cold.

Inky scoffed. *Nothing* would've stopped him from waffling the punk who'd sucker-punched *his* kid.

Oldroyd glared at Mr. Maguire, who stood nearby and had no effect on matters (as usual). "Get Connor to the Camp Doctor, Paul! The rest of you—we're gonna pitch us a tent, then have us a nice blood and thunder Mass!"

Chapter 12
Fireside chat.

"Here," Oldroyd said, depositing his son. Calvin could see pain in Jon's eyes, fear in his heart. The kid climbed into his bunk and pulled his sleeping bag up to his face without changing clothes or drying off. The elder Oldroyd waved his Mag-Lite about the Hawk Squad tent in a mean way. "Y'all put out that goddamn lamp! First thing tomorrow, we're gonna have that Kangaroo Court and sort this shit out!"

The Hawk Squad all moaned, all sighed.

Oldroyd left with a curt nod, just to show off his cowboy hat. Ryan Phillips acted for the wounded Calvin and doused the Coleman lantern, plunging the tent into darkness.

For a long moment no one moved. Not to roll onto their stomachs, nor to turn the pillow over to the cold side. They were all scared—aside from Gus, who had the honor (if such it was) of being the only kid in the Troop *not* involved in what had already been dubbed by Mr. Maguire as "Tentgate."

Calvin had been taken to the Camp Doctor: the kindly old man gave him six stitches, some aspirin, and new bandaging and head-dressing. The paintball gun had been confiscated, to be returned to Mr. Maguire's Bronco and only removed again when the man and his son next went to the paintball range back home. The ransacked possessions and garments from the Leaders tent got collected up. They reassembled the tent as best they could—Inky declared the paintball-splattered canvas would be washed out in the reservoir at first light, and then flawlessly reinstated with new tie-down ropes.

The whole Troop got to stand in ranks, in the rain, before the hissing remains of a Fire of Inky; shivering, shuddering spectators to Oldroyd's ghastly performance of barbarous shouting. Then the man did the worst thing he could have—he set the Kangaroo Court to happen tomorrow.

After a night's rest.

Father gave the Sunday Mass, already dubbed by the chronicler as "the loosest ever on record." After it was over (all of two minutes later), Oldroyd sent the Troop to bed. He hadn't bothered to post a leader in the unoccupied bunks of either the Hawk or Beaver Squad tents; he left the kids to their own devices. Precisely, reckoned Calvin, the reason this whole fucking mess happened in the first place.

If this mustachioed moron had had wit one, Troop 666 wouldn't have been late, would've loaded the trucks (plural!) with ease, would've had a roadway route ready, and would've had some mandatory activity to occupy them if the reservation didn't have one of its own planned. Camp Souviens did not, and Oldroyd's campfire chorus was voluntary. So this lot had been left unsupervised, and therefore made the most of it.

Ol' General Schultz had been an utter prick, but at least he recognized conflicts. This sort of episode never, never, *never* happened with Konrad Schultz III as Troopmaster. That man smelt the pungency of trouble a mile off. All Troopmaster Oldroyd seemed to smell was smoke from his Marlboro.

Calvin (bloodied), Gus (confused), Crowe (afraid that Troop 666 was some wild WWF version of tag), Jon (beaten—by Calvin, then Sandy, then his dad), Ryan (silently emoting something) ... this was a fun summer camp? Somewhere in Florida, the duly elected Hawk Squad Captain—Samuel "Zedz" Dzedzy—was laughing his ass off, laughing so hard his bleached blond hair was undulating, his flabby love-handles jiggling.

Here, Calvin wasn't feeling his usual self. His determination, the same hard edge that will twice help him strike out twenty-one batters in a game during his incredible major league career, was nowhere to be found right now. He felt a little woozy: blood loss? Blow to the head? Fear and anxiety?

Calvin rarely felt fear but tonight was one such occasion. A villain had already used his head for batting practice, and might desire to do so again. That same villain had been subjected to one hell of a pre-trial whipping. Oldroyd beat the everloving aloofness right out his son for his part in Tentgate.

Calvin's father very rarely hit his offspring. Art's dad never did (not even here, tonight, when Art deserved it). Sandy's dad, a ne'er-do-well failure of a folksinger, was often too stoned or wasted to lose his cool with his two boys. Calvin tried to envision what it was like to be horsewhipped by your father with everyone else around. That had to be damaging. And here, now, in this very tent, lay the publicly demeaned Jon—the proverbial wounded, cornered dog, only with blond hair and zits.

Calvin had moved to America at age ten. By the time he'd joined Troop 666 at Sandy's urging (around age twelve), Calvin wore a cerebral sheen of grease created as a defense against insults to his heritage. He changed certain elements of his Irishness immediately (such as learning to say the H in words like "thirty"), but others he steadfastly refused to amend. His first Squad Captain, Inky, had wasted no time peppering rookie Calvin with "mick" insults. Calvin came back with gruff retorts (directness) and did his best not to let the insults get to him (determination), especially when the insults were as dumb as a comparison to that "porky dweeb Benny Hill."*

Calvin was who he was; he was what he was. "Deal with it," he told Inky, and by extension, the world.

The point—if the chronicler would ever get to it!—is that Calvin had learned long ago to ignore such comments. For all his outward haughtiness towards the peons, Jon Oldroyd had evidently *not* learned to ignore taunters, and certainly hadn't known what to do when a serf stood up to him with more than bluffing words, as Calvin had done several times today.

Unseen by the others in Troop 666—the ones going to the lowly public Axsubeen School District and living in their old brick rowhomes, aging ranchers, or ramshackle farmhouses—Jon Oldroyd's life of privilege was rife with pressure. The Larsen Academy had tough obligations. His father was a mean asshole. His mother was strict and distant. And

---

* Who was *not* Irish, of course, but we're talking about stupid American kids here. Some of Calvin's peers called him a "mick" while their own last names were as unabashedly Irish as "O'Boyle."

it'd only been a couple of months since they'd divorced.

Looking down on others was an escape for Jon. His natural reaction to opposing force wasn't to wave a red sheet, but cock the hammer and shoot back.

Calvin had known none of this hitherto. He'd just decided to take a stand. And he did, and it'd ended disastrously.

"Connor, yer a fuckin' porky penis-head," Jon snarled.

Calvin could not avoid hearing the words cutting the thick silence of the dark tent, but he kept silent. He focused on the trickle of rain outside. The *tap-tap-tap* on the thick tent canvas.

"I hope your faggot head gets gangrene and you die."

Tap-tap-tap.

"And I ain't gonna fall for this old trick, numbnuts." Calvin heard Jon shuffle about his sleeping bag, then a wet thud as something hit the tent deck. Calvin had no idea what Jon had referred to, but *Gus* picked an odd time to insert his blatant fake snoring (what terrible cover—it was nothing compared to his *real* window-rattlers!).

"Fuckin' mick asshole," Jon breathed. "Get bent."

Calvin snapped. The hot anger surging to his face created a queasily electric burst from his wound. "Fuck you, ya cunt!"

"No, fuck you, Connor!"

"Fuck yourself, Jon! Give yourself AIDS!"

Someone—Crowe, probably, since he was too green to realize how heavy this all was—gave a laugh at that.

Drowning in this mire of fear and rage was too much. Calvin got up, very casually, putting on his Reeboks as if nothing had happened, and ducked out the front flaps.

He sat at the fire circle. It was vacant; the Fire of Inky had long ago drowned in the rain. He took out Spazz's pack of Marlboros, dug out a cigarette, and put it in his mouth. Only then did it occur to him that he had no lighter. As Junior Troopmaster, Inky had control over the fire-starting supplies, and had given Calvin a book of paper matches for the Hawk tent's Coleman propane lantern. Calvin had placed said matchbook in the side-pocket of his rucksack for safekeeping.

"Need a light?"

Calvin leapt.

Standing not two feet to his left—favoring the leg he *hadn't* landed on—was Art Maguire. He wore sweatpants and an old Pirates T-shirt with Bill Madlock's number 5 on the back. Art held out his awesome Swiss Army knife, the super-dooper model, with a slot for storing one wooden match.

Calvin exhaled coolly, playing like he hadn't shat himself. He waved at the packed earth beside him. "You bailed too?"

"Spazz wouldn't shut up about how he's gonna Perry Mason our asses tomorrow," said Art as he sat. "The guys were nervous—you could tell by their breathing. So I beat feet."

Calvin took Art's knife and shook it to free the match. The match head was, curiously, blue. "What the hell?"

"It's a blue-tip," Art said. "You can light 'em on things as smooth as dry wall. I guess they don't make them anymore—a guy down at Schultz's Hardware told me they're illegal now."

"So where the hell'd you get them?"

"Bought a bunch off some guy on CompuServe."

Calvin ignited the match off his shorts' zipper and lit his smoke. Noting Art's curious stare: "What?"

"Nothing." But it wasn't nothing. Art's negative feelings on smoking were not unknown to Calvin. "You smokin' for real now, Irish? Like, bringing your own cigarettes to camp even?"

"No and no. These are Spazz's: possession is nine-tenths of the law. I'm just trying to cool off a bit."

"Booze works better," Art said. "Ain't Sandy stocked?"

"He's in *your* tent. Shoulda grabbed his canteen on the way out, African."

Art smiled nostalgically. "Remember SoCo at Lucid Pond at the Klondike Derby?"

"Tasted like high-octane Kool Aid!" Calvin chuckled as he took a drag. He wasn't inhaling, much. "At Lewis & Clark Camp one time, he put gin in the coffee! And then, back when we went to Canada, he had this wine called Mad Dog."

"What a bitchin' name for wine!" Art said. "Yep, I could sure use a hit from Sandy's magic canteen!"

"Me too."

The light drizzle stopped altogether. Cool breezes swept through the pitch black campsite. Calvin, feeling guilty smoking in front of Art, tossed the butt into the campfire ashes.

Art lowered his head in dread. "We hang at dawn." He looked over at Calvin. Art wanted this to be a "moment." He was that kind of kid, looking for *Wonder Years* moments in real life.

Calvin let him have it: "We hang at dawn."

Chapter 13

Tentgate — chastisement.
Monday, July 27, 1987.

A GRAY DAWN, remnant of the night's rain, hung over the fire circle at Campsite Quatre. The surrounding foliage was wan and pale. Very few birds carried on their usual morning chirping, and who could blame them.

Calvin stood at the head of the Hawk Squad, in semi-attention, nervously awaiting his fate. The Kangaroo Court had not gone well: each member of the leadership corps had a good long shout at the boys. Even Father issued stern platitudes. It was grim stuff, with only one burst of laughter: Inky stood before Spazz, with a hand on his temple, and mocked the wild-child's ESP routine. "I see the future, Spazz … and it's got you neck-deep in shit written all over it!"

The leaders then grilled each boy on his part in last night's activity. The lies of the Spazz-led Weasel Squad quickly became evident, especially Jon's attempt to shift the blame to Calvin and company. The Weasels' "smart" choice in picking the Leaders tent to ransack (well, they'd've looked silly ransacking one of their own tents) now seemed kinda stupid.

But the Calvin-led avengers fared no better—they started the brawl, and their sniper turned a perfectly normal green tent canvas into a red mess. Washing that sucker out was a real bitch. Though it'd been soaked by the night's rain, the canvas refused to sink in the reservoir; after the kids dropped it off the jetty and jumped on it to force it to sink, the thing became almost too heavy to bear. Some of the boys' hands were stained red from scrubbing off the paint. It'd probably take all day for the canvas to dry, and if it didn't, Oldroyd warned them the leaders would be moving into unoccupied bunks in the Hawk and Beaver tents.

Calvin stole a glance at the rest of the Troop: the guys shuddered from the cold reservoir and from fear. Spazz looked like he was about to shit. Art likewise; as the gunman, his punishment would be severe. Ordinarily, Art would've reassured his pal Calvin (say, with a thumb's up). Not now. Dawn had come. Death was imminent.

Calvin turned to Sandy, who stood next to Art with his stocky legs spread, arms out at sides, eyes darting to and fro. This was the Sandmiller Special: from here, Sandy could leap on someone and drag him to the ground, or simply leap into a casual conversation on Budweiser's merits vs. other urine-based domestics. Sandy's eyes darted to Calvin's, held for a sec, then darted up when a mourning dove decided to hoot a little.

Calvin looked at Ryan Phillips. The lad actually meditated: hands pressed together, eyes shut, mouth parting then closing as if reciting some kind of prayer. The stillness of the Camp Souviens forest elevated the spookiness; remembering the Book, Calvin wondered to whom Ryan might be praying.

"Eyes front," growled Inky. With a sigh, Calvin did as told.

The two Troopmasters had taken a walk to discuss punishments, and Calvin wondered if they hadn't gotten lost. It was a distinct possibility. But a minute later, the men slogged up from the goat-path. Oldroyd smiled ear to ear, teeth poking from under his gray mustache. Mr. Maguire's bushy beard obscured flattened lips. "Ten-hut, ladies!" Oldroyd called.

The Troop snapped to full attention. Father and Inky took their places on either side of the adults. Oldroyd panned his eyes over the Troop. He opened his mouth … teeth ground anxiously during the pause …

"Spazz, front and center." Spazz left the Beaver Squad line, marched forward, and saluted his Troopmaster. "I sentence you to absolute silence for the rest of the trip," Oldroyd pronounced. "That means ya can never talk. And I mean never. Only time ya *might* be allowed is if someone's life is in danger. Anyone who catches ya talking can sentence ya to ten push-ups for each and every word. Once we reach Troop Hall again, you can talk. Got that?"

Spazz saluted brusquely and marched back into ranks. Calvin saw defeat in Oldroyd's eyes: the man had hoped Spazz would've acknowledged his discipline vocally.

"Denny, Crowe, Chicken—front and center." Slowly, the three slogged before the leaders to hear their fate. "You sideline warriors get to clean the sidelines—policin' this campsite mornin', noon, and night. Every inch of the ground; twenty feet up each tree. If I find so much as a luger, y'all do push-ups for it. Clear?"

The three nodded their heads solemnly. Crowe, though, pumped a hidden fist when back in formation. The rookie believed his punishment surprisingly minor! He'd learn. Wait 'til vengeful Inky discreetly scattered foil gum wrappers into supposedly policed areas one night so he could "discover" them the next morning. Oh yes, Crowe would learn!

"Ryan and Sandy, front and center." Both dutifully stood in front of the leaders, arms at their sides, heads back. "You two'll be Inky's fire helpers. You'll gather every bit of wood for all Fire of Inkies. If he asks for an oak branch eight feet long with no bark, ya damn well better find one. And Sandmiller? You so much as *think* about hittin' my son again, and it'll be the last thought you ever have. Understood?"

They saluted. Sandy and Ryan would be brutalized as slaves to Inky's pyro cravings (a punishment Calvin had gotten once, and never wished to get again).

"Art: front and center." Art stepped up to his Troopmaster and his dad. "You, Lee Harvey Oswald, get a very specific punishment: ya get to go to one merit badge. That's it. So pick which one and drop the rest after breakfast. Yer dad here says you were ready to make a big jump up," Oldroyd noted, thumbing at Mr. Maguire (who, as usual, stood statue-like and impassive). "Well, it sucks to be you, rifleman."

Art nodded, as bravely as he could.

"Lastly, Jon and Calvin, front and center."

Somehow Calvin knew he'd get paired with Jon. Only a moron like Oldroyd would put Luke and Vader together on some bollocksy post-battle punishment detail. As Jon sidled next to him, Calvin prayed that their penalty wasn't the—

"Latrine!" Oldroyd smiled at their dismay. "I want that there shit-stall scrubbed every mornin'! If I smell anything other than Pine-Sol, I'll drop ya's both inside the pit! And since you been so eager to clean each other's clocks, y'all get to be our representatives on the camp's K.P. crew. You boys are gonna be a pair of clean sumbitches, I tell you what!"

"Oh do us a favor, Mr. Oldroyd!" Calvin snapped. "It's one thing to hand out punishments, but you're *enjoying it!*"

Trembling something fierce: "You got a problem, Connor?"

"Jon split my skull open, my blood is all over this campsite, and I have to do punishment *with him?* Go and shite!"

Oldroyd reared up, as if about to launch forward.

Before he could, Calvin recoiled—in fact, the younger lads in the back of the ranks, unable to see over the taller kids in front of them, thought Oldroyd *had* socked him one. Not so. Calvin was socked from within, stumbling to his knees, gripping his head. Electric-static havoc sprayed from the stitches on his forehead, sharp enough to bring tears.

Numb palms flattened over the crusty gauze in a vain attempt to push his body into chemical balance. Salty tears and thick saliva dripped from various orifices in his face. He took deep breaths to still his hyperventilating heart. One weak hand moved across his body, feebly making the sign of the cross.

No one helped him. Certainly not the Troopmaster, who he'd just stupidly told off—Oldroyd would let Calvin die now if that were his fate. Father had positioned himself to help but held off actually doing so, as if waiting for permission. Where were the other loyal and helpful boys, the ones sworn to leap in during crisis situations and lend a friendly hand?

For that matter, where were his good friends? Sandy? Art? Still frozen in place. Where was their voice in the argument? Being saved for later, to complain to each other in private—achieving nothing. Remember their reaction to the maniac cop? Art flung himself to the floor. Sandy flung himself out the door. Mr. Maguire flung his hands in the air. All useless cunts.

"That's ... my opinion," panted Calvin, adding a tart, "sir!"

"I heard'ja," muttered Oldroyd. He was not deterred.

Calvin rolled from his knees to his butt. He gazed up at his conqueror, who did not look down at him. Jon Oldroyd still stood next to him, quaking, probably afraid Calvin was going to get him in more hot water. Father finally knelt to offer help. Calvin caught Inky's squinted eye, at first aimed down at him, then panning ruefully over to Oldroyd.

"I guess it goes without sayin'," the Troopmaster said, "that all you guys'll be extra good the rest of the trip?"

No one made a sound. A cricket in the woods broke the perfect silence by giving off a loud *cheep!*

"Glad to hear it. This Kangaroo Court is dismissed."

Slowly the Troop broke ranks. Calvin, who had refused Father's help, stayed on his arse until he had the energy to stand. Once he did, he wished for the energy to fly.

To fly far, far away.

Lyons rapped on Murphy's door, then burst in. He found the Camp Director standing at the larger of the office's two windows, scanning the Green Trail with a heavy pair of black binoculars. "Murph, I think we might have a situation."

Murphy turned to offer slits #476 ("If I don't like the message, I may shoot the messenger.").

"From the horse's mouth," Lyons said, opening the door a little further and beckoning a young man into the office. He was about sixteen, tallish, with a forehead's flop of brown hair and a tight little grin between his pink cheeks. "Son, this is the Camp Director, Mr. Murphy. Murph, this young lad is Mike. He told me the most interesting thing just now."

Murphy set the binoculars down and rubbed his aching wrists. His eyes formed slits #364 ("I don't think I'm going to trust you."). "Ah yes—Mike. A miscreant given K.P. duty just after supper yesterday. Mere hours after your arrival."

Mike nodded shyly.

Murphy grunted a "Thmpf" at the kid, by way of a prompt.

Mike, after getting a more histrionic *go ahead* nod from Lyons, spoke: "I was takin' a walk this morning, at dawn, down by the reservoir right behind our campsite." The kid used a strong, determined voice, without any evident nerves. "Then I stopped cuz I saw some kids up a ways a bit. I watched as they carried a tent into the water."

Murphy's eyes shot open. "They did *what?*"

"They didn't carry the *whole* tent in," Mike qualified with arched brows. "Just the fabric—y'know, the canvas. They took it to the end of their jetty and dropped it in to wash it out. After they left, this big red stain came floatin' down toward me."

"Someone *stained* one of the tent canvases?"

"Yeah. But it wasn't blood or anything," Mike noted, a little too offhandedly.

The slits #364 doubled in squintiness, forming slits #182 ("Yep, I'm not going to trust you. Not at all.").* Murphy asked, "And just how do you know, Mike?"

Mike smirked, like it was obvious. "Blood wouldn't of come out. Ever tried washing out a bloody shirt or somethin'? I think it was paint. Only thing I can think of."

Murphy took all this in. His face came alive with interest. "Any of these 'kids' a gargantuan guy with muscles and red hair? Or a big Irish kid with long hair clumped back his scalp? Another kid, maybe part-black, skinny, with a felt-tip haircut?"

"Couldn't say. I was too far away."

Murphy nodded nonchalantly. "Thank you, Mike, for your help. It will not excuse you from K.P., of course; but I am glad to see good behavior after bad. Rest assured, those responsible will be dealt with. Your name will be kept confidential."

"Well, Mr. Murphy," Mike said, "I only said anything cuz that Troop was makin' an awful noise last night. Like they was at war or somethin'. Shouting and brawling ... and then, first thing this morning, they had some kinda trial. Pronouncing sentences and all."

Lyons gave Mike a friendly slap on the back. "Thanks a bundle kid. Chow time: you better catch up with your Troop." Mike bowed slightly and exited, closing the door behind him.

Murphy drummed his fingers on the desk. "Our little criminal informant—what Troop's he from?"

---

* The next level would have been slits #91: "You're full of shit, young man."

"Troop 73," Lyons said. "They're in Campsite Trois."

"Right—so he took a walk by the reservoir starting at his camp-site's jetty. He saw the tent-washing at the *next* jetty, and the stain flowed *toward* him, following the winds out of the south from the coast. So it wasn't the kids in Campsite Deux. It was those shitheads from Quatre."

"So it would seem," Lyons frowned. "Doc George notified me he treated a boy from Troop 666 last night with a forehead laceration. Took six sutures to close it. George said it was caused by a blunt object."

Murphy bit his lip. "So it has started, then." He stood with pur-pose. "Give your daily bullshit breakfast notes and keep an eye on the caf. I'm going to Quatre to have a look around, see what other perver-sions the Devil's Troop's been up to. Did that twerp say they had a trial?"

"That's what he said, Murph."

"I almost want to have one of my own."

Chapter 14
Bullshit breakfast notes.

"WOULD THE OWNER of a blue Ford F-150 with Maine plates please see me after breakfast," Deputy Director Satan said to the crowded cafeteria, but Calvin wasn't paying attention. The plate of food before him was a bigger concern.

Never trust food made by a camp reservation's staff. Legend had it, barely sentient cretins brought putrid horse dung scarcely to a boil and slung it onto crusty rolls which came in boxes labeled LOWEST GRADE BUT EDIBLE. At every camp ever.

"... would like to reiterate Camp Souviens's policy to never leave campfires unattended, even during rainfall ... "

Calvin's dish held liquidy eggs and two very dung-ish sausages. A slice of African-American toast hung on one side of the plate, while a Caucasian slice dangled on the opposite side.

"... goes by the nickname 'Pudge-Puss.' A wallet with that name stenciled on it was found in la Maison de Douche ... "*

The previous night's turkey and stuffing had looked like freshly ground-up tauntaun innards—something Han would stick a frozen

---

* Camp Souviens's old name for the showering facility down the Yellow Trail. Prior to 1978, everything at the Camp had an authentic French name (the Yellow Trail, for example, was Le Sentier Jaune). Camp Ranger (and property owner) Richard Grant ditched most of the French to make it easier for the predominantly English-speaking kids to find their way around. The only French words retained were memorial names (like Lacroix Field), the Centre des Trois cafeteria, and the campsites' numbers (but not the French for "campsite").

When Satan let slip just now the old name for the Camp Showers to a crowd of mostly teenaged boys, their shock at hearing the word "douche" used in such a public (and offhand) fashion led to a burst of laughter, which Satan forced himself to ignore.

Luke into in an emergency—but it tasted better than any turkey and stuffing Calvin had ever eaten.

"... tonight, all you Gene Kellys out there can cut the rug at our weekly 'Across The Reservoir' dance festival ... "

It was only prudent to give one more meal the cautious treatment before declaring Souviens a culinary Mecca.

"... Lacroix Memorial Field, across from the parking lot, will be transformed into a giant discotheque. D.J. Koolie Kirk will provide the light show and the beats for your feets ... "

Calvin poked the eggs with his fork. They failed to scream in pain; always a good sign. He had a bite. And what do you know—fantastic stuff. He scarfed with relish.

"... but the real entertainment will be when our sister camp, Camp Eureka in Niantic, buses over the ten Companies of Cookie Girls they're sheltering this week."

Raucous applause. The two hundred or so boys in the caf hooted, hollered, and whooped with delight. "Cock-a-doodle-*doooo!*" Chicken called from the Beaver Squad table.

"A party!" Sandy shouted at Art. "Gorgeous Cookie Girls! You know what *that* means!" He gave a sly eyebrow waggle.

"... don't don your leisure suits just yet! More details at lunch. Enjoy your breakfast, guys!" Satan stepped down from the podium next to the caf's buffet table and made his rounds, shaking hands with Troopmasters and winking at young men.

He winked very deliberately at Calvin. "Enjoy your breakfast, Mr. Connor the Third!" he called over to the kid.

Being addressed in such a friendly way by an adult embarrassed Calvin. The Hawk Squad table grew very quiet; snide looks and hidden sniggers.

Just as the meal wound down, the P.A. system came alive with hectic bursts of feedback. Teeth gritted and flatware clanged on wooden tables as hands heaved to ears.

Calvin popped a bit of sausage in his gob and turned towards the podium. Murphy, the grumbly Camp Director, tapped the mic again and the room grew respectfully quiet.

Sandy got Calvin's attention from the next table over, and once he had it, mouthed the word, "Kermit." Calvin laughed, choking on his sausage; his vehement hacks boomed in the silent cafeteria. Gus, seated on Calvin's right, slapped him on the back. "You okay?" the blob said at normal volume, herding their table with more ugly stares.

Calvin forced down the sausage and took a deep breath. "I am," he grunted, wiping his eyes, "thank you, Gus."

Kermit was not at all happy that the Devil's Troop hogged his spotlight. "Hello!" he said into the mic, and all eyes went to the podium. The man smiled darkly. "Thank you. For those who haven't met me, I'm Mr. Murphy, the Camp Director. I do not give daily notes, but I have a few random items which merit attention." Kermit produced a note-card and glared at it. "Would the owner of a blue Ford F-150 with Maine plates—"

No one needed to actually say "We heard that one already"—the simple mood of the room told Murphy that he was too little, too late.

"Ah," he said. "Next, the one o'clock Culinary Arts merit badge session has been moved to 2:30. Make a note of it. Finally, would Troop 666 of Axzubean please—"

"Yeah?" Oldroyd cried from the Hawk Squad table.

Kermit paused, glaring viciously at him. At the man's mustache, at his black cowboy hat. At his audacity to interrupt a public message. "Please remain after breakfast for a brief meeting with me," Kermit said, rhetorically, but Oldroyd made an ass out of himself again by shouting back a "Sure thing!"

"Thank you." As an afterthought: "Enjoy your breakfast."

But the kids were done eating. Slowly, the crowd filed out the cafeteria. Satan goose-stepped up to Calvin's table and said, "Excuse me, fellas, but the two clean-up representatives Mr. Oldroyd here told me about oughta report to Chef Jim. The rest of you can stay here for that chat with Murph."

Satan winked at Calvin again, drawing a fresh grimace from the kid. Then Calvin started—something was oddly *familiar* about Satan's face.

Oldroyd said, "Calvin, Jon: get'cher asses in gear."

Popping his head through the kitchen door, Calvin found some lads sorting out rags and squirt bottles. The kitchen had two stoves, two ovens, two fridges, two banks of fluorescent lights, two stainless steel tables, two doors, two phones on the wall, and there were two sets of boys here, three to a set.

But no Camp Chef. "Anyone seen Chef Jim?" Calvin asked.

"Nope," replied a kid who, when he spun to face Calvin, turned out to be Asian. "We only saw him that one time last night. He gave us this stuff, said 'Cl-cl-clean it up!' and took off."

Jon Oldroyd came in and made a swift count. "There's only eight of us? This is gonna suck."

The Asian kid shrugged. "Actually, it'll be easier now that all you new guys are here. Ken," he said, sticking out his hand.

Calvin shook it. "Calvin. That's Jon. We're from Troop 666 in Pennsylvania."

"Troop Six-Sixty-Six? Like, Six-Six-Six? *For real?!*"

"For real."

Ken offered his hand to Jon, who shook it only because he had to. "The Troop from Hell," Ken joked. "So what'd you do?"

"Had a scrap last night," moaned Calvin. "Nasty one too. Tents wrecked, gunfire, pepper gas, condoms filled with water exploding everywhere. I would say, 'it had everything but the kitchen sink,' but here we are now."

One of the other K.P. kids tittered. Ken said, "You'll have to give us the whole story someday, Calvin. Especially the condoms filled with water part. Did you guys win?"

Jon groaned. "We *all* got a kick in the 'nads."

Calvin gave Jon a sideways glance. "It was a draw."

Ken introduced the others. "That's Hank and George. They're with me in Troop 99, Coventry, Rhode Island. We had a fight too, something dumb that just got out of hand. And that's Mike, from Troop 73 in Buffalo. And this is Jimmy and Dale—they just joined the K.P. crew too."

One of these two, Dale, chirped up. "From Troop 2, right here in New London. So no offense, man, but what the hell's goin' on with your head? That hair is something else!"

At first Calvin didn't know what they were talking about. He fingered his locks and got his answer. "Old Aqua Net mixed with rain, mixed with soda, mixed with blood." He reached up and parted the hair back, which he'd maneuvered low over his bandage as cover. "From this little paper-cut."

"Jesus," breathed Dale, "how'd *that* happen?!"

"*I* did it," said Jon, in a queerly even voice. Then his normal annoyed voice returned for duty: "If yer finished feelin' sorry for this loser, I'd like to get outta here. Whadda we do?"

"Last night I volunteered to head up the crew," said Ken.

Jimmy, Dale, Jon, and Calvin shrugged that it was cool.

Ken bit his lip. "Now that our crew compliment's eight, the assignments oughta change. There's one *big* snag, though."

Calvin said, with malice aforethought, "The dishroom girl."

"Right on. Know something we don't?"

"That she's pretty grumpy. I'll volunteer to wash dishes."

Ken took an anxious breath, looked over his crew, and fingered Mike from Troop 73. "Go with Calvin, Mike. She hasn't met you yet, and you're kinda quiet. Maybe we can get through breakfast without another scream-fest. Jon, you and me'll do the kitchen. Jimmy and Dale, get the dining room, every table and bench and the buffet table. Hank, broom or mop?"

"Broom," Hank said.

"Mop for George." Ken slapped his hands together. "Okay guys, previous best time is twenty-nine minutes. Let's assassinate that record."

Calvin and Mike took a dolly, headed back out to the caf dining room, and loaded up the bus-pans stationed by the buffet table. Nearby, the Camp Director faced off with a Troopmaster, whose charges sat as far away as possible; they looked embarrassed.

"*There's an example of what I mean!*" the Troopmaster roared, pointing at Calvin. "One of my squad captains, workin' hard to clean up your camp! So ya can take that 'irresponsible attitude toward camp property' *horsehockey* and stick it!'"

"So," Kermit countered, "you *deny* washing out a tent canvas that was covered in red paint?" The man was so infuriating. It wasn't just the words, but the calm face employed. The polite eyebrow arching. The disdainful curling of his lips when Oldroyd's saliva rocketed too close.

"Quit changin' the dang subject! You Camp Directors are all the same—*look* at you! Haven't worked a real day your whole life!"

Kermit gave the ipse dixit: "Clean up the mess in and around that tent, *thoroughly,* or you'll be fined for the damage."

Oldroyd's reply followed the typical pattern—feigned deafness, denial, confusion, claim of restitution already paid, emphasis remark: "What? There was no mess! What're ya talkin' about? We cleaned it up! Every scrap!"

"'No mess,' Mr. Oldroyd? Another tent has a broken support pole and pools of dried blood on the deck. And if you've cleaned up 'every scrap,' explain this." Kermit held up a pencil whose sharp point pierced an unfurled, and damp, condom.

Oldroyd's eyes almost poked out his skull. Rather than divulge that it had been a Troop 666 tradition (for several years now) to openly discuss condoms, considering teenage pregnancy and diseases and the boys need chips of some sort when they play poker, Oldroyd merely said, "Oh." Completely avoiding the subject of how some boys in his Troop were irresponsible with their rubbers, using them as water-filled projectiles, he merely said, "Ah." Conscious that the people ultimately responsible for this particular rubber were, in fact, the grown-ups and the Junior Troopmaster, who had supposedly double-checked after this morning's clean-up operation, he merely said, "Er."

Kermit whipped out a set of slits (#165, "enough of your bullshit!"), then showed Oldroyd the door out. As they stood in an open-air cafeteria, Kermit could do a grand panoramic wave with a tight smile on his chin-strap-bearded face.

Oldroyd, a sore loser if ever there was one, shouted a vaguely profane syllable in his Troop's direction. The boys clumsily slogged out behind him. The last to leave—Inky, whom Kermit knew as "The Two Arnold Schwarzeneggers"—spent a second looking back and forth from Oldroyd to Kermit, clearly trying to decide who deserved death more.

ᕯ

The door to the kitchen shut quietly. "Hey, Jon," Calvin grinned, "Kermit and your da just had it out. Guess who lost."

Jon looked up from the stove he scrubbed. "Who's Kermit? Whatever—who gives a shit! Get done quick, man."

Mike held the dishroom door for Calvin and the dolly.

The lead singer of the Georgia Satellites had been advised to quit probing with his appendages.

The girl, Miss Ever-Persevering in the Face of Stupid Boys, was here, unloading clean prep platters from a polished steel dishwashing machine. Steam bellowed out and engulfed her. "Good morning," Calvin cheerfully said.

Miss Ever-Persevering in the Face of Stupid Boys glanced at him from under the bill of her kelly green Whalers cap. "You again," she breathed. She stacked up the platters but one of them was wedged in the loading rack. "Murphy said you shitheads'd be on K.P. duty. Son of a bitch—he was right."

Mike, afraid to glance in the conversation's general direction, began racking dirty plates for the dish machine.

The girl took off her cap to wipe her brow. The long tresses of Johnny Rotten red hair, present only atop her scalp, sighed in relief, collapsing in bright clumps along her shaved sides and about her lovely round face. "You know, Miss Ever-Persevering in the Face of Stupid Boys," Calvin said, taking a deep breath, "you've the most interesting hair. Quite vibrant."

She moaned at his impudence. "You're *sooo* proud of your stupid nickname for me, but I remember yours—Asshole."

"That's me," Calvin beamed. Ridiculously, he bowed. "Asshole at your service, Miss Ever-Persevering in—"

"Shut up! I got just three things to say to you: one, *stop* calling me Miss Ever-Persevering in the Face of Stupid Boys." She got it out without tripping on or omitting any of the words.

Calvin was impressed. "Right you are," he said, remembering to omit the usual suffix, *love.*

"Two, we got the same hairstyle, but so what. My hair ain't none of your business."

"I see."

"And three, help me get this stupid platter out."

"All right. I've just three things to say to *you.* The first is: you grab the platter, I got the rack." They each got a firm grip and yanked. The platter gave with a jerk; Calvin and the girl had to be quick on their feet to retain their balance.

"Thanks," she said, chucking the platter atop the stack.

"Second," Calvin panted, "I was complimenting you on your hair. Not making fun of it."

"Whatever," she responded tartly, plopping the Whalers cap back on.

"But feel free to hide it under that hat," Calvin grinned.

"Leave my hat out of this too. It means more than hockey."

"Really? Like what?"

She turned full to Calvin and poked a finger into his chest. "You ask a lot of goddamn questions, Asshole. If you must know, this hat is a reminder of what dickheads do to you: it's all I have left from my last relationship. I'll *never* forget the lesson I learned on that one!"

She stepped back. In her fury she'd gotten too close to him.

Mike quietly stacked the cleaned plates on the table. Calvin and the girl ignored him. For the second time this morning—or maybe even the third—Mike from Troop 73 knew what it meant to be *a fly on the wall.*

Calvin pressed on. "Third, I'm sorry for calling you 'Miss Ever-Persevering in the Face of Stupid Boys.' You wanted to be called 'One Really Pissed Off Dishwasher.' Maybe it'd be easier if I just called you 'Miss Lyons.'"

She of No Fixed Name reacted wildly. Her finger poked Calvin's chest again. "I don't fucking believe it! Did he *tell* you I'm his daughter?"

"He did not."

"What *did* he tell you?"

"Well … you should ask what *you* just told me."

She slinked back a step. "What, exactly, did I just tell you?"

"Loads." Calvin leaned against the triple-sink unit casually.

Shivering: "For example ...?"

"For example ... I think your da dragged you here. He's probably divorced and has custody over you. No married mom would let her girl work here! And you feel you don't deserve this now. You have to put up with boys like me who're only washing dishes cuz they're villains. They probably hit on you nonstop. You'd dance for joy if the next boy you saw was lying stone dead. And being stuck here *sucks* big-time: no malls, no friends, no other girls to talk to. And your 'dickhead' ex-boyfriend—I'll bet that hat was a gift from him. Maybe the only thing you ever got from him. About your hair, you dyed it just recently to piss off your da. Mr. Lyons seems like a cool guy, but he's just covering up. You can tell he's sick of Kermit the Camp Director. And the absolute *last* thing you need is Asshole here telling you your whole life's story."

Miss Lyons stood silent through Calvin's entire utterance. Black eyebrows slid slowly down towards her narrowed eyes.

Mike quietly started on the cups.

"You frighten me," she said, after the pause began to gnaw. "I'm scared shitless. You know all that? I only met you twice!"

"It's the third time we've spoken," Calvin pointed out sweetly. "But who's counting?"

"*You* are, it seems! How'd you figure all that out?"

"Things you said. The way you, like, reacted to things *I* said. Some guesses. I know you dyed your hair in the last couple of weeks since there's no roots."

"But you don't know my natural color!" she said nastily.

"It's black. Your eyebrows are still black. And that tells me even more: you *forgot* your eyebrows are still black. There's no mirrors here? Or a ladies bathroom?"

"There's mirrors in the shower house down the Yellow Trail but that's for you boys. No ladies room anywhere. I use the bathroom upstairs, or up in the Ranger's Office, but neither's got a mirror. The only mirror here is the clean side of that," she pissed, waving her pale hand at the stainless steel dishwashing machine Mike used.

Mike kept on with his work, not acknowledging them.

The lead singer of Berlin noted that whatever you're doing was interfering with her respiration.

Her hand touched her earlobe nervously. "Okay, Asshole—what *don't* you know about me?"

"Your name. I know the rest now. Just need a name."

"First, what's *your* name?"

"Calvin Ciarán Connor III," he said brightly.

"Calvin Ciarán Connor III," she said flatly.

Through the screen door, they heard the *twishity-thump!* of rain-drops smacking the packed dirt surrounding the caf. Calvin, however, could not hear her saying her name. He'd need to ask her outright, to actually say the word "What," then "is," followed by "your," and, lastly, "name," with a question mark garnish. Was she *deliberately* hiding her name? Why? To have some privacy, or—

His face lit up. "You're ashamed of it! Like my da says, it's something only a stupid hippie names a kid!"

Miss Lyons nodded as casually as possible, then burst: "In-*fucking*-credible! Tell me how you figured that out!"

Calvin spread his hands. "If your name was, like, Cindy, you'd've said so a long time ago. But you won't tell me, and you won't for a reason."

"I have a reason, all right. It's a name I have to *explain.*"

"And, you're sick of explaining it," Calvin said.

Mike quietly pulled a rack of cups from the dish machine.

The droplets outside surged to a squall of wet applause. Miss Lyons sighed, this time in nostalgia. "I love my name but it's so totally fucking annoying. So I never give it out, especially here. These stupid boys don't need to know my name."

Calvin noted her syntax (she said *"These* stupid boys," which excluded him, and not *"You* stupid boys," which would've included him), but he didn't dare comment.

"It's a crutch," she went on. "You don't know what a pain in the ass that is."

"Oh don't I now?" he said, loosing his giant guffaw. "It's bad enough when you're foreign—I'm from Ireland, in case you couldn't tell—but I'm also a 'Third.' And just how many other Calvins have you met?"

She thought about it. "Can't think of any. Oh wait—Cal Ripken. That's short for 'Calvin,' right?"

"It is. Who's that?"

"He's a baseball player. Got some kind of streak going."

"I'm not into streaking," Calvin quipped.

She actually laughed. Mike, who was about to start the dish machine going on the silverware, paused at the laugh.

"So," Miss Lyons mused, "if I *tell* you my name is Cindy, you'd have no idea if I was lying."

"I'd know you were lying!" laughed Calvin. "But if you want, we can use Cindy."

Miss Lyons considered it. Calvin had to suppress his joy at finally connecting with her. The squall outside burst into full-fledged showers.

She turned her eyes towards his. "Okay. I'm Cindy."

"Calvin. Pleasure's all mine, love." He extended a hand.

Curling her lip in mock disdain at his precocious use of "love," Cindy shook hands. Her slender little hand was warm.

Calvin suddenly remembered why he was here. He took back his hand and turned to Mike. The flop-haired, pink-cheeked guy pulled the freshly washed silver from the steaming dish machine. The plates were stacked on the table, clean and drying. The cups likewise. Calvin ran a sheepish hand over his icky hair. "I guess I was a big help, huh?"

Mike nodded sarcastically.

"I'll put that shit away," Cindy said. "You can go now, Calvin."

Chapter 15

"HAVING FUN IS OUR CREED."

"THIS SHIT'S ALL yer fault."

"Don't be retarded, Jon. We both got punished."

"No duh—but *both* of us didn't go flappin' dumb-ass lips at my dad, tellin' him how stupid it all is."

"Which I did *after* he punished us. Didn't make things worse, so the 'dumb-ass lips' sunk no ships."

"Ya know I'm right, Connor."

A sigh. "Tell me, are we learning from our mistakes here?"

"I learned not to get punished with you again."

"No, that's not what—*ffffff,* never mind! Too high a concept for your elemental brain, Jon."

"Eat shit, Connor! I wanted to give him a piece of my mind too. But I ain't cuttin' my own head off, dude! If I said what you did, my dad woulda whupped my ass again. But good."

The roaring machine gun fire on the roof of the latrine trailed to a drum roll. "Well. It's total shite," Calvin moaned.

"And here we are, cleaning the 'shite' up," Jon said. "It's all the General's fault. Shoulda gone to Lucid Pond, man, this shit never happened there. Souviens sucks major league cock."

"No it doesn't."

"Yes it does—quit arguin'! This camp sucks donkey dick, and we ain't even been to no merit badges yet!"

"Fine, then it's all misery and chores according to you."

"What the hell are you saying?" Jon squinted. "Yer so full of shit, Connor. You don't wanna be here. Yer biggest wish is to have that asshole Zedz here, so he can deal with me and Gus and that skinny little rookie Crowe. But," Jon said, waggling his zitty chin coyly, *"something's* gettin' you hard here."

Calvin lowered a brow at him. "We're not friends."

"Nope."

"Last night you tried to kill me."

Unapologetically: "So what?"

"'So what?' Suppose I *do* have something cool going on here. Why would I ever tell you what it is?"

Before Jon could respond, Art Maguire slapped open the latrine's door. He cast a dubious eye over the scene: Jon on his hands and knees, scouring the concrete floor with some greenish water; Calvin scrubbing the wooden bench seat, working on the left-side hole.

"Yo," Art announced, stepping around Jon. The drum roll of rain quietly became the tapping of fingers on a desk blotter.

Calvin sat on the bench between the holes. "What ho?"

Art shook his head. "No ho, just Art."

"Use that hole." Calvin pointed to the left one.

"All goes to the same place." Art took out his dick and sent yellow liquid down into the pit.

"Don't fuckin' remind me," Jon groaned.

Calvin snorted, "PG-13."

"Fuck that, dude. I'll curse if I wanna."

"I think your dad's right outside," Art noted.

Jon's eyes said a very loud *Fuck you* while his lips clamped shut.

Art zipped up. "So, how's K.P.?"

"Wonderful," responded Calvin.

"Sucks a bone," responded Jon.

Art laughed at them. He asked Calvin, "Talk to that chick?"

Calvin stated, "I saw no one fitting that description."

"I see," said Art, who did (albeit a little late). "Don't let me stop you losers from cleaning." He left with all alacrity.

"The dishwasher girl!" Jon whooped. "The one that chink Ken was all scared of! *That's* what yer hard for."

Calvin smirked. "Congratulations."

The tapping of fingers on a desk blotter halted altogether.

"We're switchin' at lunch," Jon stated. "You can scrub stoves with the chink, and I'll do dishes with the babe."

"Sure, I'll go with that," Calvin said.

"Bitchin'! A hot-babe dishwasher! Give her ten minutes with me and you got no shot, Calvin!"

"Oh don't I now. Well, let's get this over. The rotting feces smell is killing my brain cells."

"You only got one left anyway." Jon got back to scrubbing.

Calvin worked his brush on the other hole in the wooden bench. Satisfied that the contact surfaces were as sterile as possible, he disinfected the pit using two packets of powdered chemicals sprinkled down the holes. Fizzling sounds rose from the pit, and wafts of dying waste stench flooded their noses.

"Holy fucking shit!" Jon pissed, hacking. He nearly puked.

"We'll survive this better," Calvin gasped, "if you stop *constantly* bringing up how repugnant it is!"

Pinching his nose: "What the hell does 'repugnant' mean?"

Calvin dusted off his hands and spread them. "All this."

"Well, this is goddamn repugnant as hell, dude," Jon said. "I ain't never pissin' in one of these again."

Calvin grabbed him by the collar. "This is your Squad Captain speaking: I order you to finish up with a smile on your face."

Jon tossed off Calvin's hand. "Don't touch me, faggot."

"You're not smiling."

"No I ain't, cuz I'm doin' this repugnant shit with you."

"Smile, goddamnit!"

Jon bucked his head, donning the widest smile he could muster. "Heer, schee?" he said awkwardly. "Ah'n schmilin!"

"Beautiful. We still have the basin and outside floor to do."

Jon kicked open the door and goose-stepped outside with his bucket of chemical cleaner. Sandy slogged up the goat-path and jumped in horror at Jon's obscene smile. "Dude, stop that!"

"Ah cahnt schto' it!" Jon gargled. "He *ahrdahrd* me!"

"That's right," Calvin said, lugging a tub overloaded with brushes, spray bottles, rags, and gloves. "Don't bug him."

"Whatever." Sandy slouched against a tree and watched the two clean away.

"*Having fun is our creed,*" Calvin sang as he slopped Comet in the wash basin. *"A warm campfire's all we need! Sing it, Jon!"*

Sandy worked the pump crank, so Calvin could rinse out the basin. "C'mon, Jon," Sandy laughed, "sing!"

Reluctantly, Jon sang: *"Ahn high, a shinin' shun / on lah, the r'vahs rhun / thoo Lushid Pahd … fuhn fuhn fuhn!"*

Calvin gave the basin a final wipe and then plopped on the damp earth next to the latrine. Jon finished with the cement stoop and relaxed his facial muscles. "Done, finally!"

"Until lunch. Remember, you wash dishes." Calvin grabbed the tub of supplies. "Hey Sandy, take a walk with me."

After five minutes of scouring with a stiff-wire brush and harsh chemicals, the bloodstains on the Hawk Squad's tent deck were gone. White bleach stains sat in their place.

"Fuck it," Calvin huffed.

Sandy, sitting in Crowe's bunk, passed a half-interested eye over the deck. "Beats blood, dude."

"It *does* beat blood." Calvin sat on his own bunk. "I think I'm in with the dishwasher girl."

"No shit," Sandy smiled. "How in?"

"Everything but her name, so we agreed to use 'Cindy.'"

"She don't want you spreadin' her name around?"

"It's some hippie name. Y'know, I think she wants me."

Sandy giggled. "I'm gettin' one of them prenimations."

"Premonitions, you mean?"

"Yeah." Sandy's face had a curved look, like arousal. "There's a dance tonight with the Cookie Girls. Kinda weird, a dance on a Monday night. Anyway, I'll bet you wanna do our little trick from Lewis & Clark Camp."

"You are no dummy, Sandy. Are you stocked?"

"My canteen *and* my water bag. Gonna bring the chick?"

"I'm gonna try. I'll ask her out at lunch."

"Cool beans. Does Art know?"

"Not yet," said Calvin. He thought it over. "Let me talk to him first. He was all fired up yesterday about Jenny and Jill and all, so he'll probably go apeshit about losing his shot at Cindy."

"Yeah, I'm pissed about that too," Sandy said with some heat. "You cheated on Jenny MacDonald with Jill Pedersen. And now yer workin' your way into this dishwasher chick's panties. Holy shit, dude—you ain't all that faithful, are ya?"

Calvin groaned at him. "Sandy, I just met her. Ain't got anywhere near her panties."

Sandy shook his head. "Not yet."

A few minutes later, Sandy left for a merit badge. Calvin stretched out in his bunk, enjoying his first moment of alone-time since walking down to Troop Hall yesterday morning. He pondered random breasts. Then specific breasts. Jenny MacDonald's. Jill Pedersen's. Cindy the dishwasher's. She was something. A sweet, round ass, and a nice face to go with it! A little weird, a little rough, but she tolerated Calvin (with definite choked-back liking). What a week this could be! But how to get her to join the party tonight ...

He sighed at the approaching clomp of hiking boots. The front flaps parted: Shawn Crowe. He was quite young, barely twelve, but maneuvered adroitly on a malnourished frame. His wispy ashen-blond hair had less than a decade to live.

Calvin nodded at him as he entered. "What's up, Crowe?"

"I'm bored. I don't got a merit badge 'til after lunch." The rookie looked at his watch, which had an illustration of Boba Fett on the face. "Got like three hours 'til then."

"Best part of summer camp, boyo. It's called 'down time.'"

"Cool. What do we do in down time?"

"Anything." Calvin rested his head on his beefy arm. "Go swimming. Hiking. Or canoeing, or read a book, or whatever."

"Hey, let's go canoeing! Ain't never done that before!"

Calvin thought it over. "All right. I gotta drop off this cleaning shite back down the Yellow Trail anyway. Let's be off now."

Crowe smiled. "How come you talk like James Bond?"

"James Bond?! He's *English!* C'mon Crowe, tell me you can name just one Irishman!"

"Uh, that little guy with the rainbow. And the pot of gold."

"Bollocks!"

They left Campsite Quatre, slogging down the Green Trail towards Centre des Trois. Crowe, ecstatic to have company, filled the air with talk. "Who's your favorite group? Mine's U2."

"See? You *do* know some Irishmen."

"You're no Bono, man."

"Thank Jesus," Calvin said, crossing himself. "You know who I like? I like the Beach Boys."

"The Beach Boys? They're like that surfer band crap?"

"That's them," Calvin said. "Heard them years ago in Ireland. It's such happy shite. Sunshine, and the sea, girls in bikinis … it's what I thought America would be like." His words drifted off; a wistful nimbus floated before the lad's eyes.

Crowe looked up at him. "Uh, *ooookay* … so, who's your favorite Troopmaster?"

Calvin returned to Earth. "Art's da, without a doubt. Most of the time, it's like he's invisible—you don't even know he's there. Best kind of grown-up, I think!" Calvin loosed his guffaw. "Who's yours?"

"I dunno. Mr. Maguire hasn't really talked to me. Oldroyd did a couple times. He's all right. Why don't you like him?"

"He's a high-falutin' gobshite," Calvin hissed.

As usual, Calvin's Irish vocab made Crowe laugh.

"You'd say 'stuck-up know-it-all,' Crowe." Calvin looked down at the young boy. "You're the only rookie this year. What made you join up?"

"My pop sez to me one day, 'Do you wanna join Troop 666 and go camping and stuff?' And I sez, 'Sure, why not?'"

"Ask a dumb question, right? So you like it so far?"

"I guess. I'm away from my parents, and I get to hang out with cool guys, and do neat stuff like build fires and junk."

"It's not all neat. Wait 'til you've had the Lucid Pond meatloaf! So you like me better than Zedz?"

"Yer nicer to me than he is. Zedz is nicer to Jon, though."

"Zedz is a fat fraidy-cat. I refuse to let Jon control me—I don't care who his da is."

Crowe shrugged shrewdly. "I see that at home; my mom is too scared to get back at my dad, so she takes it out on me."

Calvin didn't dare comment on that awkward comparison. "I had to take a stand with Jon. This is *my* Squad, not his."

"But when Zedz is here, Jon isn't that much of a dick," Crowe pointed out. "You stood up to him, and *now* he's a dick."

"I like to say, 'be your own man.' Don't let dicks like Jon hold you down." And with that, Calvin let the discussion die.

They rounded the last turn in the Green Trail, reaching Centre des Trois. Calvin waved at a Johnny Rotten-haired girl leaning out the back door of the caf's dishroom. She was smoking a cigarette and enjoying doing so on the campgrounds.

"Hiya, Calvin!" the girl called out to him.

Calvin nudged Crowe. "Wave to her, boyo." The kid waved.

Cindy waved back. "Who's yer cute buddy there?"

"This is Crowe," Calvin called.

"A little young for me, but I love blond guys." Cindy stamped out her smoke. "See ya at lunch, Asshole!"

Calvin just had to laugh at that.

Crowe trembled with excitement. "She said I was cute!"

"Take it from me," Calvin said, "compared to how she treats other guys ... she practically jumped your bones!"

Chapter 16
SIGNING A FREE AGENT.

LUNCHTIME CAME AND went. The K.P. crew had started to divide up the cleaning tasks seven ways just as Calvin burst through the kitchen door. "Sorry I'm late, Ken. Went for a canoe ride—what a lake this camp's got, lads, I totally recommend it."

"Well, I recommend the fried chicken," said Ken. "That hippie chef knows what he's doin'. Got leftovers there if you wanna munch out." Ken briefly eyeballed the other Troop 666 kid in K.P. "Jon here tells me you're switchin' jobs with him."

"We made a deal."

"Don't do that without asking me." Ken brusquely handed Calvin some rubber gloves. "I'm not a power hog—I just don't want to hear a girl screaming like at dinner yesterday."

Calvin showed remorse. "Sorry."

"Let's see what happens. But to teach you a lesson, you get the grease traps." The K.P. crew chuckled. "Guys, we took seventeen minutes at breakfast. Let's shoot for fifteen." Jimmy, Dale, Hank, and George trudged out to the caf, tools in hand. Jon Oldroyd and the kid Mike from Troop 73 grabbed the dolly and headed out to collect the bus-pans of dirty dishes.

Calvin got to work on the grease traps. It was a loathsome job. He and Ken chatted to kill the boredom and found a quick common denominator: immigration. Ken was born in Japan (formerly Kenji Aizawa, now Ken Izerman). "It's cool being different from the rest of the pack," Ken said.

"I'm still white," cautioned Calvin. "I blend in as long as I never talk. Mate of mine in the Troop is one-quarter black and you'd never know it unless he told you. We're not in the same boat, Ken."

"You're saying I stick out cuz of my skin," Ken said.

"It's the truth." Calvin gave an empathetic nod. "Can't be easy for you. Don't Yanks act funny?"

"Most don't, or not to my face. You just learn to let it go."

Jon and Mike burst in the caf door with the loaded dolly and headed for the dishroom. Jon, exuding confidence, declared: "Now she's playing with power!"

Once Jon was gone, Calvin muttered, "Stupid prick."

Ken sighed in concurrence. "I got a bad feeling about that guy. Yesterday, Hank and George washed dishes, and pretty soon the girl was throwin' trays around like crazy."

"That's girls for you. All mental. Got a girlfriend?"

"Yep. Her name's Tara. How about you?"

"I do," Calvin said. "Jenny."

"Lucky guy."

"Aren't we both now."

"Tara's white, you know."

Calvin shrugged. "You say that like it matters, Kenji-san."

Ken gave his scrubbing partner a smile. "To the white kids at school, it matters! I always say, a Jap in her lap makes the Yankees reach for hankies."

"Ha ha! Put 'er there!" Calvin high-fived Ken. Bits of gunk hurtled from their rubber gloves.

A piercing shriek from the dishroom, followed by two strings of vulgar language. Jon kicked open the door and scurried into the kitchen as if pursued by a ravenous bug-blatter beast. Cindy came out after him and actually threw a plate. All three boys ducked under a stainless steel prep table.

"Goddamn pig!" roared the girl. "Ken, don't *ever* let that cocksucker in the dishroom again!"

Ken snarled at the cowering Jon. "Consider it done," he called out.

"Calvin!" she shouted. "Get in the dishroom, Asshole!"

Calvin clambered out from under the table, gave his stiffest Trooping Salute, and sped into the dishroom. Cindy knelt down by the table to glare at Jon. "I'll crush your little weenie with a meat tenderizer! Maybe serve it on a hot dog bun too!" She stomped out; the dishroom door swung shut triumphantly.

Jon, after leaving a poltroonish pause, got to his feet. "What a stuck-up cunt."

"Breakfast was so quiet," Ken sighed. "I thought Mike and Calvin had tamed her. You turned her back into a monster."

"Fuck you, chink," Jon snorted, heading for the caf door. "I'm outta here. Sick of doing chores all day."

Before dismissing the Kitchen Patrol, Ken double-checked with Calvin for his Troop's number. "Six-Sixty-Six, how could I forget," he said. "Sucks but I gotta report Jon for skipping out."

"Guess we seen the last o' him," Dale said. "He'll be polishing shit-stalls from now on."

Dryly, Calvin noted, "We already got *that* job too."

"You guys are friggin' war criminals! Himmler and Göring in the house! You gotta tell us about that fight you were in!"

"If I did, Dale, you wouldn't believe it. I was *there* and I don't believe it! See you guys at supper."

"See ya," the others mumbled, departing the kitchen. Calvin was the last to go. And, in fact, he didn't leave at all.

This guy from the Cutting Crew entered a terminal state whenever a) it was after sunset, and b) he was held by you.

Cindy stood by the yellow fridge, sipping a can of her precious Dr. Pepper, and pretended not to notice him. She still steamed over whatever Jon had pulled. The dishwashing session had been tense and quiet. Pink-cheeked Mike had, once more, done most of the work.

Calvin shut the door behind him and walked over to the automatic dish machine, a large contraption with two sets of doors to allow racks to be slid in and out simultaneously. The far side of the machine was unspoilt by soap resin and water marks. As Cindy had said, it quite nicely doubled as a mirror.

And what a sight! Face haggard. Lip and nose swollen, still carrying a twinge of pain, much like sticking a tongue on a dying nine-volt battery's terminals. Icky hair pushed down over forehead and ears to cover his bandage and gauze.

He carefully experimented with pulling his long hair back, as he normally wore it. The locks stuck to his fingers queasily. He hadn't washed his hair since Saturday night and made to instantly remedy that. He turned on the triple-sink's tap. Remembering the cold water line was broken, he shut it off.

Cindy came over to him. "Turn around."

Calvin's mouth opened.

"Don't talk."

His mouth shut. He turned around, his back to the sinks.

She set her soda can on the icky shelf above the sinks, fired up the tap, and used her hands to guide him into position. "Now lean back," she bade him.

His skin was alive, tingling and hot. He couldn't believe this was happening (whatever it was!). He leaned back as told.

She turned to face the sinks and put a hand on his chest to push him back. "Further down," she said.

She meant to put his head backwards in the sink, so the tap would run water down his scalp, like at a hair salon's washing station. He bent his knees and reached back to grab the sink edge for leverage. During this maneuver, his left hand bumped into her lower back.

She calmly moved his hand to its proper destination, which made his underarm brush against her belly. "Almost there," she said. "I'll try to keep it off your forehead."

He looked at the grease-spotted ceiling. Flickering fluorescents tickled his eyes. She pulled the long bits of his hair away from his head and fluttered them in and out of the steaming jet of water. "No shampoo like Dawn, right?" she said.

"W—"

"Don't talk." He felt pressure on the roots; she may have been pulling his hair apart, or scrubbing it. Drops of near-boiling water sprayed on his forehead and the back of his neck, but he gritted his teeth and silently endured their heat.

"You're doing great," she purred. "Almost done."

She moved closer to scrub the hair on the back of his head, and now her hip dug into his ribs and his view of the ceiling suddenly included what might've been a bit of T-shirt-covered breast. He tightened his grip on the sink edge and locked his leg muscles so he wouldn't slip, and commanded his cock to stop hardening. He didn't know how much longer he could—

She slapped the tap off. "All done," she said, squeezing out his hair one last time. She went to fetch a roll of paper towels.

Slowly, Calvin untwisted himself to stand normally. His back smarted and the wet hair was hot on his neck. He felt the water soaking into the back of his T-shirt.

After drying her hands, Cindy held up the used paper towel— pink/brown from soda and blood. "Gross me out!" she declared, handing him the roll. "I can't believe I just did that."

"Neither can I. Thank you," Calvin smiled, running some towels through his locks.

"I tried to keep the bandage dry. Why do you have it?"

"Just a flesh wound."

"Even with your hair pulled down, everyone could see it." Her black eyebrows curled. "I couldn't let you keep walkin' around with that filthy hair anymore though!"

"Again," he said, "thank you."

She laughed. "If there's one thing *I* can figure out about *you,* it's that you're not vain about your looks."

Calvin shrugged. "Except when gore forces me to."

"Gore blows." She took off her cap. "Here, try this instead."

Gracefully, Calvin accepted the Whalers cap and adjusted it to fit his head. He pushed back his damp hair, slipped it on, and looked at himself in the dish machine's "mirror."

"Can still see the wrapping from behind," she pointed out.

"But it does the job up front." Calvin smiled at himself. He looked normal. He took off the cap and made to hand it back.

"You can keep that," she said.

"But this is all you have from your last rela—"

"Fuck him and his hat. I'm better off without it."

"… thanks. Again. I keep saying that!"

Cindy hoisted herself up on the dishroom's stainless steel table to sit with her short legs dangling. Her eyes told the tale of weary feet.

"No problem. I think I'll let my hair flow in the breeze."

"Good for you, Cindy."

The lad from New Order spun a tale about this nervous dude who genuflected whenever he saw his mate putting the theory of gravity to the test.

"Cindy!" she burped, laughter exploding out. "So weird to have a normal name for a change!" Her brown eyes smiled at him. "Why'd you pick Cindy?"

"Just popped in my head. I used to have the hots for this girl named Cindy in my school."

More laughs. "I'm sorry, it's just *sooo* weird to hear 'I have the hots' in your accent!"

"Everyone loves an Irish brogue," he nodded.

Rolling her eyes: "Do they. So let me guess—your Cindy was blond hair/big boobs?"

"No, black hair, like yours used to be. And her boobs are ... underdeveloped." His mind drifted. "Blonde hair/big boobs—that's such a shite stereotype, Cindy."

"Shite," she tittered to herself.

"I mean it! Not every lad looks for blonde hair/big boobs."

"But every lad looks *at* blonde hair/big boobs! Deny *that!*"

"I deny nothing!" he chortled.

She raised a warning finger. "Spare me your next line about how perfect I am." An aloof grin grew on her lips.

Calvin let a pause go by. "Not sure how you knew, but—"

"Always the thing you guys say. Guy looks at the TV: 'Brooke Shields is hot.' Then guy looks over at me: 'Not as hot as you, though. You're perfect.'"

"Huh," was all Calvin had for that. "Guess it *is* predictable."

"It's corny, is what it is," Cindy said.

He looked at her aloof face. "It's a shame."

"What's a shame?"

"In a few days we'll go home, and I'll never see you again. You're the most perfect girl I've ever met. I'll miss seeing you."

Her jaw dropped. "Okay, less corny, but more sleazy!"

"That's not fair!" Calvin coughed, letting his emotions run free. "You asked me to spare you the corny lines, and—"

"You just said it anyway, so how's that 'sparing' it?"

"I had a legit reason *why* I said it! Please listen to the words I say, Cindy, it's totally worth it."

Desperately trying not to laugh: "I get it. But why Cindy? If I'm the 'most perfect girl ever' but your Cindy from school is an under-developed Plain Jane ... why use her name?"

"Plain Jane, I like that. Some lads call our Cindy 'Sigourney' behind her back cuz she looks like the woman in *Ghostbusters.*"

"Now why would you 'have the hots' for a girl who looked like Sigourney Weaver, Calvin?"

"Cuz I liked her. And I come on to women I like." Before he could stop himself: "She was a girl onto which I tried to come."

She almost shit. Did this guy *really* just structure his sentence that way?! "You did that on purpose!" she whooped. "It's not just dork-talk, but like, *porno* dork-talk! *Come on to her,* like hitting on her, then *cum onto her.*" She mimed jerking off.

He flashed his shite-eating grin which she nearly fell for. "You want to have English class or hear my story?"

Concerned she was laughing too much, Cindy choked the latest batch back. "Your story. What's her whole name?"

"Cindy McKee."

"And, what'd you guys do for your first date?"

"We never went out. After months chatting her up, I got bored of her not taking an interest in me."

"So you were obsessed with her? Hanging out below her bedroom window like Romeo?"

"Whatever! I just moved on. I *have* a girlfriend, you know."

"Maybe you do," Cindy smirked. "Or, maybe not."

"Maybe her name is Jenny."

"Jenny. Who *did* take an interest in you."

"She did."

"Why'd Jenny say yes but Sigourney say no?"

Calvin bit his lip. "Jenny liked me, I guess. Our very first conver-sation was an argument in Gym class. And it was obvious she liked the way I fought back. We just clicked."

"There's more to it than that," Cindy intoned. "How long you two been going out?"

"Since February. That's when she moved to my town."

"There's the answer! You ain't the only detective, Sherlock!" Cindy piqued up to explain her deduction: "Cindy McKee knew you from years of being at the same school. This Jenny was brand new to your act, your accent, your confident way of speaking." She waved a hand up and down at him: "This whole *thing* you do, Calvin."

"You make me sound like a carnival freak. *And* you're assuming I'm the only boy from Ireland in my school!"

"Stop it," she barked. "Jenny probably just felt grateful that some guy was standing up to her, instead of all fawning and drooling and offering to show the new girl around town."

"Explain why we're still dating," Calvin challenged. "My 'act,' the whole 'thing' I do ... woulda gotten old, fast. Right?"

"Maybe yer more than that," flapped Cindy. "Maybe yer a great kisser with a huge dong. That'd keep her coming back."

"That would get old fast, too!" Calvin laughed. "Admit it!"

A particular member of Genesis wanted to alter things, but couldn't, since he was at a depth over his head.

"Sounds like you got lucky, Calvin. I bet Jenny's a real cunt. That no one else at school even likes her."

"That's, uh, a good guess. But I don't care what people say about her." A fading smile. "You sound like my ma. She thinks Jenny latched on to me too quickly, so everyone would talk about her. Make her instantly popular."

"In other words, using you."

"What bollocks."

"What *what?*"

"Bollocks. *Bullshit.* I don't put up with people like that—fakers and users. Jenny says she likes how I don't give a crap about what others think. That I make my own waves. Tell me—is that something a user would say?"

"Yes," Cindy admonished, genuinely concerned. "Jenny's using you just right, Calvin. Users always make the people they use feel like they're the most important person in the world."

"What do you know?" Calvin said dismissively.

"Oh I know. I know enough. How old are you?"

"Fourteen."

"Fourteen?! Shit. I thought you were older than me, like sixteen or something. Well, I'd keep an eye on this Jenny if I were you, and don't get too attached. Is she hot?"

"Blonde hair/big boobs. I'm the envy of my grade."

Cindy's whole body bucked as if to say, *Bullshit!*

Out came Calvin's leather wallet again.

"Gonna pay me to believe you?" Cindy teased.

"Shut up," Calvin said. He poked through the wallet and found half of a photo booth strip: two black-and-white frames of Calvin hugging and mugging with a bright-eyed blonde bombshell of a teenage girl. He handed it over with relish.

Cindy looked the photo strip over for a long moment. She examined the back, then ran her finger along the torn bottom edge. She handed it back without a word, and looked away.

Calvin put the photo in his wallet and became aware of her mood change. Clearly he'd fucked up at the end there, and needed to switch topics. "Leaf," he said softly.

"What?" she chanced, her eyes bent in puzzlement.

"Your name is Leaf, right?"

"No, but—and I fucking hate to admit it—you're on the right track. Was that just a guess?"

"Just a guess," grinned Calvin. "Give me a hint."

"It's got something to do with leaves, but—" (she raised her dark brows tightly) "—not really."

"*Ooookay:* Branch?"

"No."

"Rings."

"No!"

"Sap."

"Definitely not!"

They laughed. Settled down casually. Paused in silence together. Calvin fiddled with the brim of the Whalers cap. "So. Going to this dance tonight?"

"Not if I can help it," Cindy said. "They have one every Monday night and I've managed to miss them all so far. You?"

She'd returned the question! Good sign. "I love dances but I hate pop music."

She was appalled. "Really? Even rock and roll?"

"S'all shite. Well, the Beach Boys."

"Wow, nothing from this century even."

Calvin made himself casual. "Me, Art, and Sandy—mates of mine in Troop 666—we've got a routine for this. Every spring we go to Lewis & Clark Camp near Gettysburg. Tons of Troops *and* Cookie Girls go. They put on a party Saturday night, with pairing off of boys and girls for square dancing, and then they go to your Def Leppard and so on. Me, Art, and Sandy find it in-fucking-tolerable: the girls who camp like us boys tend to *look* like us boys. So, what we do is, go for about ten minutes—then sneak back to our tent and get drunk."

Her eyes lit up. "Get drunk?!"

"Sure," Calvin purred. "Sandy's famous for it. You never know what'll be in his canteen!"

Her amazement grew. "I've seen some wacky boys here. A lot of assholes. But never one who says he gets drunk."

"True."

"Now you're speaking my language, know what I mean?! But it goes so much against Trooping ideals!" She was dubious. "I'm sorry, Calvin, it's just hard to swallow."

"Care to join us and see for yourself?"

She ruffled her lips. "I don't know." A polite *no.*

"Come on," he egged, "you must be sick of this dishroom. Listen: while you're there, you can prank Jon's stuff. Maybe piss in his sleeping bag or something."

She didn't seem thrilled with this idea.

"Cindy," said Calvin warmly, "we just have a good time. You can too, if you join us. No one will hit on you or treat you bad; and you will smile."

Her flat expression continued unabated. "Oh, what the hell. You're on." To herself: "I must be on crack."

Chapter 17

GOD AND JON.*

MONDAY NIGHT'S DINNER was lasagna. Fresh tomato sauce; soft noodles; the choicest blend of cheeses; a splash of oregano overtop. "This is really good," said Calvin. The others in the Hawk Squad were too busy stuffing their faces to agree.

Except Gus Jacoby. "Yeah!" he burped, casting an excited shower of red, white, and yellow goop across most of the table. A latecomer noodle, grappling valiantly with Gus's bottom lip, slipped and came to a rest in his lap, and so igniting a fury of "Bwah-hah-hah!"ing and "Look what you did to my shirt!"ing.

Red-faced, Gus flicked the noodle off his lap to the floor.

"Hey!" barked Oldroyd. "Do I hafta get my can of Raid?"

The bug-eyed upper half of Gus's face made tricky maneuvers; the slack-jawed lower half oozed sauce. "Huh?" he said.

Oldroyd pointed at the deceased noodle at Gus's feet. "Pick that up, litterbug!"

"*Some* of us have to mop this place later," Calvin noted.

Father dutifully collected napkins from the dispenser by the buffet table and began wiping the lasagna spatter onto Gus's tray. Crowe, seated across from Gus, gladly took napkins to mop his chest. His white U2 T-shirt had taken a large blow. "Ruined!" he proclaimed. "You ruined my shirt, Gus!"

For the first time in his Troop 666 career, Gus had seniority over someone. "Shut up, rookie! I said I was sorry!"

"Soak it in water," Father told Crowe calmly. "It'll be fine."

"It's not fine! Gus, you're a freakin' slob!"

"Crowe!" roared Calvin. "Gus is your Lieutenant! He said he was

---

* Two separate topics, obviously.

sorry! I'm sure he'll wash your shirt for you. Right?"

Gus moaned in childish shame; everyone was yelling at him all of a sudden. "'Kay," he whined.

"Good," Calvin said. "Now everyone belt up before Father takes back grace and gets God upset." He winked at Father.

"God won't *get upset*," the teenage Junior Chaplain said. "You talk like He's a character in a book, Calvin."

"He is—or haven't you heard of the Bible?"

"He's not *just* a character in a book," Father corrected. "God is ineffable. That means it is beyond human compr—"

"Father, I'm from Ireland. I *know* what 'ineffable' means. Your point is, God lives off the page as well as on it."

"That's a great way to put it. But don't place human emotions on God. He doesn't get upset."

Ryan Phillips suddenly spoke, issuing Father a challenge: "Explain the Tower of Babel." Jon and Gus jolted; their common neighbor so rarely spoke that he was usually invisible.

"I'm sorry?" said Father.

"The Tower of Babel," Ryan said. "God wasn't upset?"

"No. God confounded the language so people couldn't understand each other, but you can't paraphrase that as *God was upset*. There's no emotions. He just punished the overzealous."

"How about when He wiped everyone out with Noah and the Ark? God was pretty upset then, I'd bet."

Father warmed to this challenge, grinning tightly. He was still a few years from seminary school but would become one of those men of the cloth who relished in converting the heretical. "I see what you're doing: picking events where God acted with force. There's a lot of them in Genesis. But that's what *that* book's about: what happens when Man is dissident."

Father's speech was fluid. Others at the Hawk Squad table scratched their heads, confused. Not Ryan. He'd gotten it.

Father went on: "When your dad punishes you, it's not cuz he wants revenge, or he's upset. It's cuz you've strayed from the path. God's the same way; he wants you on the right path."

Ryan folded his muscled arms defiantly. "So God, at least your

God, punishes us to benefit us? The mere mortals?"

"If God's actions are beneficial to us, that's His business. If they are harmful, well, that's His business also."

"Gimme a break! That can't get any more ... " Ryan looked to Calvin. "What's the word?"

"Subservient?" Calvin supplied.

"No. Well, that too. I mean it's not an answer. You know!"

Calvin did: "Ambiguous!"

Ryan put the word to use: "That's as ambiguous as it gets, Father! 'God does what He wants, why He wants, and don't you dare question it!' Whatever, man!" Ryan took a breath to quell his irritation. "Lemme give you *my* opinion on God."

Father knew little about Ryan and subscribed to the rampant occultist theories regarding the kid's spiritual beliefs. (Remember Ryan's Book.) But Father was Father, the dutiful Junior Chaplain, always willing to listen: "Go for it."

"I read most of the Bible," Ryan purported. "I skipped the boring crap like all the 'begats,' but I read the rest. You know what I saw? Wickedness. As much wickedness as kindness."

"Who's to say what is wicked?"

"I am! *I'm human!* I have emotions, so I can judge them!"

"It doesn't matter if *you're* human, because *God* isn't! He's God! Who are you to label His actions as wicked?"

"Killing everyone with a flood—that's not wicked?!"

"Nearly everyone. And we grew again."

"So if I kill you, that's cool. Someone will take your place."

"Wrong. You're not God."

"Neither are you!"

No one was eating anymore, nor tempted to intercede—not even Troopmaster Oldroyd. This was a whopper of a show!

"Admit it," grinned Ryan. "'God' is just an easy way to answer hard questions."

Father sprouted a frown. "An atheist's argument. It's silly."

"Is it? Explain creation."

"You know it already, Ryan, you've certainly read Genesis. God created Heaven and Earth in six days, then—"

"Yeah yeah, now show me some evidence."

"The Bible is Truth." Father said this with determination.

"Sure it is." Ryan said this with sarcasm. "See, I use my *brain* to think, not my Bible!"

"I never use my Bible to think. I use it to guide me, to console me. There's a wealth of wisdom on its pages. Even *you* should've noticed that." This was Father's first statement with a decided *I'm better than you* tone.

Ryan was not oblivious. "Oh, I noticed a lot of things. Seas parting, talking bushes—slave owners!"

"Don't make that mistake," said Father sternly. "In American history, slavery was the chaining-up of black people. In the time of Christ, slavery was a class of society; a job, really."

"If that word means something different now, how many other words in the Bible mean something different?"

"Not *that* many. The time period is relevant to the story. Any history teacher'll tell you that!"

"Sure. They need some reason to be around."

Father, always willing to listen, was less willing now. "Look, those who fail to understand history are doomed—"

"—to repeat it," Ryan growled. "Which is true: *we* don't have slavery anymore! Modern people—*us*—know better!"

"You are focusing too much on the messengers, the ancient and modern Biblical messengers, and not on the message itself. The message is timeless. The Bible *is* that message."

"Men *wrote* the Bible! Men, who owned slaves, sat down and wrote it! The message and the messenger are the same!"

"No they aren't, you little—" Father stopped. He visibly retracted from arguing. "Okay: let me show you why logic doesn't work. I'll use *your* logic, with something that just happened." Father cleared his throat. "*Gus* tells someone to shut up, and they keep talking. *Calvin* tells someone to shut up, and everyone gets quiet. The message is the same: 'shut up.' But the messengers are different: no one takes Gus as seriously as Calvin—Calvin is older, and much bigger, and holds a rank."

"Of course, you left some facts out," Ryan quickly countered.

"Gus told Crowe to shut up because Gus was embarrassed from his goof. But Calvin told Crowe to shut up cuz the rookie got disrespectful! The message is *not* the same."

"You're wrong, Ryan. Wrong. Whatever minor things you add to it, it's still 'shut up' from them both. Thing is, Calvin's message is respected and Gus's is not."

"Here's my message," Calvin pissed: *"shut up!"* He gave each debater a scornful gaze. "I'm the Squad Captain here, so when I tell you to shut up, you better do it!"

Acknowledging (but utterly ignoring) him, Father cried, "That's my point!" He looked at Ryan. "If the message came to you through someone you had respect for, or thought was cool, you'd never question it. But you're so focused on the ancient ways, and what you see as harsh emotions—there's no convincing you of the message's truth!"

"You use the King James Bible? Whose words console you, Father: God's, or some inbred British king's?"

Calvin the Catholic didn't laugh—Calvin the Irishman did.

"The King James Bible is for Anglicans, Ryan. Down at Saint Brigid, we use the New American Bible." Looking for the endgame, Father said, "At least we use *something*. Whose words console you?"

"Truthfully?"

"Yes. I'd like to know."

Ryan needed a second. "Words console me. Not God's."

Father was dumbstruck. When the pause began to gnaw, Calvin leapt in: "You mean the Devil?" he asked, dead serious.

"I don't know," Ryan said.

"Gimme a break," Jon said.

"I hear the voice every once in a while," Ryan went on, "and what it says is always the truth. Even if it ain't happened."

"What're you, Spazz with the fake ESP?" Jon dissed.

"No, it never fails me. It's always right. But it's not God." Ryan looked at Father. "God sucks."

Quite a statement to make—everyone at the table was Catholic. With a meditative breath, Father looked at Oldroyd for backup. The man's face basically said, *Yer on yer own, kid.* "I won't try to change your mind," Father said at last. "If you want to accept Catholicism, fine; if not, fine. It's in the Constitution. It's what makes America great. We all have choices."

"Not anymore!" Calvin barked, slapping down his fork. Neighboring tables motioned to camp staff to put an end to the noise. Calvin didn't care—he stood and shouted on. "We're not in America, we're at my supper table! Enough soapbox skullduggery, insulting Catholicism and pissing on about how God sucks—you suck! Both of you suck!" He crossed himself. "Jesus, save us all! To think I *started* this argument!"

"You boys need to quit your arguing," said Deputy Camp Director Satan, sauntering behind Calvin and laying a gaunt hand on the big lad's shoulder. "The fellas around you think you're making a little too much hoopla."

"The argument is over, Mr. Lyons," Calvin stated. He glared at his tablemates. "Isn't that right, lads?"

The table was silent from that moment on.

"Ahem," came a familiar gruff voice over the loudspeakers.

Boys spun to face the podium: the short, preened figure of Camp Director Murphy (known to some as Kermit) stood at the mic, resplendent in tailored jeans, a red and black flannel shirt, and a Camp Souviens fitted cap. He looked Troop 666's way sternly. "Uh-oh," groaned Oldroyd, "what we done *now?*"

Kermit waited for perfect silence, which he got in seven long seconds. "Thank you. I have just two announcements tonight." He contrarily shuffled twenty note-cards. "First off, the dance tonight starts at eight, at the Lacroix Memorial Field. Up the Red Trail." He cleared his throat. "During the dance, no minors are permitted at any other location without an adult supervisor. So you'd be wise to not go exploring."

Kermit shuffled his note-cards, cut them, then shuffled again. "Lastly, would Jon Oldroyd of Troop 666 report to my office? Thank you." He marched up the stairs, out of sight.

Oldroyd looked across the table at his malcontent son. "Wha'ja do, boy?"

"Nuthin'," Jon said, looking intently at his empty plate.

"That's the problem," Calvin muttered under his breath.

Ken passed a hand through his fine black hair. "Guys, we go no longer than fifteen minutes this time. There's a dance with girls going on tonight." Coyly: "I need to get a shower and find out the right threads to wear."

Calvin couldn't resist: "You're going to pick up chicks with poor Tara alone at home?"

The K.P. crew chuckled. Ken handed Calvin two mildly irritated eyebrows. "And you're in the dishroom taming the shrew, with poor Jenny alone at home?"

"Jaysus," Calvin blushed. He purposefully marched right out to the caf to begin loading up the bus-pans of dirty dishes. He then felt totally stupid for coming out without the dolly.

His dishroom partner, the tall, older lad Mike, pushed the dolly through the kitchen door and brought it over with a tight little grin on his pink-cheeked face.

"Sorry, Mike," Calvin uttered, "lost my head there."

Misconstruing what Calvin had apologized for, Mike said, "You were keeping Ken in check. That's cool in my book."

This was the third time Calvin had worked with Mike, yet now was the first time he'd heard the guy speak. Mike had a strong, determined voice, just like Ryan Phillips. Both rarely used their throaty voices, while Calvin used his crackly one far too much. The irony was so naked, it might as well have worn pasties and slid its ass-crack up and down a brass pole.

"Although," Mike furthered with a smirk, "Ken's a long ways from Rhode Island. His girlfriend would never know."

Calvin eyeballed him. "True," he said neutrally.

"I ain't gonna squeal," Mike said, reading Calvin's mind. "You got a girlfriend too, right?"

"Actually," said Calvin, stopping his half of the bus-pan loading operation. He popped off Cindy's Whalers cap and put a hand to his wounded forehead. "Jenny and I separated. Happened Friday night, right before my trip here. I haven't told anyone yet. Not sure why I'm telling you."

"Me neither. She find someone new?"

"She just wants a short break from our relationship."

"No shit. You're a free agent." Mike fixed on his tight little grin. "Go pork that dishwasher chick. I would, if I were you."

Calvin loosed his huge guffaw. "Sounds like a plan!"

Dull clomping came from the stairwell in the corner of the caf's large open room. Jon Oldroyd sullenly slogged away from the foot of the stairs. "Hey, Jon!" Calvin called.

Jon turned. "Screw you, Calvin. This is all your fault." He raised his upper lip, forming an ugly stare.

Calvin tried not to laugh. "So what did Kermit say?"

"Who's *Kermit?!*" Jon snorted, raising the lip higher.

"The Camp Director. You know, Murphy."

"Why do ya call him 'Kermit?' It oughta be 'Asshole.'"

"Long story." Calvin watched ruefully as Mike took it upon himself to push the dolly away. "Now, what'd he say, damnit!"

"I can't go to the dance. It's my last warning. I hafta stay at camp with a grown-up—which'll be my dad, you watch."

"What? Kermit's way out of line!"

"Damn right he is!"

"You don't understand, Jon! If you stay at the campsite—oh, shite on a shingle!"

Jon adopted a suspicious gait. "Whadda you care?"

"I'm your Squad Captain. You and I knock heads once in a while, but I won't sit back while that tyrant takes you away from the dance. You live for dances."

"That's what I said. Your friend Kermit didn't listen."

"He'll listen to me." Calvin headed for the stairwell.

"Wait up!" Jon intercepted him. "It'll make things worse!"

Calvin raised his eyebrows at Jon.

Who gave in. "All right. Things can't get worse, I guess."

"Never say that!"

Calvin marched up the stairs and skulked down the hallway. The lacquered maple door at the far end bore a monstrous brass plaque, shrieking "CAMP DIRECTOR."

Calvin knocked. "What?" a voice called roughly.

"Mr. Murphy, it's Calvin Connor from Troop 666. We met yesterday. Could I have a word in your ear?"

A muffled obscenity, a sigh, then a "Come in."

Calvin entered Kermit's office. He noted the subtle pale blue wall-papering, the plush faintly golden carpeting, the many award plaques, the stately old bookcase, the behemoth oaken desk in front of the larger of the two windows. He especially took notice of the air conditioner keeping things cool.

Kermit sat in a padded leather throne, the bill of his fitted Souviens cap pulled down, shading his slits.

"Thank you, sir." Calvin settled into one of the two chairs facing the desk. When he looked up, he found Kermit wearing a new (but no less histrionic) expression: nonplusment.*

Kermit had drawn back and fixed wide eyes on something above Calvin. Oh shit—Calvin was *wearing Cindy's hat!*

Laden with contempt, Kermit took charge. "Mr. Connor, what can I do for you?"

Calvin opened his hands. "I'm a Squad Captain. I know my lads well. We've been a close-knit bunch for—"

"Get to the point. I have things to do before the dance."

"Jon and I have been in the same Squad for years, and—"

"Is that why you're here?" Kermit interrupted. "Jon is banned from the dance. There is no appeal system."

"Begging your pardon, sir: you opened Pandora's Box."

Kermit remained stoic for exactly two beats. "Have I?" he grinned. "Let me guess—Jon will wait for his hillbilly father to fall asleep, and sneak off to the dance anyway."

Oh, Kermit was good! So much for Calvin's plan.

Oh, but Kermit wasn't *that* good! Calvin went ahead and called the bluff: "Mr. Murphy, why would you tell me that unless you mean to use me as a harbinger of doom?"

"Very good, young man," the grown-up nodded. "If Jon doesn't

---

* Nonplusosity? Nonpluscence? Nonplustiture? Whatever, you know what the chronicler means.

listen to you, I'll bag him at the dance. If he does listen, he stays put at camp. If you don't tell him, I'll bag him. So you see, now it doesn't matter what you do—does it?"

"That's evil," Calvin hissed. "There's no other word for it."

Kermit sighed. "Mr. Connor, you have wits, but not enough. To maintain complete order over two hundred teenage boys in twelve Troops every week, I must occasionally resort to shady methods." Kermit's manner was matter-of-fact. "What one or two kids perceive as a bad deal also ensures the other hundred ninety-eight are keeping clean noses." Kermit shook his head at Calvin's flummoxed face. "Don't give me that look. Your verbal dexterity and keen eye tell me you're no dumb hick, even if your Troop is damn well full of them."

Calvin jumped on that. "Then *eliminate* the problem, don't play games with him. Just send Jon to the dance!"

That started the ball rolling. Calvin did not look back.

At last, Kermit was miffed. He'd seen all of Calvin's moves in advance up 'til now. "Excuse me—*send* him to the dance?"

"Every year at Lewis & Clark back home, we have a dance just like this, with the Cookie Girls. And some Cookie Girl always ends up punching Jon's lights out or kicking him where the sun don't shine. Or both, last year."

"I see," Kermit said, a degree of levity visible in his slits.

"Jon starts a lot of trouble," Calvin admitted. "Still, I am not allowed to fight back, because I'm his Squad Captain." He omitted Jon's father as a further reason. "I have to set the example. Captains can't punch out the guys, right?"

"Right."

"However, pissed off Cookie Girls *can*. And then you'd have a real crime worth punishing." Calvin put his hands in his lap. The rush from such deceit! Calvin felt so alive!

Kermit looked sold. And, for that very reason, he smelled a rat. "I get this feeling you're using me, as I'd use you."

"What if I am? Suppose you pardon Jon and I convince him to behave. Then he's no longer a problem for you, is he?"

"True. But you named him 'Jon the jerk' in the registration book. I *know* he's not your friend." Kermit squinted. "You have a motive here which I cannot quite discern."

"My motive is revenge." Calvin took off the Whalers cap. "See this? Jon did it. Clocked me with his flashlight."

"Doc George was right," Kermit said to himself. He gripped his desk and donned some light slits. "Look, Mr. Connor: if I don't hear a kid's name, he's not getting into trouble. But the very idea Jon might grope Cookie Girls bugs me. I *would* hear his name then, and nowadays, sexual harassment lawsuits are as common as dandelions."

Calvin bit his lip. "Er. I see."

"On the other hand," Kermit reasoned, the savvy rich in his voice, "were I to *catch* this troublemaking son of the Devil's Troopmaster just as he was about to make such a move … "

"You did tell him it was his last warning," Calvin noted.

"I did. He was bad and got K.P.; then skipped out on it. The third chastisement would be the last: confinement in the Chamberlin Memorial Building. The Cell. One little room with a cot and a toilet. Three meals on trays. Once a summer I get a Rambo and have to use that route."

Calvin winced, for Kermit said "route" like Inky would. Good thing old man Oldroyd wasn't here. For many reasons!

"You'll give him that rather than ban him from the dance?"

"No. I thought I was clear—Jon hasn't earned that yet." Kermit made his decision. "Tell Jon he can go to the dance. He is to return to Kitchen Patrol duty at once. Remind him this is his last warning. If you want, tell him about the Cell, so he'll be a good little boy. Or don't tell him; I really don't care."

Calvin wasn't sure if he'd won or lost. "Thank you, sir." He stood and saluted, a move that Kermit clearly loathed.

That, if anything, was Calvin's cue to exit. Immediately.

The lad trundled down the stairs to the caf proper and found Jon sitting at the bottom. "It's fixed," Calvin said, hurrying past him. "You're back on K.P. and going to the dance."

"Really?" Jon's face brightened with joy. "What'd you say?"

"I'll have to tell you later—I have dishes to wash. I'm sure Ken needs a hand with those fucking grease traps."

Calvin sprinted through the kitchen to the dishroom.

A guy from Crowded House thought it'd be a great idea not to imagine things had ended.

Mike and Cindy dried their hands after a job well done. Stacks of clean dishes and cups lined the dishroom's table.

"Oh bollocks," Calvin sighed at their rueful faces.

"Neighborly, my ass," Mike pointed out.

"Thanks for nothing, Asshole," nodded Cindy.

Chapter 18
ARGUING THE CALL.

TROOPMASTER DICK OLDROYD wasn't even born in the same month as his presumed delivery date. So began the trend of his being late for everything. *Everything.* Even the introduction to this chapter (viz. the very words you're reading right now) got added very late in the creative process.

Tardy. Overdue. Dilatory. Oldroyd's favorite card in the deck was the late of spades.

"I'll be there at six," he'd say, and show up at seven.

"I'll be there at seven," he'd say, tacking on an extra hour to cover his ass, and he'd show up at nine.

"I'll be there at five," he'd say, cutting himself an hour short as self-imposed motivation, and he'd show up at eleven.

"I'll be there tomorrow at four o'clock sharp," he'd say, and he'd show up about midnight next Tuesday.

"I ain't comin'," he'd say, a month after the fact.

On those rare, almost accidental occasions when he *would* show on time—like on page 1 of this chronicle—those around him, influenced by osmosis, would pick up the slack.

Lazy. Laggard. Procrastinating. The way he met his future wife at the supermarket (she just walking in, he hotfooting it out in a rush) was merely a twist of late.

"Be here at five," old Troopmaster Schultz used to tell him, meaning seven, but making two hours' allowance for Oldroyd's customary lateness. When the mustachioed moron finally arrived, at ten-thirty—out of breath and stinking of the peppery sweat of extreme hustle—he claimed to have been held up after getting his bolo tie caught in the coffee grinder.

Excuses. Alibis. He never went on dates; he went on lates.

"I was unavoidably detained," he'd lie.

"I was held up in traffic," he'd lie.

"My dog ate my homework," he'd lie, as a joke. Ha ha.

"Caught my bolo in the door," he'd lie.

"Caught my bolo in the dishwasher," he'd lie.

"Caught my bolo in the VCR," he'd say, absolutely telling the God's honest truth.

On the event of his death, God will commemorate Richard V. Oldroyd's legacy by showering the Axsubeen area with tornadoes and flooding, thereby ensuring the one o'clock burial does not commence until about quarter past six.

Sometimes, like here at Camp Souviens on Monday evening, Oldroyd's lateness was like some kind of magic trick: people would see it with their own eyes, and *still* couldn't figure out how it's done. After the dinner meal—ninety minutes before the dance started—he laid out a plan. Troop 666 followed it to the letter: they'd gone in groups to la Maison de Douche down the Yellow Trail to get showered up; they'd returned to their campsite and selected their finest T-shirts and shorts; they'd spit-polished their hiking boots, slicked their hair, and tightened their belts; they'd gotten in ranks, called roll, and marched hurriedly the two-thirds of a mile or so from Campsite Quatre to the Remy F. Lacroix Memorial Field up the Red Trail, near the parking lot. At no point did the Troop or its leader delay, dilly-dally, or fart around.

And *still* they showed up twenty-nine minutes late.

"What a gyp!" roared Oldroyd's son Jon with disgust: the punch bowl was already dry; the place already rocked in their absence; and (most importantly) the good-looking Cookie Girls were already taken. "All the ass is gone! Only ones left are the thunderthighs!" Jon launched into a colossal frown.

The others responded with vulgar taunts (except Spazz—he was, remember, under strict orders never to speak).

"We should feel lucky we got here before it ended," Inky grunted. "If only we had *real* leadership ..."

"Go slow dance with yourself," Oldroyd fired back, getting a genuine laugh from the others.

"ARE WE ROCKIN' TONIGHT, PEOPLE?" came a rich voice through the speakers. The teenage crowd, massed mostly in the center of the field, screamed and waved. "I'M YOUR HOST FOR THE EVENING, THE MAN IN BLACK WHAT GOT YER BACK, D.J. KOOLIE KIRK! I'M JAMMIN' AND SLAM-MIN' THE WHEELS OF STEEL HERE AT THE CAMP SOUVIENS 'ACROSS THE RESERVOIR' DANCE! BOYS, WON'CHA SAY A BIG 'HELLO!' TO THE GIRLS OF CAMP EUREKA!"

The boys in the audience woofed like dogs.

"WE'LL BE GROOVIN' 'TIL TEN, PEOPLE," Koolie Kirk noted, "PLENTY OF TIME FOR SOME BON JOVI ACTION!" The night came alive with whining guitars and chants about only existing with the help of an invocation.

Oldroyd and Maguire took their cue to stand to one side with the other Troopmasters and the Cookies' Chiefs. Inky planted his feet, folded his arms, and glowered at the boys.

Calvin scanned for Kermit and found him keeping watch with the rest of the camp staff on the far side of the "dance floor." He turned to his friends, flattening out his shirt and cracking his knuckles. "Let's mingle." He made a beeline for the crowd, Art and Sandy close behind. Ryan Phillips headed after, followed by the others. Jon came last, dropping the frown—it didn't work unless there was an audience.

Once firmly imbedded in the crowd, Calvin slowed down and made his path windy. D.J. Koolie Kirk mixed the end of the Bon Jovi song with the beginning of a Bob Seger song, hollering, "SHAKE YER BOOTIES TO THIS BEAT!"

Calvin brought himself to a halt at the far edge of the "floor" and looked over the crowd. They weren't in class A uniforms, tying knots, or selling overpriced baked goods. But it was obvious they were Troopers and Cookie Girls. These teenaged boys and girls really ill-fit a dance setting. Calvin couldn't get away fast enough.

Art and Sandy made hurry-up motions, *the others are catching up!* Calvin swam back into the crowd, poked into a clearing, and arrived at the right-channel speaker stacks.

Adults slouched here. Calvin's eyes met with Kermit's. Kermit raised an eyebrow in return.

"Uh-oh," bleated Sandy. "We're dead, aren't we?"

Calvin glanced over his shoulder. *"Relaaaax,"* he sang.

Kermit caught Calvin's glance and followed it: the line of Troop 666 kids worked its way along Calvin's path towards this corner. Jon, bringing up the rear, charged through the crowd with his hands by his belt loops to pinch many passing asses.

Art grabbed Calvin's meaty arm with his gangly hand. "Oh shit! Did you plan this, Irish?"

"The second Kermit goes to bust him, our coast is clear."

Murphy's thick brows dipped low. "We have a situation."

Lyons sighed. "Now what?"

"Look," said Murphy.

Lyons looked: there was that 666 miscreant, the Troopmaster's son, Jon by name. The kid slyly ran his mitt over a Cookie Girl's buns as he shuffled past her on the dance floor.

Hot blood rushed to Lyons's heart-shaped head. He had a daughter the same age as the accosted Cookie Girl, working next to this little bastard in the camp's kitchen, no less! "Excuse me!" the man raged, pushing Murphy aside.

"Right behind you," Murphy said.

Calvin took careful steps in the dark pathless forest, Art and Sandy following, making their way as the crow flies back to Centre des Trois. "I admit it was a pretty great setup," Art said. "And Jon wouldn't be in trouble if he wasn't an asshole."

"But ..." Calvin prompted, rolling his eyes.

"Your mom's butt," Sandy muttered with a laugh.

"... but it was a bit over the top," Art went on.

"Jon was in our way tonight," Calvin pointed out, "and after last night, he deserves all the punishment he gets."

"Nope, over the top," Art repeated. "You can just ignore Jon and all his bullshit. Try it. I do it with Spazz all the time; it totally works. Jon's all talk."

Calvin popped off the Whalers cap to flash his bandage. "I got six stitches of 'all talk' right here on my fucking face!" he roared. *"You're all talk, Art! And soft as shite!"*

Sandy hissed, "Shut the fuck up! We're near the Red Trail here—sittin' ducks if you assholes keep yellin' that loud!"

A long quiet period passed among the friends. Then Art blurted out, "What happens if Jon fingers you?"

"Nothing happens. He was caught red-handed. Dick'll totally think *Kermit* is the villain here, not me." He turned to sneer at Art. "Now belt up, the pair of you—we need to be fun around Cindy. It's time to drink!"

Chapter 19
TWIN BILL.

CALVIN POKED HIS head in. Cindy sat on the dishroom's stainless steel table, decked in bright orange jeans, pink Chucks, and a black T-shirt that screamed **INXS** — the **I** and **S** wrapping 'round her breasts. Her Johnny Rotten hair lay to the left side. Her eyes were shut.

A song by U2 came out the boom box. The bass had a strong effect on Cindy, gripping her above the sternum, moving her back and forth with gentle precision. Something in her sway indicated she noticed him, and *hi,* and *how are you,* and *be right with you once this tune is finished.*

Calvin ducked back outside. "She'll be a minute," he said.

"That's a minute wasted, dude," Sandy huffed. "Nuthin' oughta be wasted but the four of us. I'm headin' back."

"Best we stick close, Irish," Art warned, "case you need to cover our asses, or vice versa." He turned, sprinting to catch up to Sandy.

Calvin watched them hoof it down the Green Trail until they faded into the crisp night. He, Art, and Sandy had forged a complex set of relationship circles. At the core, them in private settings; one layer out was them in Troop 666 together; the next layer was school; then the crust, their social lives beyond each other. Each layer was built upon the strength of the one under it. The bond of friendship was quite strong.

It was not uncommon for one of them to bring a girlfriend along for a night at the movies or a day wasted in Art's room playing cards: Art, Sandy, and Calvin (with Jenny); Art, Calvin, and Sandy (with Bonnie, later Julie). This would be the first such instance in Troop 666, but what could go wrong?

Cindy kicked open the door and lobbed a half-gallon carton of milk at Calvin. He just barely made the catch.

Calvin: This'll be fun. Thanks for coming tonight, love.

Cindy: Stop calling me that! And tell me again why we need milk?

Calvin: To mix with the brandy.

Cindy: Brandy and milk. And, you drink it?

Calvin: It's called a Brandy Alexander. Ever had one?

Cindy: Never had *brandy*.

Calvin: It's … it tastes like, well, brandy. And milk.

Cindy: [laughter] You're jabbering, Asshole.

Calvin: Just nerves, I guess. We're on the lamb, with a girl, on our way to do some underage drinking. How can you *not* be nervous?!

Cindy: What can they do to me? Give me K.P.? I'm actually looking forward to this. Being cooped up in that dishroom … it's totally burnin' me out!

Calvin: "Being cooped up." I know someone who'll be cooped up!

Cindy: Um, what?

Calvin: I set a trap for Jon. Kermit busted him at the dance grabbin' girls' butts.

Cindy: Good! They ought to fry his tiny dick off—that'll teach him. What's *that* face for?

Calvin: We have a rule: no talking about castration!

Cindy: Jesus, you guys and your ding-dongs!

Calvin: I'm pretty protective of mine. You would be too if you had a big one like me!

Cindy: Ha ha, shut up! You're so paranoid.

Sandy: Quit lookin' over yer shoulder, dude!

Art: Got a bad feeling about this. Calvin told me that chick is Satan's daughter.

Sandy: Really?

Art: I'm afraid she's gonna tell her dad and we'll end up in the clink with Jon.

Sandy: Relax! She's cool. She wants to drink with us. Calvin wouldn't invite the enemy over!

Art: He did it to Jon!

Sandy: But not to himself!

Art: Whatever.

Sandy: Besides, Jon's a dickhead. He got what's comin' to him. I say, let Kermit nail his ass to the wall. Stuck-up son of a bitch!

Art: Kermit wants to bust *all* of us. Remember his fight with Oldroyd in the caf? And that look he gave us yesterday when we met him on the Red Trail?

Sandy: Yeah, Kermit's real snooty. Looked just like that faggot Mr. Smythe at Lucid Pond, dude. *Just* like him!

Art: Right. Looking down his nose at us. Kermit hates us. Y'know, I think he's got something nasty up his sleeve.

Sandy: Like tonight, ya mean? Shut up. Kermit didn't set this thing up with Cindy. That's so fuckin' ridiculous.

Art: It's possible!

Sandy: No it ain't. She ain't gonna fink on us, dude!

Art: Sandy, you assume we know who Cindy really is. Or who Kermit really is, for that matter.

Cindy: By the way, who's Kermit?

Calvin: Mr. Murphy.

Cindy: Doesn't look like a frog.

Calvin: It's … a long story, and you like hockey. Trust me, you don't wanna know.

Cindy: Not anymore! [laugh] You guys are dorks!

Calvin: "Dorks?" Now see here, we are classy gentlemen, I'll have you know!

Cindy: Classy my ass!

Calvin: What about your ass?

Cindy: Watch it, buster. If you start staring at me like your pal Mr. Buzz-cut-Guy up there, this'll end real quick!

Calvin: Buzz-cut-Guy is Art, but it's not a buzz-cut. He's got a flattop afro.

Cindy: *Nooo!* Afros are what black people have!

Calvin: Art *is* black. He is one-quarter black. If you get a chance tonight, look real close at his hair. You'll see it.

Cindy: No shit! I'da never noticed it. He's, like, really white-looking. Does he have the black guy ding-dong?

Calvin: [Cindy voice] "Jesus, you guys and your ding-dongs!"

Cindy: [laughter] I'm only kidding! I'm not that type of girl, Calvin.

Calvin: Never said you were … but you do like talking about them ding-dongs!

Cindy: [looks at him] You're actually cool with that. The way I talk, I mean.

Calvin: It's like us lads talk.

Cindy: It's good to meet someone who gets me. Who knows what I'm about.

Sandy: *I'd* like to know more about who Cindy really is. She's a total freak but that fact gets me hard for some reason!

Art: Yo, you ever talk to her? That'll kill your boner! [Cindy voice] "Fuck fuck fuck, look how tough I talk, just like a guy!"

Sandy: *You* ever talk to her?

Art: I *can't* talk to her—Calvin went in the dishroom first so's he got to talk to her first! Irish's hogging all the chicks lately!

Sandy: So what, he's good with chicks. Maybe he can get her shirt off to-night and we can bug-eye some boobage.

Art: Yo, the brandy might help!

Sandy: Calvin get some milk?

Art: He's holdin' a jug of something.

Sandy: I hope it's milk. Brandy and milk is a good mix.

Art: If you say so.

Sandy: Art, *relaaaax!*

Art: I'm sorry, Sandy. Really.

Sandy: Here's something else to think about: Gus told me Spazz was talking today at the Navigation merit badge.

Art: No shit! What'd Gus do?

Sandy: Nothin'. He's Gus!

Art: Chickenshit. Yo, do me a favor: after everyone's asleep, sneak on over to the Hawk tent and lean right up to his ear and whisper, "Gus, show some balls! Don't be a fraidy-cat!"

Sandy: Ha ha ha, that shit ain't never gonna work!

Art: It only works on the really dumb ones.

Sandy: Dumb ones like me, you mean? Shit, I'm wearin' earplugs tonight! [laughs] Thank God yer my friend!

Calvin: You must have other friends. You aren't *that* difficult to get along with!

Cindy: Wait, I'm "difficult?"

Calvin: Not to me. I love having no fuckin' idea what'll happen next!

Cindy: I'll punch you in the face, that's what'll happen next! Now shut up and tell me who's the other guy up there? The white one.

Calvin: [laughter] The "white" one is my best friend Sandy.

Cindy: Is he dating anyone?

Calvin: Not right now. Girls get upset over his partying. Bit of a boozer. An alcoholic.

Cindy: But he's single. He's a cutie—don't you think?

Calvin: Um … Cindy, I'm not into butt-piracy.

Cindy: [long, loud laughter] Oh my God—"butt-piracy!" That is *sooo* funny!

Calvin: Belt up, or I'll knock you out.

Art: Remember Calvin bashed Gus's head into the Bronco?

Sandy: Kinda. Calvin says you guys faked his mind out about it. I was like, "Bullshit!"

Art: Nah, it's true. We planted a story in Gus's head that he ran into the truck cuz he was concentrating on his Snickers. When he woke up, *that's* what he thought happened!

Sandy: Pretty cool. Where'd ya come up with that?

Art: Some psychology journal in the library.

Sandy: So ya want me to plant an idea in Gus's head?

Art: That's it. Tell him, "don't be afraid of nothing." He'll wake up a changed man, totally fearless.

Sandy: That's dangerous shit, dude. Jesus Christ, girl! Listen to her laughing, all loud and shit. She could wake up the dead!

Art: Don't tell me—tell her!

"HEY CALVIN! TELL HER TO KEEP IT DOWN!" "WILL DO, SANDY!"

Cindy: [giggle] Yer a Squad Captain … on a ship of butt-pirates!

Calvin: Cindy, that's enough.

Cindy: You're a great speaker. I love listening to you … even when you sound gay.

Calvin: I'm not gay!

Cindy: I hope not, or I'd be wasting my time with you.

Calvin: [oblivious] You know what's a waste of time? Trying to hide your real name from me—Fern! That's it, isn't it? Ha! You couldn't hide it forever! Ha ha!

Art: Now *he's* laughin'. People back in New York City can hear us! We're spose'sta be hidden here, covert and quiet!

Sandy: Ain't no one here! We're in the woods! I'm gonna plant an idea in *your* head, that you gotta relax. Unwind your ass a bit.

Art: Unwind my ass? You homo, I'm gonna plant the idea in *your* head that you wanna hump Inky!

Sandy: I *did* win a bunch of condoms during poker. They'll come in handy.

Art: Jesus …

Cindy: ... Christ, who'd name their daughter "Fern?" Shut up!

Calvin: I need a hint. Animal, vegetable, or mineral?

Cindy: No way, too obvious! It's bad enough one of the letters in "Fern" is actually right.

Calvin: Something to do with leaves, but not really; obviously animal, vegetable, or mineral; and shares a letter with "fern." What th—I got it! *Walnut!*

Cindy: No, no, no, no!

Calvin: Yes! It falls off a tree, like a leaf! And it's a vegetable! And the N is—

Cindy: Walnuts are *nuts,* not vegetables!

Calvin: Thought I had it there.

Cindy: But now you have *two* letters right.

Calvin: Really? Can I ask a different question? Why am I kept in the dark, but dickheads like Mr. Whalers Cap and everyone else gets to know your real name?

Cindy: Maybe my real name's only good *for* dickheads like Mr. Whalers Cap. The one we use, Cindy, that's special. Special to us.

Calvin: Oh, we have something special now?

Cindy: Yes, Calvin, we do.

Sandy: "Do me!" That'd be Inky later, all "Do me, Sandy!"

Art: Goddamnit, Sandy!

Sandy: Speakin' of, think Calvin's gonna put a move on Cindy?

Art: I think he'll try something.

Sandy: What *I'm* thinking is, Truth or Dare might come up! I could dare them to—

Art: No, you'll ruin it for him.

Sandy: It'll be fun to torture the guy. He's been on a high horse lately. Needs to come back to Earth!

Art: [pause] After he said that shit yesterday about Jill ...

Sandy: Uh-oh. He told me ya might take the Cindy thing the wrong way.

Art: No, I'm not jealous. What I really am is concerned.

Sandy: About what?

Art: My future with chicks.

Sandy: Dude! Do *not* start that shit right before drinking! You'll end up bummed out!

Art: I can't compete with you two. I don't even know what I'm doing wrong. It's like I'm retarded.

Sandy: Okay, you ain't even listenin' to me.

Art: I think deep down, we all know it— I'm just a loser.

For a brief moment, their eyes met.

Calvin: This is our campsite. Let's have some fun.

Cindy: Yes, you promised me some fun.

Sandy: This is fun-time, dude. Bury that shit.

Art: Fine. I'll be all happy for fun-time.

Chapter 20
GETCHA COLD DRINKS HEE-YEH ...

THEY SAT IN an oval on the wooden deck, a fat citronella candle clouding the Hawk Squad tent with its sour yellow vapor. Cradling his deerskin water bag, Sandy measured out ginger brandy into four tin camping cups. Calvin poured the milk; Art stirred the concoctions with a pen.

"Gentlemen," Art said, "and lady, of course: cheers!" He clanged chalices with the others.

"Sláinte," Calvin said, sipping.

"Here's to us," Cindy said, gulping.

"I'll drink to that," Sandy said, guzzling.

Art squeezed his cheeks together. "Ugh! Milk, awesome—brandy, awesome—both, gross!" He set down his cup firmly.

"Actually," Cindy beamed, "this is good! Great recipe!"

Calvin indicated Sandy. "Thank him, not me."

Sandy bowed. "You're welcome. C'mon Art, drink up!"

"Yo, I don't like it!"

"Don't even, dude."

Art took the water bag and had a hit from it. "Happy?"

Sandy laughed. Art laughed. Calvin laughed. Cindy, feeling left out, chuckled. "So, you guys do this often?"

"Whenever we can," Art chirped.

"This is, what, our fifth go at this?" Calvin asked Sandy.

"*Errr,*" Sandy said, thinking hard. "No, sixth. Three times at Lewis & Clark, once at Lucid Pond, then Mad Dog in Canada."

Calvin noted Art's act; all their acts, to be honest. A chick was with them, so their laughter had gotten louder; their talk, fluffed up; they showed off. Sandy's curly black locks practically stood up.

Cindy was used to this act—better than the pure boasters, mind you, far from honest. "Ever been caught?" she asked.

"Nope," Sandy said. "I'll *drink* the evidence first!" He toked on his tin chalice once more. "Who needs a refill?"

The conversation died off. Awkward smiles on dim candlelit faces. "Truth or dare, Cindy?" Calvin suddenly said.

"Truth." Cindy leaned back onto a bunk and let herself go.

"What's **INKS**?" he asked.

"What's what?"

"**INKS**. On your shirt."

"This one's an **X**. It's IN'·ecks·ess."

"You're such a moron," Art snickered.

"You never heard o' INXS?" Sandy asked.

"Guess not," Calvin gave him. "So, it's a pop group. Good, are they?"

"Oh no," warned Cindy. "You know the rules: one question per turn. Now I get to go." She locked eyes with Calvin and licked the milk slowly from her lips.

Calvin pulled the brim down on the Whalers cap.

"That's like torture," Art muttered.

"Sandy," she said, "truth or dare."

"Dare," Sandy told her, as if there was no doubt which.

"I dare you to go ten minutes without another sip."

Sandy looked up from his chalice. "You serious?"

"Yep," Cindy said. "I hear you're, like, an alcoholic. So let's see you go ten minutes."

Sandy neatly set his chalice by the one from which Art had refused to drink. "Irish, time me."

Calvin glanced at his Swatch. "You got it."

"I'm no alky. And I'll prove it. So, truth or dare, Calvin."

Calvin caught sight of Art, wiggling one eyebrow. "Truth," was Calvin's rigid choice.

"What did you say to get Cindy to come here?" Sandy intoned, tilting his head at a spooky angle.

Calvin seethed into his tin chalice, the milk bubbling up and bouncing onto his nose. "Meaning what?" he said, wiping his face with the back of his hand.

Sandy shrugged. "Ya hadda say something."

Calvin gave Cindy a curved look. She returned it. "I told her she could prank Jon's stuff," Calvin admitted. "Do something to his sleeping bag."

Sandy looked at Cindy. "And that was what convinced ya?"

"Nooo!" Cindy laughed.

"That's a fucking awkward question," Calvin blurted.

"No, it's a perfectly good question," Sandy replied. "Your answer is what's awkward. Sounds like 'bollocks' to me!"

"Oh boy!" Cindy teased. "Are you boys gonna fight?"

Calvin gritted his teeth at Sandy for a second, then turned to Cindy. "Sandy here has broken a cardinal rule in our circle. In fact, this rule is the Pope: we don't undermine each other."

"Nice speech," Cindy said, with an annoyingly tight smile on her round face. "Now say it again, in English, please."

"Sandy's trying to embarrass him in front of a girl," Art put in. "That's called 'undermining.' Isn't it, Sandy?"

Sandy's response to Art's own breaking of the rule? A nonchalant shrug. "Better have them earplugs in when you hit the sack tonight, Art."

"Why? Gonna try my subliminal suggestion trick?"

"Maybe."

Art smirked. "It only works on *dumb* people, Sandy."

Calvin, remembering when he and Art had used this trick successfully on Gus, gave a loud laugh. Cindy made dismissive *Stupid boys!* noises.

Sandy shrugged again and made for his chalice, intending to drink his irritation away, but caught himself. "Goddamnit!"

"Eight minutes," Calvin noted.

"And counting, dude. It's your turn again."

"So it is." Calvin looked them over. "Cindy, truth or dare."

"Dare."

"I dare you … " He was counting on a truth. "I dare you to tell us your real name."

Cindy needed a drink of the brew first. "I can't do that," she reported at last.

Calvin pushed his face closer to hers. "You can't *not* do it."

"I'll tell you my name," Cindy said, pushing closer to him, "if you tell them what you *really* promised me to get me here."

He pushed even closer. "I told them already."

She pushed even closer. "No you didn't."

They were only inches apart. They could smell each other's milky, flammable breath. It was Calvin's turn to talk, but he simply stewed. This was most unlike Cindy, manufacturing something to hold against him—or, maybe he'd made a promise amongst the billions of words he used to convince her to come and had since forgotten it. "Someday, I'll tell them," he said lamely. "But not now. I'm supposed to be having fun."

Cindy leaned back, acting ever so smug. "Fair's fair: you tell them the truth, I tell you my name."

"Blackmail. Speaking of—six minutes."

"Shit, dude! This is takin' forever!"

"You'll live," Cindy said, taking a stage-gulp.

Sandy muttered, "Yeah, fuck you."

The girl drew back in horror. "Oh my! That's not funny ... not even funny if yer bein' sarcastic!"

"It's yer own fault, girl. If you didn't dare me to stop, I wouldn't be sayin' 'Fuck you' to ya."

Cindy socked Sandy on the shoulder, and not playfully. Sandy reflexively brought up a retaliating fist, holding it at head height. "Good thing for you I got a rule about hittin' girls."

"Useful information to know!" she said, hitting him again with her small yet pointy fist.

Sandy fired a glare at Calvin. "I suddenly don't give a shit what ya promised her. Send this bitch back to the dishroom!"

"Bitch!" she whooped. "I haven't *begun* to be a bitch yet!"

"Trust her on that one," Calvin added, rather evenly he thought, but she socked him one too. "What? I'm just saying when you fly off the handle, you're like the Concord!"

She hit him again.

Art took a pull from the water bag and proudly told everyone present that he was the only one not to be hit by Cindy—and Art did it without saying a word, making a face, or using a gesture. Cindy flung a fist at him to punish his pride but it accidentally connected with the water bag, popping it into the air. Art juggled it, splashing a jigger's worth of brandy on Sandy's collar. "Ain't even allowed to lick it off," Sandy whined.

"That's it." Calvin guzzled his drink and stood. "She's drunk. Got to toss her in the reservoir now. Sober her up."

"Bullshit!" Cindy yipped, getting to her feet and placing her fists between her and Calvin. "I had *one* drink. You ain't throwing me anywhere!"

"Oh aren't I now." Calvin moved right in on her, grabbing both her fists. He used her knotted hands to twirl her around, allowing him to wrap an arm around her stomach. He could feel the bottom of her bra on his forearms.

"No!" she shrilled. "Let me go!"

"Back in a flash, lads." Calvin heaved the pair of them through the tent's front flaps. Art and Sandy listened to her "No!"s, the sounds of bodily movement and shuffling feet ... and the silence afterward.

"Fun girl," commented Art.

"Bitch," Sandy spat. He roofed his chalice; then, for an encore, roofed Art's.

"I think he's telling the truth, y'know," Art said. "He promised her she could trash Jon's shit. That's all."

Sandy thought it over. "Maybe there's more. She must be tryin' to get him to open up in front of us or something. Then she was flirtin' with me, right in front of him ... typical girl."

Art's long gangly face suddenly opened wide with laughter. "You call that flirting, Sandy?"

"Yeah."

"What would it be like if she was actually pissed at ya?!"

"You don't know shit about chicks, Art. If they get grumpy at you and leave, they're grumpy for real. If they do it and stick around, and want you to do it back, then it's flirting."

Art blinked. "Maybe she wants to boff ya both!"

Sandy made another drink. "Calvin wasn't too happy when they was arguin' just now," he said to himself. Then, without another word, he stood and went through the flaps, knowing Art would automatically follow and bring the booze.

Calvin flung Cindy as far down the goat-path as he could. She stumbled about six steps but did not fall. Her pink Chucks dug into the packed dirt, allowing her to heave to. Spinning to face him, she brought up her fists … but her face wore the remnants of a wide smile, as though she couldn't shed it once it'd been unleashed.

"I dare you to try," Calvin breathed.

"I'm not going to," Cindy replied, almost instantly.

"You can't *not* do a dare. It's in the rules!"

"What's the rule when people *lie* when they're supposed to tell the truth? You promised me more than revenge on Jon's stuff. You distinctly said, 'you'll have a good time.'"

Calvin held open his mouth.

She laughed at him.

"Jaysus," he said, "I did. I said that."

"Yup. You never once told them that—and that bothered the shit outta me. What *did* you tell them? Why *did* you bring me along?" Cindy lowered the fists; the smile had been replaced by an irritated frown. "I like your honesty, which is why I came. Now I'm not sure it was the right move. You brought me to show me off."

Calvin smiled at her. "Not really. They clearly don't like that I brought you now. And to set the record straight, I invited you so I could be with you. Because *we* have fun."

She pushed closer. "I am *not* having fun," she said, mock-serious.

He pushed closer. "You're feeling what I'm feeling."

She pushed even closer. "Just what am I feeling?"

He bridged the last gap and gave his shite-eating grin. "I'll show you." He put his hands up to hold her, moved his face in to kiss her—

"What about Jenny?" she suddenly asked.

"What about her?" he returned, not halting his movements even a little bit. He wound his arm around her, tilted his head down, arced her back, and kissed her. She let him twist her into this position and, after a few seconds, kissed him back.

It lasted a bit longer than your garden variety first kiss.

When it ended, Calvin slid his hands from her shoulder blades to her sides.

She licked her lips again. Her brown eyes locked with his gray. "Yummy," she said quietly. "Milk and brandy."

"A little sugar coating helps," he said, matching her volume. "That was awesome. The whole thing. You're the—"

A burst of noise behind them shattered their lovey-dovey bubble: Sandy stumbled out of the tent, followed quickly by Art. The two kissers separated shyly, as if nothing happened. Sandy came right up to them, gave his drink to Calvin, and started talking.

Chapter 21
SERIOUS SHIT.
TUESDAY, JULY 28, 1987.

MORNING REPORTED FOR duty. On time. Bright and clear.

His mouth was dry; his lips, cracked. The chilled sleeping bag felt funny to his dead fingertips. Eventually he found the zipper; more eventually he got it to work. He could make out peach-ish molding around a white blob, and he took this to be his legs and arms poking out a T-shirt and Y-fronts. He tried to speak, but the noise was less like a word and more like he'd gargled a shot of hydrochloric acid and a tuning fork. He silently scolded himself for not wearing sweats in the night chill.

His head slid off his pillow and he found himself staring at a dim, very close view of his bunk mattress. With every breath he could smell something clinical, like a medicine chest. His scalp sizzled. Silence, loud silence, played bongos on his eardrums. He hocked up what mucus he could and washed it around. His mouth went from feeling dusty to sort of shrink-wrapped. No matter how hard he sucked back on the mucus, it refused to catch on a small patch of sandpaper-ish throat in the back. His left arm panged with pain. Had someone punched him there very hard last night?

Immediately he stamped that thought to death. Whatever happened last night, and he had a large bowl of confetti on the matter to piece together, would wait. He needed to take a piss, and then release the violently stirring creature holed up in his stomach. He threw his whole right arm over his body; when his right hand gained purchase on the side of the bunk, he yanked. He plummeted to the deck, landing pretty hard.

Sheep.

The word hopped on a pogo stick and galloped through his mind.

His vision went all white on him. Long, thin, vertical shards of the out-side world (presently, the wooden deck beneath him) filtered through, but otherwise, white. "Jaysus," he said. His Adam's apple stung— somehow, *it* had hit the deck first. A cool breeze swept through the crack between the tent's two front flaps and grabbed the hair on his legs.

He'd heard the expression "feeling the rotation of the Earth," but had always doubted it as an actual feat. He doubted no more as he got to a standing position and watched the tent move eastward around him at a rate close to nine hundred fifty miles per hour. Did the Earth create sonic booms in space? He would need to check that in his massive astronomy tome back in his room in Axsubeen, PA. Said tome, though perhaps useful just now as a counterweight for his swaying, would not solve his aching bladder, sore nuts, or leaky dick.

The plan: mad dash for the first bush willing to accept a gallon's worth of urine. He took a baby step, wobbled, took a giant Nazi soldier step, reached the front flaps, and parted them clumsily. He celebrated the bright forest view by stepping rather idiotically out of the tent without compensating for the twelve inches of ground-level difference.

Thud went his body, as it impacted on the goat-path's packed dirt … or so it would have, had not a pair of pink meaty hands caught him. The hands, which resembled Panzers in their size and forceful movements, tossed him on a ninety-degree yaw. He landed softly on his bare feet and stumbled back into the tent's front support pole.

A bloody collage of red eyes, red hair, a black T-shirt, and black denim shorts blocked the sunny morning view. This new hideous image seemed quite interested in what the hungover lad's head might taste like. Calvin expected the image to clear up, like in the movies, when the focus puller did his job.

The focus puller was not there.

Calvin assumed, by the sight of black denim shorts, that he faced his Junior Troopmaster. "Inky," he said.

"Calvin!" Inky shouted back through an orifice half a foot above Calvin's eye-line. Definitely slavering teeth in there.

"Don't shout! I'm right here!"

"Douchebag," Inky said; the dancing teeth in the orifice said a different word altogether. "You're missing breakfast. Fat-asses like yourself shouldn't miss a meal. Food's your only real friend."

"Other than you," quipped Calvin.

"Some Captain you are. Right now the Hawk Squad's being led by *Gus*, for Christ's sake! It'll be a miracle if they don't all end up dead!"

Calvin wheezed, *"I* didn't vote for him. Not on purpose."

"Listen," Inky growled, producing the pink Panzers again and using Calvin's collar to shake him. "You got five seconds to explain that—" (he indicated with his head something to his right) "—or you get dunked in the latrine cesspit!"

"I'm—you're—what?" It made no sense. None. And he might even be killed based on how this conversation went. *Why fear it?* he thought. *Face death like a man! Death cures hangovers, right?*

"What are you talking about?!" Calvin shouted back. "Inky, you're babbling like a mad monkey!"

"I'm talkin' about that, goddamnit!" Inky said, motioning with his head again. "That bloody rag there! This campsite should sparkle, and you're leaving your used tampons out in the wild for the Camp Director to find!"

Shrieking because of the clenched fist on his throat: "Used tampons?! What the hell is this all about?"

Inky's eyes grew large. Calvin curled up, bracing for the green planet-killing laser to burst forth and destroy him. But no laser came. The Junior Troopmaster merely wiped his brow with a Panzer before dropping Calvin to the ground.

"That bet we made?" Inky said darkly. "Shit, that dollar is all mine." With a rueful huff, he departed.

Calvin decided lying on the packed dirt was a welcome change from all the hullabaloo and choking. The dirt was comfortable. It was warmer than the tent deck. Slightly softer. It was, near his stomach and groin, pleasingly damp.

So Calvin lay there a while.

A long while.

A long, long while.

A black leather boot stepped on the ground Calvin had been scrutinizing at precisely the moment when the lad realized the "pleasingly damp" feeling near his stomach and groin was, verily, the result of a boiled-over bladder. The same sweaty Panzers lifted Calvin up, and the same loud voice shouted: "Calvin, what the fuck did you do to your hair?"

"What!"

"Your hair! It was stupid before, but now ... *holy shit!* You are a piece of work, ya mick!"

"And you're a piece of shite, ya kraut!"

"Oh forget it." Inky disgustedly shook his head. "You know, it actually fits a cowardly asshole like you." He dropped the perplexed Calvin again and trampled out of view.

The ten minutes did not go quietly. This was the time requirement Calvin had needed to stand; enter the tent; tuck his wet clothes under his bunk; change into his Reeboks, clean tighty-whities and sweats, and a goofy sky blue T-shirt depicting Oscar Wilde guzzling an XX bottle; and slog to the latrine. The ten minutes kicked and screamed the whole way. They held their breath, and, when Calvin wasn't looking, doubled their usual length.

Once at the latrine, Calvin produced and deposited several mouthfuls of sizzlingly hot, painfully acidic, and wildly colored stew; and when he was finished, he did it again. He crashed on his arse, which registered cold from the latrine's concrete floor. Puke congealed on his chin. Later this morning, he'd have to clean this very latrine over which he'd just sprayed barf! Calvin let out several dry retches at the irony.

The violently kicking creature in his stomach was gone, probably enjoying its new home underground. His head, however, did not appreciate all the stretching and twisting it had had to do. He needed aspirins, and he needed them last week. He stroked the bandages on his forehead sutures; they made crunchy noises. Was it safe to get the wound wet yet? He decided to find out. He slipped out, worked the pump six times, then shot over to the latrine's wash basin to let four seconds of cold spring water cascade over his head. The wound tingled slightly but otherwise seemed fine with a bath. The water also curbed that odd sizzling sensation in his scalp.

The rookie Crowe materialized out of thin air on the other side of the basin. "That's neat," said the scrawny kid.

Chagrined that so many pumps had produced so little water once he'd managed to get to it (modern plumbing is a fucking Godsend, isn't it?), Calvin sighed and whipped his head back. Cold water streamed in a flashy mohawk-shaped arc, hosing Crowe, the tiny roof over the pump and basin, and several bushes behind him. "What's neat?" asked Calvin, pressing his mane back.

"The hair. Neat-o." With that, Crowe slogged off.

Calvin lowered a brow. He'd met two people this morn. One mentioned a bloody tampon. Both mentioned his hair.

And the penny dropped.

Rowdy conversation and trampling feet: Troop 666 returning from breakfast. He spent a second panicking, another second going over options, and a third crashing back through the door. The latrine reflected his sewage-like language.

Years of pulling on his hair had taught those parts he hadn't had shorn close to his skull to flow back naturally from his face and scalp, cascading along to fall on the back of his collar; with Aqua Net, he could make the bits above his forehead defy gravity. This style *was* something close to all the rage amongst white youth in 1987. Calvin sat between the holes in the latrine bench and shook his head as roughly as his bandage and headache would allow. Time to get to the bottom of this.

Unfortunately the thin white veil was his only view. Again.

The door opened and someone stepped up to one of the holes, nonchalantly taking out his pecker. Calvin failed to do anything as the person urinated loudly one foot to his right.

"Well well," the person mused—it was Sandy. "Ya musta had one hell of a hangover to miss breakfast, dude. You okay?"

"I was," Calvin squeaked. His voice was on holiday.

"I see ya ralphed it out. Best thing to do." Sandy shook, then zipped up. Calvin heard him snort. "I wasn't gonna say nothin', but now I gotta."

"What?"

"The mop on your head. I know yer dedicated to cleaning up the shit-stall and all, but—"

"It's not a mop."

"... yer right. Jesus Christ! What *is* that?"

Calvin crossed himself when Sandy mentioned Jesus, then used his right hand to part the white veil. "I think it's my hair." He saw utter shock on Sandy's squat face. "My hair's white!"

"I can see that, dude. It's white as a goddamn sheet!"

Calvin scrubbed his knuckles through it—the motion brought back that odd sizzling feeling in his scalp, but only where he'd rubbed. He brought his hands down to his lap and stared at them: no white powder or residue. Curtains of white hair framed his view. He started sobbing. "What the fuck happened last night, Sandy?"

The door opened and Mr. Maguire stepped in. "Having a party, boys?" he joked—then froze. The man stepped up and grabbed a hunk of the white hair in his dark hand. "What happened to your hair, Calvin?"

"You tell me, Mr. Maguire," Calvin said, casting pleading gray eyes upward. "You tell me."

"You mean ... *you don't know?!*"

"I don't!"

The man turned and left the shitter post haste. "What the fuck?" Calvin bucked.

"Fuck him," Sandy said. "Who did it? Who did this to you?"

Calvin got flustered. "I don't know!"

"This is serious shit. Looks permanent, too."

Fluster became anger: "I'll find out." Determinedly, Calvin steeled his face: "Then I'll kill him."

"You and me both, dude."

"Sandy, I mean it—death."

"Whoa," Sandy heaved. "Killing him won't cure your hair."

"Easy for you to say! No one's fucked with *your* hair!"

The door blew open. "Now what?!" Oldroyd roared, his cowboy hat looking very disgruntled. The man fixed a stare towards Calvin's head. "What in the Sam Fucking Hill happened to your hair, Connor?!"

"I don't know! But I know what'll happen to the pusillanimous retard who did it—I'll kill them!"

Oldroyd frowned. "Calvin, killing someone won't—"

"All of you are a bunch of broken records!" Calvin stood, shoved Oldroyd and Sandy aside, and crashed through the latrine door, not heeding their calls of "Stop!"

Calvin marched down to the fire circle, where, to either side of the cold plateau of ashes that had once been a Fire of Inky, stood Troop 666, in ranks and at attention, with Gus Jacoby before the Hawk Squad and Art Maguire before the Beaver Squad. The two older kids in the leadership corps—Father, looking worried, and Inky, arms folded—faced them. Mr. Maguire, who had fetched Oldroyd and ordered "Ten-hut!" to the others, wandered towards the goat-path, literally turning his back on it all. There was no sign of young Jon Oldroyd.

Calvin planted himself between Inky and Father, grabbed his hair with both hands, and held it up. "Who did this to me?!"

Stares of utter shock from Gus on down to Art—except in Spazz's case. "Calvin the friendly ghost!" he hooted, doubling up. An outstretched finger aimed at Calvin's white mane.

Moving forward, Calvin faced off with Spazz. Words came through grinding teeth: "Who did this?!"

Spazz tucked the happy face away, in favor of a very solemn face. "Don't know," the kid muttered out of thin lips.

Calvin looked Spazz up and down. *"Six* words! *Sixty* push-ups! *RIGHT NOW!"*

Obsequiously, Spazz dropped to the ground and silently counted off push-ups.

A cricket broke the thick silence by uttering *cheep!*

Oldroyd stood near the by-way, a comfortably safe distance away. "Do something!" Calvin urged.

"I WANT SOME ANSWERS, DAMNIT!" said Oldroyd.

No one said a word.

The Troopmaster shouted on with a typical selfish bent: "You guys're enough to make me quit this job! *Every single night* there's somethin'! Shootin' guns at each other, tearin' the place apart, that stupid Camp Director lockin' my boy up, midnight skinny-dippin', and now this! If ya know who did it, you'd better speak up! I want an explanation—now!"

"I can explain it," Inky growled, unlidding his Death Star eyes and panning them across the Troop. "More bullshit from idle boys, who don't get enough guidance from their 'leader.'" Inky's eyes locked on Oldroyd's mustachioed mug. "Kind of a pattern here, wouldn't ya say?"

Oldroyd flung his arms to the sky. "Shut the fuck up, Inky."

"Nice talk from the Troopmaster," Inky replied. "If the man with that job had the last name 'Schultz,' none of this—"

"SOMEONE TALK," Oldroyd roared, cutting Inky off. "OR WE'LL STAND HERE ALL DAMN DAY!"

Calvin waited for someone, anyone, to crack. Or at least claim they didn't do it. But nothing. Not a bloody peep. He took a breath and marched to the by-way for the Green Trail.

"Where are you goin'?!" Inky hollered.

"I'm taking a shower," Calvin's voice echoed through the forest, "then maybe I'll go hang myself."

Chapter 22
La Maison de Douche.

ONE OF THEM did it. Spazz did not.

The guy's reaction had been so natural … genuine shock for the briefest of instants; then, once his mind had gotten its breath back, laughter and finger-pointing. If Spazz was predictable in any sense, he took credit for his shenanigans: beaming smiles, deliberate sniggers, or plain boasting.

But if not Spazz, then who? When? How? Why?! Calvin finally tried to recollect what had taken place twelve hours ago. He found a large gap in his memory, from about 8:30 last night 'til twenty minutes ago. Ordinarily Calvin's memory was digital: infinitely capacious and flawlessly testimonial, the sort of thing Microsoft programs need in obscene abundance to function properly. So why the sudden terminal error?

Had he drunk *that* much?

A gaggle of boys swaggered down the Green Trail towards him. Their faces screwed up at Calvin's visage. When they were twenty paces past him, they made comments.

Calvin grumbled, "Go and shite."

He probably looked like a sheep. He certainly felt like one.

At the mouth of the Green Trail, Calvin beheld the Centre des Trois cafeteria. Dozens of teenage boys milled about. He broke into a mad run, sprinting past the caf for the Yellow Trail and la Maison de Douche beyond, not caring that he'd attract more attention this way. He took out a small red-haired kid standing stupidly in the way; he didn't even apologize over his shoulder.

Calvin crashed into the small, squat Maison to find more kids. Two near the urinals. One grunting in a toilet stall. One just exiting the shower room. Calvin raced to the bank of sinks and looked at himself in the nearest mirror.

They hadn't exaggerated—a good deal of Calvin's hair shone a sickly pale white. A very contemptuous streak an inch wide, starting at the top of his skull and going down past his right ear, was still sandy brown. Most of the back—what he could see—was also still brown. The rest was an awful shade of white, lifeless and wan, like the hair on a cadaver at a haunted house.

Calvin loosed a hideous scream. One of the teenagers at the urinals, who was zipping up, caught himself and loosed a scream of his own. Calvin tore a hair out of his skull and scrutinized it: white all the way to the fucking root. He parted his hair at every conceivable angle and spazzed at the damage. It was a haphazard job: around his ears, the buzzed-close bits were still brown. His limited sideburns too. Small consolation.

"Fuck!" The word created a petrified silence in la Maison de Douche, adding to the torture of the moment.

He'd have to hide under the Whalers cap from this point forward. At least until he could get home and dye his hair (or, God forbid, cut it off). Here, at Souviens, he was totally screwed. Imagine the gawks! Imagine—

—Art.

Calvin could still see Art's shocked face at the fire circle just now, so amazed, so stretched out with stupefaction. Art *certainly* had the means to do this, since he brought a little bag of tricks called the "portable lab" on every camping trip, and the portable lab was full of the sort of liquids and devices which, when put to work, could do crap like turn hair white. But Art was a friend; more than that, a worshipper. Art loved being Calvin's friend. His behavior could be downright unctuous; even when a line got crossed (like the little brawl on the Red Trail over Jill Pedersen), Art always made sure the friendship hadn't gotten fucked-up. He was above suspicion.

But someone else could've found his portable lab. Who? And why?! Calvin shook his head to clear it. Laying blame had to wait. Dealing with a white mane was the priority here.

He rocketed into the empty shower room and peeled off his

clothes. The showerheads lined the near wall and he violently cranked the knobs on the closest set, bleating "Come on!" when the HOT knob stuck. He dove under the water and let himself get wet. A choir of cells busily repairing his forehead wound sang in disapproval, since they'd gotten wet twice this morning, once over the collectively bargained limit.

He scrambled to the bench along the far wall, where complimentary hotel-sized soaps and shampoos sat in plastic baskets. Calvin grabbed one of each and danced back, much to the shock of a boy passing by the shower room entrance. According to the boy's long face, it wasn't every day he saw a chunky buck-naked teenager with sickly white hair dancing about, juggling toiletry implements.

Calvin tore at the wrapping on the Ivory soap so roughly that he broke the little bar in half. He emptied the bottle of Prell over his skull and scrubbed. The remnants of sizzling on his scalp died a quiet death, strangled by over-the-counter detergents. The gauze headwrap got in the way, so he tore it off.

He rinsed. The wet hair falling over his eyes was, stubbornly, still white.

With a savage chop, Calvin shut off the shower and fell to the floor, warm and wet tiles snuggling his butt-cheeks. He found a leftover lost-and-found towel by the clothes cubbies and groaned to note that it was damp from recent use.

He swathed the towel across his body and slogged out to the sinks. Punching the fat silver button on the hand dryer, he let scalding hot air erupt over his dome. It took several punches to dry all his long locks. He went back to the mirror. His hair was now sickeningly clean, an annoying contrast from when it was covered with caked blood and sticky soda shite. But it was still white. He sighed in brutal finality.

The exposed cut on his forehead shone purple and red, crunched together with black threads. After probing it a bit, and wondering how awful the scar would be, he stomped to the shower room to pull on his clothes.

He heard la Maison de Douche's door slap open and several pairs of feet. Huffs of irritation. "We gotta talk. It'll be safe in here," came a voice. Calvin thought it sounded like Art's.

"I ain't gettin' in no stall with *you,* dude!" That was definitely Sandy.

Calvin silently yanked on his Reeboks and sidled up to the archway. Peering into la Maison's main room, he saw Father, Art, and Sandy slouching by the sinks. They hadn't seen him, so he ducked back out of sight.

"Oldroyd's gonna search the campsite," Sandy said. "Hope none of you brought porno mags. But whoever hosed Calvin ain't stupid enough to leave evidence. I'da chucked whatever it was in the lake, dude."

"Well, what could do that to your hair?" asked Father.

Next to Calvin, a bead of water from the showerhead dripped to the tiled floor.

"Peroxide," Art offered. "It's in every first aid kit."

"Those tiny bottles?" Sandy said. "Would that be enough?"

"God knows," Art said. "My mom don't bleach her hair!"

"*God* knows, yes," sighed Father, "but we *all* know now. I feel sorry for Calvin. That's a dirty trick to do to anyone."

"Let's think about this," Sandy said firmly. "It hadda be done this morning, dude. Last night, when you caught him skinny dipping—he had brown hair. I went to his tent this mornin' at first light to check on him—brown hair. We came back from breakfast—white hair."

Calvin checked his gasp. He'd gotten caught skinny dipping last night! By Father, of all people! Wasn't there something in 1 Corinthians about skinny dipping being a sin? Had Cindy skinny dipped? He hoped so—for his own heterosexuality's sake. If he'd skinny dipped and been caught, why hadn't he been chastised for it? Or had he been and he forgot!

He felt dizzy at the un-knowledge abounding.

"So if Calvin was fine right before we went to breakfast," Art said, "it happened in the next half hour. But we were all at the caf, except Calvin."

"Not true," Father pointed out.

"Yeah!" Sandy agreed. "I kept an eye out for Calvin—I figured he'd show, so he could wash dishes with Cindy—so I noticed it when Inky, Gus, and Crowe came in late!"

"Remember when we called roll?" Father added. "Gus was really giving Crowe the business about something. I think Inky kept them behind to set 'em straight."

"So when did they show at the caf?" Art asked.

"I dunno, like five minutes after us," Sandy said.

"It's more than that," Father noted. "I sit at the Hawk table, and Ryan was the only guy there for all of breakfast. He and I had a little 'discussion' yesterday, maybe you heard about it, and now he's being awkward and quiet around me. So that's why I know he was the only one there the whole time. Gus and Crowe were late; Oldroyd came and went, looking for the Camp Director; and Calvin didn't come at all. Jon wasn't there either, of course, but that's another story."

"Was Inky with Crowe and Gus that whole time?" Sandy proposed. "He ain't exactly Calvin's number one fan!"

"I don't buy for a minute that Inky did it," Father said.

"He had the time, coulda been alone, he's smart. And like I just said, he totally had the motive, dude."

"It's too dirty," Father said. "Inky will just confront you directly. He'd never do something sneaky like that."

"So who did?" Art flapped. "Crowe? Gus?"

"Gus?!" Sandy laughed. "Yeah, right!"

"Gus was real fired up this morning," Art noted. "Maybe working through his nerves? Cuz of a guilty conscience?"

Calvin lowered his eyebrows.

"Were Gus and Crowe with Inky the whole time?" Sandy asked again.

"Even if they were," Art proposed, "it'd only take ten seconds to dump a bottle of H_2O_2 on Calvin's head."

"*Another* Kangaroo Court," pissed Sandy. "Holy shit."

"Sandy," Father droned, "feces is rarely holy."

A moment passed in silence.

"Hey Father," Art said, "did Oldroyd say anything about Jon at breakfast?"

"Did he ever. The story is, a girl complained that Jon touched her at the dance. The Camp Director and the Deputy Director both witnessed it. When Mr. Murphy tried to take Jon away, he took a swing at him. So now he has to spend the rest of camp in the Chamberlin building in some small room."

"So we'll never see Jon again the whole week?"

"He can have visitors. We gotta bring him meals on trays. But no time outside."

"That's so stupid!" Sandy spat. "This is summer camp, not Alcatraz! We shoulda gone to Lucid Pond, dude!"

There was panic movement. "Is that the time?! I gotta bolt!" Art yelled. "Lifeguard started five minutes ago, and I can't be missin' my only merit badge!"

Father: "I'm supposed to be at Insects. We'll talk later."

Paddling of shoes and then silence. Calvin's back ached from leaning on the tiled wall. He trudged to the vacant main room and stared in one of the mirrors at the sheep resting on his head.

Chapter 23

REVELATION.

FOR THE FIRST time, Calvin entered the dishroom and the boom box said something worth paying attention to:

"—severe storm warning for coastal Rhode Island and Connecticut, and Block Island Sound. Thunderstorms and gale-force winds expected. The system should reach Q105's broadcast area late this afternoon. Batten down your hatches!"

Cindy leaned on the yellow fridge, close to the greasy gray boom box. On seeing Calvin, she bleated, "What the hell!" The girl wore a face of complete bewilderment.

"Big storm coming?" Calvin wheezed. *"Greaaaat."*

"Calvin, what happened to—"

"Sorry I missed the washing up. I don't think I've washed a single dish yet!"

Cindy came over and simply gawked up at him. She was considerably shorter. He lolled his head down to her. "Eagle. Has the E of *fern* and the A of *walnut*. It's an animal. They make nests up on cliffs, so it's got nothing to do with leaves."

"Close, in a way—but nope. God, Calvin." She reached up and stroked his sickly white hair. Her touch summoned goosebumps all over Calvin's body. "You didn't do this on purpose," she whispered.

"Sure I did," he said, a ghost of a smile playing over his mug. "Now you and I can shave our heads bald, and make a giant Red Cross flag from our hair."

She laughed, mostly shock from the unexpected humor. "Where's the Whalers hat? And you lost the bandage. Holy shit, that cut is bad!"

He said nothing for a spell. Then: "What a mess."

"What a mess. See what getting drunk does to you?"

"This didn't happen cuz I was drunk," he said with sass.

"Are you sure? Do you even *remember* last night?"

"Do I remember it now?" he repeated, lamely. He debated lying, then went with the truth: "I don't remember anything. You started punching Sandy and Art, and I grabbed you and took you outside, and I think we had a snog ... and after that it's a blank. I don't remember skinny dipping, or getting caught, but rumor has it I did both. Like I said—what a mess."

"Oh," she said. She opened her mouth to speak. A second later, words finally came: "I don't remember anything either."

His jaw dropped. "What?"

"Heh!" she said, a single, loud, embarrassed laugh. "Does *snog* mean *make out?*"

"It does."

"Okay—*that* happened. Then Sandy and Art came out and we had a big drink together, and another, and then ... I can't remember. We went skinny dipping? Really?!"

They giggled. Then pointed fingers, covered mouths, and stifled belly-laughs. Cindy said, "So we were both naked in the water, and neither one of us remembers what the other one looks like? How fucked-up is that?"

Calvin wiped a tear from his eye. "We were probably playing Marco Polo!"

They chuckled softly, exhuming the last laughter the situation could bestow. They rubbed their aching cheeks and shook their heads disdainfully at each other.

Then, looked at each other very feverishly.

"'Bollocks,' you're going to 'snog' me again," she grinned.

"Oh am I now."

"Yes."

"Your fate is sealed, then." He pushed closer to her—

Fine time for Kermit to come marching through the door to the kitchen. "So the portly mick peckerhead from the Devil's Troop didn't show today," he smiled, casually, to what he thought would be an audience of just Cindy.

He caught sight of Calvin and was all business. "Just the young man I want to see. Mr. Izerman informs me you were a no-show." The man made his lips flat. "You'd convinced me you were smarter than that. Got an explanation?"

"As a matter of fact, I do." Calvin shuffled hands through his hair. Long sickly white strands dripped down his face.

Although he couldn't have possibly missed it, Kermit reacted as though he'd just now seen it. "Jesus," he purred with genuine concern. "How did *that* happen?"

"Malfeasance. But I got no clue who the perpetrator was."

Kermit's left eyebrow yawed at Calvin's vocabulary. "Someone in your Troop, no doubt."

"Why would anyone from *another* Troop do it?"

"Good point. I'm sure your Troopmaster is grilling suspects as we speak."

"Oh, then I'm in good hands, aren't I now?"

"You don't trust Mr. Oldroyd's ability to settle the matter?" Kermit said with a wry grin.

"We *are* talking about the same person, right?" Calvin cracked. "The Cowboy King Dumb-Ass of all Dumb-Asses?"

Kermit refused to laugh at that. "You should have the Camp Doctor take a look at your hair. He'll want to follow up on your forehead sutures, too."

The lad nodded. "I'll go see him. Thank you, Mr. Murphy."

"Not at all." Kermit turned, and with perhaps a half of a half of a half of a half of a nod, made for the kitchen door.

"Heard about Jon," Calvin called out.

Kermit stopped, revolving his chin-strap beard around to his shoulder, in order to cast Calvin one thin slit (#287, "I don't mourn those deserving of death."). "Yes, shame about him, cut off from the law-abiding world for the rest of the week."

Sarcastically: "I'm crying, sir."

Muttering: "As am I." Kermit promptly left. A moment later, Calvin swore he heard the man laugh.

Cindy bore a wild face. "Jon's in Chamberlin?"

"He got the Cell," Calvin confirmed.

"Oh, yes!" Cindy jumped like an excited kindergartener. "Yes yes

yes! I love it!"

He waited for her excitement to drain with a crooked grin. It did, eventually. She looked at him, looked around the room, then asked, "Why're you looking at me like that?"

"So," he grinned, "I'm about to snog you again, am I?"

She smiled shyly. "Are you?"

Calvin pushed closer to her—

Kermit stormed back into the dishroom. "Don't you have *merit badges* to go to, Mr. Connor?"

Knowing Kermit could check his merit badge schedule (and, more importantly, Kermit seemed the *type* to check), Calvin played a discretion card over a valor card. "I do, actually. Thank you again, sir." With a wink at Cindy, he ducked out the back door.

Fully seething in his reborn dark mood, Murphy aimed his slits at Cindy. He studied her red tresses and sporadic acne. "I told Lyons to leave you in Norwich," was his salvo, and having fired it, he stormed out.

Cindy popped him the finger, but only after he'd gone.

The kindly old Camp Doctor, George, declared Calvin's hair permanently white and almost certainly stripped of its color via a chemical agent. Doc George cleaned the forehead sutures and applied new gauze dressing, eschewing the headwrap; he thoughtfully dispensed a few aspirin for the pain.

Standing outside the First Aid Shack, Calvin eyed the sliver of sky between the tall trees bordering the Yellow Trail. It was a sun-shiny day; was there really a major storm coming?

Calvin decided he'd skip his merit badge after all. It'd been one hell of a morning, and promised to be an even worse day.

He slogged to Campsite Quatre to find everyone gone. He went to his tent and traded his sweats for cut-off jeans. His rucksack had been searched.

Pulling on his Swatch, he caught sight of the kelly green Whalers cap under his bunk. He got to his knees, groped—

—recoiled in shock!
He got flat on his stomach to have a look: also lying under the bunk were his urine-logged shirt and Y-fronts from this morning, and his towel and class A uniform, thrown there two nights ago after getting soaked through with his blood.

Had Oldroyd *really* searched the campsite? How could such odious items, in such an obvious hiding place, escape detection? That lazy bastard: all he did was search the unguarded backpacks! Ol' General Schultz would've strip-searched *the entire camp*. If such an episode occurred in a movie, no one would believe it. When looking for criminal evidence, you always search under the beds! At least glance there!

Disgustedly, Calvin plopped the cap over his mane. He snagged the hidden clothes—the bloodied ones were rather brown and crusty at this late hour—and made for his rucksack again to fetch a Hefty trash bag. This was not an officially required Trooping International Tribunal camping item, but one no Trooper would dare forget. A Hefty trash bag could see service as an impromptu water collector, a poncho, a rope, an emergency flag, a pillow, a booby trap, a close-quarters weapon, a laundry basket, a tourniquet … a million possible uses. Calvin flapped open the bag and used it for its designed purpose. He ambled out the tent, wondering where to throw out the bag.

He suddenly remembered the *other* bloodied towel: Jon's, which Art had used during the desperate first aid moment, and which Calvin had tossed out the tent in a fury. A quick search through the thorny brush landed the encrusted rag. Oh—*this* was the "used tampon" Inky referred to this morning!

Calvin averted his eyes when grabbing this second towel—he wasn't squeamish, but there was only so much congealed Calvin-juice the lad could stand to see!

Then he recoiled *again*. In averting his eyes, his view included the Hawk Squad's tent … and its wooden deck … and the low space under the deck. *Something was hidden there.*

Dropping the now full Hefty bag, he slinked on all fours 'round to the tent's side for a better look. And there, under the deck, was a camouflage satchel—Art Maguire's portable lab.

Calvin reached for it, but stopped himself.

His hand sat there, inches away.

Time passed slowly while he lay motionless in the weeds.

Of course, he was about to fetch the lab and check for hydrogen peroxide vials, full or empty (or if nothing of the sort was present; then a *real* mystery would emerge!).

But something really didn't make sense here. Why was Art's portable lab under the Hawk Squad's tent? Why not under the Beaver Squad's tent? That would've been the likely place Art would've hidden it. Nearby, but out of sight. That's what a smart person like Art would've done.

Right?

Right.

Ah.

With the realization came revelation. Calvin knew who had bleached his hair.

Chapter 24

CARDS ON THE TABLE.

JIM, THE BUG-EYED hippie Camp Chef, made chicken nuggets and French fries for lunch. Calvin sat at his table aware that plenty of bugged eyes were on him. The Whalers cap covered his dome but swaths of white hair spilled down the back. The Hawk Squad and its chaperones Oldroyd and Father ate quietly. "Pass the salt," was all Calvin heard. Whenever he looked up, he caught a face briskly tilting down to a plate of food.

Just before lunch ended, Troopmaster Oldroyd got up. "Hey Calvin," the man said quietly. "Got a minute?"

"I suppose, sir."

"Let's go somewheres private."

They slipped out the caf and went 'round the back of the building, to the milk crate stack by the screen door. Calvin heard pop music coming from the dishroom.

Oldroyd tweaked the angle of his black cowboy hat; this tiny adjustment successfully made him appear sympathetic. "After you split, I got loud and rough on the guys, tryin' to find the sumbitch who bleached your hair. I searched the whole dern campsite. Backpacks, everything: but I found nothin'."

Calvin frowned. "So you stopped looking?"

"There ain't nothin' to find, kid. Whoever did it must've thrown the murder weapon in the reservoir, or the latrine."

"And, no one came forth with information?"

"Nope."

"Not even Father or anyone?"

Oldroyd gasped. "Father?! Ya don't think *he* did it, do ya?"

"Father is a man of the cloth," Calvin said. "People with guilty consciences confess to them, right?"

But men of the cloth, it seemed, confided to no one. "He ain't said nothin' to me," Oldroyd shrugged. "No one has."

"Oh well, never mind."

"Bullshit, 'never mind!' We both got dumped outta the fryin' pan and into the fire here. Inky thinks this is his big chance to assassinate me and take over! And when yer folks see yer hair, they'll go apeshit. Especially yer mother!"

"None of that is what I meant. We'll figure it out another way. I'm sure of it. Thanks," the lad said, omitting *for nothing.*

"Ya don't *know* who did it, do ya?" Oldroyd's hat snapped down, successfully making him appear mean. "We're talkin' about an asshole here, Calvin. That's what he is—an asshole." He pointed at Calvin's head. "Ain't no friend did *that* to ya."

Oldroyd's attitude was damn near adult-like, on par with General Schultz, or Father Sean at the church, or Principal Fartin' Martin, or any other actual authority figure with which Calvin had experience.

But in this matter, it meant nothing. "I don't know who did it," Calvin stated. "I just figure it'll come out eventually."

xXx

After lunch, Calvin popped in the kitchen to find it empty. He heard voices in the dishroom, so he headed there.

The singer of Eurythmics announced the impending repeat of some precipitation, and her lack of argument over that fact. (With a major storm approaching, this was surely but one in a clever, or damn clichéd, parade of rock songs with lyrics concerning rain. Wouldn't be long before that one by the Doors came on—about journeymen surfing on the coattails of a tempest—and Calvin hoped to be far away by then.)

He found the K.P. crew huddled near the triple-sink unit, laughing. They turned to Calvin and offered salacious looks ... then freaked at the sight of him. "Holy shit, dude!" whooped Hank from Troop 99. "Didja see a ghost?"

"Actually, I saw your ma naked," Calvin zinged.

Laughter. "You get worse every time we see ya!" noted Jimmy, trading a look with his mate from Troop 2, Dale.

"Hopefully the worst is over," said Mike. The pink-cheeked kid gave Calvin a spooky look, like he knew something. But what could he know? How could he know it? Well. It was shady shit from the usually silent kid from Troop 73.

The K.P. foreman, Ken Izerman, had a twinkle in his eye. "Leave him alone, guys, he's in enough trouble as it is." He held up a folded sheet of Souviens letterhead, sealed with Scotch tape. "That girl Cindy, or whatever the hell her name is, gave me this. Said to give it to you. Then she took off."

Calvin accepted the note with a smirk. "How long ago?"

"Five minutes, tops," Ken said.

"She's pro'bly at lover's lane, waitin' for ya!" Dale teased.

Calvin broke the note's seal and passed an inquisitive eye over the scribbling therein. All the while, Jimmy sang, *"Calvin and the cunt / sittin' in a tree! / F-U-C-K / I-N-G!"*

"Envy is the Devil's work, boyo," Calvin smiled. "Cover for me." He headed out the screen door. As it shut behind him, he added, "At least one of us is getting some this trip."

"Aw, shit!" screamed Hank and George. They high-fived.

Calvin slogged up the Red Trail, his stomach in the spin cycle. A show-down awaited—it might be a bluffing situation. The gastronomic end-arounds made him dizzy by the time he reached the Racine Memorial Amphitheater.

The structure was immense and mentally sobering. An outer wall of blackwashed wood stood ten feet high and made a long circle in the forest. A plaque by the entranceway claimed that Luc Racine had been a great Troopmaster and a caring man ... and (most importantly) the father of the Camp Ranger's wife. As Calvin slogged inside, he wondered if there would ever be a Calvin Connor memorial building.*

The amphitheater was large enough to seat four hundred people.

---

* Little did he know. And, he would even live to see it.

Benches, crafted from long thick logs cut down the middle and sanded, formed two sets of rows stepping downward to the stage. Two totem poles, thirty feet high, supported a long bank of weatherproof lights and speakers. A wall of thick oaks and maples lined the back of the stage area, arrogantly standing with their leafy arms crossed.

Cindy sat halfway down the right-hand section, smoking a cigarette. Calvin trampled down the aisle to her row, shuffled across as if dancing in front of seated patrons, and plopped down next to her. He callously took the cigarette from her hand and inhaled a long drag. The smoke corroded his lungs ... the pure oxygen flow to his mind was briefly cut off ...

He exhaled. A tingly Selsun Blue feeling galloped from the top of his skull down his chin—the true, grammatical impact of the word *head-rush*. He nearly lost his equilibrium.

"I got this note," he said. He dug it from his cut-offs pocket and read it aloud ...

> Calvin,
>   Meet me at Racine. I'll be inside.
> Will explain there,
>   Love,
>   "Cindy"

... adding, "Love the quotation marks!"

"Knew you would." She folded one leg under her so she could turn to face him, and Calvin had a gander at her short-ish, soft-ish, pale-ish legs. They curved this way and that out from lavender hip-hugging shorts. He wanted very much to set his hand on those legs. Maybe the other hand on the shorts.

"I'm here," he grinned, returning the cigarette. "Explain!"

She gave him a half-curious look. "Do you like me?"

"Do I like you?" he said, or nearly scoffed. "What kind of question is that? Of course I like you!"

"Why?"

"Tons of reasons. Mostly cuz you're honest—I live in a world of fakers and liars, so your honesty is a very sexy thing."

She half-smiled at this. "Thanks."

"What I'd give to have a girl like you—to have *you*—live down the road back in Axsubeen. How great would that be?"

She took half a drag, and lowered a half-dubious brow at him. "Are you really in a relationship, Calvin?"

"I am. We talked about it, remember?"

"Yeah, this Jenny. *Buuut,* you're a boy. And more than that, you're kind of a weirdo boy. Dorky weirdo boys lie about being in relationships—that way they won't seem so weirdo dorky."

"Be that as it may," he chuckled, "I *am* in a relationship. Jenny MacDonald is quite real, and we're really going out."

Cindy was miffed. "You know that by making out with me, you cheated on her!"

"Well … not really. We're separated for the moment."

"So now you're separated? For the moment?" No more "half"-anything in Cindy's emotions: she was 100% dubious. "Which is it?" she demanded.

"A few days ago, Jenny said she wanted a break."

"But officially, you're still boyfriend/girlfriend."

"We are."

"Show me that picture again."

"Heh?"

"The photo booth thing." Snapped fingers became an open palm. "Out with it."

Calvin drew his leather wallet and handed over the photo.

"Okay," Cindy said, holding it up so they could see it. "You got the top half. The first two pictures." Her finger traced along the tear in the strip below the second image, a move she'd made the first time she'd held it. "Every time *I've* done a photo booth with a guy, he wants the bottom half, cuz he always tries to kiss you for the last picture. Didn't *you* try and kiss Jenny?"

"Ahem," Calvin burped, quite astonished at her detective work. "I did; except I also grabbed her."

"Grabbed her? You mean her tits?"

"She didn't want me showing that off to the lads, so she took the bottom two snaps." He couldn't believe the honesty that passed between them. Why'd he tell her that?!

One long nod. "Let's play a little game, okay?" Cindy held the photo strip near his eyes, covering Jenny's face with a thumb. "Imagine that's you and *me,* and not you and her."

"Easy enough," he smiled.

"Now," she said, switching thumbs, "imagine it's her and some douchebag jock named Brett or something." She focused on his face for a reaction, and he had one, all right. "Ah-ha! *That* means you're cheating on her! If she did what you're doing, and you react like that, *that's cheating.* So vice-a versa!"

"Jaysus," he flapped, snapping up his photo strip so he didn't have to actually see Jenny's happy doe-eyed face while having this discussion. "So I'm fuckin' cheating, Cindy. Sue me." He slapped his wallet away and chuffed at her. "And, you know ... it wouldn't even be the first time."

"No shit." Her shoulders fell just a little bit. Softly, she said, "Guess you ain't the weirdo dorky boy I thought you were."

"Is this about me, or you? Or us?" he asked, a bit testily. "Are you feeling something here? Is that the problem?"

She bit her lip and silently flicked the cigarette away.

"I think you are," he said. "Someone so completely different from the rest of the asshole boys comes along. I'm a different kind of Asshole!" he laughed, referencing his nickname. She didn't react. He went on: "So, being lonely and deserted here, you wanna have it. For me, someone like you comes along, a completely different kind of girl, and I wanna have it too. We seem attracted to each other. I'm attracted to you, for sure!"

"I'm attracted to you too, Calvin," she blurted, "but we are *sooo* totally *not* in the same situation. You think I'm the most unique girl ever. I think you're the most unique boy, too. But you came here for a week, and there's only me to meet. I *stay* here, and meet millions of 'asshole boys' every week! And you get to go home in a few days. To your room, and your bed, with your bathroom with all your stuff in it, your books and magazines and a phone to call friends with ..." Her brown eyes pleaded with him. "I have to stay here, and do it all ... over ... again. Then, like, four more times after that."

A drop of rain impacted sharply on her bare knee. As he peered up at the gray sky, Calvin said, "It must totally suck."

"*That's* what this is about. Why we're flying along here, doing what we've done already, sitting here having this talk only, like, two days after we met. I'll admit it," she whooped, pointing at herself, "I'm desperate! It's so awesome to meet someone like you! I don't want it to end!" Her black eyebrows sank. "But *you're* not desperate. Sounds like you have *choices.*"

"I guess I do," he muttered.

"Where do you live again?"

"Axsubeen. Near Altoona, which is near Pittsburgh."

She wanted to do something with her hands. "That's a long ways away." Like, maybe punch him: "But not far enough."

"I'm sorry?" he pipped, feeling the hot tingle of blame.

"You're the Devil, Calvin. The Irish Lucifer. You're a snake, and a schemer, and a cheater!"

He didn't say anything just now.

Cindy raged, "You're the answer to all my prayers here—but *God* didn't send you. I see you doin' the sign of the cross, like a good Catholic, but that's just cover." She looked away, flushed from her outburst; when she turned back, she started talking about something else. "Back home, I have a few friends and they're all boys, and they're all more or less like me. I don't date them—I relate better to them than I do to dumb bitches. I *hate* dumb bitches. Is Jenny MacDonald a dumb bitch?"

"Jenny's a smart bitch," said Calvin evenly. "We're kinda the same that way. We're smart and don't care what others think. Ha—I think we enjoy knowing people don't approve!"

"So if you're such a perfect pair," she said, confused, "how come you're separated?"

"I don't know. We don't really relate."

"Oh, relate *this:* Jenny knew you were comin' here, that you'd be away for a week. So what's the *real* reason why she wanted a break? What's the *other guy's name?*"

"The other guy's name." Calvin nodded at her perception. "Sean Corgan. He's the most popular guy in my grade, throws the wildest parties, his da's a hotshot. The girls all love him." He smirked. "I see the way he eyes her up at his parties."

"You're so calm about this, Calvin! Jenny could be fucking this Sean right now! Don't you even care?"

"Of course I do," he bucked. "But what can I do? I hadda come here for camp. I don't wanna lose her, so I agreed to it."

She shook her head at him. "She don't want you anymore."

"We're still official!" he barked.

"Wake up and smell the coffee, Calvin!" She gave him a slap on the cheek. "I can't believe you're letting her use you!"

Calvin's only response was a crooked lip.

"I think she's been doing it from the start: just moved to town, met a confident boy, now looking higher up the ladder. Calvin, what the fuck?! You're smarter than that!"

Feeling insulted, he came back with immature bragging. "Dear, lovely Cindy: I have the hottest chick in school as my girlfriend, the girl every lad has a rock-hard boner for. And I've already cheated on her once. And now, I'm trying to cheat on her again." He spread his hands. "Is *Jenny* using *me?*"

"Fuckin' A, you're using each other!" cried Cindy. She looked up at the drizzly gray sky. "You two are like second grade enemies or something—competing at everything! You'll probably compare notes on who you cheated with, to see who wins!" She laughed hollowly, slapping her knees. "I *thought* you were different. But you're just a boy."

Calvin swallowed a dry gulp. "Am I now? Can we make this cards on the table time?"

She nodded. "Please, tell me your side of it."

"All right." He started, then stopped. Just when he was about to say it! "I love girls. I *really* love girls. Girls are what I'm about. And not just tits, I mean talking to them, being around them, the way they laugh, the way they coordinate the colors of, like, nail polish and barrettes. The way they pretend not to like the corny little shite I say. I even love what girls smell like!

"So when me and Art came in the dishroom, and you and I started talking … I was amazed. I wanted to get to know you so badly, and now that I *do* know you, I wanna know more." He wiped the light rain off his arms nervously. "But I'm a snake, I admit it. I invited you to the party last night to feed you booze."

"So why didn't you make it just the two of us?" She was very calm right now. "You coulda snuck off alone from the dance and met me somewhere. I woulda said yes."

"That ... never occurred to me." He gritted his teeth. "All I was thinking was having Sandy and his booze there." He suddenly felt guilty—for the very first time—for having set up Jon Oldroyd so he'd be out of the picture.

"The booze was the key, then." Dangerous knowledge glowed in her eyes. "You're not saying the words 'I wanted to get you drunk and screw you,' because you don't wanna scare me off, to look evil. But that's what you wanted. To use me. Like you use Jenny. Like you used the *other* girl you cheated on Jenny with."

"Jill Pedersen."

"You're all about getting what you want. If you use girls, it means you don't really like them," Cindy noted. "You like 'being around them, the way they laugh, the way they smell.' All that shit turns you on. But you don't like the girls themselves. If you did, we wouldn't be here."

Calvin literally couldn't face such whole-cloth truth, and looked at his shoes instead.

Cindy looked at hers too. After a spell, she took a deep breath. "My turn. I hate it here. I fucking hate every youth organization in the whole world. You boys, you ask me where I'm from, what's my favorite band, do I have a goddamn boyfriend—oh! It's torture! Troopers are always portrayed as these great kids, helpin' old ladies across the street. *Bull...shit!* Remember, 'Trooper' rhymes with 'pooper.' They use dirty words and make pranks and pick on each other and even get drunk in their tents. And they follow their dicks, and when I'm, like, the only burger left at McDonald's, they'll do *anything* to get me."

"Two weeks ago, I had a kid grab my tits in the dishroom."

Calvin drew back. "There's some shite! What did you do?"

"Punched him. He stumbled back and his face smacked the table. Chipped one of his teeth." Cindy shrugged, defeated. "I shoulda reported him to Murphy but that asshole thinks I'm a brainless whore, inventing stories about getting groped. And my dad ... he saw it as me trying to get back to living at my mom's. I hate living with my mom as much as being here! My parents can't even look at each other without screaming. I'm in a corner. And that son of a bitch groped me ... and I just reacted."

The leafy summer trees outside the amphitheater's walls encircled the sky like a wavy green picture frame. The sky swirled gray; middling rain grazed them, warm and slick. Their two-man show, all dialogue, had taken them out of this wide natural world and into a tight cocoon of teenage angst.

She bit a nail, staring idly at her kneecap. She always made eye contact, so it said something that she suddenly didn't want to. "I hate it here, man," she whispered.

"I get it," he said softly.

"You probably do." She stopped biting her nail and cracked her knuckles. "Okay, here's the tale of Mr. Whalers Cap. We both live in Norwich—it's like half an hour up north. He goes to my school. His name isn't important."

"Whose is?" Calvin joked.

"Right. He's kinda popular; everybody knows him and he hangs out with different crews; but he's basically a loner. James Dean and shit."

"The type you fall for, but hate yourself for doing it."

"I guess. No, that's *exactly right*, Calvin. God, you can read me like a fucking book. So when he started showing me attention, I kept wondering, why me? I finally broke down and went out with him, but it was like a secret relationship. I went to parties with him but never got to talk to his pals. We were always hiding in closets, making out; or sneaking out the back door without saying goodbye.

"Shoulda realized if a guy don't like me hanging out with his friends, he's embarrassed by me. *Everyone* knew we were goin' out, but he wouldn't even kiss me in the hall at school."

Cindy's whole body language spoke of exasperation. "What a sucker I am. I got tired of it, confronted him, and he dumped me; I'm 'too selfish and needy.' After it was over, Mr. Whalers Cap started talking about me, about what a slut I am, and worse shit than that. Apparently, I used to beg him to do me in the butt. That's what everyone thinks now."

"Wow," Calvin said, recoiling. "There's a ..." Cindy looked at him expectantly. He had to go on. "There's a girl in my school who gets talked about like that. That exact same rumor. It makes me feel sad just thinking about her right now, after hearing your story. I know what they say about her is lies. But ... "

"Have you said it too?" Cindy asked. "Just, like, joking?"

Calvin's bloodless expression was answer enough.

"You get it—the power of rumors. How they destroy people. Why'd he do it? There's no need to push my face in it! I told myself I'd never get in such a fucked-up situation again, and I ain't gone on a date since. Going with you for a drink ... that's the first date-like thing I did in months. Pathetic, right?"

"Not really," was his lame comment. "I bet it was awesome compared to the Mr. Whalers Cap rollercoaster."

A rueful laugh. "Sure—'awesome.' Let me fill you in on a few things." She wiped back her wet hair to expose a malicious face. "I *don't* lose my memory when I drink. But I felt bad for you, so I pretended I blacked out too."

Kinda shady. Calvin anxiously asked, "So, what'd I miss?"

"Tons. We went out to 'snog.' Sandy and Art came out with the booze. You drank five cups of brandy, then finished the water bag! You didn't stop! I hope you don't *usually* drink like that! Then, Sandy said we should go to the jetty and jump in. I knew what he was doing: he wanted you outta his way."

"Outta his way to what?"

"Outta his way to *me*. You were too shitfaced to figure it out. You sure that Sandy's a friend?"

"My all-time best friend, both here and in Ireland."

"Oh don't be too sure, Calvin. He wasn't your friend last night. He conned you into taking off all your clothes and jumping in the reservoir. Art loved that you were being embarrassed. You didn't even care that your guy-friends were there." Her round face wore a salacious look. "'Member I said maybe you get girls cuz yer a good kisser and got a big ding-dong?"

"Vividly," he said.

"You're two for two, Calvin. Don't think I didn't notice."

He turned red. "I'm just as God made me," he joked thinly.

She took off the salacious look: "Art sat on the jetty, keeping an eye on you so you wouldn't drown. Sandy didn't care. Now he had a clear shot at me."

"This is so ... " Calvin trailed off. "Sandy hit on you?"

"Yes. But I didn't want no part of it. I wanted to run away. I felt surrounded. You were only one of them I trusted, so I got in with you. I got down to my underwear, jumped in, and took the rest off once I was next to you, cuz the water was deep there and Sandy and Art couldn't see." She shook her head. "If they couldn't see, why'd I bother getting naked? I'm so dumb."

Shrugging, she went on: "Art suddenly didn't care if you drowned. He just stared at my chest. He's never seen tits. Sandy kept nudging him—'look, boobs!' What an asshole! I know his type: put a few drinks in him, he's fuckin' Superman."

Calvin wanted to dispute that.

"You were struggling to stay on your feet, so I got us to come in a bit, to water deep enough to hide my tits. I hate the reservoir—the water's always cold, and just doesn't feel clean, and you never know what you're stepping on. Ugg!"

The rain was for real now, wetting them nicely. Neither of them moved for cover.

"I know what happened after that," he said. "Father, that's Matt Duffy, our Junior Chaplain, he came back from the dance—I guess early, since parties aren't really his scene."

Cindy nodded. "Father heard our noise and called out. Sandy and Art ran and hid. We couldn't get out in time, so we got busted. But you put on a pretty good imitation of a sober guy, and we got dressed with Father's back turned. He told you to walk me back to the caf. We got, like, halfway down the Green Trail when you fell. You were like, 'Don't leave, Cindy! Don't leave!' I didn't know what the fuck your problem was.

"You had to puke. I held back your hair so it didn't get all icky again. Then we moved in the woods so we didn't have to smell it, and sat there. We didn't talk. You didn't try anything; we just held each other. You were really warm. I was cold from the reservoir. It was nice to have you there to warm me up.

"Then the other Troops came by, for what seemed like for-fucking-ever. Finally they stopped. I said I'd be okay on my own. You kept insisting on coming, but I told you to relax. And you went back to your campsite and I went back to my room."

Calvin soaked all this in. "So," he said at length.

She let him think in peace.

"Why did you do it?" Calvin's gray eyes were earnest. "Really— why? You held back my hair, got naked in the reservoir, said 'yes' and came for drinks, rinsed the blood out of my hair. You've done all this stuff for me—the Devil. Why?"

She issued a humming sigh. "I really like you. I know you like me too. That's how I want things to be between us."

They took a long, long moment to let the previous one pass. The rain held its steady course.

She clicked her cheek. "Are all the cards on the table?"

"Not all of them," he warned.

She smiled guiltily. "Oh, right—Wren."

He didn't get it. "Say again?"

"My first name. Wren."

"Wren," he said. The name infused him with some fresh energy. "With a W, the bird *wren*, right? The W from *walnut*, the N from *fern*. Something to do with leaves, but not really. Obviously an animal. It's a cool name though."

"That's all my cards," she said. "You got any more?"

"I got one I'm gonna shove up Sandy's arse when I see him," he urged. He looked into her eyes. "So, what now?"

"What now?" She considered it. "Why don't we start by dropping all the bullshit, all the hidden agendas and 'bollocks,' and admit that we have a pretty hot thing going here?" Grinning, she reached in a pocket and withdrew a Trojan, its red wrapping standing out against her white hand.

His face grew long. "What? *For real?*" He took the condom but kept his eyes locked on hers. "In light of all this?!"

"Oh it's not a good idea," she agreed. "But I wanna fuck you so bad. I'm *sooo* turned on right now by all this honesty."

"What if *I'm* not turned on?"

"You're not?" she scoffed. "Fine—is there something I can say to convince you to fuck me?"

He shrugged. "I'm sure there is now."

"Then pretend I said it. And get over here and fuck me."

" ... easy enough."

She reached out her hand. He took it.

Chapter 25

Chaos and carnage.

"It's really bad out here. You need to get me goin' again."

"What? This was yer idea!"

"No, it was yours!"

"And it was a stupid idea."

"It was not."

"Ha! It *was* yer idea!"

"Fuck Jon. I don't wanna go visit him anymore."

"It ain't that bad. Ain't seen Noah go by in his ark yet."

"We're liable to get picked up by a tornado!"

"Shut up, Art, yer one serious whiner."

"Yo, this is one serious storm, Sandy. Stop being a dick."

"Am what I got, Art."

"What you *eat* is more like it!" Art broke off running. He only had a half-step on Sandy. Bounding up the Red Trail on his gangly legs, he took a sudden, sharp left into the forest, heading for the Racine Amphitheater ahead of them—

And collided with Cindy. Their combined speed, and unbeknownst beeline trajectory for one another, made for a wicked crash. Art ricocheted and his left shoulder attempted to cut through an oak tree. (It failed.) Cindy's face slapped Art's chest, then slapped a maple. She hit the ground with an awkward splat; she spat out blood and crusty maple bark granules.

"You guys okay?!" yelped Sandy, screeching to a halt. Art's face bent downward. Cindy climbed to her knees, checking if her teeth were all there. Unlike the boys, she was not wearing a poncho, and her sopping wet Ocean Pacific T-shirt clung to her body ... so it was obvious she also wasn't wearing a bra. Sandy's hormones momentarily stunned him, and he was nearly thrown to the ground by a blast of thunder.

"Holy shit, I *felt* that!" he screamed. "Too dangerous out here! Let's get in that amphitheater and find a dry spot!"

Cindy's eyes were a little askew. She wiped some fresh blood from her lip and called out, "We need help!"

"Obviously!"

"Not me!" She bridged the gap between them. "Calvin!"

"What happened?"

"He's back there!" Cindy flailed her arms towards the forest behind the amphitheater. "A tree fell on him! I can't move it!"

Sandy peered where she pointed: tall trees moshed in deluges of water. He looked over at Art; the kid rolled on his back, clutching his left shoulder and making rueful noises.

"You get Art somewhere dry!" Sandy huffed. *"Don't* touch his arm!" He ran, dashing deeper into the forest with reckless abandon, adroitly avoiding the branches strewn about. The stinging rain—or was it hail?—did not help any.

KER-BOOOOM!

And neither did the thunder.

Sandy rounded the bend of the tall blackwashed wooden wall and arrived behind the amphitheater. It was a calamitous maelstrom; everything here was riotous green or pissed off brown ... except for Calvin, lying face-up in a muddy patch between two venerable northern red oaks. A large branch, twenty feet stem to stern, sat on him. The split-off end of the branch had crushed the lad's right arm, spearing into it. Making Calvin all the more obvious was his fully naked state.

"Jesus Fucking Christ With Ranch Dressing!" Sandy yelled.

Calvin squirmed a bit. Sandy knelt beside him and wiped back the white, now sludge-filled hair to reveal ... a giant smile.

"Are ya all right, dude?!"

"Sandy?" said Calvin. "Go away. The last time I was naked in front of you—are you hitting on Cindy *right now*, too?!"

"Are you shitting me with that shit?!" wailed Sandy. "Right *now*, you wanna talk about that?! C'mon, focus!"

"Been tryin' to move for like five minutes," Calvin said, turning his body. The broken branch, maybe a foot in diameter, made plain its intention to use gravity to sink through him.

Sandy shimmied in the mud and squinted at Calvin's right arm. Fat and bloated; raw red flesh shone where the cracked wood had knifed in his inner elbow. Sandy swore he saw bone.

"Do I leave it in or pull it out?!" Sandy squeaked.

"Like I fucking know?" Calvin said.

"Goddamnit—THINK, Sandy!" the kid yelled at himself. He looked around, extreme desperation in his stocky face. He refocused on Calvin and remembered Art's first aid before Tentgate. "Art worried about blood gushin' out in a big stream. That ain't happening here. Hardly bleeding at all!" He took a determined breath. "I'm gonna pull it out. Then we haul ass into that amphitheater. Where are your clothes?!"

Calvin sighed. "I was so close, Sandy! *Sooo* close!"

Sandy blinked. "So *that's* why yer naked! Strike last!"

"Strike fast!"

"Get h—"

A tree near them hopped off the Earth a half-inch, blanketing the two lads with a fury of tiny splinters.

Everything after that was a blur.

Then blue.

The shore of his mind.

Something washed up to it.

It turned a soft, watery light on in his brain.

Moisture dripped from his hair.

Cold, damp fluid.

It stung his skullcap.

His nose emitted bubbles.

He could taste salt on his lips.

He didn't know how much longer he could take it.

He threw up all over himself.

The Comedie of King James' Jimmy
Act III

SCENE IV

Enter KING JAMES
and SQUEAK,
attended by GUARDS.

King James. Disease plagueth our people. Shall ours be the next cadavers?

Squeak. 'Tis bowel-dancing that doth bewitcheth thee, for a speech thou soon giveth.

King James. I repaireth to my chambers, to don fresh trousers.

Exeunt KING JAMES.

Squeak. Alack, here cometh the sixth Earl Douchebag.

Enter [BYRON,]
EARL FROBISHER.

Frobisher. I beseech thee.

Squeak. As do all of simpler minds.

Frobisher. Insult me not! I herald all armies, men who would thrash thy spotty seat at an utterance from mine own lips!

Squeak. Lips only employed for close-gathering upon James' hind-glands! Such utterances reek of the Royal Trouser-Seat.

Frobisher. False words! His Majesty is bathed nightly. No cleaner Royal [Arse] there be!

Squeak. Yet stinketh the man like no other, save thyself. Brothers-in-law—ha! Brothers-in-fetor more like!

Frobisher. I should strike thy noggin off its stool!

Squeak. Even thy shadow daren't strike me! King Cad needeth me more than he needeth thee.

Frobisher. Didst thou just call James a "cad?"

Squeak. Be there an echo hereabouts? Aye, I doth that thing. The King have naught but two organs: his heart and his dagger. The man's mind is rivaled only by the wit of encrusted inner britches.

Frobisher. Exercise thy gift for menacing silence!

Squeak. Know only this: I be the mind of this Kingdom. King Cad be naught but the loins!

Frobisher. The King haveth no mind indeed to prefer thy company over any other.

Squeak. Understand ye at last!

Frobisher. Stop! We shan't add another page to the infernal book on how great thy mind may (or mayn't) be.

Squeak. So great be my mind that we commit to parchment this very thing.

Frobisher. Sendeth thy book into the flames! I beseech thee for another reason.

Squeak. Beseech away, then.

Frobisher. 'Tis but a sneeze's time 'til standeth we on the balcony, overlooking the masses.

Squeak. Not e'en so long.

Frobisher. Yet have we no sign of my sister, our Queen! When addressing the peoples, never be a King without his Queen; lest he a bonnie be, and our James is certainly no molasses-miner!

Squeak. Queen Kalina matters not. Only the speech. James must spake his drivel.

Frobisher. Didst thou just call our discovery, which may save our plagued people, 'drivel?' 'Drivel,' didst thou say? Nay!

Squeak. Yay! The moniker fitteth like tailored britches.

Frobisher. Dispenseth of thy metaphor of malaise! A distraction only be thy britches-fetish. A wasteth of time!

Squeak. Mayhap we have all wasteth our time; for thy sister, Queen Kalina, hath declared our discovery an affront! "The man donneth the discovery, but the woman beareth all brunt!"

Frobisher. 'Tis the way. Woman cannot screw man!

Squeak. But could sheep screweth woman?

Frobisher. ...what?

Squeak. Thy tremendously tittieth sister regardeth the discovery based wherefrom it came. "A bestial encounter," she calleth its use! Sex with a sheep!

[*Frobisher.* 'Zounds!

Squeak. 'Zounds is correct,] for only last night, did it occur to King Cad, His Majestic Feeblemind, that testeth the discovery we hath not!

Frobisher. 'Twas my understanding that randy Duke of Umberton testeth the discovery, abounding his girth atop and within many a whore—strictly in the name of science!

Squeak. Proving once more that thee understandeth little. Umberton knew whores carnally, yes. Yet "forgeteth" the horny Duke each time to tote the discovery upon what I have heard tell is known in the brothel region as "His Grace's slight ear of maize!"

Frobisher. "In the heat of the moment," he sayeth? In the heat of the moment! Hath none worn the discovery in combat?

Squeak. None save James. And he, only during the night just past.

'Twas a royal rumble! The Queen grew angered at him! And clippeth did she the Royal Jewels, her sharp fingers grinding the pouch! Headeth she for the hills thereafter.

Frobisher. Kalina is a Frobisher indeed! Taketh a strong bitch to defy thine own King! Yet it only adds to the total disaster that our discovery hath become!

Squeak. I harken to mine first words on this whole discovery nonsense: "'Tis a shitty idea, your Majesty." Words that ring loudly true; as do all my words.

Frobisher. Her Majesty hath reacted as if James doth brought an entire sheep into the bedchamber of love rather than a tiny portion thereof!

Squeak. But if the *masses* react as violently ... 'tis your slovenly asses first 'gainst the wall.

Frobisher. Not thine own?

Squeak. Hell no, I shall rideth the first horse-cart outta here!

Enter KING JAMES
and [*the* DUKE OF]
UMBERTON.

Umberton. All hail the King!

All. Hail King James!

King James. We haveth no time for such bovinal fecal matter.

Frobisher. I bid you good tide, Majesty. May God guide us!

King James. Pray thee only that God holdeth mine bowels!

Squeak. I commit ten such prayers to God.

Umberton. I have the discovery here, Majesty!

Squeak. Ah, remembereth you at last! And lo, no whores in sight! Umberton, thy be as ass-backwards a thing as a man with buttock-cheeks for lips.

Umberton. Heh. Lord Squeak jests to ease thy jitters, Majesty.

King James. Good lad. Let us marcheth now to our destiny!

KING JAMES *stands on balcony, addressing his peoples.*

King James. Friends, peons, mama-sans! Surviveth we many demons: bubonic, hunger, war! Now we face two new devils: birth, and vee-dee! Bushelfuls of mouths to feed, borne by women who did not want them, from men who did not pull out in time. And then there are those fearfully cringing when they spy thy genitals and note green growths!

But soft!, we four wise men, the great minds of the kingdom, hath discovered the cure! Behold! The new future! Behold! A device which alloweth man to gallop as long as his horse doth not tire out, and yet produceth no offspring!

Behold—the condom!

Stareth thee now at a portion of a sheep's bladder, one end lacerateth, the other fuseth! A scabbard for man's dagger, or "sword" if thy be a Moor. Funnelth it will man's milk, ensuring getting off whilest preventing whipping up any buns in that most sacred of ovens, the bakery of a woman's snatch.

All the while, our discovery also prevents the syphilis and the crabbes from grasping thine pubes! Shouldst thy wife possess titanic titties to grapple with during battle, as doth your fair Queen Kalina, [hubba-hubba!,] then the screw be just the sweeter! And if thee desireth a romp down the Hershey Highway, needeth thou only a scoop of simple pig lard, nature's lubricant, to grease the motherfucker up—

KING JAMES *is pelteth on the noggin by a tomato.*

Needles. A tree branch. Some unnaturally red hair.
   A hilarious moment with a stubborn condom wrapper.
   A soldier with a rifle. Flying underneath the sea.
   A tiny bird. A quizzical look. A circular light.
   A shoelace tourniquet. A king, with tomato on his face.
   A blur. A blue. A shriek. Hot pain under cold rain.

What the hell was going on? *Had* gone on? There were no answers, only nuggets. Oh look, this one is a crowded ride in some heavy truck, like an Army personnel carrier. Lots of close faces. Lots of paperwork and questions. Lots of "Just sit back and rest, young man."

   Too much information. Little knowledge. No connections.

   Focus dropped on him, leaving him with the blue blur again. He could see the mists forming into shapes, the figures of people, who would talk nonsense for his enjoyment. Like the last dream. Silly drivel. "Drivel," didst thou say?

   Maybe he was high. He couldn't feel anything. He couldn't hear anything. And he definitely had scab workers subbing for his eyes.

   Yeah, he was high.

Chapter 26

THE MAN IN BLUE.
WEDNESDAY, JULY 29, 1987.

HE HAD COMPANY. Quite a bit of it: someone snored in the bed next to his, and two men sat in the visitors' chairs. Something was attached to the inside of his left elbow. Something was attached to the entirety of his right elbow. As he moved, a white linen sheet slid down his arms, and he barely felt it.

Calvin blinked. He was in hospital.

He retrieved all the information possible. He looked at his Swatch for the time—gone. No cut-offs or goofy sky blue Oscar Wilde T-shirt; now, a long pale green smock with no back or sleeves. He reached down with his right hand to throw off the thin linen blanket, but things felt very unnatural during the moving process, so he stopped dead.

A thick cotton sling knotted up behind his neck held his right arm frozen in place. Also, there was a … thing over his right elbow. It looked like a bubble, like a sock, like a soccer ball, like a rubber. A brace, he mused, some kind of inflatable brace. He tried moving his right hand; the fingers kind of twitched after some queasy and difficult effort, like making a fist while his hand was buried in packed snow.

His left arm was still free and working, so he used that instead, flicking the blanket off. His bed had guard rails, intriguing him. Do people fall out of hospital beds often enough for guard rails to be advisable? He gripped the left rail and yanked; it shifted and dropped out of sight. "That's handy," he said, nearly drunk at the piercing sound of his own voice.

He stood, incurring no discomfort. Unbeknownst to him, his right arm registered distinct pain. Appropriate signals got sent to the brain; gangs of opiatic muggers beat them up.

The lad made for the I.V. stand to which he was connected. Clear fluid in the clear bag, dangling from the drip-stand wistfully. The bag bore a white label belching forth bar codes, nonsense words, and numerals. He gripped the stand, which happily had casters, and began a little reconnoitering mission.

Two beds, one empty. He chuckled—that bed was his! A lump lay in the other bed, with a sheet yanked completely over it. Another I.V. stand fed a tube under the sheet. The lump, while human-shaped, had an awkward bump near the top.

A large window covered by a blind revealed a daytime scene, possibly morning. He saw a parking lot outside, and a river or harbor in the distance. A tall wooden wardrobe case in one corner—empty. A mobile dining tray sat in the other corner, with the sports section of *The Day* on it. Calvin looked for the date at the top of the page:

Wednesday, July 29, 1987.

The young lad suddenly felt very tired.

He wheeled his stand past the beds, past the visitors' chairs (two of which, as the chronicler has already recorded, had men sitting in them), and headed for the doors. One certainly led out; the other, off to the side, was the loo. The mirror in the loo showed Calvin Ciarán Connor III with sickly white hair. Of all the revelations, this was the most disconcerting. He hadn't been dreaming all this time. *So,* Calvin wondered as he made a quick deposit in the toilet, *where'd Tuesday go?*

He flushed.

It had been Tuesday, about two in the afternoon, when the tree fell. Or split. Or blew up. And here he was, in hospital, on Wednesday ... or, quite possibly, later. He exited the bathroom and finally decided to focus on the two men sitting in the visitors' chairs. One was white, wore a blue uniform with a shiny badge, toted a gun on his belt, and was wide awake.

The other was black, bearded, beefy, and sleeping. Eureka! Mr. Maguire's presence logically meant the nearby presence of one other person—Calvin hustled to the occupied bed and tore back the sheet. And there was Art! He had suffered some whopper of an injury to his left shoulder or arm: both were wrapped in a strange, beige, hard plastic encasement; and, as a result, Art was probably on the same drugs as

Calvin.

"Fuck you, Irish," the kid cursed, crashing awake. "I am totally not happy with you right now."

"Oh aren't you now?" asked Calvin. "What'd I do?"

Art scoffed. "Like you don't know?! This is all your goddamn fault. And you'll be dead if you don't give me back the sheet." His gray gangly hands fumbled blindly.

Calvin flung the sheet over him and let out a long sigh. No talking to the grumpypants Art or the sleeping Mr. Maguire. That left the unidentified white man in the other visitor's chair.

Who was a cop.

Calvin had rarely interacted with cops. When he, Sandy, Art, and Ryan Phillips had been busted blowing up a mailbox, it was the Maguire residence the police visited ("Of course," Art ranted, "they went straight for the black suspect.").

Axsubeen had one law-enforcer, Sheriff Stefan "Steve" Schultz V, who could often be found at Corgan's Pizzeria on Railroad Street. "Hey Calvin, how's your dad doing!" Sheriff Steve would shout as he tossed French fries down his swollen gullet.

"Fine." Calvin would pay for his hoagie and depart.

Decidedly *not* a world of experience upon which to draw!

Calvin must have been higher than a kite, doing all this exploring, talking to Art, and suchlike without even acknowledging the men in his room. In particular, the *armed* one.

"Excuse me," the lad said, "but who are you?"

The cop, who wore tall black boots and had a white motorcycle helmet in his lap, took a long look at Calvin. Calvin looked back. He could see himself in the mirror shades resting atop the cop's sharp blond crew-cut.

"Sergeant Robert White, of the Connecticut State Police."

"Okay," Calvin said highly. "Then ... am I in trouble?"

"No."

Calvin waited for the man to say more. He did not. So Calvin blurted, "I'm a little weirded out! I was at summer camp, minding my own business; then *bang!* Here I am in hospital, with a policeman guarding my room."

"I'm not guarding your room," the cop pointed out. "I was waiting for you to wake up."

"Well ... I'm awake now, aren't I?"

From under Art's sheet: "There's cops here?! What'd you do *now*, Calvin?!"

"Go back to sleep," Calvin told him.

A grim look of consternation crossed the cop's mug. He stood, set his shades and helmet on the breakfast tray, and moved closer.

As he was already pressed against the wall, Calvin lamely shielded himself from the cop with his I.V. stand. The cop was short but carried himself with a restrained menace. He wore an M1911 and not some limp-dick service revolver; that was no good! Another step brought him in arm's reach. "I heard some kids were injured at the reservation and brought here," he said. "I radioed the captain, offering to check it out. He said yes.

"And I recognized you."

"You ..." Calvin's blood ran cold. "You recognized me."

"We met three days ago," the cop breathed. "At Joe's Gas & Food right off 95. *That's* one of the fools who was behind the wheel," the cop said, waving a hand at the dozing Mr. Maguire. "You were in the mini-mart when I had my little ... episode. You didn't duck or put up your hands like the others did—so I took note of you."

Calvin's blood nearly froze solid. He recognized this man now. Oh yes, that grim look was unmistakable.

"You were on your way to summer camp," Sergeant White hissed. "And since then, you've been assaulted."

"Assaulted?" repeated Calvin.

The cop pointed. "Your head wound. The docs said it's blunt force trauma. Might even be a brain bruise."

Calvin made to reach up with his right hand, but the sling caught him. He settled for using his left and discovered the forehead wound was, once more, bandaged. "It was this asshole in my Squad," he said dismissively.

"Was it." The cop clearly doubted this story. "And then there's your hair."

"Yes," squeaked Calvin. "I know, it's pretty white now."

The cop's grim face got grimmer. "Wasn't before."

Calvin's squeaky voice got squeakier, almost guiltily so. "Guess not!"

"Sit," the cop demanded.

Calvin could not come up with an adequate reason to defy the man, so he did as demanded by sitting on the corner of his bed. The cop slid his visitor's chair across from Calvin. "We both have questions," he said. "We both have answers."

"Oh do we now?" Calvin wheezed. "That's a fucking relief. Let's trade off then, Sergeant."

"You first, young man."

Chapter 27

BLOOD, SWEAT, TEARS.

THINK *YOU'VE* HAD a bad morning?

Spazz started off his Wednesday slogging down the Green Trail to Centre des Trois with what remained of Troop 666 (three boys and one grown-up were absent). The blond headbanger quietly ate his bacon and eggs surrounded by two hundred other kids. He felt safe in the crowd, but being under orders never to talk, he dared not express his relief.

Then Oldroyd told Spazz to sub for Calvin and Jon on K.P. So he cleaned a few ovens with some chink. One of the K.P. guys (who had unnervingly pink cheeks) gave him looks; probably another straight-lace dork freaked out by long hair.

When Spazz rejoined Troop 666 at Campsite Quatre, Oldroyd wondered aloud who'd clean the latrine. Beaver Squad Captain (Acting) Sandy volunteered, as did Hawk Squad Captain (Acting) (Acting) Gus. But Oldroyd made Spazz do it.

So he trudged down to Centre des Trois and further on, along the Yellow Trail, to the Supply Shack. Laden with utensils and detergents, Spazz hiked back and cleaned the latrine. Despite the reek, he enjoyed it: he could let down his guard.

Spazz had to return the cleaning utensils whence they came, so he trudged down the Green Trail past Centre des Trois again. On his way back, that tall dude Satan said to pass word that Troop 666 should report to the caf in an hour; they were on the second shift of today's storm clean-up crew.

Hooray, Spazz thought, *more damn work.* Then he made his mistake. He decided he'd marched the Green Trail enough for one day (this was already his third round trip), so he took the long way to the campsite, cutting through the forest.

Once he was safely away from the trail, Spazz got the shit beat out of him by four teenage assailants. One of them went *cheep!* at him.

Bloodied and woozy, lying on the damp earth of a grassy knoll ten yards from the Beaver tent in Campsite Quatre, Spazz felt he'd had enough of this shit. The Troop 666 novelty—a headbanger actually in Troop 666!—had gotten old. As the blood dripped, Spazz counted off reasons to quit:

He liked Metallica. *Drip!* They preferred "Kumbaya."

He liked to smoke. *Drip!* While tolerated in Troop 666, cigarettes brought ugly stares. Only campfires should smoke.

He liked long hair. *Drip!* He rarely saw other Troopers with long hair. Buncha Aqua Net-using dorkaroonies.

He liked to tinker with cars. *Drip!* Cars had to be the single least outdoorsy thing on the face of the Earth. The tee-eye-tee ignored the automobile completely.

He liked having fun. *Drip!* In the new Oldroyd era, Troop 666 was anything but. Spazz's one outlet to combat these woes had been taken away, and he lay in a pool of his own blood without permission to even cry out in pain. *I can see the future,* he thought, *and it's got me bleedin' out, dying a most heavy metal death, written all over—*

But wait! Dumb ol' Oldroyd said Spazz would be allowed to speak *if someone's life was in danger!* "Help!" he wailed.

No response. He was, remember, deep in the woods, privately dying. "Is somebody there? Help! HELP ME!"

Spazz heard talking, but far off. He assaulted the air with anything that'd get their attention: "Hey ya stupid motherfuckers, the Spazz-ster's lyin' in the grass bleedin' and shit! HELP!"

"Over here!" came a call, very close at that. Spazz eased his head back and watched an inverted Gus Jacoby walk towards him on a sky of grass. "Spazz, yous better shut up!" chided the tub o' lard. "Oldroyd heard ya, an' he says you better—WOW!"

Gus twirled, cupping plump hands around his mouth. "Get the first aid kit! Get a doctor! He's bleedin' all over the place!"

"Thanks a million, fat-ass," Spazz said, passing out.

Two ranks of skinned, sweaty boys moved in a phalanx through the woods near the Yellow Trail, stepping deliberately: front rank moving first and stopping, rear rank following. At each stop, they scrutinized. Any foreign, mislaid, or deceased objects got raised into the air, and runners from a distant third rank scurried forth and collected them.

"Neckerchief!" came a call.

"Sock!" came another.

"Dead chipmunk—damn!" came a third, unable to check the mild profanity in view of his discovery.

The third rank's boys stuffed the trash in bags and dragged them to the Yellow Trail. Kevin the Camp Fix-It Man heaved the bags on a flatbed gondola towed by his Golf Cart From Hell. The salvageable personal items would be ferried to Centre des Trois for a grand Lost and Found party.

Camp Counselors and Troopmasters pitched in when an adult's strength came in handy. Every ten minutes, the ranks rotated, so no kids had to do the trash hauling all day. Troops rotated in and out: one hour on, two hours off.

Standing off to one side in his designer Souviens threads, Camp Director Jake Murphy performed no work other than divvying. His mirror shades panned to and fro. He wanted to fetch his rifle so he could complete the look of the villain from *Cool Hand Luke*. His entire adult life revolved around managing youth organizations, and this moment struck him as a perfect one. There was something incredibly coming-of-age about it. Manly maturity. A group of boys doing men's work, outdoors, in the woods … the sun shining on their shirtless skin …

Perhaps too manly. He deliberately looked away before he could drown in the inappropriate testosterone … and leapt a foot in the air when he discovered the carrot-topped biker from the Devil's Troop—the Two Arnold Schwarzeneggers—standing behind him. *Directly* behind him, like a couple inches away. "Please respect my personal space!" Murphy squeaked, hoping it had sounded manly but knowing it hadn't.

"There's been an assault and battery," the Two Arnolds reported, his pale lips barely peeling off his locked-tight teeth. "One of my boys was the victim. Four kids he didn't know kicked the living shit out of him. He's with the Camp Doctor."

Murphy, still cradling his heart from the shock, did not have the facilities to process what this black-clad behemoth had just said. "Are you saying your Troop is fighting again?" he retorted, his mind switching to automatic backup.

"I did not say that. I will repeat what I said, word-for-word; and this time, you'll forget your obvious bias against us."

Operating on automatic, Murphy whipped off his mirror shades, ready to give a piece of his mind to the Two Arnolds for his churlish impudence. The man's conscious mind fought to prevent that, lest it lead to a pounding and perhaps death; in the deadlock, Murphy simply stood still with a blank face.

"There's been an assault and battery. One of my boys was the *victim.* Four kids *he didn't know* kicked the shit out of him."

"And he's with the Camp Doctor," Murphy finished. "Is he in any life-threatening danger?"

"He's not," the Two Arnolds snapped.

"But the alleged assailants *are?"* Murphy fired back, once more losing the struggle with his automatic personality. "Perhaps 'revenge' should be added to the twel—"

"You will deal with this, or *I* will!" The top half of the Two Arnolds's face began a long, slow slide downward. "When you locked up Jon, you practically locked up his father too. Now, *I'm* in charge." The young ogre folded his massive arms. "What are you going to do, Mr. Murphy?"

"I'm sure you want an investigation started right away. But in case you haven't noticed, I'm busy with the clean-up." The man remembered something the Irish kid in the Two Arnolds's Troop had said. "Why would anyone from *another* Troop do it?" Murphy risked pointing a small finger. "Even if that's the case, there will be *no revenge,* no taking the law into one's own hands. *I'm* in charge here."

"Chickenshit."

"Excuse me?!"

"You heard me. Troop 666 has been fucked with for the last time. From now on, we will return fire. Shooting to kill."

Murphy's automatic systems recalled this kid's predilection for using the word "kill" in a most literal-sounding sense and voted to call him out on it. His conscious self vetoed that shit, and even took a step back in caution. "I think this discussion is over, young man."

"Goddamn right," the Two Arnolds said, turning his beastly back on Murphy and stomping away.

Murphy watched him rumble down the Yellow Trail towards Centre des Trois. With a gasp that was half-relief, half-chapped ass, Murphy popped on his shades and swiveled 'round to resume *Cool Hand Luke*-ing this clean-up ... and leapt in the air again to discover the portly Camp Fix-It Man, Kevin, standing not three inches away. "Jesus Christ!"

"Oh, don't bring *him* into it!" Kevin smiled. "Who the hell was that, Murph? I was about ready to tackle him!"

"Him?" Murphy drew a sharp breath. "He's one of the scourge. Perhaps the scourgiest of the bunch."

"Step on in, Matthew," Lyons said. "Pardon the mess! We've been insanely busy since the storm, especially after the National Guard took the injured kids to Lawrence + Memorial."

"I understand," young Father said, entering Lyons's tiny office/records room and taking a seat in a creaky metal chair.

Lyons circled his gunmetal desk and flopped his gaunt bones into a creaky chair of his own. Despite the stress of the storm and its cleanup, and despite Father's pea-soup-colored uniform showing the block numerals of **666**. Lyons projected his usual jovial self. "What can I do for you, young man?"

Father folded his fingers together pleasantly. "Mr. Lyons, we need to discuss the mishap earlier this morning."

Lyons duplicated the finger fold. "With your boy 'Spazz.'"

"Yes. The Troop in Campsite Trois is responsible."

Lyons cocked his heart-shaped face. "I'd've readily believed you a few days ago. But after the brawl the first night, and the behavior I witnessed at the dance—Troop 666 isn't exactly an angelic bunch. And now to cast blame on others ... "

"I won't deny our sins," Father said. "But in Job 11, it says God *will make us answer for our guilt.*"

"And has He? I have a daughter, right here in this building, the same age as the girl Jon felt up. For all I know he tried that shit on her, too. Do you have a Bible quote for *that?*"

Father slumped his shoulders a bit. "Mr. Oldroyd let you keep Jon in the Cell. After all his fuming at Mr. Murphy and swear words, he understood that Jon needed punishment." The young lad spread his hands. "Even the guilty feel that the guilty need punishment."

Lyons soaked that in. The kid before him, not yet eighteen, had the calm and understanding of a well-adjusted adult, and made a compassionate case with only a few words. Either he was a fantastic liar, or a future cardinal. "Okay, I'll listen to your side of the story. Why do you suspect Campsite Trois?"

"A witness, but he stayed away cuz he was outnumbered."

Lyons opened his mouth to be trite ("So much for 'bravery.'"). A little quiet air came out instead; any trite remark would've been Murphy's by proxy. "He can identify them?"

"He already has," Father said. "I'm sorry, thought that was obvious. It's how we know the folk at Campsite Trois did it."

Lyons churned options in his head. The most appealing was suicide. "Our course of action," he said, trying to make one up. "Would be," he said, failing. "Asking Troop 73's Troopmaster," he determined, then glanced yearningly at his wrists.

"I took the liberty. I visited Campsite Trois on my way here and met with him. Mr. Dixon."

"Ah," Lyons said, recalling the name. "What did he say?"

"That he didn't know anything about it, and please leave."

The door to Lyons's office slapped open. "We got a call from Ranger Rick," Murphy said, attentively shuffling a hundred sheets of paper with practiced fingers. "Chef Jim answered it and said Tricky Dicky got his airline to—"

Murphy halted. His slits (#240, "What are *you* doing here?") stared down at Father. He looked over at Lyons and said, "Ah, this is about that thing. You're dealing with it?"

Lyons chucked his list of options. Time to face the truth: Murphy would do nothing to help Troop 666, and they may actually have been victims here. "I am dealing with it, Murph."

"Very good. I need the AL-2 forms on those injured boys ASAP. When Ranger Rick gets back and 'takes command,' he'll wanna browbeat the insurance rep personally."

"Will do," Lyons said.

Murphy walked out and yanked shut the door.

Lyons waited a second. Murphy's signature footfalls (from his crummy Nike hiking boots) went along the corridor and down the staircase. "We're booked up, so it's not like I can move you to another campsite," Lyons said softly. "I need to speak to Mr. Dixon. Personally. I'll switch Troop 73 to third shift so your Troop and his aren't put on clean-up detail together. In the meantime, watch over your boys."

"I've been trying," Father sighed. "Mr. Maguire's at the hospital with our wounded. And Mr. Oldroyd has lost control of the Troop. Our Junior Troopmaster took over and he's the avenging type. He might *lead* us into battle." Father aimed folded hands at Lyons. "This is why I need your help, sir."

"The chances of retaliation will get smaller as time goes by, so *now's* the time for vigilance," Lyons said. He got to his feet. "Watch your Troop 24/7. I'll watch Troop 73."

Chapter 28

THE RETURN OF ART, THE AVENGER.

ART MAGUIRE SHUT his eyes as the van veered down Camp
Souviens Road. It was early Wednesday evening. Art had managed to
lose about twenty-four hours of summer camp because Calvin was
getting laid!

Well, there was more to it than that. A branch fell on Calvin; Cindy
ran for help; Art ran into her; and now Art had a class III shoulder
separation with a torn ligament; and no one actually got laid. Still, Art
had his scapegoat!

Camp Souviens's lunatic-looking janitor, Mick, "drove" the van
past the Ranger's Office. The muscled maniac bypassed the parking lot
and went straight down the Red Trail, far too fast along such a thin path
for anyone's comfort. The van skidded to a graceless halt across the
packed dirt of Centre des Trois and the passengers hurriedly debarked:
nine injured boys and three Troopmasters/dads who'd accompanied
them to the hospital in nearby New London.

"Hiya, fellas!" Satan said, goose-stepping their way. Art and the
other patients turned over the insurance papers that should go to the
camp (and later, their liability insurance company). The remaining
twenty sheets (!) Art would have to lug back with him to camp, and
eventually give over to Gus's dad, Claudius Jacoby, D.O., back in
Axsubeen.

Satan gave them an update on the camp's condition. Art didn't
care. Satan told them there was a dodgeball tournament in progress at
the Remy F. Lacroix Memorial Field. Art didn't care. Five minutes of
this rambling! Satan finally offered them specially cooked chicken
nuggets in the caf and told them to take care of themselves tonight.

Art and his dad scarfed a couple plates of food. To stand from the picnic dining table, Art needed to push up with his right hand, maintaining the balance lost to the heavy plastic cast on his upper left arm and the sling which held it close to his chest. It totally sucked.

The Maguires slogged down the Green Trail. A breeze from the reservoir fluttered the insurance papers in Mr. Maguire's hand. A bottle of pills rattled in Art's pocket. The boy's chest was sore where the sling was tight. The walk took forever. Passing down the by-way to Campsite Quatre, they found a latrine which smelt of fresh chemicals and a Fire of Inky blazing. Inky sat by himself, gazing into the flames.

"Where is everyone?" asked Mr. Maguire.

"Biding their time," growled Inky.

Despite this odd answer, Art kept his apathy going. "Bedtime," he said, meandering down the goat-path to the Beaver Squad tent. The canvas flaps were shut but a Coleman lantern glow came through cracks. Art poked his head in.

"Artichoky!" yelped Spazz, sitting up in his bunk. "Join the walkin'-wounded!" In the sharp propane light, Art saw crimson-splotched bandages on Spazz's face and bandage-like lumps under his tight-fitting AC/DC shirt.

Art climbed into the tent. "Yo, what happened to you?!"

"Not much, Artillery," Spazz hiccupped. "I was walkin' *over the river / and through the woods* when four ninja assmunches pounced! *Ffft! Ffft! Wham! Bang!* And I'm bleedin' like a gall-dern waterfall. I even passed out. So's they tell me!"

Art sat in his bunk—then recoiled in fright. Not only was Father lying in a bunk across the aisle, fast asleep, but Ryan Phillips lurked in a dark rear corner of the eight-man tent. And lurked *well!* "Yo, Ry— what's with you?"

"They're bodyguardin'," Spazz said. "Can't be too careful!"

Ryan, calmly jotting notes in the margin of his Book, acknowledged Art with a raised eyebrow.

Spazz flicked back his blond locks. "Where's Calvincible?"

"Still at the hospital. Fucked up his elbow real bad—the branch cut this ligament here almost clean in half." Art pointed with his good finger towards his slung arm's inner elbow.

"They gotta amputate?" Spazz grinned. "He'll hafta switch hands when he's churnin' his butter!"

"He's gotta have an operation when we get back. But they also think he got a brain bruise when Jon clocked him."

"A brain bruise?" Ryan said. "You can *bruise* your brain?"

Art explained: "It's when your head gets hit so hard that your brain actually *smashes* against the inside of your skull."

"Holy shit," Spazz said, "Now *that's* bangin' your head!"

"He didn't seem *that* bad," Ryan registered.

"Ain't like he was all scrambled-eggs and shit," Spazz said.

"I'm sure he'll tell ya all the gory details," Art sighed.

"That's cool shit *you* got bolted on, Artisan-Fartisan!"

"It sucks dick," Art reported, "but I'll live."

"What's it for? Broken arm?"

"Just a separated shoulder."

Spazz affected a haughty voice. "Yez. Juzt a zeparated zhoulder. Trivial."

"When you're on these," Art smiled, rattling the bottle of pills in his pocket, "it's pretty fuckin' trivial."

"Cool beaners for pool cleaners! Give the Spazzster a hit!"

"No way. You might be allergic."

"Come on, Raiders of the Lost Art, I'll take that chance! I'm hurtin' more than yer mama's snatch after I boffed her!"

"Oh yeah—good to be back!"

They sat in silence for a bit. "Why is Father here?" Art asked in a conspiratorial tone. "Who beat you up? Chicken?"

The circus in Spazz's voice took a rare lunch break. "Wasn't any of us," he said calmly, like a normal kid. "There were three or four of them. We think it's them jerk-offs from Campsite Trays, or Troys, or whatever—Campsite Three."

"Really? Why would some other Troop attack you?"

"Got me. I only know's what he said," Spazz shrugged, pointing a thumb over at Ryan.

Art looked at him. "And how do you know?"

"I was there," Ryan urged, in a dark voice. "A little ways off, getting wood for Inky's Fire."

"So, you saw it happen?"

"I didn't 'see' it."

"Then ... I'll ask again: how do you know?"

Ryan hunched his eyes up from the Book, chin against his chest, a look seen in every Stanley Kubrick film.

"Y'know," Spazz laughed, "I don't even blame this heiny-hobbit for not getting involved."

"Shit, Ryan's muscles coulda tipped the scales in a fight!"

"He ain't a fan of the Spazzster. I accept that. But Inky's got my back. He's running the show now—Dick'll's out of a job!—and Inky's ready to nuke them noodle dicks." He tilted his head towards the dozing Father. *"He's* being all 'love thy neighbor' about it, though."

Art bent over to take off his boots—with only one hand. Life would be miserable for some time. "Tomorrow," he declared, pulling his sleeping bag over his head. "I'll have a plan worked out by then. We'll totally avenge you."

Spazz made Ronnie James Dio horns. "Awesome, gnarly, and tubular! Spazzmattacks will abound!"

Camp Souviens had four memorial areas, all named after an in-law of the Camp Ranger (who owned this whole property). When Mr. Grant designed Camp Souviens, he got a list of names from his wife. Most were easy to assign: Racine the father-in-law/actor for the amphitheater, Chamberlin the mother-in-law/hotelier for the staff quarters, and Clement the great uncle/Olympic swimmer for the swimming shack. Remy Lacroix had been his wife's first cousin once removed, and after spending all nine of his years incessantly terrorizing his parents by setting fire to everything and leaping off everything else, one day he decided to try both at once. When Mr. Grant couldn't immediately find a thing to name the late pre-teen pyro gyro after, he said, "Eh, that field over there'll do."

The Lacroix Memorial Field was just a field. A flat bit of land with low grass. No paths, pavement, marked areas, light standards, sign-posts, or structures. Just a spot to have parades and play sports. Dodgeball raged there this early evening. Several Troopmasters moved their trucks to the field's edges to fling lights on the action.

One Troopmaster—who had never owned a truck—felt a tug on his sleeve, and agreed to step away to the adjacent parking lot. "Thanks for giving me a minute," Lyons said.

The stubby Troopmaster, Dixon by name, gave a slight shrug, the sort of motion one can only pull off correctly if one comes from *real* money. "The benefit of having a small Troop," he said, "is I know my boys can be trusted if I'm not around."

Very choice words, thought Lyons, *almost prescient to a fault.* "They're right over there, playing dodgeball," he said aloud, waving a gaunt arm towards Lacroix Field.

"As I said," the man said. And that was all he said.

"You're the only Troopmaster in Troop 73?"

"I'm all they need," Dixon nodded.

"How many kids are in your Troop?"

"Six, at the moment."

"*Six?* In the whole Troop?!"

"At the moment."

"What about the minimum roster requirement?"

Dixon gave the slight shrug again. It might as well have been a thousand-dollar bill wrapped around an extended middle finger. "It's political. We are a very proud Troop. I've managed to keep our tradition despite roster policies. It's made us a few enemies of late, but let them kick up dust. We persist."

"Funny, you bringing that up. Have you met Troop 666?"

Dixon made to lean his arm on the nearest vehicle, but noticed it was a Volvo station wagon and pulled the arm back as if afraid of contagion. "I know what this is about, Lyons."

Lyons's bald head roared with flame. "Then I'd very much like to hear your opinion on it."

"The attack happened at about ten this morning, if their J.C. is to be believed. My—"

"Is there any reason to doubt him?"

"We're talking about a representative sent by their T.M.—this Oldroyd character. I hear that 'man's' own son was locked away in some sort of confinement yesterday." Dixon coughed darkly. "Starting a battle, skipping out on K.P., sexually assaulting a Cookie Girl. If the acorn didn't fall too far from *that* tree, can any of the kid's father's hangers-on be trusted?"

Lyons needed a moment. "But he was their Junior Chaplain. *His* character can't be questioned."

"One wouldn't think."

One wouldn't think?! "Can you account for your whole Troop at ten o'clock this morning?" Lyons asked directly.

"My boys were cleaning up our C.S. at that time."

"You can prove this?"

"*I* was there," urged Dixon, this time with a dose of tartness. "I'm not sure how these morons from Pennsyl-tucky got the deranged idea that any of *my* boys is responsible."

Dixon made it a point to end that paragraph there, then start another: "Because they're not."

"Your very first words to me were an alibi statement," Lyons said. "I hadn't even brought them or the fight up yet."

"We are the accused." Dixon walked away. "The burden isn't on us. Prove I'm lying, Lyons."

Chapter 29

JESUS FUCKING CHRIST (OUR LORD) RANGER RICK.
THURSDAY, JULY 30, 1987.

ONE MINUTE BEFORE dawn, a black Ford F-250 roared down Camp Souviens Road piloted by one Jesus Fucking Christ (Our Lord) Ranger Rick. Alternatively known as Rick "Nature Boy" Flair, Tricky Dicky, That Big Prick Grant, Ranger Dick, Dickhead Rick, Rick the Prick, and Bitchy Richie. "Mr. Grant" was what everyone called him to his face — the other monikers only saw employ under Camp Director Jake Murphy's breath.

Mr. Grant had been in Florida on his first summer vacation in twenty years. After a stirring Tuesday afternoon's activities with Mrs. Grant (golfing, dining, and humping), Mr. Grant slouched on the hotel bed and clicked on the Orlandoan six o'clock news; next to the rug on the anchorman's head sat a superimposed box depicting video of damage done by a storm to lands "east of Long Island Sound."

Before the toupéed anchorman could utter another syllable, Mr. Grant was on the phone. As the sports anchor jumped onscreen with news of Bill Buckner signing with the California Angels, Mr. Grant suffered through the slow, stuttery delivery of Camp Chef Jim, who mentioned the National Guard's invasion of Camp Souviens. While a large-breasted weatherperson cheerily told the greater Orlando region that sunshine and 93° was the forecast once again, Mr. Grant had booked the next plane to New Haven.

Mrs. Grant would have none of it. She'd spent her first thirty years in Quebec City, and the next thirty with her husband in a Connecticut forest; she wouldn't end her first trip to Florida early for all the Tim Horton's in Canada. "Use sunblock," Mr. Grant urged, packing his bag in ten seconds. "And stay away from that nude beach." He kissed her goodbye.

Mr. Grant took the stairs eight flights down to the lobby, where he left a large pile of cash with the check-in man to cover the inevitable drinks tab his lush of a wife would run up. He slammed open the hotel's door to the street, and in the process knocked over a fifteen-year-old kid with flabby sides and waves of bleached blond hair. The kid's parents were most upset. "Sorry," Mr. Grant said, leaping in a cab.

As it turned out, the next plane from Orlando to New Haven wouldn't leave until first thing Wednesday, and even then it needed first to stop in Chicago, Wichita, and Pittsburgh, in that order; there was an excruciating delay in Wichita when the ground crew could not empty the "blue ice" tank. Then the plane got grounded at Pittsburgh when a stupid flap went on strike. "We're sorry for the delay," the captain announced, as the sun set on Wednesday. The passengers sat in a departure lounge twiddling their thumbs angrily. At nine o'clock, they were taken one at a time to a counter to speak to a tidy gray-haired lady in a cobalt blue airline sport-coat and skirt.

"New Haven," Mr. Grant told her sternly, "or else."

She handed him a pass and Mr. Grant was in New Haven by midnight. He got his truck from the park-and-fly garage and got as far as New London before noticing his gas gauge. While refilling at the nearest Texaco station, he was astonished to find, one pump down, his old high school prom date, Margie Horne, feeding gas to a Buick. One thing led to another which led to another hotel room and another hasty departure and another collision with a teenaged boy outside the lobby. The boy watched from his prone position on the asphalt as the front right tire of Mr. Grant's Ford F-250 flattened the kelly green Hartford Whalers cap which had popped off the boy's head. "Sorry," Mr. Grant said, burning rubber back to camp.

As dawn broke on Thursday, Mr. Grant exited I-95 at Rte. 117 and made two lefts. Seconds later he turned onto Camp Souviens Road. He was quite relieved, so far. The sign featuring the mascot Lefty still stood. Mr. Grant roared up the road to the Ranger's Office, an addition to his modest ranch house.

Hustling into his Office, he remembered that Lyons's daughter would be sleeping in the back room; so Mr. Grant kept the noise down while he brewed up some coffee in the lobby. Rounding the counter, he checked his desk. His "in" bin had ten AL-2 forms; ten kids had been hospitalized.

"Jesus," breathed Mr. Grant, grabbing his key ring off a wall hook. He found a bleary Wren at the Office's counter, stealing his coffee. "I need a cup," he urged, filling his prized *I'm A Ranger—You're a Stranger* Thermos. "The rest is yours."

"Thanks," the young girl said, but he was already gone.

Mr. Grant got in his truck and zoomed down the Red Trail to the Chamberlin Memorial Building. Marching into the west wing, he found neither Murphy nor Lyons was in quarters. He filed over to the east wing; Chef Jim, Janitor Mick, Lifeguard Aaron, Doctor George, and Fix-It Man Kevin were gone too.

He stopped. The door to the Cell was closed!

Mr. Grant jingled his considerable key ring, unlocked the door, and found a teenage boy with bright blond hair and an acne problem blowing Z's on the bunk. In one corner sat a heap of dirty laundry—so he'd been in here a couple of days, at least. "Christ," Mr. Grant said, hustling out.

Mr. Grant drove down the Red Trail to the Racine Amphitheater. Just past it, he came upon Kevin's Golf Cart From Hell parked in the Red Trail's accompanying drain-ditch. The Golf Cart From Hell had a custom chassis, painted glossy black and engineered to accommodate everything Kevin needed to be an effective fix-it man. Twenty-four storage compartments, a dozen per side, held everything from monkey-wrenches to chainsaws to dried guava halves, Kevin's favorite snack. A cable wench jutted out the front; a trailer hitch jutted out the back; a blue police light adorned the roof. The bumper sticker read "I Brake For Nobody." Kevin himself was nowhere to be found. Mr. Grant discovered why the cart had been parked here—the scorched carcass of a passed-on oak lay about a hundred fifty feet into the forest, just behind the stage. It looked like the tree had exploded. "Almighty," he said, quickening his pace to Centre des Trois.

He parked at the caf and took a detour to the kitchen in search of a snack. Alas, breakfast ingredients lay, uncooked, on Jim's stainless steel prep table. Mr. Grant climbed the stairs, stormed down the hall, and threw open Murphy's door.

"Mr. Grant!" Lyons said, standing. "Welcome home!"

The Camp Ranger nodded to Lyons and the other chief staffers (Mick, Jim, Aaron, George, and Kevin). Murphy, sitting at his immense oaken desk, held his face in a frozen position, indicating histrionically that Mr. Grant *was* interrupting.

Mr. Grant set his Thermos on the venerable wooden bookcase. "Hello, Jake," he prompted with agita, his long lumberjack beard standing on end.

Murphy stood up against his will. "Mr. Grant. I got word you'd be back ASAP."

"*I* only got word from Jim. He mentioned the National Guard ... but not kids going to the hospital."

Murphy glared over at Jim, as if it was all the googly-eyed chef's fault. "He didn't want to upset you, that's all."

"I'm sure. Were they taken to Lawrence + Memorial?"

"Yes. They're all back except the one. He's getting discharged later this morning. I'll send Mick to get him."

"Oh no. You'll see to the job personally."

"What?!" Murphy bellowed.

"I called *three times* yesterday. I'm sure Jim passed on all the messages." The Ranger didn't bother to look at Jim's worried, bearded face for confirmation. "You plainly ignored them all, so this is your punishment."

"You've no idea the kind of strain I've been under!"

"Surprise surprise, you have a tough job."

Murphy gave the special custom-fit slits (#687, "If you weren't my boss, why, I oughta ... ") that only saw duty with Mr. Grant: half-open eyes with very little malice to them. Then he gave full-blown, lethal slits (#2, *"FUCK OFF!"*) to the rest of the staff. The staff took their cue and exited with due haste.

"Start with the kid in the Cell," sighed Mr. Grant.

"No," frowned Murphy. "I'll start with the Devil's Troop, from which that kid spawned."

Chapter 30

THE RETURN OF CALVIN, THE REVENGER.

JON OLDROYD SAT at a little desk, staring at his copy of the *Handbook for Troopers*. The Cell sucked, man. His dad had just left to take the breakfast tray back to Centre des Trois, leaving Jon alone once more. Some of the other Troop 666 guys occasionally dropped by, every once in a while, on their way to having fun somewhere ... but for the most part, Jon's life since Monday night was equal parts 1) alone in the Cell, or 2) alone in the Cell with his mean-ass dad, who'd spend hours telling the kid what a fuck-up he was. "Hopefully yer learnin' a lesson."

Jon learned a lesson, all right. He slammed shut the book and was about to embark on yet another engrossing study of the ceiling when the door opened. Mick, the deranged-looking Camp Janitor, leaned in. "Hey Charles Manson, ya got a visitor."

Mick stepped aside and held open the door, which normally would've swung shut and locked automatically.

A tall kid slanted into view, filling the doorway with his wide shoulders. By his gait, the kid didn't seem quite awake. "Thank you, sir," he told Mick.

"Knock when yer done," Mick said, letting the door shut.

The kid flopped his body into the visitor's chair.

Jon stared at him: the flowing mane of sickly white hair; the smaller but professionally applied bandage covering the stitches above his eyebrow; the faded red New England Patriots T-shirt, clinging to his bulky torso unappealingly; the large blue sweats on his legs, which had "C.S.P." in white letters silk-screened on them; and his right arm encased in a sling of white cloth, holding it in place across his chest. The slung elbow was itself swathed in a tight bandage wrap. This kid was not having a fun week either. He appeared haggard—maybe stoned!

"Hello," Calvin Connor said, blankly.

"What's up," returned Jon Oldroyd, softly.

Calvin eased back. "Just got back from hospital, thought I'd say hi on my way down." He looked at Jon and said, "Hi."

"What happened to you, dude?" Jon burped. His eyes went wide, crunching up the acne on his forehead. "You break yer arm? And yer hair's white as a fuckin' sheet! What the hell's been goin' on out there?!"

Calvin sucked in a breath. "It's a long story, Jon. Hydrogen peroxide, trees exploding, doctors, cops. You name it."

"Cops! You ain't in trouble, are you?"

"I ain't in trouble."

Three seconds passed.

Calvin then leaned forward. "But *you* could be."

Jon pushed his chair back from the desk. *"Now* what? Whatever it is, you know I didn't do it! I been sittin' in this—" His mind added two plus two. "You told 'em *I* hit ya, didn't ya?"

"I did," leered Calvin. "The cop wanted to know how my head got dented. I told him everything. See my outfit?"

Jon took another look at Calvin's duds. "The Patriots? Or the sweats—C.S.P.?"

"Connecticut State Police. But they like to say 'Crush Stupid Perps.' The cop gave me these clothes. He was really interested in what goes on here at Souviens—he visited me twice."

Jon put up his palms. "I'm sorry, dude! I didn't mean to bash your brains in! It was an accident—"

"Stop!" Calvin shouted. He planted his free hand on the table. "That goon only gave me five minutes so I gotta get to the point: Sergeant White wants me to file assault charges—with, like, the camp staff charged too. *That's* what he wants, revenge on the camp. Revenge for something long ago. He can't do anything to them—or you—unless *I* agree to it."

"Then don't!"

"I won't! Under *one* condition."

"What's that?" Jon gulped.

"I got a plan to annihilate the dick who bleached my hair."

Unsure and unmoved, Jon asked, "Who's that?"

"No way, José," Calvin said firmly. "With your da here, I don't dare tell you. Oldroyd must not know *anything*. My plan needs to be secret. It includes me, Spazz, and you."

"Spazz?"

"And you."

"But I'm here! In jail!"

"How often does your da visit?"

"After every meal," Jon sighed. "Stays for like two or three hours. I think Inky is running the Troop instead of Maguire."

Supper was at 5 every night, so ... "I'm busting you out tonight at eight sharp. Got a watch?"

"No."

Calvin took his Swatch off and slipped it to Jon. "Don't have it on your wrist where your fuckin' da will see it. You'll learn the rest of the plan at 8 tonight. Be ready."

"Sure," Jon said. His zitty face sprouted the tiny saplings of hope. "We'll be even then? What're you gonna tell that cop?"

"To fuck off. Without me he's got no case. He'll have to bust Camp Souviens another way. And you and me'll be even."

"Great! So how ya gonna break me out?"

Calvin got to his feet. "I gotta work that out. But it's like ten hours away. You're going to have to trust me now."

Jon hesitated. "If it means we'll be even, and I'm gettin' outta trouble with the cops—sure."

"Good. See you tonight."

The furniture in Murphy's office had a conversation: the chairs told the oaken desk what an odd week it was. The master chair welcomed this break in the action; better than giving Murphy's break something to sit on! The bookcase, older and wiser, haughtily droned, "The worst is yet to come."

The maple-wood door slapped open, bleating in pain. Murphy marched in fuming. Mr. Grant sauntered in three steps behind, reporting, "Careful! I'm not buying you a new door."

"Buy me a new job." Murphy flopped in his throne (which also bleated). "You know what happened in New London?"

"You didn't say. Too busy stomping around in a huff."

"A complete massacre." Murphy flipped off his fitted Souviens cap, exposing a sour purple nose and a bruised right eye.

"Ouch," volunteered Mr. Grant.

Murphy blew irritated air through bitter lips. "I got to the hospital and parked in front, in the loading zone, since I was only to be there two minutes, tops. I go inside and there's Mr. Lab-Coat-Hair watching *Hogan's Heroes* in the lobby."

"Who—"

"That mick from Troop 666, now let me finish!" Murphy crushed the desk blotter with irascible (but manicured) hands.

Mr. Grant zipped his lip, but made plain he'd chosen to.

"He sees me and gets up," ranted Murphy. "He wasn't even dazed—brain bruise my ass! God knows why they kept him there *two* nights, except to run up the bill."

"Well, he did have a broken elbow."

Murphy slapped his desk and spun his chair 'round.

Knowing the guy wouldn't continue until he was allowed to do so uninterrupted, Mr. Grant took his cue: "So what happened nex—"

"We go outside to my car," Murphy went on, without turning back around. "Then who the hell should lay a hand on my shoulder but Bobby White!"

Mr. Grant's face drooped in mild horror. "Bobby White?"

Murphy spun around with wild eyes. "Only twenty years older, a hell of a lot thinner, and in a state police uniform!"

"Yeah, someone told me the guy was a statey now."

"A goddamn disgruntled one at that! He called me by name then blasted me for parking in the loading zone. He went on shouting for five minutes. Then he popped me with his baton and gave me a six-hundred-dollar ticket!"

"He hit you?"

Arms gesticulated frantically and eyeballs sprung from sockets. "Look at my face, Mr. Grant! He's scarred me for life!"

Darkly: "You scarred *him* for life."

"Accidentally! But that does not justify use of the baton, certainly not at this late date! Even if I, for example, told him to go fuck himself, I would have done so politely. Besides, he has a code of conduct to—"

"Wait wait: how do you *politely* say 'go fuck yourself?'"

Murphy made one slit (half of #384, "Watch it, pal!"). "Another comment like that, and I will demonstrate," he hissed. "White cursed first and cursed worse. He dredged up expletives unlike none I've ever suffered. And cops simply aren't allowed to cold-cock law-abiding citizens!"

"'Law-abiding?' You said you parked in the loading zone!"

"F—" Murphy bit his tongue. *"Six ... hundred ... dollars!"*

Mr. Grant rubbed his bushy beard. "Seems exorbitant."

Actually leaping in the air: "EXORBITANT! I've never gotten a parking ticket bigger than twenty bucks in my entire life! You realize I'll need to tap the operating expenses account—"

"Oh no you won't," Mr. Grant said, definitively. "You admitted to parking illegally, so pay from your own cash. We can ill-afford another expense in the wake of this storm."

"Fu—" Murphy bit his tongue once more. "I'll take you to court. Any judge'll side with me, plus restitution and interest."

The Camp Ranger folded his arms defiantly. "Then call your lawyer. I'm sure he'll remind you that stupidity does not hold water in court. Witness your divorce."

"Fuc—" Murphy ground his teeth so hard that several hairs from his thin chin-strap beard plummeted to his lap. "I blame you for this, Mr. Grant! I mean, sending the director of a major camping reservation to a hospital in a distant land, just to pick up a brat with a broken elbow! We have lackeys here!"

Mr. Grant sat his woodsy ass on Murphy's desk and picked up the name plate: CAMP DIR. J. MURPHY. "This means," he said, pointing at the title before the name, "Head Lackey."

"That Calvin got injured in the woods near Racine with two of his Devil's Troopmates," Murphy surged on. "But Wren was with them when the National Guard got there. I'll bet she was giving herself up to all three of 'em, even the mulatto. Why else would they be deep in the woods, during a storm?"

"That's disgusting," Mr. Grant said. "You got no way to prove that. Don't blame the girl for what your mouth caused."

"And that mick didn't say anything the whole ride back," Murphy plunged on. "I suggested to him that Lyons's daughter may not be the best company to keep—and he ignored me! Me, with my blackened face, which happened cuz I came to give *him* a ride!" The man flung his hands up. "It *all* comes back to Troop 666! *Everything* comes back to the Devil's Troop! The goddamn storm was probably their doing—black magic!"

"Murph, you're getting hysterical!"

Murphy sighed a sigh so gargantuan that it needed ten whole seconds to complete. He nearly slid out of the chair.

"When you've relaxed a bit," the Ranger said, "come find me at the clean-up operation. *Do not* speak to our customers while you're still in this mood." With that, the man left.

Murphy's office was oddly quiet.

"Told you so," the bookcase said.

Calvin slogged down the by-way to Campsite Quatre's fire circle to find the two adult leaders having smokes and cracking jokes. "And here's our Purple Heart recipient himself!" Mr. Maguire announced. The grown-ups warmly asked about his condition. Unable to recite the complete tale, being sick and tired and all—and dubious of their sudden interest in his well-being, considering Oldroyd's usual antipathy and Maguire's usual apathy—Calvin used an expurgated version of four succinct sentences. He never mentioned painkillers. Then Father trotted down from the latrine and asked how he was doing. Calvin was suddenly very sick and tired of being sick and tired. He curtly headed off for bed before anyone else could show up.

He sloped up to the Hawk Squad tent, peering in to find Sandy reading his hardcover of *IT* in Ryan's bunk.* Art sat in Calvin's bunk, dozing lightly. Sandy's brother Denny was in Jon's vacant bunk, bang-

---

* He'd made it to page 14.

ing his hairy head to his Walkman. Why were all these Beaver Squad kids in the Hawk tent?!

Calvin made his left hand flat and whacked the deck floor with it. The three Beavers sprang up and bombarded him with questions. Calvin was, by now, extremely sick and tired of being very sick and tired about being sick and tired. "Don't take this the wrong way," he said, "but fuck the lot of you. I'll tell you *everything* at lunch. I'm so exhausted. Go away."

"We heard you were on yer way back, and we been here waitin' for ya," Sandy said. "We gotta talk."

Calvin kicked off his Reeboks, ejected Art from his bunk, flopped his arse in it, and closed both eyes. "Sleep," mused he.

"We got some real shit going on," Denny said ruefully.

"Sleep!" mused he.

"We're officially at war with Campsite Trois," Art added.

Calvin popped one eye open and cast it at the three guys standing over him. "We're *what* now?" he breathed tartly.

"At war. For real," Art said. "And some of us are sneaking away at lunch, since phase one of my plan happens then."

"Another war?" roared Calvin. "What's that make this one, World War IV? World War V? *World War IX?!"*

"They beat the shit outta Spazz, dude! We—"

"Fuck that, Sandy! Count me out!"

Sandy exhaled angrily.

Calvin growled, then sat up in his bunk. "Thanks, you cunts. I'm too pissed off to sleep. So. Your story, then."

Chapter 31
WORLD WAR IV, PHASE ONE.

AN HOUR LATER, Gus shook Calvin's good arm. "Lunchtime, Calvin!" He got up and had Gus help untie and re-tie the sling so the lad could put on a shirt that fit. Calvin went through his rucksack and dipped into his poker chip supply, stuffing one in the pocket of the C.S.P. sweats. He headed to the fire circle and joined the leaders of Operation World War IV (Art Maguire, Ryan Phillips, Spazz Watson, and the Sandmiller brothers). Eventually, Junior Troopmaster Inky Schultz yelled, "Fall in."

Once in ranks, Inky called roll and the Troop marched down the Green Trail in pretty rigid formation. The two adults, Oldroyd and Maguire, brought up the rear. The latter contently lumbered along making small talk about the Pirates and how bullshit *Platoon* was, while the former sucked down a Marlboro and whined about making the long walk to the Chamberlin building and back to see his son ... while his predecessor's son pretended to be the Big Cheese.

Inky slowed his pace to march beside Gus. "Might as well be the Hawk Squad's official Captain now. Not like your superior's been around much." Inky gave Calvin a look.

Calvin merely pursed his lips in response.

Gus, apparently having lost what little mind he'd had to begin with, flared his bulbous eyes at Inky and snapped, "Who died and made you God? Leave Calvin alone!"

Inky blinked in surprise. "Watch your mouth, *Acting* Lieutenant!" He fell back to terrorize the Beaver Patrol next.

Chef Jim's lunch meal was grilled hot dogs and sausages, with optional roasted peppers and onions or sauerkraut. Like all meals minus those eaten during arguments about God, this was a quiet affair;

everyone was too busy scarfing to chat.

As Calvin munched on what he lovingly called "a banger in a bun," he thought about his revenge. Talk about tricky—Operation World War IV, Art's plan to avenge Spazz, included the very target of Calvin's own plan (Operation Nuclear Payback); and Spazz himself was a vital cog in both. And since Campsite Trois had attacked Spazz when he was alone, he hadn't been left alone at any moment since. Worse still, Spazz openly feared spooks hiding in every tree, ready to kill him.

Calvin toyed with the idea of volunteering for bodyguard duty (allowing him to get Spazz alone), but in Calvin's current state, he'd hardly be able to defend himself! Ergo, Calvin needed a plan just to ask Spazz about his plan!

With fifteen minutes left in lunch, Oldroyd fetched a tray of food for his son and slogged off up the Red Trail. A few minutes after that, Spazz mimed washing dishes to Art, who turned to Inky and said, "Spazz wants to head to K.P."

Inky glared at them. He yelled over to the Hawk table for Calvin. "You and Art both have one good arm. You can wash dishes as a team. Take that headbanger trash with you."

The three of them made a defeated trudge to the kitchen and passed through the door. Suddenly everyone involved in World War IV broke character: Inky (along with Sandy, Denny, and Ryan) widened their eyes and watched the crowded caf for their enemies' reaction; while in the kitchen, Spazz took off running, out the dishroom's screen door and down the Green Trail, leaving Calvin and Art to deal with the bug-eyed, bedraggly bearded, and curiously present Chef Jim.

"No offense," Art said to the chef.

"N-n-none taken," the man stammered. "If he g-g-got the runs that f-f-fast, it didn't come from m-m-my cooking!"

Art and Calvin laughed and popped in the dishroom. Cindy wasn't there, but she often showed up just as the meal was ending. "What a break!" Art smiled. "Inky set that up perfectly."

"No way your da or Father will suspect us," Calvin nodded. "I gotta say, Spazz's paranoid act had me fooled!"

"It ain't all an act, but I'm glad he had the balls to do this."

Spazz booked as fast as his teenage legs could manage. Hooking down the by-way to Campsite Trois, he held up his buck knife, ready to strike … but the place was vacant. Spazz tucked away the blade, drew a small notebook and pencil, and made a rough sketch. From his laden pockets he fetched a length of thin nylon cord (as used for tying tents to pegs); the cord was exactly ten feet long, and Spazz stationed himself at various points, holding one end and flinging the other this way and that. He also hurled it upward at various tree branches above the fire circle's edge. After recording measurements, Spazz flipped the notebook over and tore off a sheet on the opposite side that already had writing on it. Leaving this sheet in the ashy fire circle, Spazz did an about face and ran.

Art used his calculator watch to time Spazz; he came back in the door just over eight minutes after going out. The headbanger bent at the waist, hands on kneecaps, sucking air. "Ain't run that fast since the last time I porked yer mama and yer pops came home early," he wheezed, looking straight down.

"Gotta be talkin' about *your* ma," Calvin said to Art cheerfully. "My da *never* comes home early!"

"Shut the fuck up!" Art said with a laugh.

Cindy popped in the kitchen and jumped to find all these boys here. "Calvin!" she shouted, very happy to see him.

"Hold on," he told her, turning to Art. "How about you go back with the Troop? Tell Father that Ken said he didn't need ya. Then you can get the dirt from Inky and all."

"Okay," Art said, a twinkle in his blue eye. "Ready, Spazz?"

Calvin almost panicked—he'd meant for only Art to leave. But Spazz waved Art off. "Ken *always* needs me!" he hissed. "That nip's mama's makin' sushi for me right now!"

Art nodded. "We'll go over your notes when you guys get back." He took rueful note of how Cindy didn't wait for this conversation to end and gave Calvin a long hug, tucking her body and arms away from his sling. Without another word, the kid ducked back through the kitchen.

A second later, the K.P. leader Ken Izerman came in the dishroom. He exchanged pleasantries with Calvin and asked if he was fit for duty. "I have a broken elbow," Calvin said.

"I'm on it," Spazz said, a heartfelt comment that came with a friendly hand on Calvin's shoulder. "You two go suck face."

Everyone laughed. Ken shrugged and said, "Might as well stay here in the dishroom, Spazz. Mike'll go get the dishes."

Ken left, and Calvin looked at Spazz. "Thank you," he said. On a whim, he returned the cigarettes he'd stolen from Spazz on the first night. "Only two left," he said sheepishly.

"I can see the future," Spazz said, hand on temple. "It's got us catchin' a smoke and you tellin' me more about what a totally awesome dude I am written all over it!"

"Oh my God," Cindy said, rolling her eyes but in a friendly way. "This *must* be the famous Spazz!"

"Famously just done wit'cher mama!" Spazz winked.

"That's enough ma jokes," Calvin smiled. "We totally *do* have things to talk about."

Troop 666 limbered back to Campsite Quatre, going on about how great the ballpark franks and spicy sausages were. Camp Souviens's food rocked! At the fire circle, Art flopped down to sit Indian style even though there was no fire. Denny joined him. And Sandy. And Ryan. Inky waited for the others to stop lingering and head to the tents or back out the by-way. Once the conspirators were alone, Inky slipped into a dense cluster of trees and thorny bushes, kneeling down. His meaty hand rested on the hilt of his Bowie knife.

Six minutes later, an older, sober-looking Trooper with fleecy hair over his ears and a navy blue polo shirt embroidered with the numeral 73 trotted confidently down the by-way. "You dropped this," he said, tossing a crumpled sheet of loose-leaf into Troop 666's ashy fire circle.

The guy turned his back on them and left.

Sandy spoke first. "He came alone."

"No fear," Denny nodded.

"He's their leader," Ryan noted darkly.

"Good," Inky said, emerging from the woods, "now we have a target." He fetched the paper and passed it to Art, who dug out his Swiss Army knife and shook out a blue-tip match.

"Phase one is over, guys," Art said, striking the match on his shoulder brace. The sheet of notebook paper, which had the words *WE KNOW WHERE YOU LIVE* penned on it, burned into nothingness.

Twenty minutes later, Calvin and Spazz returned and the seven went over Spazz's notes. Art used this data to finalize Operation World War IV: where, when, and how to enact phase two; and what to do when phase three broke out.

Chapter 32
RELATIONS WITH THE LYONSES.

CALVIN HAD ONLY spent a few minutes chatting with Cindy as they, Spazz, and Mike had gotten the work of the dishroom done. It'd been small talk. Like how she'd gotten the Whalers Cap back (during the Lost and Found party) and how Sandy had taken time to stop in and give her news about Calvin's hospital stay. They'd spoken blandly, clearly aware that they had company. Spazz had sung some Maiden to himself as he scrubbed serving pans. Mike hadn't said a word; the dish machine's steam made his pink cheeks wet with sweat. When all was done, Calvin escorted Spazz back to camp (the headbanger faked *some* of his paranoia … not all of it).

Now Calvin slogged back down the Green Trail towards Centre des Trois. His mind wandered, woolgathering about Lisa De Leeuw's wah-wahs. The caf came into view. As his beefy hand settled on the dish-room door handle, Calvin ditched the dreamy doozies dancing about his dome.

Phil Collins had resulted to begging, pleading, please baby please, could I possibly be granted another evening?

Cindy had been caught unawares earlier, showing up at work in a frumpy ol' shirt and shorts. Now she stood ready to make a good impression, sporting her best lime green shorts and the black **INXS** shirt Calvin had so comically mispronounced a few nights back. Her bright round face no longer glistened from kitchen grease, and her dyed-red hair sat properly towards the left with the kelly green Whalers cap atop it.

He felt ashamed that he hadn't stopped to pick a flower or something. "You look wonderful," he said softly.

"I do?" she said, laughing. A hand popped to her chin and both cocked in opposite directions; she affected a Southern belle accent. "Why Calvin, you *do* embarrass me so!"

He came closer and they stood for a while, taking in the sight of each other. No hug, no small talk.

"So, uh," Calvin eventually said, wiggling his slung arm, "got to stay in hospital for a couple nights."

"Sandy told me," she nodded. "Your elbow or something?"

"Sorta. You weren't kidding: Sandy brought you news."

"A couple times. I guess Art's dad called here. Jim and my dad were on the phones a lot that day, and everyone had to run messages down the trails to the Troops."

She was acting funny. Anxious. "But you heard it from Sandy, not your da," Calvin pointed out.

Sandy—she was awfully nervous saying it—had been so friendly. And, like before, the guy had tried to move in while Calvin was gone.

Calvin smirked. "Did you tell him *fuck off* or *fuck you?*"

She didn't respond at first.

"Hold on now." Calvin felt his skin grow hot. "What exactly did he do? What did *you* do?"

"He ... " She trailed off. "His updates had a price."

"A *price?* Oh, tell me you kicked him in the 'nads!"

"All right, I kicked him in the 'nads."

Calvin ground his teeth. How dare Sandy? And she agreed to it?! In light of the way he'd treated her out by the jetty ... "Did he stop by here before lunch," Calvin spat, "and let you know I was back? When I was gonna be here, like, ten minutes later?"

Cindy's pale face also turned hot, a mix of embarrassment and annoyance. "Don't be like that," she said, in a stern voice. "Besides, it's not like I *like* Sandy. Sure he's cute, but he's a big-time asshole." Her black eyebrows became chevrons. "I *sooo* desperately wanted to know how you were ... you jerk!"

An unhealthy silence blanketed them.

"Please believe me. Nothing 'real' happened. I told you cuz I thought you'd understand. Savage honesty, right?"

It was quite awkward, this reunion. Being teenagers, they didn't have the software to handle this problem. Both apologized. They spoke in simple words to ease the tension. Short sentences. Topics breezed over. Old tales retold.

Calvin spoke of the bastard who'd bleached his hair, and his clever Operation Nuclear Payback. He didn't reveal the bastard's name, and she let him have that secret.

Cindy whined about Ken's stupid K.P. crew (no previous K.P. had named a foreman) and Chef Jim's constant absences.

"Wanna take a break?" Calvin asked. He used his good arm to open the screen door. "Time off for good behavior."

She stared at the open door. "Where would we go?"

"For a canoe ride. Can you paddle?"

"I've never done it. You won't even be able to help, right?!"

"I won't, but it's easy. Trust me."

She burped out a couple empty laughs at that.

Lyons left his office, clomped down the stairs to the caf, and made for the kitchen to check in with Wren. He found Murphy at the grill, whistling a small tune, a white apron over his designer flannel and jeans. "What'cha doin', Murph?"

Murphy twirled a spatula. "I like burgers with *meat* on them, you know? Don't get me wrong, Jim's good—best chef we've had since Kirby, God rest his soul—but his burgers are the pits." Murphy gingerly flipped over a sizzling slab of beef. "I use a little onion. Peppers. Like my mother used to make."

"Never found out why," Lyons said, leaning his gaunt butt on the grill's edge, "but my mom mixed an egg in the beef."

Murphy tilted his head. "Not into the cholesterol scene myself. Got some chuck left over. Want one?"

"Sure." Lyons swiveled his head to watch Murphy pat together a burger the size of a flattened volleyball. Then he recoiled in mild horror: "What the hell happened to your face?"

Murphy pulled his fitted cap down. "Bobby White happened to it. I don't want to talk about it."

"*Bobby White?* You mean *the* Bobby White? He was here?"

"I won't repeat myself." Murphy slapped the second burger on the grill. Hissing and fresh grease scent filled the air.

Lyons drew a breath. "Listen, earlier today I saw you having a private chat with Mr. Dixon of Troop 73."

"I already know where you're going with this, and I don't like it," Murphy urged. "I merely probed him for information about that kid in the Devil's Troop who got beat up."

"Oh? Let's combine our efforts. Did you learn anything?"

"Dixon claims his boys aren't guilty. I believe him."

"Well, can you explain you and him laughing up a storm afterward? Were jokes about the assault told, maybe?"

Murphy tapped the spatula against the grill.

Lyons knew what was coming, so when Murphy gave him the slits (#130, "Pathetic little man!"), the Deputy Director could not withhold a pedantic sigh.

Murphy pointed at Lyons's burger with the spatula. "That represents the camp. The grill represents Troop 666. See what the grill is doing to the burger?" Murphy chopped the burger in half with the spatula's edge. "And the spatula represents—"

Lyons tore the spatula from Murphy's hand and tossed it on the stainless steel prep table behind them. "Murph, I'm so sick of your horseshit! Let me tell you what *I* think."

Murphy raised a brow at the spatula, then raised a brow at the sizzling burgers, then raised a brow at Lyons, who stood in between. "Nothing's stopping you."

"This camp makes money," Lyons huffed. "More than any other in the council, in the whole northeastern corridor, even. We got a good write-up in *Trooping Update* last year. Despite your static with Mr. Grant, your job is secure. These are facts."

"Yes," agreed Murphy, glancing at his burgers. He juggled with the idea of using his bare fingers to flip them over.

Lyons slipped a scowl on. "Now here's my theory why you get upset when a 'scourge' Troop comes here: *you're perfect.*"

Murphy blinked.

"In your eyes anyway; not a blemish on you," Lyons went on. "Troop 73 is Jake Murphy's kind of Troop. Perfect kids with perfect hair. Higher-income, no-divorce type of adults. Dixon drinks wine, not beer; wears Preferred Stock, not Hai Karate."

"You sound prejudiced, Lyons. Is it Troop 73's fault they look like they fell out of a Norman Fucking Rockwell painting?"

"Jesus, Murph! Where have you *been* all these years? Troop 73 is the exception, not the rule! *Troop 666* is what normal Troops look like! Lower-income, rural families. Their Troopmasters are blue-collar men who used precious vacation time for this trip. Why can't you deal with them properly?"

"I *am* dealing with them properly," Murphy said, reaching out for the spatula. "Scourges are, after all, my speciality."

In a lightning-quick movement, Lyons grabbed Murphy's wrist with both hands and slammed it against the table. The move brought the two men's faces to within an inch of each other. "You're deliberately making things worse for them, aren't you?" Lyons bellowed, casting spittle on Murphy's nose.

"Bullshit!" Murphy roared back. "I had nothing to do with that brat getting beat up!"

Lyons shook Murphy. "You're really crying for that kid!"

Murphy shook Lyons. "He probably deserved it!"

"Cold-blooded bastard!"

"Better than a shithead-sympathizer!"

"Join the real world, Murph!"

"This *is* the real world, Lyons!"

Lyons pushed Murphy away.

Murphy skittered in his Nike hiking boots but did not fall. He straightened himself out and distributed some top-rank, noxious slits (#5, "*Death would be kinder!*"). "The real world will not include you much longer, Lyons."

"The real world includes your burnt hamburgers."

With theatrical aggravation, Murphy swiped the spatula and scooped the burgers onto a plate. The bottom of the original burger was black as a hockey puck; the two halves of the second burger were simply well-done. "See what you've done!"

"Poor baby." Lyons kicked open the door to the dishroom and ducked through it.

Murphy heaved the plate and its contents into the large trash bin beside the table. "What a goddamn waste."

The dishroom door kicked open. "Where's my daughter?"

Murphy lazily scooped the remainder of the chuck out of the mixing bowl. He patted it into a chintzy oval and tossed it on the grill. "She spends her free time with one of the Devil's Troopers. You know, Mr. Lab-Coat-Hair: 'Calvin Ciarán Connor the Third.' Haven't you noticed? They were just in there, flirting up a storm." He suddenly broke into overdone laughter.

Lyons balled his hands into fists. "What's so funny?"

"Nothing." Murphy flattened the tiny burger with the spatula, still tittering like a small child. "Just envisioning your grandkids, coming from a white-haired boy and a red-haired girl. Would they have pink hair? Or striped, like a barber—"

Lyons belted Murphy with a fierce right, paused to watch the small man slump to the floor, then bolted from the kitchen.

Murphy's face, already bruised, now stung like a motherfucker. He wiped the apron over it: blood stained the white cloth, blood from his nose. As he finished cooking his snack, he composed in his head Lyons's dismissal report.

Aaron, the Camp Lifeguard, slumped in his beach-front shack, keeping one eye on the dozen or so kids swimming near the gangplanks, and the other eye on an issue of *Muscle & Fitness*. Calvin and Cindy stepped up to take out a canoe.

The dirty blond young man bucked. A boy with his arm in a sling wanted to take a canoe out! "No!" he bleated. "You can't even paddle, much less swim. ¡Lo siento, amigo!"

Cindy took command. "Aaron, *I'm* taking out the canoe. This useless lump is just a passenger."

Aaron debated with himself. It was a battle for the ages. "Okay, Wren," he said, slapping down his 'zine. "But you guys wear lifejackets. And don't tell nobody, or I'll sic Mick on you."

Calvin had as much trouble helping move the canoe to the reservoir's shore as he did getting into it. Cindy launched the canoe solo (Calvin situated inside, yelling, "Push!") and hopped in herself. "Paddle!" she shouted, hopping out. She sprinted to shore, gathered up a paddle, and lunged into the water again. She found entering a canoe when the water was waist height a difficult task. "It's easier," Calvin laughed, "closer to land."

"Fuckin' A," pissed Cindy, towing the canoe back ten feet. "I already hate canoeing." She relaunched the canoe and hurtled herself in. She worked her paddle and they were off.

"It's not that bad," he said. "You grab us some lifejackets?"

Cindy buried her face in her hands. "Fuck it," she sobbed. "I don't care. Let's just go."

"Can you swim?"

"Not really. Can you?"

"With a broken elbow now?"

"So we drown together, Calvin. How's that for romantic?"

Calvin shrugged. "Crowe and I went canoeing a couple days ago." He pointed eastward. "See there, where the reservoir splits up? We found a nice spot there. Quiet and private."

"I'm *sooo* lucky it missed the artery," Calvin said. "It's literally next to the muscle, and the branch just missed it."

"So you can't move it at all?" Cindy asked. Her words seemed quite loud all of a sudden.

"I'm not supposed to," Calvin replied, lowering his voice. "The muscle's cut pretty deep. But it's not too painful cuz the nerve's pinched. It feels numb, like I hit my funny bone. The worst bit is where the skin's torn; that *still* stings like hell!"

"Can they fix it?" Cindy said, voice positively deafening.

"It's some major procedure," Calvin whispered. "They take a muscle from somewhere else and tie it onto my elbow."

"But not 'til you're home?" Cindy whispered back.

"My ma insisted. She wants to be there. It won't get worse as long as I keep it in the sling and don't move it."

"Cool. Why are we whispering?"

"Cuz, listen." Calvin cupped a hand to his ear. "Hear that?"

"No."

"Exactly. Nice, isn't it?"

Cindy took up her paddle, moving the canoe further into the lagoon. Tall trees on three sides formed a dark enclosure, a bubble of bleak shade; the overcast sky only added to the crepuscular atmos. In here the reservoir skulked, littered in lily pads and weed-stalks. The water was still and clean; Cindy peered over the side of the canoe and saw bottom. She made out tiny black tadpoles, doing frivolous aquatic line dances.

"Let's stretch our legs out. Shame we didn't pack a lunch."

"Just what I need," Cindy moaned. "More dishes."

Calvin laughed, then laughed as the laughs bounced off the tall trees and echoed about them. "Heave to!" he warned.

"What the fuck does that mean?" she snapped.

The canoe jolted as its bottom scraped the land. "It means 'stop,'" Calvin snorted. He planted his left hand on the canoe's lip and used it to thrust himself out; he tumbled onto the dirt shore, crashing on his arse. Cindy chucked her paddle and pulled the canoe on shore a few feet. She sat down next to Calvin and wiped water from her legs. Her tiny pale bare feet picked up loose brown dirt from the embankment. Her toes wore the remnants of long-ago-applied lime green nail polish.

"Wasn't that bad, was it?" Calvin asked.

"We didn't sink," she responded. Calvin's raised eyebrow brought her defenses up: "I'm trying to look at the bright side."

"We're sitting on the bright side. No dishrooms."

"This has been my whole life since school ended. Nothing but trees." A raindrop tapped the dirt near her feet. "See?" she sighed. "It's like I've been out in the rain all summer!"

He waited for the next raindrop; it didn't take long. "You're not really cut out for the country-type life, are you?"

"Nope." Accepting the fact that she'd be wet again soon—with no redress—she simply lay back. "I'll take my Norwich life in a heartbeat. City, smoke, and metal beats forest, rain, and leaves any day."

"I like that." He smiled at her. "We're the same that way, Cindy. I came from a tiny village in Ireland, and I live in a tiny village in Pennsylvania, but I love cities."

"Where do you live again?"

"Axsubeen."

"Axsubeen! Funny name."

"Your name is Wren and you have the nerve to make fun of something else's name?!"

Her endearing round face smiled tightly.

He poked her in the ribs tightly.

"Asshole!" She bombarded him with pokes and prods.

"Stop!" he said, curling up to shield himself. She tweaked his unguarded ear, leading him to take a wild retaliatory poke that caught her right breast quite by accident.

"You pervert!" she wailed. She socked him on the chin, then climbed on him and pinned down his good arm. She was careful not to crowd or jostle his slung right arm. He leaned up to kiss her, quite a rough kiss at that. She pushed his head into the dirt and smothered him with a big wet one. Their front teeth scraped together, a sensation neither enjoyed, and the bill of her Whalers cap pressed into his forehead bandage.

And then it was over. She released his left hand, sat up on him, and folded her arms across her chest. "You behave," she breathed furtively. Calvin flicked his wrist to get the blood going again. She tapped his gut ominously with a forefinger.

"Quit it." He made to grab the prodding forefinger.

She pulled it back, then used it to brush the long white hair off his face. He stroked her red hair; despite its clumpy, frumpy appearance, it felt quite soft, if a tad greasy from lack of washing; the locks fell through his fingers. An electric surge rushed along his bloodstream, tingling his various lacerations. His cock started to get hard. If she noticed—how could she not, she was sitting on it!—she did not reveal it.

He arched his brows. "Is there something I can say," he purred, "to convince you to fuck me?"

She punched him.
He rubbed his cheek.
They rubbed each other.
He got out the rubber.

Chapter 33

POST-COITUS.

CALVIN HAD HEARD a smoke tastes better after sex. Well. He inhaled, and it felt (as always) like getting slugged in the chest. He exhaled. Soon the buzz arrived. The head-rush was lesser now than earlier times, but still alive and kicking. Maybe it tasted better after sex because, you know, you just had sex.

Cindy lay next to him, smoking as well. He lay with his T-shirt pushed up to his sling and his C.S.P. sweats and Y-fronts still down to his shins. She'd replaced all clothing shucked for coitus: her black **INXS** shirt, plain white bra and cotton panties, and lime green shorts. The drizzle clearly gave her a chill.

He had needed to do most of the work. He'd spent five minutes trying to get her bra off,* then spent a like amount of time with her lovely tits. They weren't the zeppelin-size zaboombas he usually dreamt about, but they were warm, soft, and tasty. Working his way down, he ate her out. This, however, tasted terrible; the summer heat, moist dish-room air, and general lack of shower facilities made it dreadful (in contrast to the air conditioned pussies of Jill Pedersen and Jenny Mac-Donald).

He'd had to remove his own clothing when she didn't leap to the task. But he let her take a moment to examine his cock. She was obviously a fan of it, but not enough to have a taste. After some fiddling with his poker chip (the Trojan), he got on top of her. Uncomfortable moments passed and he had trouble lining up his peg with her hole (rookie mistake), then had trouble getting it in (Cindy was so incredibly tight). Once firmly ensconced inside her, his nerves went orgasmic—

---

* Cut him some slack, Lothario. Calvin was fourteen and only had one working arm.

literally! She went through spells of limp limbs followed by spiky spasms. She mounted him as their second, and as it turned out, final, position. By the end, all of four minutes later, he grunted like a wounded dog as she mooed like a cow with a slight udder blockage. These were the only noises they'd made: for two kids who rarely shut up, it'd been a pretty quiet hump. In the end, he came like a shaken-up New Coke; the condom barely held all the white goop. It'd been fucking awesome, everything he'd hoped it'd be, and more besides.

There had been no cuddling, no hugging afterward. Cindy had said nothing after "Pass me my shirt." She'd lit smokes and they smoked. Her body still skittered: the experience lingered. Getting fucked was still, semantically, getting fucked.

He'd gone further with another girl than Jenny had ever let him get with her. Totally ... awesome. Calvin Connor had achieved his goal.

Determination.

His conscience tried to haunt him: fade up his mother's shrill Irish voice, bleating, "Women are not objects, boyo. You treat them with respect, or I'll put a wallopin' on your arse."

Calvin took another drag and pondered that. Treating girls with respect for fourteen-plus years had gotten him nothing. Taking over this afternoon got him laid. Ah, victory!

But *had* he disrespected her? He didn't even know. He leaned over to Cindy and stroked her red hair. She didn't pull away; only leaned aside to put her cigarette out in the wet dirt.

The silence grated on him. "How're you feeling?"

After a moment's thought: "I don't know," she sighed, making deliberate eye contact. "Please don't."

"Huh?" he said, pulling his hand away from her hair.

"Not that. Don't be all brooding."

"I'm not. Maybe you are," he said, a little accusingly.

"No I'm not," she said, a little too defensively.

"It was the right thing to do—we both wanted it."

"Yeah." She bit her lip. "We did. Didn't we?"

"*I* think so. Sex doesn't come from here," he tapped his temple; "it comes from here," he thumped his heart, "and here," he waved a hand over some genitals. "Those bits feel good right now."

She blinked. "I guess I'm embarrassed after the fact."

"It's an embarrassing thing, showing someone your naked body."

"Then letting them stick something in it! I'll admit it—I'm *sooo* totally embarrassed, Calvin."

"You didn't waste any time getting dressed!"

She cocked her head. "Being embarrassed is normal."

Calvin shrugged. "We just said."

"But brooding can't be. Who'd even *want* to fuck, then?"

Pause.

A monstrously large penny, like the one in the Batcave, fell a mile to the ground. "You mean you don't know?"

"I ... " She didn't finish.

Jaysus: Cindy and Calvin were *both* virgins! His brain beat on some bongos, yippee! So why wasn't she ecstatic? Regret?

Yes, he got what he wanted. But he felt he should convince her that *she* wanted it, too. It'd be disrespectful not to.

Calvin continued stroking Cindy's hair, but with trembling fingers. "I don't know, Cindy. This is my first time. Being embarrassed is probably natural."

"Yeah. We should do what we did before—it'll help."

"Cards on the table?"

"From the heart. Me first." She reached up and stroked his hair too. "You got a lot outta me, Calvin, more than any other boy ever has. I'm not complaining; I'm just tryin' to figure out why. It's so stupid. Usually I hate boys. Even when I like them, it's never this deep. Just laughs, flirting ... making out. You got me naked, had sex with me, got me to bare my inner feelings."

"You gave a lot, and so did I. It's called sharing."

"Oh? So how do *you* feel?"

He smirked. "I feel great ... and a little afraid. You're so awesome, upstairs and down; it's a really cool combination. To get to feel you— from all angles—wow, I'm a lucky cunt, aren't I? It's rapturous."

"Rapturous!" she cried. "I could only *dreamed* to hear a word like that after my first time!" She soaked in it for a short period. "So ... what are you afraid of? We used a condom."

"Not that," he said. "You let Sandy get kisses from you for news of me, and that's not right."

"Don't let that shit bother you," she replied. "I told you, I only did it to find out about you. And *you* have a girlfriend! That makes me the other woman, you know."

He thought about it. "I'm sorry. You're right. But this is more than an affair, isn't it? I thought affairs were just about fucking. What we have going here is more than that."

"Think of how *deep* this got. How much of each other we got to see. It's like we held nothing back—we touched souls."

"Touched souls. I like that idea." He chewed on his tongue. "Our future together is most likely nil—we're so far away from each other— but I got memories to last forever. What an awesome experience!" He pushed closer and kissed her.

When she'd caught her breath, which he'd taken from her, she whispered, "I feel like I'm free."

She paused. He hung on every millisecond.

"Like I've been in jail and then set free. This goddamn camp *is* jail for me. The time with you, where we … connect, is so great. Rapturous! It puts me back in my real life, in Norwich, talking to people who know and understand.

"I wish you were there, Calvin. I really do. Remember what you said about wishing I lived down the street from you?" She smiled, showing teeth. "The same! I mean it!

"Don't take this the wrong way, but it's not you yourself I like— it's your perspective. You ain't afraid to be direct, to reveal embarrassing shit, or speak the truth. The way you talked to Murphy in the dishroom? Not afraid to use bad words, being direct with him? That got me wet, Calvin.

"And so … I let this happen, even though I know I'm just another vagina in a chain. Poor Jenny. I feel bad for her. Whoever she's fooling around with, that Sean or whoever—he ain't nowhere near the man you are."

His eyes lit up at that.

"But hey, you played your hand right. Guys like Sandy do the same thing, but they're slimy. I don't feel good when I talk to him. I feel *great* when I talk to you. That's why all he got was a couple kisses, and you got to totally fuck me. God!"

She laughed. "And I'm no longer a virgin. Awesome. I mean, I poked out my hymen years ago—it's amazing how far a banana can go up in you. But here it actually happened, actual sex, and I'm *sooo* glad it was with someone like you. I see you differently. You're a special person, you know that?"

He hung on these words, then hung after she finished.

"So your turn again," she said. "What're you thinking?"

"Honestly?"

"Yes."

"I'm thinking, *why didn't I bring another rubber?*"

She laughed. "Sorry, dude: safe sex or no sex."

"I guess. Well, we got all week."

Chapter 34

THE LAST SUPPER.

WHILE THE CAMP Dishwasher was off getting fucked, the bug-eyed Camp Chef reported to the Centre des Trois cafeteria to take weekly inventory. The more Jim fussed about in the walk-in cooler, the more his unwashed beard stood on end: supplies were low, and most of the foodstuffs available had reached or breached their expiration dates. Jim grabbed the left-hand kitchen phone (the sky blue one) and dialed the number for the right-hand phone (the red one). Upstairs, on Camp Director Murphy's desk, one of the two phones rang: it was his private line (the red one). Jim made clear he was downstairs, on the Centre des Trois main line (the sky blue one), and fucking pissed off. "Why can't you keep the fucking food order up to date?" the ex-hippie lashed out without a single stammer.

"No time for that," Murphy muttered over the clack of his typewriter keys, "I have an important discipline report to—"

Jim said, "To hell with you," slammed down the handset for the main line (the sky blue one), and—just to be a dick—took the handset for the Camp Director's private line's extension (the red one) and let it dangle from the curly-cue cable.

The Chef started preparing the dinner meal at once. He cooked everything in the walk-in that had today's or a previous day's date on it but wasn't obviously spoilt or rancid. Maniacally, the chef grilled and broiled and fried and boiled. He sautéed and roasted and broasted and toasted. He even did some quick marinating. At the 5:00 p.m. suppertime, Jim gathered it up and dumped it out on the buffet table, needing to make seven trips: raviolis, meatloaf, hamburgers, hot dogs, grilled chicken breasts, steeped turkey slices, freshly sliced beets with hardboiled eggs, a bowl of browning lettuce, sixty meatballs, a red sauce, pancakes, loaves of bread, a pile of corn dogs, some red delicious apples, French fries, chipped beef, two pounds of tater tots, and four breakfast sausages.

Camp Ranger Mr. Grant made an aside to the portly Fix-It Man, Kevin, that if Jim could have fit the kitchen sink into the deep fat fryer, that too would be on the buffet table. "All that," Kevin nodded, "and a partridge in a pear tree."

Jim stepped up to the mic and said, "Come and get it!" The couple hundred young lads thundered up, aghast at the selection. The collective joy on their teenaged faces outweighed all the chagrin Jim carried. Still, the bug-eyed fellow vanished to his quarters in Chamberlin with all alacrity, knowing a certain female dishwasher would rage over the increased workload.

Troop 666 rejoiced in the grand supper atmosphere. They ate and joked and laughed. Mirth and mayhem abounded.

Calvin sauntered in, dampened sweats stuck to his legs, Whalers cap perched daintily on his skull. He got the news of the day—merit badges had resumed, and Denny Sandmiller had executed the world's coolest cannonball off the gangplanks—then coyly demurred when asked where he'd been.

Inky came over to Calvin's side. "What's Crowe been up to? You *have* been spendin' time with your rookie ... *Captain?*"

"I dunno, and not lately. Is this part of World War IV?"

"This isn't a fucking play, Connor. In case you missed it, I'm the Big Cheese." Inky sniffed the air. "I smell something."

"What?"

"That dollar." He stomped back to his table.

Rolling his eyes, Calvin got the Hawk Squad's attention and proposed a toast to absent friends: Zedz and Jon. The table raised cups of soda into the air and heaped loud praises that the two absentees would never hear. The neighboring tables gave an obligatory telling-off about the noise.

In the midst of this joyous atmos, the Operation World War IV conspirators gave knowing glances across the caf at the Troop 73 table. The direct contact between 73 and 666 made one group visibly irritated and the other downright giddy.

Art nudged Sandy. "Yo, they're shaking in their boots."

Sandy grinned. "Your plan is totally working!"

"You pick the lock on the yellow fridge?"

"Yep." Sandy exposed the two cans of New Coke nestled in the pockets of his tan Trooping shorts.

"Cool." Art noticed Spazz was at the Hawk Squad table, seated next to Calvin, having fun (Calvin's guffaw was loud, as usual; but Spazz's laughter forcibly silent).

"Is that part of World War IV?" Sandy asked.

Art said that it was not.

Murphy's office was quiet. Again.

"Wait for it ...," the bookcase droned.

Murphy marched in, strode to his desk, and fetched the disciplinary report sitting neatly on the blotter. "Here, Mr. Grant: read this, sign it, and give me some justice!" He popped off his cap, exposing even darker, more swollen eyes.

Mr. Grant looked at the eyes, then the report. "Lyons punched you? I can only assume you said something stupid."

Murphy pointed at the report. "Read it, it's all in there!" He flopped into his throne and turned it to face the window. Mr. Grant duly filed the report in the trash can.

Lyons stalked in. "Finally found Wren. She *was* with that Irish ki—" He felt the mood of the room. "What're we talking about?"

"You," Mr. Grant shrugged.

"Good." Lyons looked Mr. Grant in the eye. "I quit."

Mr. Grant choked. "You quit? *Why?!*"

"Trying to beat me to the *punch*, Lyons?" Murphy hissed.

Lyons counted to ten in his head but still felt irate: "Due to irreconcilable differences with my superior. Specifically, his quiet policy of undermining the quality of some Troops' stays."

"Undermining?!" Murphy hooted, whirling 'round.

Lyons glared. "Your behavior toward our guests endangers them. And you let that brat go to the dance knowing he would molest those girls ... just so you could catch him."

Mr. Grant's weathered eyes grew narrow. "You're just burning out, Horace. Take a week off, and reconsider."

Lyons said, "I've done enough considering. And I'm not saying anything else. He's your problem, Mr. Grant." He skulked out the door. "You'll pardon my apathy. I'm going to my quarters to pack. I'll expect a final paycheck before I leave."

Mr. Grant menaced over Murphy. "What's going on here?!"

Lyons poked his head back in. "I'll be taking my daughter too. You'll need a new dishwasher starting Sunday."

Murphy's office was oddly quiet.

"I'm too old for this shit," the bookcase said.

Chapter 35
World War IV, phase two; Nuclear Payback, phase one.

6:42, Art's calculator watch said. He forced himself to work faster. "Someone shake up those sodas."

Sandy worked the two cans of New Coke up and down. When Denny made a crack about masturbation, Sandy "accidentally" jettisoned a can into his younger brother's face.

Spazz lobbed the can back to Sandy. "All shook up now!" he grinned. Denny wiped his sore chin with a snarl.

"More light!" Art groaned. Denny tilted his tiny pocket flashlight to a better angle over Art's shoulder.

"Fuckin' stinks in here," said Sandy, as he shook.

Spazz looked around the latrine and said, "Who's responsible for cleanin' this motherpuker up, anyways?"

"You are, asshole."

Spazz reeled at his own words. Singing: *"There goes stupid Spazz / what a dumb mouth he has!"*

"Yo, shut up!" Art pissed. "I need to concentrate!"

"Well, *excuuuuse* me!"

"You're a dick, Spazz."

"I am's what I got's, and my dick's been itchin' like crazy." Spazz jumped on the opportunity to use his catchphrase: "And when *that* happens …," he started.

"… someone gets pregnant," laughed his sidekick Denny.

"Besides, the Spazzster's done a better job of tidyin' the shitter than that Cookie rapist and the Irish dingle-dong!"

"Speakin' of Calvin," said Sandy, giving the others a crooked eye, "I'm gettin' one of them prenimotions. Something about Calvin and one of Troop 73's douchiest bags."

"What makes ya say that?" asked Denny.

"Rem'ber when Oldroyd and Kermit were arguin' in the caf, the mornin' after Tentgate? Calvin and some other kid on K.P. were there too, gettin' the dishes together."

"Yeah," said Denny. Art nodded too.

"Well," Sandy said, "that kid suddenly looks familiar."

"I just saw that fool at K.P. today," Spazz hooted. "He ain't one of the speds who jumped me."

Denny burped. "What if you're wrong? Calvin coulda been leakin' our plans to this guy after every meal."

"Fuck that, dude," Spazz snapped. "Calvin ain't no stoolie."

"Ain't what ya said at the Kangaroo Court!"

Art took Spazz's side: "Why would Irish fuck with our plan just cuz he's on K.P. with some Troop 73 ass-nose? For all we know, *they're* the dickheads who bleached his hair!"

"I mean, I could see him sellin' me out," Spazz said. "Like Ryan did. We ain't butt-buddies. But he'd never sell out his *real* butt-buddies: Pound-Sandy and the Black Panther!"

"Racism!" yelped Art.

"Whatever," pissed Sandy. "I just got a feeling, is all."

Spazz said, *"I* got a feelin' about my dick and yer muddah!"

The door to the latrine thumped twice.

"That's my cue. Give me five minutes," Sandy said. He handed Spazz the Cokes and tore out of the latrine.

Art snapped shut the casing on the minor contraption in his lap and tossed it in his satchel. On top of the contraption he carefully placed a small clock, a tight bundle of closed cardboard tubes, and a pair of fireman's gloves. Spazz shuttled the Cokes into the satchel's side-pocket. Denny shouldered the satchel (Art had had trouble keeping his balance with the satchel on one side and his braced arm on the other). Spazz handed the Troop's collapsible spade over to Denny.

"Brothers," Art barked, "let's do it."

The three conspirators gingerly exited the latrine, passing by Ryan Phillips, who stood at the plugged-up basin discreetly washing his hands and face in the same water for the last five minutes. Ryan pointed down to the fire circle.

Calvin, whose conspirational job during this phase was to keep Father distracted, had apparently failed—the Junior Chaplain glanced up at the latrine with curiosity in his eyes.

"Shit," Art said. "You take Father. Denny, stick close."

The conspirators fanned out at the fire circle. Ryan sat on Father's other side and ignited to conversational life, arguing for the merits of playing Dungeons & Dragons. Spazz sat nearby and gave silent supporting nods on the thieving and murdering aspects of the game. Father was not amused.

Calvin shook his head at them. "Enough of that bollocks," he urged. "I have a real question for you. For *all* of you."

Father, Ryan, and Spazz turned to look at him.

Calvin noted obliquely that he was the only non-blond of the bunch, but now his hair was lighter than all theirs. "This is about Trooping," Calvin said. "I know we're Troop 666 and all, but don't you think we do an awful lot of sinning?"

Blank stares. "What?" Ryan asked with a chuckle.

"We do sin a ton," Father noted. "But we also do God's work. That's part of Trooping." He glanced sidelong at Ryan. "Some think it's an *optional* part."

"Stop," Calvin said. "Leave Jesus out of this. I haven't lost faith," he said to Father, "and I ain't turning to the dark side," he said to Ryan. He noted Spazz's Iron Maiden T-shirt with its zombie-like mascot. "And I ain't getting into bed with Eddie."

"Eddie's no homo!" Spazz roared, making guitar noises.

Father swiveled his head. "Three words: thirty push-ups."

Spazz killed the Maiden, snapped his fingers like some swell 1950s kid who just got caught, and did his push-ups.

Father said, "We're young so we act childish. 1 Corinthians 13:11 and all. But Trooping's about growing into men."

"Learning leadership skills," Calvin said, rolling his eyes.

"Personal advancement," Father nodded, "the road to—"

"Tying knots," Ryan added. "All the better to hogtie us."

"I hear all that now," Calvin said, "but it's all *Handbook* shite. None of that's why Spazz is here." He looked at the headbanger, who'd finished his push-ups. "You're here to hang out with your friends and have fun. Right?"

Spazz plopped next to Calvin and high-fived him.

"Me too," Calvin said. "You're all my friends, I guess. But we've done some terrible stuff. Commandment-breaking, even. I don't think saying Hail Marys'll cover them."

"You aren't worried about God pardoning you," Father said. "You're worried about *you* pardoning you."

"I am," Calvin nodded, pondering the roaring, five-foot-tall Fire of Inky. "I did a pretty big sin just a few hours back. Felt good at the time. Now ... " He trailed off.

"Catholics ain't ever happy," Ryan said. "Always feeling guilty about being alive. Calvin, just have fun. Don't let the weight of the Pope's hat pull ya down!" he joked.

Father dismissed Ryan with a tongue-click. "Calvin, is this about the Troop, or about that girl?"

Calvin looked up sharply. "Both," he sighed.

"Seek forgiveness with God," Father stated evenly. "But, as you get older, you'll learn how to let go of your guilt too. Just having guilty feelings is a good start. It means you're a kind soul." The Junior Chaplain smiled. "It's heartwarming to see you go through this, and still your faith isn't wavering."

"Never has," Calvin beamed. "Just call me Job."

"Job was a blind idiot," Ryan said. "Y'know how much suffering coulda been avoided if he just took the offer from—"

From far off, they heard a deep bell chime three times.

Art and Denny had taken four steps down the goat-path towards the tents. When confident they were out of sight, they cut into the woods. Denny handed the spade to Art and pulled out a length of yellow rope from his drawers; he began to coil it along his arm, twisting it 'round and around in one direction. Art stared at his calculator watch as they slinked through the woods. A couple minutes later, he hissed, "Damnit, c'mon!"

"Relax," said Denny. "My brother's so fuckin' fast—"

From far off, they heard a deep bell chime three times. The sound snaked through the forest, making everyone at Camp Souviens turn their heads in alarm.

Then the commotion started. "Three times!" they heard Inky scream. "There's an emergency to go to!"

"Head out, double-stat!" they heard Mr. Maguire holler.

Denny smiled at Art. "Told you he's fuckin' fast."

The heated exchange in Murphy's office, ceaselessly raging from the moment Lyons had left, abruptly went on pause. Three chimes! Murphy grabbed his Souviens cap. *"Now* what?!"

"That's my line!" yelped Mr. Grant.

The two men hustled down the stairs, out of the caf, and made a beeline up the Red Trail. The basketball court sat a few hundred feet away, and next to it was a thirty-foot bell tower made of blackwashed wood. The rope attached to the bell's clapper fluttered this way and that, slowly coming to a stop. Murphy and Mr. Grant hailed the gaggle of basketball-playing kids. "Who rang the 'All Camp' alarm?!" Murphy yelled at them.

"Dunno," said one.

"Think it was some kid," said another.

A third added this pearl: "We was playing ball."

Murphy shut his eyes. A pipe in his brain started hissing.

"A prank," Mr. Grant said, though not uneasily. "If it really *was* an 'All Camp' alarm, someone would be here."

"Hrrrm," Murphy offered. The light breeze of early evening carried the sound of nagging, anger, annoyance, and aggravation— indeed, the sound of many feet headed for Centre des Trois. The de- sired result of an "All Camp" alarm.

That mustachioed, cowboy-hat-wearing demon from the Devil's

Troop, hitherto sauntering down the Red Trail with a tray bearing the detritus of his incarcerated son's dinner, reached the bell tower first. He cracked, "Where's the fire?"

Murphy brushed Mr. Grant out of the way. "You tell us," he snapped. "Everyone in your Troop accounted for?"

"Now just how in the hell would *I* know?" Oldroyd said. The chrome buckle on his cowboy hat made a noise like grinding gears. "I was just up at Chamberlin visitin' my son—who's in jail! Or don'cha remember *framin'* him?"

"Somebody pulled a false alarm here, Mr. Oldroyd, and the *last* thing I need is lip from some mountain-bound hick—"

Mr. Grant clamped a hand on Murphy's shoulder; the enraged Camp Director nearly started swinging. "Excuse us," Mr. Grant said to Oldroyd, pulling Murphy aside.

Infuriatingly, the basketball players giggled. This was funny to them! *Vile slobs! I'll kill 'em! I'll—*

Mr. Grant's bearded face filled Murphy's vision. "Horace was right. You're going crazy. Now apologize to that man."

"I think not! I'm going to find the brat who pulled this—"

"I don't care who pulled it."

Murphy had reached his limit: he gave Mr. Grant the most vicious slits in his repertoire: #1 with bullets, the dreaded *"FUCK YOU, MOTHERFUCKER!"* variety. Slits this evil had only seen duty twice before—when then-Camp Counselor Murphy opened the certified letter informing him of the White family's civil lawsuit against him; and when the then-married Mrs. Murphy informed her spouse that the papers in her extended hand were of the initiating-proceedings-to-cease-being-Mrs.-Murphy variety. The #1 slits involved snarling, gritting, squinting, barking, and drooling, and were quite painful to sustain.

"This is the sort of bullshit I've put up with all week!" Murphy gnashed. *"You're* only relaxed because you spent the worst of it in Orlando, playing golf and screwing your wife!"

"I know," Mr. Grant said, unapologetically. "But it's your job to be nice to our customers. *No matter what.*"

Murphy nixed the agonizing slits #1 and growled like a petulant

Chihuahua. He turned to face the enormous crowd of boys and adult chaperones which had gathered around the bell tower. "Sorry, folks!" he shouted. "False alarm!"

He stomped over to Oldroyd. "I'm sorry," he mumbled.

He stomped back to the bell tower. "FALSE ALARM!" he screamed. "THERE'S NO EMERGENCY! WE'RE SORRY!"

The crowd expressed relief (adults) and disappointment (kids). They spent a minute or two milling around, wondering who would do such a dastardly thing.

In the milling crowd, Sandy had absolutely no trouble slipping out of hiding and rejoining his Troop.

In the milling crowd, Calvin had absolutely no trouble slipping a set of keys off the belt-loop hook of a certain Troopmaster. Said Troopmaster scanned the crowd, looking for his son—and, according to the shrug-like look on the man's bearded face, was only semi-concerned not to find him.

Spazz skirted round to Calvin's side and they exchanged the keys. "You know the plan?" whispered Calvin.

"Yeah, fuck around 'til eight and meet Jon at the caf. *Don'choo worry 'bout Spazz / he's down with that revenge jazz!*"

During the mass-march back to the campsite, Calvin noted a bizarre over-the-shoulder look from Sandy. He quickened his pace to come alongside his best pal. "Sandy," he said.

"Calvin," Sandy returned.

"We haven't talked since I've been back. Maybe we ought."

"Okay, dude—is one of the K.P. guys from Troop 73?"

Calvin frowned. "I don't remember. Troop 99, Troop 1—or is it

Troop 2? Jaysus, having a brain bruise sucks."

Sandy analyzed Calvin's face for treachery, but the Irish lad wasn't faking: he genuinely couldn't remember.

"I think so," he said at last. "Troop 73. Sure. Why?"

"*Seriously?!*" Sandy yelped. "WW4's all about whalin' on Troop 73! I wanna make sure yer on *our* side."

"*Seriously?!*" Calvin mocked. "You steal kisses from my girl, then test *my* loyalty? '*Are you shitting me with that shit?*'"

Sandy sighed. "You'll never believe this, but she was the one who made the offer. All's I did was poke my head in the door of the dishroom to tell her what'd happened to ya."

"Hold up now: you went to tell her, but *she* made the offer to kiss you for it? Is that how it went on the jetty too? How do you ever win at poker, Sandy? What a fat load of shite!"

Sandy was red-faced. "Whaddaya want, dude, blood?"

"I want," Calvin crowed, "my friend to act like one."

"All right, asshole, I did it all. The night of the dance? I 'under-mined' you in fronta her to embarrass your ass. Then she argued back like flirting, so I tried to get in her pants. And I made out with her yester-day. So what! You're spoken-for. She's a free agent in my eyes. For all we know, she pro'bly does this with a new guy every week! Are we going to fight about some stupid slutty dishwasher chick?"

Calvin laughed. "Oh are we now? I don't think so. All your work to ruin me only made me look better in her eyes."

"What?"

"You and her shared tongues; me and her shared *souls!*"

Sandy didn't get it, but found himself laughing anyway.

"I think," Calvin went on, "it's best summed up by the phrase, 'Strike last, strike fast, get hard.'"

"No way!" beamed Sandy. "No freakin' way!"

"All true—you cunt."

"Good job, dude!" Sandy slapped Calvin's back. "So does that mean no hard feelings?"

"Oh, I had a few 'hard' feelings, all right."

The old pals boomed guffaws into the trees.

Art was on tenterhooks. Setting up the two traps in the Campsite Trois fire circle had taken much longer than he'd anticipated. It turned out (when it had counted the most) that Denny had zero tree-climbing ability; so he got relegated to boost-duty and kept sore hands on Art's ass while the injured kid shimmied up a tree on one good arm. Art then had to hold on with his bad hand while he rigged the soda-helicopter and set its timing device with his good hand—very painful stuff.

Setting up the soda-helicopter took seven minutes.

The other gizmo, the Eat-At-Joe's fireworks bomb, had been a breeze—Troop 73 had doused their campfire before racing to answer the alarm. So while Art was up a tree, Denny uncollapsed the spade and dug. When Art returned to earth, he gave detailed coaching and Denny had planted the gizmo in the damp dirt directly under the doused fire.

Setting up the Eat-At-Joe's took five minutes.

The half-mile-or-so trip from Campsite Trois to the bell tower (hustling there, and strolling back), with a minimum pause there of say two minutes, took fifteen minutes total. So Art and Denny had finished with no time for a double-check. They hastened through the forest back to the Green Trail. After a few deep breaths, Art relaxed. No sweat, really. The countdown to 8:21 p.m. was seventy-nine minutes.

The kids crouched down in some undergrowth ten feet from the Green Trail. Troops already marched along, on their way back to their falsely interrupted lives; the first was Troop 73, adding to Art's residual anxiety. 73 consisted of a snobby, stubby adult; the fleecy-haired older kid who'd confidently confronted them in their own campsite; and five others of varying younger ages and hairstyles.

They passed by without noticing Art and Denny.

A minute later Art spotted Inky leading Troop 666, with his dad and Oldroyd bringing up the rear as usual. With no difficulty, Art and Denny slipped in with them. Art saw Sandy and breathed a mighty sigh. "Yo, are we cool?"

"We're cool," Sandy reported. "Are we cool?"

"Yo, we are cool!"

Art looked over at Calvin. "How about you, Irish?"

"Just fine, African," returned Calvin. "Though all this running around is painful. I popped another pill to stop that."

"Me too! Try climbing a tree with a separated shoulder sometime!" They tittered at their high state. "Stay frosty though, Calvin. Things are gonna get crazy."

Darkness enveloped Campsite Quatre. Proposals were made to either a) engage in an AD&D session, letting the boys attack Asmodeus en masse with their +1 guisarme-voulges and *magic jar* spells; or, b) tell ghost stories by the Fire of Inky.

Ghost stories won out, to Father's delight and Ryan's dismay, so everyone in Troop 666 gathered at the fire circle ... except the rookie Shawn Crowe. He gave a quick pan with his flashlight to ensure his solitary state, then dug through his backpack and donned a baggy pair of navy blue sweats and a black U2 T-shirt. He grabbed the Whalers cap Calvin had discreetly left under his bunk, adjusting it for his smaller head.

He left the Hawk tent and slogged up to the fire circle, telling Inky he wanted to visit Jon. Inky nodded, and Oldroyd added, "Good idea, kid." As he trudged down the Green Trail, Crowe wondered if he'd picked the right side. Earlier, he'd allied with Spazz and Jon because his impression of Art, Calvin, and the "leader" kids was elitism: rookies picked up trash and got sent off to find apocryphal bullshit like the left-handed smoke-shifter. Otherwise, shut up and go away. But with the "cool" kids, he feared he'd get in trouble. And he did.

Crowe later hung out with Calvin, who turned out to be cool after all. He wondered if their canoe ride was "bonding."

Guys like Spazz and Jon wanted to kill Calvin, but why? Cuz Calvin told Jon to shut up all the time? Was that reason enough? And *yet,* tonight Calvin had hatched a plan to break Jon out of jail. Isn't that weird. "The reason I'm asking you," Calvin had explained, "is tonight'll end badly. You know Art's 'secret' revenge plan? Bollocks. But if you do this for me, you'll be safe from the certain death we'll all suffer tomorrow morning. And all you need to do is spend a few hours away from the campsite ... and lend me your watch. What do you say, Shawn?"

The speech sold Crowe. Of course, with all the double-crossing and junk going on around here, Crowe knew this could be another trap. Jon and Calvin had very few kind words for each other (more like none at all!), even when one was around and the other not. Crowe had a nemesis like that at school—a goon called "Doseman," since he dosed out beatings like a pharmacist. Nothing in the world could *ever* get Crowe to lend Doseman a hand ...

Crowe's doubt of Calvin's compassion was strong.

Everything about this puzzled Crowe. Calvin had given him a message to pass on. Gibberish, by design no doubt, so if Crowe was caught and sweated down, he wouldn't have the right information to spill. Calvin stressed, "Get to Jon before eight." Crowe no longer had his beloved Boba Fett watch but he knew time was pressing—he quickened his pace.

Crowe reached the Chamberlin building and stuffed a stick of Juicy Fruit in his mouth. "Hi," he said to the first adult he saw. "I'd like to visit Jon, please. He's in the Cell." The adult was a woodsy man wearing a big brown beard, decked in well-worn jeans and faded flannel. Crowe had seen the man at suppertime. Was he the Camp's Lumberjack?

"Sure," the man sighed; upset and covering it up. This scared Crowe a little. Maybe they were on to him!

The Lumberjack led Crowe to the opposite wing of the building. They arrived at a blank door and the Lumberjack searched through the largest collection of keys Crowe had ever seen. "Five minutes. Don't let the door shut until you leave: it will lock automatically." The Lumberjack marched back down the hall, still upset at something. *This is gonna be easier than I thought!* Crowe smiled to himself, popping inside.

Jon sat at a desk, alone in a tiny little room, looking focused. "Crowe! Yer the last one I expected, but whatever! What's the word, rook?"

Crowe took the Whalers cap and jammed it in the doorway to prevent the door from clicking shut. "Meet Spazz at the caf. The douchebag will be rained upon at the fork."

"Say what?"

Crowe cleared his throat and recited again, "Meet Spazz at the caf, and the douchebag will be rained upon at the fork." He shrugged. "Calvin made me memorize it. He said you'd understand and Spazz'll have more instructions."

Jon chuckled. "I don't get a goddamn word of that! But Spazz'll know what's up, and he'll be able to say it in English."

"You gotta hurry, though," warned Crowe. "You two gotta get back there by quarter after."

Jon checked the Swatch Calvin had given him. "That's fifteen minutes. How ya gettin' me out?"

Crowe pulled off his shirt. "Jon, yer *walkin'* outta here!"

Chapter 36
WORLD WAR IV, PHASE THREE;
NUCLEAR PAYBACK, PHASE TWO.

THE SUN HAD left them. So had Mr. Maguire, gone to bed early complaining of pot-belly overextension brought on by the dinner feast.* Oldroyd strummed quietly on his Martin guitar. Inky was present but silent—less grim than usual. Father, so convinced someone would slip off and start a war, kept his head swiveling around like the girl in *The Exorcist.*† The soon-to-be-realized fruitions of two separate plans grew closer. Fingers skittered. Eyeballs bulged. Bottoms shifted nervously.

The ghost story, by contrast, was laughable.

It was Chicken's turn, and he spun a yarn of a lost soul hitchhiking along a dark highway, endlessly stalking a woman driving alone. It was all cliché, and even Chicken's unusual accent failed to liven it up! So he added vampires, escaped convicts, kung fu masters, police detectives, Nazi soldiers, spaceships, CIA agents, Satanic preachers, buxom angels, werewolves, dragons, rock musicians, time machines, Mafia hitmen, the sword Excalibur, Martians, the zombie of Cleopatra, a heart of pure gold, a man who'd lived for a thousand years, and a poor sap who always saw the green light go yellow just when it was too late to hit the brakes ... into what was ordinarily a story told in one act with just two characters. And *still* his fireside crowd of Oldroyd, Inky, Father, Calvin, Gus, Ryan, Art, Sandy, and Denny appeared maddeningly bored.

Chicken added Judas Priest and Joe Montana to the yarn.

---

* There was a lot of talk of "waffer-thin meents."

† There was also a lot of talk of "your mother sucks cocks in hell," but teenage boys did that fairly often, so it was just a coincidence.

Art turned to Sandy. "You ready?"

Sandy, having fielded the question a hundred times in the last hour, sighed. "Yeah I'm ready! Yer moltin' up a storm!"

"I'm high on the adrenaline, that's all." Art pulled at the brace on his bad arm, then ran his good hand along his perfect half-inch flattop. "Woo! I'm excited, bro. When this shit goes down, I might wet my pants."

Sandy chuckled. Chicken, disturbed by the chuckle ruining a dramatic moment, added Darth Vader and King Arthur to the fray. This brought chuckling from all.

Art gave his calculator watch a glare. "You seen Spazz?"

"No. Just find Denny: those two are closer than homos."

"Denny's right there. Where the hell's Spazz?"

"I dunno, takin' a leak maybe—chill out!"

"He'd better hurry. We only got, like, eight minutes."

Calvin overheard that, checked the Boba Fett watch he'd gotten from Crowe (what a silly item), and pulled himself to his feet. "Off for a piss," he announced.

Chicken sighed loudly. "Hurry up! You don't wanna miss part about Megatron versus the Hell's Angels!"

Calvin slogged up the path to the latrine. In the dark, dank shitter, he sat on the bench between the two access holes.

Two thumps came from the thin wooden wall behind him. "All clear!" he hissed. The door opened. Jon Oldroyd wore the navy blue sweats, inside-out black U2 shirt, and Whalers cap Crowe had given him; he toted Crowe's cheap plastic flashlight. Spazz wore his usual blue-jeans and black Iron Maiden T-shirt, but he'd taken the effort to rub dark mud (or something) along his exposed arms and neck. He'd tied back his long blond hair and concealed it in a dark wool cap. He carried a large something with a black sweatshirt draped over it.

Calvin nodded at Jon. "Did Spazz tell you the plan?"

Jon held up some fold-up traveling scissors. "How much?"

"Don't get crazy—a couple snips from the front is fine. Give me

Mr. Maguire's keys, Spazz."

Spazz flicked the key ring over. "How ya gonna return 'em unnoticed, CAL 9000?"

"Let me worry about that," Calvin said, instantly worrying about it. He checked Crowe's watch, which reminded him: "Jon, I need my Swatch back." Jon returned it; Calvin strapped it on his wrist next to the Boba Fett watch. "Spazz'll show you the spot, Jon. We only got four minutes until Art's plan goes off, then Troop 73 will head our way, lookin' to have a go."

"Troop 73?" Jon said.

"Yeah, didn't Spazz tell you?" Panicking at the fuck-up: "No, *don't tell him!* Jon can't join in. He supposed to be in jail!"

"Okay, whatever," Spazz shrugged. He looked at Jon. "I can't tell you about Troop 73. There, that was easy!"

Calvin wondered if they'd missed anything. "You gotta get back to your cell on your own. Crowe gummed the lock, right?"

"Yeah yeah, we even tested it before I left." Jon cracked his knuckles. "Everything's covered, dude! Let's go kick ass!"

Art felt a prod at his back and whirled around. Calvin stood there. "What's up?" mouthed Art.

"Come here," Calvin mouthed back. "Important."

Chicken leveled a dark eye on the two and rapidly introduced the Loch Ness Monster, ridden behind the ears by ten naked Valkyries. This caught the attention of Oldroyd, Sandy, and Gus—*finally,* stunt-casting that worked!

Art got up and followed Calvin down the goat-path, one eye on his calculator watch, the other on the woods to the south, the general direction of Campsite Trois. "Yo, what's up?"

"We have a big problem," Calvin hissed back. He slogged to the fork in the path and stopped.

"We only got like a minute, Irish! It better be good!"

"Oh it is, buddy."

That came from a bush alongside the path. Art twisted around and found a zitty face wearing a Whalers cap rising up.

For two seconds, Art felt panic: a known felon in their Troop had busted from his cell and been lying in wait for them! "Ambush!" Art tried to wail, squaring off with Jon—a selfless act to shield his good friend Calvin while he himself took the brunt—but Art never got the word out

POP POP POP!

because he was shot three times in the back from close range. Accustomed as he was to a drug-induced, pain-free existence, the violent reintroduction of hurt felled Art on its own. He landed awkwardly on his shoulder brace and tasted dirt.

He remained conscious for two more seconds, and spent that time stewing over being betrayed.

Jon Oldroyd stepped out to the path and knelt down. "Nobody fucks with Calvin but me!" He clocked Art on the nose with a snapped fist, then pulled out the scissors.

Far away to the south, Operation World War IV's phase two went off: a fizzing, splashing sound that cut out at regular intervals; several dim *poof!*s of explosions; and yells of surprise and horror. Art missed it all.

Calvin thanked his Operation Nuclear Payback coconspirators for a job well done, bade them disappear at once, then discarded the hair trimmings Jon had thoughtfully handed over (thinking Calvin might want them as weregild). The lad made his way, alone, back to Campsite Quatre's fire circle. He felt very proud of himself: Art had thought the ambush was Jon's doing, and had valiantly moved to shield Calvin.

"That's what you get, boyo," Calvin said to himself.

The lads of Troop 666, hitherto hanging on every word of Chicken's new ghost story character (a bikini-clad Christie Brinkley), had roared with delight a moment ago as something just short of a 4th of July fireworks show rocketed skyward from the dark woods to the south. They were still buzzing about it when Calvin returned.

"Holy crap, that was cool!" Sandy turned to Calvin. "Didja see that, dude?!"

"I missed it."

"Dude! It was totally awesome! Fireballs goin' sky high!"

"Really."

With dangerous alacrity, Sandy assumed the Sandmiller Special stance. "What's wrong with you? Where's Art?"

"Oh," Calvin said, tilting his head towards the goat-path, "down there somewhere."

Sandy couldn't decide whether to investigate or start swinging. A loud battle shriek forced his mind down a third path. He—and Calvin—and everyone—looked to the south.

Six very pissed off kids emerged from the dark forest into the blazing cone of campfire light. They wore soggy, sticky clothes, bore scowls of animosity, and two of them carried aluminum baseball bats. "Here we go!" Sandy screamed.

Chicken, standing in the storyteller's spot, was but an arm's reach from the intruders. A towering kid, twice Chicken's height, brought up his bat. Chicken smiled—a chilling, triangular beam—and punched the bat-wielder's nuts.

"Oh shit," Oldroyd moaned. He was ill-positioned to prevent the skirmish, so he jettisoned his Martin and heaved himself right in, standing next to Father, and they did their best to corral the brawling Inky, Gus, Chicken, Sandy, Denny, and Ryan. "Break it on up!" Oldroyd shouted.

Face alive with queer rage, like something from a previous evil life reemerging, Denny aimed over Father's shoulder and sucker-punched one of the bat-toting Troop 73 hooligans. Oldroyd hurled his thin body at Denny. "Damn ya's, *quit it!*"

From the goat-path, Mr. Maguire issued forth. "The hell's all the noise down here?" he asked blearily. In short order he stood aside Oldroyd, peacemaking. "Back off, all of you!"

The six Troop 73 hooligans inched to the lip of the woods, huddled together for safety. The six brawlers from Troop 666 took a few steps back towards the Fire of Inky. The two grown-ups and Father stood in the no-man's-land between them.

The standoff spanned several seconds. Quietly, without ceremony, the massive monster Inky drew his Bowie knife. No one missed him doing it. The polo shirt, fleecy-haired hooligan motioned to one of his mates, saying, "Bring it out."

The hooligan so indicated—tallish, with a forehead flop of brown hair and a tight little grin sandwiched between pink cheeks—reached back and drew out a steel machete.

The two silver blades held orange gleams from the fire.

"Who dies first?!" the pink-cheeked hooligan challenged, in a strong, determined voice.

"You just volunteered," Inky replied.

Suddenly Chicken's lean frame appeared between the bladesmen. "No way, José!" he yelled. The world around him went on hold. Panicky faces on both sides watched with wide eyes as the 5'5", 120 pound ball of rage flew, Superman pose and all, at the hooligan's machete.

Chicken's face reverberated when the body and bridge of a Martin acoustic suddenly smote it. He careened sideways from the blow, crashing to the ground. His forward momentum carried him out of the fire circle like a flung bowling ball, knocking him about the head with the trunks of old trees. Physics finally exercised a firm grip on him and Chicken lay, stomach down, head buried in the bark of a maple's trunk, legs sticking in the air. Steam hissed from the poor kid's ears.

Troop 73's hooligans turned. Troop 666's lads turned.

Calvin lay on the ground between them. "Stupid cunt," he breathed, frowning at the remains of the weaponized guitar in his left hand. It had split in two: the neck and body were only still held together by the three strings which hadn't snapped.

He dropped the thing and turned a contemptuous eye towards Troop 73. "You're lucky I did that, Mike."

All the gin Sandy had left in his canteen might not be enough for this one! He helped Calvin up—just so he could grab the kid by the shirt collar. "Please tell me you didn't just do that, dude!" he pleaded. "You didn't just cross us, did ya?"

"I didn't *cross* you now!" Calvin said, jutting a thumb at Mike. "This one's in K.P. with me."

"I *knew* it!" Sandy gnashed.

"This albino cripple is from K.P.?" the fleecy-haired hooligan queried Mike.

Mike lowered his machete to a less evil position. "Yep."

"Okay," fleecy-hair said, hefting his aluminum implement of destruction. "We'll spare him."

"Bullshit!" The roar came from Inky, garnering the attention of everyone present. The ogre pointed his Bowie knife at Mike. "This is war, not Woodstock! *We spare no one!"*

"Relax there, Inky," Oldroyd warned.

"Go to hell, you stupid hick!" Inky returned.

"Mike," Calvin mumbled, sidling next to him, "put it away."

Trembling, Mike dropped the machete to the ground.

Father took a step into no-man's-land. "Betrayer!" he cried, looking at Calvin. "Get back to *our* side, now!" His ordinarily pious hands now held fists.

Calvin looked at the fists. *"Put your sword back into its sheath! You know what book that's from … Matthew?"*

"You just killed Chicken! Right now I quote Exodus: *eye for an eye!"*

"Sounds good!" growled Inky, standing by Father. "Move your ass, Connor! We got cocksuckers to murder!"

"You lay offa Calvin!" spat Gus. The young blob trotted limply to Calvin's side. "He's right! Fightin' ain't the answer!"

"Beat it, fat-ass!" Inky spat.

"Fuck you, Inky!" Gus screamed, a wobbly rage in his bulbous eyes. "I'm bein' loyal here! I'm on his side!"

"This ain't your fight, man," fleecy-hair muttered to Gus.

"It's *nobody's* fight!" snarled Calvin, his face turning flush.

"It's my fight now!" shouted Sandy, standing aside Father. "Where the hell's Art?!"

"Maybe we should be going," Mike mused.

Inky had had enough of the patter. He brought up his Bowie knife, wielding it with both hands like a knight gripping his longsword.

"You're not going anywhere!" The laser weapons in Inky's eyes were primed and ready to fire. For real.

"Inky!" Calvin yelled. He turned to the dumbfounded grown-ups. "Would you *do* something?!"

Oldroyd, noticing Inky's severe attitude, buckled at the chance to intervene. He had been on the receiving end of an Inky attack and obviously didn't wish to relive it.

Mr. Maguire, who'd seen action in Vietnam and had no particular beef with Inky, did not yet buckle. He eased into the no-man's-land and put up his hands. "Inky, give me the knife."

"Fuck you," spat Inky through his clenched teeth.

And, having been told off, Mr. Maguire cycled through his collection of take-no-shit faces. He opened his mouth to deliver a rebuke. But, facing a gargantuan young man with a deadly weapon, whose temperament was known to be violent, Mr. Maguire did what he always did: back down.

Calvin fetched Mike's machete and stepped to Inky. The blades nearly touched. "You don't scare me," he stated firmly.

Inky's shiver-inducing eyes flickered; his lip dipped down; his grip on the knife got tighter. "Killing you won't bother me."

"Then go ahead," Calvin challenged, flinging away the machete. He stepped forward so the Bowie knife's blade pointed at his ribcage, half an inch above his slung right arm.

"Don't be stupid, dude!" Sandy cried desperately.

Calvin did not look away from Inky's Death Star eyes.

Oldroyd shook. Mr. Maguire stood frozen. Gus's mouth gaped. Ryan Phillips, usually stoic, seemed all out of sorts.

"Go on," Calvin said. "Kill me."

Inky quivered. "Last warning, Connor!"

Calvin's determination did not falter. He would win this confrontation, at any cost. His good hand moved up to Inky's throat and he squeezed with all his might. "Put down the fucking knife, Konrad!"

Their embrace drew gasps of horror from all: Calvin throttled Inky, bulging the guy's glowing eyes; Inky kept the enormous Bowie knife blade firmly against Calvin's ribs.

Inky gave out a gasp; Calvin gave out a growl.

Simultaneously Sandy and Mike cut in. Mike swooped his arms around Calvin's stomach, pulling him back; Sandy ducked under Calvin's outstretched arm and swatted the Bowie knife from Inky's sweaty grip. Inky, now disengaged, fell to his ass, massaging his throat and taking huge gasps of air. Calvin, hyperventilating, fell into Mike's arms, his limbs drooping dead.

Pudgeball Gus flopped to his knees and grabbed both blades. He held one in each hand with a fierce paranoia, daring anyone to make a grab for them. He hopscotched backwards, keeping all in view, until he neared Chicken's wheezing body.

Having seen enough, the fleecy-haired hooligan bolted into the woods for his campsite, followed by a few of the other Troop 73ers. Instinctively Sandy went after them—but Mr. Maguire's anxious hands restrained him. "Stop, Sandy! You go rushin' in there, you'll end up kicked to shit like Spazz was!"

Mike, who'd stayed behind, broke his silence. "Why don't we all go back to our bunks," he said, his deep voice tearing at their weak hearts. "I'm willing to call a truce."

"Truce my ass," Inky croaked, the words limping out.

"You cunt!" Calvin said. "Let it fucking end!"

Sandy gathered up a luger and deposited it at Calvin's feet. "You sure shocked me, backstabber! Siding with the enemy!"

Calvin crossed himself left-handed. "Jesus weeps at your behavior, Sandy, you fuckin' ball-bag!"

Father, releasing a savage sigh, stepped into the standoff. He said to Sandy, "Calvin's right."

"He's a whiny little dick-sucking traitor," Sandy replied.

"But he's also right," Father stressed. "Let's not spend all night trying to make everyone dead by morning."

"Dead," wheezed Chicken, climbing to his feet. He aimed a finger at Calvin. "The choice of a new generation—*death!*"

Mr. Maguire took his cue and flapped his arms. "Come on, time for bed. Let's end this shit, stat!" Oldroyd, still worthlessly shaking, steadied the frowning cowboy hat atop his head.

Gus chucked the machete towards Mike's feet, the Bowie knife at Inky's feet, and ran off to the goat-path like the Devil Himself chased him. Inky slogged away with a threatening glance over his shoulder. The others followed. Sandy's final, spiteful glance back grated at Calvin's sore heart.

Mr. Maguire nodded at Calvin. "For your safety, you better sleep in my tent tonight."

"Not happening," snorted Calvin. "Pretty soon, *you'll* want to kill me too." He grabbed the machete and offered its hilt to Mike. "I hear your Troop is really small. Got any bunks open?"

Mike gave a crooked smile. "If you want, big guy."

Calvin looked at Mr. Maguire—maybe for the last time as a friend. The lad pulled out a set of keys and tossed them on the ground. "You dropped these earlier," he lied.

Mr. Maguire stared at the keys, checked the quick-release snap on his belt where the keys should have been (and obviously were not!), then looked, dumbly, back up. Mike and Calvin disappeared into the dark woods.

And then it was over. Like the firefights Paul Maguire had experienced in 'Nam, this felt like it'd lasted twenty minutes but had only taken three, beginning to end. The man picked up his keys and chewed the inside of his lip, wondering about his son's absence. That ever-present circle—Art, Sandy, and Calvin, often seen at the Maguire apartment playing cards or doing homework—might be over.

His bladder begged for relief; he made a deposit on the Fire of Inky. The quaking Oldroyd came to a stop and joined in.

"That mick traitor owes me a Martin," Oldroyd noted.

Mr. Maguire stared at him. "I heard about this thing in 'Nam," he said softly. "Called *fraggin' the sarge*. Heard about it a lot, but never met anyone who had it happen to their unit. I figured it was a rumor." He rubbed his scruffy beard with a dark hand. "And then," he said, "someone did it to *my* sarge."

As he zipped up, Oldroyd stared at the thin sliver of starlit sky between the trees above the fire circle. By the time he'd composed his nasty retort and looked down to deliver it, Mr. Maguire was gone.

Chapter 37
EXPLAININ' THIS SHIT.

WITH DENNY'S HELP, Sandy got Chicken to the Beaver Squad tent. The kid had hazy eyes, cradled a swollen nose, and made a baleful hissing noise as he lay in his bunk. "I sleep now," Chicken purred, rolling over. "Tomorrow, I bring justice."

"Cool," Sandy said. He went to his backpack, fetched his canteen, and had a good swig from it. His face scrunched up at the grit of warm gin. He said to his little brother, "I'm gonna find Calvin and end this. You stay here and watch him."

"If ya see Spazz, tell him it's safe to come out," Denny said.

Sandy stepped out the Beaver tent and scrubbed his curly black hair. This night was far from over—Dick'll be gettin' punishment ready already, and Kermit'll be involved before long, a real inquisition this time, and what's our alibi? Oh, just telling ghost stories by the campfire … damn this whole Operation World War IV was stupid! Sandy knew he needed to finish it now, or he might not get the chance.

He trotted to the Hawk Squad tent on the off-chance Calvin was there. He quietly held aside one flap and looked in. No Calvin. No Jon. No Crowe. Only Ryan Phillips and Acting Squad Lieutenant Gus. "Is he here?" Sandy muttered.

"Who, Calvin?" Gus said dumbly.

It was answer enough. "He ain't coming back," Sandy stated. "He's got a billion people ready to whip his ass right now, me included. Ain't nowhere safe for him in this campsite tonight." He looked at Ryan. "Where the hell is everybody? Spazz, and Art—and I ain't seen Crowe for a while, neither."

"Something happened," Ryan intoned, lowering a brow. "Involving all three. Let's just say, justice was served."

Sandy felt the need to shudder. "I heard enough B.S. about justice!" He booked from the Hawk tent. What the hell did Ryan mean? Was the kid molting ... or was The Lord Low Almighty speaking to him? Sandy had a feeling—a premonition—that he'd only get more pissed off as the night went on.

As he slogged along the goat-path towards the fire circle, dangling his lunchbox flashlight at the ground, Sandy caught sight of a hunk of plastic in the brush off to one side. It resembled, in color and shape, the brace that Art had been wearing. Closer inspection led to the amazing discovery that Art was, in fact, still wearing it! The kid lay passed out on his back; a trickle of blood ran down his chin, mixed with dirt and leaves.

"Jesus H. Christ with Thousand Island!" Sandy gasped. He knelt down and slapped Art's cinereous face.

The kid's blue eyes switched on and his free hand deflected the blinding light. "Who the fuck's that?" he croaked.

Sandy clicked a switch on his lunchbox flashlight, killing the beam and activating a soft glow from the side panel. "It's Sandy. You okay, dude? Anything busted?"

Art grabbed Sandy's arm and pulled himself up with it. "Just my pride, Sandy."

"What? Let's get you to the pump. You look like shit."

Holding on to Art's waist, Sandy shuffled the pair of them down the path. He felt something wet against his bare forearm where it contacted Art's back, and held it up to the light.

"That's paint," Art said. "Three shots in the back, point-blank, with my own gun. Hurts like a motherfucker."

They reached the fire circle. It was empty, and the dying Fire of Inky's lingering, frail light spooked them. "What the fuck?" Art choked, pointing. "Is that Oldroyd's guitar?"

"Yeah," Sandy said, "long story." He got them to the latrine and worked the pump crank until cold water trickled out the tap. Art splashed his face, wiping the blood and dirt off and having a nourishing drink. The boys slogged back to the trembling Fire of Inky and flopped to their asses, heads in hands.

Sandy recoiled, pointing a wild finger. "Dude! Your afro!"

Art jerked his hand along his perfect half-inch-high flattop and found a notch on the very front (from the center towards the right, extending back his scalp about an inch). "Holy shit!"

"How the—start explainin' this shit!" Sandy demanded.

Art looked his friend over. A long pause followed. "Don't get lit when I tell you. You just asked to hear it, remember."

"Tell me, goddamnit!"

A sigh. "*I* bleached Calvin's hair."

Sandy's emotions collided with this knowledge; it was a horrific wreck. "*You* did it? But ... but ... why?!"

"I was pissed off at him. He was scoring with Cindy, like, right in front of us. And what he did to Jon really got me going."

"So, just that? He didn't do anything to you!"

"Don't give me that. I was justified." Art's gangly face rolled in pent-up frustration. "I'm so tired of Calvin getting his way, while I don't get mine and I work hard for it. Look at Jill Pedersen—he got her by fuckin' accident, just shoppin' at the mall. But I worked on her for a whole night, feedin' her drinks, and I didn't get shit. Don't you realize how frustrating that is?"

Sandy issued a long sigh through his nose.

"Remember I told you to use that subliminal thing on Gus? I thought you'd do it, then tell Calvin—let him in on the joke."

"I *did* use it," Sandy said, tilting his head in confusion. "The morning after we got drunk. Went down to the Hawk tent at first light to check on Calvin, and told Gus's stupid sleepin' face to show balls and be a man. Think it even worked: you shoulda seen him here, telling Inky 'fuck you!' But I never told Calvin about it. I mean, we joked about it while we was drinkin', but otherwise, never came up. Are you sayin' *Gus* cut yer hair?"

"No," Art snapped, "just listen. That same morning, right before roll, I hit Calvin with super-strength peroxide from my lab, then hid it under the Hawk tent. If you'da told Calvin about the subliminal thing, and *then* if he woulda found the lab there and not under *my* tent, he woulda thought Gus did it."

Sandy worked that over. "But you told me about the subliminal thing *before* Calvin made out with Cindy—when we was walkin' back here!"

"He was gonna bag her, you could fuckin' see it coming. But if it looked like he wouldn't of … I woulda just let it go."

Sandy was pissed. "Are you fuckin' crazy?! I can't believe I'm sidin' with Calvin on this, but just for the moment!"

"What's that mean?" Art asked.

"What's that mean?! Cindy's a slut, dude! *I* made out with her just this morning! She gets a new guy every week! She ain't nothin' special—and for *that,* you bleached Calvin's hair?"

"For a lot of things. Jill … Jon … bottled-up, you know."

"No. I *don't* know." Sandy aimed a perturbed look at him.

Art shrugged. "Go to hell. I was righteous. Remember when Oldroyd threw us outta the campsite? I took charge and led us to the Camp Showers cuz I knew Calvin'd be there. He'd just found out about his hair, and he'd go shower and shampoo and probably get upset and cry, and then try to hide."

"What're you smokin', dude? He wasn't there!"

"Yo, he was! In the shower room still, listening. I could hear his breathing. So I ad-libbed, bullshit about my mom don't peroxide her hair, maybe Gus should be a suspect … " And as he said the words, Art's righteous form collapsed. "I left thirty clues to blame Gus. Way too many. Five woulda done the trick. And Calvin waited 'til during my masterpiece to pay me back!"

"But how did he—when could he of—I don't know whether to scratch my watch or wind my ass!" Sandy rolled his head around to cool his overheating brain. "How'd Calvin fire the paintball gun with a bum arm?! Ya need two hands!"

"Wasn't Calvin. I actually shielded him from whoever did."

"You mean he had others helpin' him? Holy shit—Crowe! Crowe's been missing for like an hour!"

"There you go." A frown. "No wait, Crowe went to see Jon in jail. And Jon ambushed us on the trail, but he was in front of me and I got shot in the back."

"Okay, the only missin' person left is Spazz!" Sandy's jaw dropped low. And stayed there. "I can see why Crowe helped Calvin: he's a dumb rookie. And Jon's always up for violence. *But Spazz?!* What a fuckin' dickhead—you was gettin' revenge for him against Troop 73, and he shoots you for it?!"

Art smirked. "That's Spazz. I shoulda seen it comin'!"

"This is … unforgiveable! Calvin broke the circle!"

"Sandy, *I* broke it first."

Sandy made fists. "Listen to this shit—*your* plan went off like a charm. Fireworks sky high. We could see 'em from all the way up here. Then the shitheads from 73 came straight here lookin' for trouble, carryin' baseball bats even. So Inky got out his Bowie knife, and one of them pulls out a machete!"

"Whoa."

"The guy says, 'I'll kill you!' So of course Chicken goes ballistic … and Calvin roofs him with Oldroyd's guitar!"

"No shit! Why the hell would he do that?"

"Take a guess, dude."

Art cocked his head in disbelief. "Come on—really?"

"Yes, *really*," Sandy gnashed. "Calvin called one dude by name! Took *their* side in the fight! He got hold of the machete and faced off with Inky, then nearly choked him to death!"

"Calvin … *choked Inky?!* And he lived to talk about it?"

"Inky *backed down* afterward. Calvin made him give up!"

Then Art laughed, long and hard, like someone who'd just heard a joke. "Yo, I'm in awe! Look at how it all played out: Calvin gets his revenge on me; he makes up for puttin' Jon away; Jon gets to have a little fun; Spazz gets *his* revenge on me for shooting him in the throat; and Calvin gets Inky back for all them years riding his ass, calling him a 'mick.' And he ruined my plan too! It's, like, so perfect!"

"Perfect, my ass! He's a fuckin' traitor!" Sandy snarled. "You totally worship him, Art. You oughta be rippin' his head off! Where *is* that asshole? Do I got some shit to say to him!"

"Hidin' somewhere—with Cindy I bet," Art proposed. "Gettin' his dick sucked. He always gets away with it."

Through gritted teeth, a long stream of words left Sandy's mouth: "She's gotta have a room somewhere. Shit, he's got like a twenty-minute lead on us—and he knows where he's going! We got no god-damn idea. He'll stay with Cindy all night too. He ain't comin' back here with only Ryan and Gus to back him up—Ryan can't take us *all* on. And he ain't goin' near *your* tent cuz of what he did to you and Chicken, and he *sure* ain't goin' near the leaders' tent, with Inky and your dad!" Flush with fury, Sandy punched his open palm. "Fuckin' A! Calvin betrayed us all, and we lost World War IV! *We lost!*"

"You said it yourself: Troop 73 got spooked by the fireworks bomb!" Art barked. "So Calvin didn't leak nothing. Besides, when could he have told them?"

"He found out 'bout you being the guy who bleached 'im," Sandy stated, "and kept that a secret for like fuckin' days, all the while gatherin' up a posse!"

"Stop it! You're *purposely* tryin' to turn me against him!"

"You'll turn on him yourself once you look in a mirror."

"I bleached his hair, he paid me back! We're even!"

"Fuck that! Let's find that dickhead and settle this shit!"

Art rubbed a hand through his notched afro flattop. "No. Game over." He shoved himself to his feet and took a breath of the forest's air. "And even if it's not, I'll settle for losing."

"Fuck that!" Sandy yelled. "I ain't goin' to bed a loser!"

"Then have fun stayin' up all night," Art shrugged. "Wake up and smell the coffee, Mr. Sandmiller. We lost." He looked down at Sandy. He very nearly added the words, "For now."

Chapter 38

PICKOFF ATTEMPT.

MILK CRATES BORROWED from Chef Jim's monstrous stack sat atop Lyons's soon-to-be-former gunmetal desk, filled with the myriad minute knickknacks with which the man had, over the years, decorated his pathetically secondhand office. Polaroids. Neckerchiefs. Awards. A movie poster for *The Year of Living Dangerously*. A flute whittled for him by a Trooper. A framed dollar bill, withdrawn from his first Camp Souviens paycheck.

Lyons stared blankly at the junk. He was overdramatizing. He did that sometimes. Osmosis—years of gauntly tripping by Murphy's side, watching the bastard put on a one-man show.

This was it. The last time Lyons would be in his office.

Unless he needed to come in tomorrow, or Saturday morning. But it was the last time he'd be in his office while it still had all his junk in it—while it was still *his* office.

Seven years spent in this little windowless room: eleven weeks over summer and early fall, then eight weekends in the winter. He toiled the remainder of his year in Norwich as a plumbing contractor. Counting his early time as a Counselor, Lyons had spent thirteen years total at Camp Souviens. Thirteen years of putting up with the self-righteous, nasty snob Jake Murphy, and his crassness, pettiness, anti-smoking, anti-woman, anti-black, anti-everything beliefs. Thirteen years spent away from his wife and daughter, perhaps a contributing factor to the ugly divorce last year. Lyons had taken the Deputy Director job in part due to his inability to have a son. One daughter was all his striking sperm had managed. One daughter, who'd gotten arrested this past May, pissing off her mother so much that the mean cow forced the kid on her dad for the entire summer. One daughter, who'd dyed her hair apple red in response to being stuck in a boys' summer camp.

"What a waste," Lyons said aloud. He stood up, packed the crates on a hand cart, and wheeled it out to the hallway.

He stopped dead. His nerve-endings sang a sharp chord.

Two boys stood three paces down the hall in dark clothing and hats pulled down low. One had mud smeared on his face. He carried a rifle; the dangerous end zeroed in on Lyons's chest.

"This guy?" the rifleman grunted. He fully intended to blow Lyons away right here and now.

The other kid, whose Whalers cap was similar to Wren's, stared at Lyons in the limited light. "No," the Whalers cap said. "That ain't him. Connor calls him 'Satan' but he ain't the guy."

"Er," Lyons said, feeling he should do *something* before his execution. "Can I help you boys?"

"Where's Murphy?" the Whalers Cap urged.

Lyons licked his dry lips. "After the false alarm, the Camp Ranger reamed him out and he stomped back to his quarters at Chamberlin like a little baby. He locks the door, you know."

"Shit," cursed the rifleman, finally lowering his gun so he could snap his fingers in defeat. "And I wanted ta murderize the mothahumpa! Guess I gotta pop off my juice in the stupid bastitch's office. Which one is it?"

The Whalers cap pointed. "At the end." They obviously didn't care if Lyons heard. "Make sure to get the stupid desk!"

"Is that … " Lyons pointed at the rifle. "… a paintball gun?"

"Sureby-derby!" the rifleman said. "Coat'cher friends in red, instead o' making 'em dead!"

"A few hours ago I quit my job, and the straw that broke the camel's back was Murphy had it in for you fellas. Pretty sure he ordered the hit on you." Lyons fingered the rifleman.

"Fuck me!" the rifleman said, feeling fear's sting himself.

"Holy shit! I knew it!" The Whalers cap turned to the rifleman and stomped a foot. "Murphy's been targetin' us from the moment we showed up! I shoulda slugged 'im when he took me down at the dance! C'mon Spazz, let's do it!"

The rifleman made heavy metal guitar chord noises.

The Whalers cap took ill-note of Lyons. "You got a problem with that, pal?"

Lyons shook his head. "In fact, can I fire the first shot?"

The rifleman cocked his head at the Whalers cap. They shrugged in unison. The rifleman put a hand to his head. "I can see the future," he said, "and it's got you takin' the first shot written all over it, Darth." He proffered the rifle, grinning.

Chapter 39
CHEEP!

MIKE SETTLED IN by the meager campfire. "Guys, this is Calvin. Calvin, the guys: Terence, Ric, Jack, Gray, and Doug."

"What's up?" the guys said.

"Hi," Calvin said.

"And dozin' away there," Mike said, pointing at a distant shadow in the Campsite Trois share of the woods, "is Mr. Dixon."

Calvin shrugged. "Hi," he said to the shadow. "What'd he say when the booby-traps went off?"

"He's been sleepin' like a baby since like eight," said Mike. "We drive him nuts on camping trips, and he gets tired of coverin' for our asses. So he takes Valium after dinner."

Doug—a bushy-haired kid with a rotund face—arched his brows. "Your Troop gonna take another shot at us?"

"They don't got anything else planned," sighed Calvin. "But *I'll* be a target now too." He eyeballed the hooligan kids in Troop 73. "Is *your* Troop going to take another shot at *us?*"

"Yes," said Ric matter-of-factly. He was the older, fleecy-haired, polo shirted guy, leader of the pack here. "And on that note, I don't like you bein' here. So what if you saved Mike?"

"Fuck that," Mike spat.

Ric put it to a vote. "All those in favor the albino splits?"

No one but Ric.

"Shit," he summed up. "So which one of you hicks set up the traps, Calvin? *That's* someone I wanna keep an eye on."

"My mate Art," Calvin replied. "You didn't see him just now cuz I had him ambushed."

Mike burped, "Ambushed?! What for?"

"He's the one who bleached my hair. You don't think I did this to myself, on purpose?!"

"I thought *mate* meant *friend,*" asked Jack, a tall kid with black hair parted to one side.

"It does," nodded Calvin.

"Some friend."

Terence—short, stocky, with a wide chin and dark curls—gave an irritated growl. "What's he want, to kill us all?"

Calvin leveled a gaze at them. "Listen to you sore losers now. Art's something of a genius. He's been working on that Eat-At-Joe's fireworks bomb for as long as I've known him."

Jack grinned maliciously. "Well, your ass-buddy 'mate' just made the top of our target list. Whaddaya think about that?"

"Gonna kick his teeth in like you did to Spazz? Why the hell did you do that, anyway? It started all this shite!"

Troop 73 looked at each other. Ric flailed a *what-the-hell* hand and told the tale: "We heard all the noise you guys were making on the first night and snuck up to have a look. There was that kid with the long blond hair, what'd ya call 'im?"

"Spazz."

"Spazz—he saw Gray standin' there in the dark. He reacted so weird to it, though. We spent the next few days making noises in the woods near him, so's he'd shit his pants."

"We've been spying on you guys pretty regular," Terence added. "We saw your Kangaroo Court, saw you and that red-haired chick go skinny dipping ... we saw it all, man."

Ric went on: "I thought Spazz was gonna freak out and attack us— he was totally paranoid!"

"I almost shit when he came into K.P. yesterday," Mike said. "He was subbin' for you, Calvin. He caught me watchin' him, and I thought for sure our cover was blown."

"We took no chances," said Gray—a towering kid with gawking eyes, flat blond hair, and what could only be accurately described as a penis-tip for a nose. "Ric rounded us up and we waited to get him alone."

"Jaysus," Calvin said, "no one's safe with you lads around."

The guys chuckled proudly. When the laughter died, Jack asked, "So where you from, man? Australia?"

"Australia?! Try *Ireland,* you cunt!" There was laughter from Calvin's left. He ignored it. "We moved here when I was ten. I have dual citizenship. I'll ask about getting a third passport from Australia, though." Giggles from Mike. Calvin looked at him. "What did you do to get in K.P.?"

The guys started laughing again. Mike cleared his throat. "Well, Ric's our J.T.M., and—"

"He's your *what?!*"

"Junior Troopmaster. Anyway, he spent the whole ride from Buffalo pickin' on me, calling me gay, a super-faggot, all kinds of shit. So I mooned him and asked him if he liked it."

Ric nodded. "Mike's totally gay way of getting back at me."

"Dixon didn't want us acting up all week—cuz we've been known to do that. So he sent me to K.P. as an example."

"What did *you* do to get in K.P.?" Doug asked Calvin.

Calvin rolled his eyes. "Punishment for Tentgate. You guys were at the Kangaroo Court. It was all bollocks."

"At least you *earned* a trip to K.P.," said Mike. "I didn't! And neither did Ken and George and Hank! Totally shafted."

"What'd those guys do?" asked Ric.

"They were playing Dungeons & Dragons," Mike explained. "They got into a fight. Their T.M. blamed D&D—he's a total Bible-thumper, and thinks D&D is the work of Satan."

"Well, Gary Gygax *is* Satan!" Jack laughed.

"No, he's *God!*" Terence replied.

"Satan!"

"God!"

"Satan!"

"God!"

"Jesus save us," Calvin said, crossing himself and giving the laughter a new target.

Mike shrugged. "I like those K.P. guys. I think Ken's cool."

"Ken's all right," Calvin agreed.

"It sucked until you and Jon came along. Then I could spy on you guys totally up close, without you even knowin' it."

Sarcastically: "Must've been a real thrill."

"Nah, in the end it still blew. I still hadda wash dishes with that bitch going nuts on us. You seem to get along with her."

"We saw you guys skinny dippin'," Terence said, wiggling his eyebrows. "She's got an awesome ass, man."

"And nice tits," Jack added.

The guys made grunts of approval.

"Don't talk about her like that," Calvin snapped.

"Like what?" Mike smirked. "You got some, didn't ya?"

"I did," Calvin smirked back. "But still, don't talk—"

"No shit!" Mike yelped, cutting him off. "Congrats, man. I'd high-five you, but your arm's busted."

"A verbal high-five, then—strike last, strike fast ..."

Mike looked lost.

Calvin finished off himself: "... get stuffed."

"Talk about gay," Ric laughed.

The guys had a titter. Then, they got quiet. Troop 73's campfire, a limp thing compared to a Fire of Inky, crackled a little. "You'd never know there was a scrap like fifteen minutes ago," Calvin noted quietly. "You're all pretty calm about it."

"Probably cuz we're stoned," Gray smiled.

"Seriously?" Calvin burped.

"Yeah," Mike said. "Gray there grows it in his back yard."

"Farming merit badge did you right," Calvin said. "But I mean, shouldn't one of you be on the lookout right now?"

"You said your Troop didn't have anything else planned tonight," Ric pointed out.

"I also said I'm a target. They might come lookin' for me."

The guys turned to peer into the darkness of the Souviens woods. Then, faced front with a collective shrug.

Calvin squinted. "I'm not thick. You got some kinda defense set up. Or your next attack plan!"

"Yep. You can even show him if you want," Ric said to Doug confidently. "Not like he can stop us using it."

Beaming wide, Doug took something from his tan shorts' pocket.

"We were gonna plant this at nine o'clock sharp, but the false alarm and your boyfriend Art's bullshit here got in the way." He lobbed the thing over.

Calvin caught it—a half-dozen small metal tubes whose open ends had been sealed with wax; lengths of green cord poked out of these ends; and the tubes had been lashed together with bands of bailing wire. Calvin dropped the thing in the dirt next to him with all alacrity. "Fucking cunt!"

Doug feigned ignorance. "Why are you scared, Calvin?

"This is *six* CO_2 cartridges!" Calvin raged. "With only like five seconds' worth of fuse!"

Troop 73 beamed at themselves. "You obviously seen 'em before," Jack said. "We got like four of those. Bitchin', right?"

"We're at a *campfire* here!" Calvin roared. Then the lad's eyeballs bulged. "Hang on! What in the name of Jaysus's bollocks were you gonna do with it?!"

Ric spread his hands. "The vote was a split. Jack saw you throw out a bag of clothes and we snagged it. Him, Gray, and I wanted to put that cluster in your bloody uniform and blow it up on your jetty. You guys would find the uniform and freak out, thinking someone died. Mike, Terence, and Doug said that was stupid. They said, we should toss one down your—"

"Stop, just stop!" Calvin buried his face in his hand. "A guy like Art is a genius cuz he thinks things out. Guys like you are just stupid, cuz you don't." Ignoring the disapproving grunts, Calvin picked the bomb up and carefully placed it as far from the campfire as he could while still seated. "We're in the forest here. You can't alibi your way out of arson!"

There was a dangerous pause ... ended by Doug going *cheep!* Mike did the *cheep!*, as did Gray. Must be some little thing with them.

Ric said, "This guy's too intense, Mike."

Mike shrugged. "K.P. does that to you."

"Yeah," Terence said. "He's got me all worried and shit."

Calvin bugged at them. "You should be 'all worried and shit!' That's a fucking bomb now. Try growing up in Ireland—bombs like that go off all the time and people die! For real!"

"Who cares," Ric spat. "You're in America, asshole."

"Ain't no one gonna die," Gray added.

"At least," Doug said, "won't be any of us."

"I don't want to know anything else about it," Calvin said, shuffling up to his feet. "And I thought *my* Troop was off their nut—you're all fucking mental!"

The guys made insulted noises, bombarding him with wide angry eyes. Calvin didn't back off his attitude, despite being seriously outnumbered—and unable to brawl with both fists. "It's the truth now. *You* attacked Spazz, without getting attacked first. Now you want to blow us up? You're lunatics!"

Ric announced, "I'm done listening to this douche. Let's try again—all in favor the albino splits?"

Everyone but Mike ... who eventually raised his hand.

Calvin turned his back on them. "Fuck all you nutters." He swiftly moved up the by-way from the Campsite Trois fire circle to the Green Trail.

"I vote we stick the bomb down his pants," Gray said, releasing an ungainly garbage-disposal laugh.

"Shut up," Mike said. "He did save me back there. He's actually all right."

"Says his gay lover," Ric laughed. "Ah, fuck 'im. Hey Gray, go get your stash. Let's smoke another one."

Chapter 40

New lodgings.

THE RED TRAIL was quite dark. Calvin slogged up the gradual incline, struggling to breathe. Twice he paused for a rest-bit; it was still his first day out of hospital. His right shoulder and back were stiff from the sling, and the painkillers had worn off.

He soldiered on, passing the Racine Amphitheater, the mostly dark and quiet Chamberlin Memorial building, and finally Lacroix Field and the parking lot. Calvin saw no one during his journey. Even the forest's insects sounded sleepy.

He continued down the paved Camp Souviens Road, and at length came to the ranch house called home by the Ranger. A newer-looking addition to the home served as the Ranger's Office, with a covered porch, a large front window, and a door; a wooden sign near the door gave the Ranger's name and the office's hours of operation.

Calvin stared at the building. A light was on down the far end of the house-portion, but being a ranch home, those windows were high off the ground. No lights could be seen in the house's main section or the office. Calvin left the roadway pavement and peered in the office window: one large room with a counter, posters on the wall, and a desk. The office's back wall had a pair of doors—presumably, a bathroom and a private room. So Calvin crept around the corner of the building and was delighted to find, towards the back, a much lower window. It was shut and mostly obscured by green curtains. He knocked softly on the glass. "Cindy?" he hissed.

No response.

He knocked a bit harder, said "Cindy?" a bit louder.

He heard movement.

"Cindy, it's Calvin," he said to the window. "Let me in."

The curtains moved just slightly, and Calvin saw Cindy's spooked face between them.

"Holy shit!" she heaved. Her eyes showed both relief and annoyance. "What the hell are you doing here?"

"Long story," Calvin said. "Can I come in?"

"Okay. At the front, the office door," she nodded. "But be quiet— Mr. Grant's home."

Calvin slinked back around to the office entrance; Cindy quietly unlocked and opened the door. She hadn't switched on the lights, and the dark office strongly smelt of old coffee. They stood before the counter, facing each other. She was wrapped in the blanket from her bed (and, by all appearances, wearing little else). Her red hair was more askew than usual.

"It's like ten o'clock," she said, in a quiet, tired voice. "Why aren't you at camp?"

"There was another scrap," Calvin said, matching her soft volume. "My Troop and the one next door. I smashed Chicken with a guitar, then I choked Inky."

"You know their names? Their nicknames, I mean?"

Flatly: "Chicken and Inky are in *my* Troop."

"Oh."

"But I got back Art for bleaching my hair."

"*Art* bleached your hair? Stupid little part-black Art?"

"He was the one."

She nodded, once, then placed a warm little hand on his cheek. "You get into so much shit … "

"I'm in the Devil's Troop, after all," he said crookedly.

She laughed, then checked her volume. "So let me guess—you wanna hide out here."

"I'm not hiding at all. I just don't want to be with them. Any of them. Everyone's a betrayer or a loony."

"But, of all the places to go, you came here. To me." Cindy put a sarcastic smile across her round face. "I don't remember telling you that I sleep here."

"You only said you use the bathroom here," he said.

"Good job, Sherlock." She hiked up the blanket, as it'd started sliding off her naked shoulders. "It's not much of a bed. Kind of like your bunks."

"I didn't come here to sleep with you."

"We don't have to *sleep.*"

"I didn't come here for that, either. Don't even have a rubber. 'Safe sex or no sex,' you said."

"Well ... you have to promise you'll pull out. And I mean *looong* before you cum. I'll totally kick your ass if you don't."

"Cindy," Calvin sighed, reaching out and pulling her close.

She would've hugged him back, but his slung arm smashed against her hands, which she'd had gathered high across her chest to hold up the blanket. She let her face settle on his body. "Oh. I get it," she muttered.

"You do. You get it." He took a deep breath. "Je—I mean, *other* girls never understand. They tell me to stop thinking about things, or just don't bother them with it. But you understand, Cindy."

"It's good to find someone who understands."

They stood in this embrace for some time.

"C'mon," she said. "But we gotta be very quiet."

She pulled away and led him back to her room.

Their bodies entwined on the slender bunk. Their faces sat against each other. The room was small, dark, and very subdued. The pace of their breathing matched up, and they simply lay together quietly.

Many minutes passed.

Then she mumbled, "This ain't very comfortable."

He chuckled. "It's comfortable enough."

"If only we weren't in this goddamn place," she sighed.

"If only."

"This needs to move." She squeezed a small tube in his pants.

He needed to de-pretzel to free his left hand and remove the bottle of painkillers from his pocket.

Her eyes lit up. "Ooh are those space pills?"

He put them right back in his pocket, his ass pocket this time.

"I wasn't going to take one," she said huffily.

"I wasn't either," he said, "but then a tree tried to cut my arm off."

Many minutes passed.

"Want to hear a story?" he asked, suddenly.

She adjusted herself, repositioning numb limbs, and laid her head on his stomach. "Sure. I'd like that."

"Usually summer camp is at this place called Lucid Pond, which is the opposite of here. We have to bring our own tents, and there's no cafeteria. They got a trailer thing where they cook food, and we stand in line then sit in the mud and eat it. And the food's fucking rancid. Merit badges are held in, like, little fields, and if it's raining, we're all jammed in under a tarp. Totally in the woods, the whole time. But I loved it. Goofing off with my mates, just having a good time, y'know?"

He chewed his tongue in dark thought. "Not this week. You got actual buildings. Electric lights. This house has conditioned air! I've barely spent any time in the woods: I'm in a big tent, or the dishroom, or hospital, or la Maison de Douche ... "

Cindy burped a raucous laugh into Calvin's belly.

"Our old tyrant Troopmaster quit, so we got this gobshite cowboy instead. And I'm Squad Captain. I don't know what I'm doing half the time. I'm not even *there* half the time!

"And my mates ... I'm on this side, that side, getting revenge, betraying people." He vented air through flapping lips. "This summer camp is a lot different!"

"Of course it is!" she laughed, reaching down to pat his penis. "You got laid, Calvin!"

"I did," he sighed, "and y'know, I'm not trying to ... ignore that. But sex doesn't outweigh all the shite. I'm not the same person now. I came here without a shredded elbow, without white hair, without a brain bruise. I had loyal friends and archenemies. It's all changed. You know how grown-ups say 'Nothing will be the same after this?' That's how I feel about it.

"What's going on, Cindy? Is this what life is really like?"

His gray eyes looked down at her for an answer.

She looked up at him, her brown eyes curling sadly. "I don't know. I don't have any idea. In my experience, life sucks dick. I can remember a happy time, like you were saying about that other summer camp ... but it was years ago. My parents were married, and I had a girlfriend named Rhonda who always hung out with me. We were gonna take over the world!

"But she's gone. All my friends are gone. I haven't had a real friend, or even a real enemy, in forever. A lot of bad shit happened recently, and I ended up stuck here. So, to answer your question ... yeah, this is what life's really like. Life blows. You can't trust anyone— you're pretty much on your own."

"I wasn't, until I came here. Fucking Camp Souviens."

"Fucking Camp Souviens," she agreed.

Many minutes passed.

His left hand moved a bit, and came to rest on her right tit.

"I want to fuck," he said.

"Yeah, okay," she said.

Chapter 41

MURPHY'S LAW.
FRIDAY, JULY 31, 1987.

BONG, PAUSE, *BONG,* pause, *BONG.*

Murphy, standing at the bathroom mirror in his quarters a third of a mile north of the bell tower, pulled the razor from the edge of his chin-strap beard. "Was that the ... "

A second later, he crashed through his door into the hall, juggling his hairy legs into a pair of khaki shorts. The last thing the Devil's Troop would do is repeat themselves—so *this* "All Camp" alarm is for real! As he hopped down the stairs, he acknowledged the worst aspect of Troop 666: their creativity.

At the front door of the Chamberlin Memorial Building, Murphy found Janitor Mick, panting and sweaty. "Smoke on the horizon!" Mick screamed, his deranged face made wide by fear. "Whole camp's on fire!" Mick thundered down the main hall and kicked down the door to a supply closet. Murphy zipped up his khakis to a melodious chorus of steel scraping aluminum and wood clanging off tiled floor.

Mick emerged with two fire axes and two fire extinguishers, hurling one of each towards his boss. Murphy, agile when unencumbered by his Nike hiking boots, ducked down to avoid the ten-pound fire extin-guisher, which sailed over his head to dent the wall behind him; and slid aside to avoid the sixteen-pound axe, which pirouetted by him at waist height to clang blade-first into the third step in the staircase. Mick bounded out the door wielding the remaining axe and extinguisher, leaping, hollering bloody murder, squirting milky white clouds of gas into random air pockets, etc.

Murphy got to his feet and was nearly bowled over by Lyons, charging his gaunt limbs out the front door at top speed. "Did I hear

right? The whole camp's ablaze?!" bleated the soon-to-be-former Deputy Director. Lyons followed Mick's slowly rising trail of gas bursts.

Murphy peeked out the door, saw no fire or smoke, and sighed
histrionically to his appreciative audience of one. He pushed himself
back up the stairs to gather a shirt and his Nikes. Before heading out, he
picked up the axe and extinguisher with which Mick had thoughtfully
tried killing him.

The Camp Director began the arduous trek down the Red Trail
towards Centre des Trois. He must look a real schmuck, hustling along
with an axe over one shoulder and an extinguisher over the other, but
he was thankful that his audience of one was forgiving in the (rare)
moments of weakness.

AAAAOOOOGAH! The boisterous blast sent Murphy ten feet
into the air, scattering the axe, extinguisher, and Nikes in the four principal compass directions. Again dexterous while unshod, he executed
an Olympic-caliber triple somersault with a twist and landed facing the
opposite way, just in time to see the Golf Cart From Hell barreling
straight at him.

Fix-It Man Kevin applied all 350 pounds of his girth on the brake,
which, ha ha, broke. The Golf Cart From Hell lurched, chucking Kevin
out the left side then crashing onto its right side. All manner of panel
hatches on the Golf Cart From Hell's custom chassis popped open, and
all manner of miter saw blades, canisters of WD-40, dust rags, fuzzy
dice, and quart bottles of Jack Daniels hopped out—an insane array of
jacks-in-boxes. The various items bounced and rolled and showered the
Red Trail for at least fifty feet.

After the obligatory heart grabbing and "What a close call!"ing,
Murphy found himself alongside Kevin, righting the Golf Cart From
Hell back on its wheels. When they did, the dozen side panel hatches
on the vehicle's *right,* hitherto kept shut by the packed earth of the Red
Trail, flew open. The two men could only watch as their feet got pelted
endlessly by ball-peen hammers, battery-operated screwdrivers, telephone cords, welding masks, and ten pounds of loose dried guavas.

"Get in!" Kevin said as he hitched up his pleated work-pants and
bent over to scoop a handful of dried guava halves into his gob. The Golf
Cart From Hell seeped forward. Murphy dove in and made to stomp on

the brake. Except, no pedal.

"Scoot over!" said Kevin. The gargantuan guava-chomping man took a running jump through the open doorframe, landing in the driver's seat and making the Golf Cart From Hell skitter momentarily on two wheels in a maneuver seen weekly on *The Dukes of Hazzard.*

The Golf Cart From Hell returned to four-wheel motion; Kevin turned the key, firing up the engine. He blew the custom-installed Edsel horn for shits'-and-giggles' sake. Whatever junk that *had* still occupied the chassis' storage hatches, including a wet/dry vac, a bowling ball, a year's supply of Windex, a tin box of wing-nuts, and a spare tire, now occupied a place at the end of a cluttered stream of crap-laden Red Trail behind them; said trail of crap would, in the coming minutes, impede a racing team of firefighters riding in a truck that will suffer a front-tire flat after striking the tin box of wing nuts.

The Golf Cart From Hell traveled three times its normal cruising speed when unhindered by the quarter-ton of bullshit previously stored within; so much faster did it now move that Kevin said (much to the demise of Murphy's underwear), "It's like bein' at Daytona! Too bad we ain't got no brakes!"

"Slow down!" Murphy pleaded. His eyes shut themselves.

"Can't, Murph!" Kevin worked the wheel in a herky-jerky way to steer around (and avoid smooshing) the hustling Lyons and Mick. "We're just gonna hafta roll with it! *Yeeee-ha!*"

Kevin looked through the windshield from horizon to horizon. "So where's this fire? The way Mick was screamin', you'da thought the whole camp was burnin' down!" He calmly stuck one boot outside the Golf Cart From Hell to try and ease the barreling monster up.

"You'd've thought," Murphy said, eyes shut.

"Probably coked up again. I'd shut my eyes if I were you."

Murphy, whose eyes were already tightly shut, opened his eyes at this comment. Centre des Trois was upon them. The two-story cafeteria building loomed larger and larger with each passing tick of the inexplicably slow-moving clock.

Not inexplicably. Time slowed because death approached.

For a moment, Murphy figured he might survive. The cafeteria was an open-air facility; and at their current point of trajectory, the Golf

Cart From Hell might leap *through* the dining room in a single bound, rocketing in that precarious space between the tops of the dining tables and the surface of the stucco ceiling, flames spewing out of Kevin's boot from his Fred Flintstone-esque brake attempt, leaving a trail of smoke along their flat parabola; smoke which might still hang about the ceiling in a couple hours when the boys came to breakfast.

Murphy, possessing a brain that computed physics realistically despite indigenous theatrics, knew the Golf Cart From Hell would never sustain the perfect, proper altitude to clear all fifty feet separating the north side of the caf from the south. Moreover, the Golf Cart From Hell likely wouldn't even survive the ground level difference between the packed-earth roadway surrounding the caf and the building's concrete base/floor, a difference of four inches, far too much to act as a ramp for the barreling Golf Cart From Hell's ten-inch wheels. More moreover, bug-eyed Chef Jim stood between them and the caf, floppy faggot chef's hat waggling from his manic Mexican-jumping-bean act: Jim's gesticulating, with an egg-whip in one hand and a two-gallon aluminum mixing bowl full of interfused pre-fetal *gallus gallus domestici* in the other, seemed to indicate (in a frozen moment of clarity just before absolute catastrophe) that something very sensitive to Chef Jim's wavering attention span had happened somewhere to his left ... to the west ... where, as Murphy's eyes panned right, lay the kitchen and dishroom of the caf ... where, pan-pan, also lay the Green Trail ... where, pan-pan, *also* lay Campsite Quatre ... where, within, the indomitable bastards from some one-gnat town in west-central Pennsylvania were staying ... and, (towards the end of this moment of clarity), when Murphy shifted his westward-gazing head upward, he clearly saw black smoke billowing into the dawn sky from a location which triangulation would no doubt (and to Murphy's everlasting chagrin) confirm was Campsite Quatre, as those indomitable Devil's Troop assholes tried blowing up the camp as 1) a checkmate move in the wildly destructive bad-behavior game of chess they'd been playing this week, and 2) a kill-shot, perfectly centered on Murphy's forehead, blasting the poor man's wracked brain clear through the back of his skull.

The moment of clarity ended with Kevin returning to his usual frantic self: the fat Fix-It Man, faced with death at left (himself), death at right (Murphy), or death in front (Jim, Murphy, and himself), valiantly chose death at left, violently yanking the steering wheel that way. The Golf Cart From Hell again tilted on two wheels, then crashed on its side with crazy force. For a lifetime and a half, the tipped-over Golf Cart From Hell rocketed along the packed dirt road, and when Murphy dared himself to take a peek out the windshield, he saw the thick concrete stanchion of the caf's northeast corner hurtling towards him, sideways.

Kevin had gallantly sacrificed himself when death came a-knockin'. Oh, did he regret it! With no doors on the Golf Cart From Hell, Kevin's substantial left arm, left torso, and left leg dragged over the Earth—and because of this fact, the Golf Cart From Hell slowed from hyperspace to docking speed.

But not soon enough to prevent a collision.

The concrete stanchion crushed the Golf Cart From Hell's hood, severely mangled its engine, and burst the windshield. Inertia carried the flashing blue police light, formerly adorning the cabin roof, on a blazing course a hundred feet forward, where it smashed into tiny pieces against the side of a northern red oak tree at the edge of the surrounding roadway. Inertia did not carry the passengers out of the cart, thankfully.

Panting and deep breaths. A lot of "Yow!"ing from Kevin. A strange hissing noise from the deceased engine, part of which protruded through the dash. Then the clanging of an aluminum mixing bowl on the packed-dirt ground, followed by the twang of the egg-whip, followed by the goose-steps of a panicking Chef Jim. "B-B-Bob Marley's ghost!" the ex-hippie screamed as he screeched to a halt near the wreckage. He leaned up and peered down through the open right-side doorway, his bug-eyes bugging like they'd never bugged before.

Kevin wept, not moving anything unnecessarily; Murphy lay crumpled atop him. Jim stuck his hands in and grabbed Murphy's right arm. "G-g-get out before it b-b-blows!"

With that errant comment, Murphy instantly sprung off Kevin's right hip and flew out the doorway. Turning as he landed, he ogled the distance they'd slid: easily a hundred feet. *Easily.* The mere thought of what Kevin's left side looked like …

"It's no good, I c-c-can't reach!" Jim cried to Kevin.

"I'm on the ground anyways," Kevin whimpered to Jim. "Tip the cart back on its wheels."

Murphy grabbed the right rear tire; Jim took hold of the right front; they heaved back. The Golf Cart From Hell crashed upright. The caf's corner stanchion tore off pieces of bumper. Plexiglas nuggets spewed everywhere and leaky engine hoses whipped about. A dusty Atari 2600 console plopped out of a hitherto-stuck right-side chassis hatch. An *E. T.* cartridge slid onto Murphy's right Nike.

Kevin lay on the ground in the same fetal position. His right leg and arm moved, both up and out. "Pull!" he cried.

Jim and Murphy did. When Kevin came off the dirt road to stand on his feet, a nausea-inducing noise—a *WRRRECH!* noise—came from his left side. Jim puked all over his beard.

"It ain't that bad," Kevin muttered slowly. *"YES IT FUCKING IS!"* he hollered quickly. His rotund body blasted by Murphy, showing him the gross damage—dust-packed, bloody cakes of flesh; flaps of torn and burnt skin, flailing like a T-shirt tied to a speeding car's radio antenna; torn and burnt-off pant leg pieces, falling to the road in his wake. Wailing something bloodcurdling, Kevin tore past the caf to the south, heading directly for the Clement Memorial Swimming Shack.

"He's g-g-gonna jump in the reservoir," Jim moaned.

"I'll call an ambulance!" Murphy said, heading for the caf.

Jim wiped his face with his chef's hat. "Some k-k-kids came up a minute ago to report a f-f-fire—a latrine blew up!"

"One of the latrines has *blown up?!*" Murphy pictured a LucasFilm explosion: a flaming latrine hurtling skyward (eventually achieving orbit); a blast crater a mile wide, its circumference lined with burning trees and scorched corpses.

"They r-r-rang the alarm bell and Aaron g-g-got 'em organized for a bucket brigade!"

Murphy whipped his eyes to the distant billowing smoke. "The camp could actually burn down!" he wailed.

"Dunno. I think only the l-l-latrine pit was on fire, but—"

"Only the pit? *Only* the cesspool afire?!" belched Murphy, jumping up and down. "You sure the Space Shuttle won't crash in

Lacroix Field in five minutes, with half a latrine stuck in its hull?! Should I just get the National Guard back here or what!"

"Calm down!" shouted Jim. "Call the ambulance!"

From the south, from the reservoir, a roar erupted; loud enough to rattle the windows in the caf's second story offices.

Murphy happily ran to the caf, away from this inexhaustible bad news. His brain boiled as he sped upstairs to his office.

He opened the door and fell into a bizarre indifference.

Had anyone asked Murphy last week how he'd react to opening the door to his office only to find the room awash in red paint, Murphy would've gruffly responded, "I'm not sure. Never had anything like that happen before. Why do you ask?"

Murphy *was* facing an office, belonging to him, that was awash, from wall to wall, carpet to ceiling, in red paint. His stately bookshelf, his leather-bound chair, his oaken desk, all of it—red. Distinguishing depth perception was difficult, as everything in the office was uniformly red.

And it wasn't just the color. It was paint! A toxic haze stung his eyes. The dawning sun, shining on the two painted-over windows, turned this room into an oven bearing an ungainly breakfast casserole.

The sheer preponderance of industrial oddities suffered in the last ten minutes (the past week notwithstanding) had evidently beaten Murphy's sense of shock into an apex of complete submission. He considered his reaction to this latest in a series of cataclysms. He *should* be bouncing off these veneered walls right now, tugging tight clumps of immaculately lacquered brown hair from the base of his skull with flawlessly manicured fingers. His Nike hiking boots and the L.L. Bean knee-high woolen-socked feet within should be executing Kyptonian bounds, shaking the cafeteria building to its very foundation (or, at the least, causing stucco from the ceiling of the dishroom one floor down to plop into the sinks).

Nope.

The fact that, in his head, he did *not* envision a teenaged Trooper with shoulder-length hair (who, when his cerebral dolly grip pulled the camera back, was found to be dangling from a most taunt noose) bothered Murphy greatly. Slaughtering scourgy Troopers in his mind was the man's favorite stress release. He needed to have *some* reaction to this!

Nope. Calmly, like nothing happened, Murphy walked to his desk. His Nikes went *squik-squik!* on the carpet, slipping a bit on the myriad malted milk ball-sized plastic shells littering the floor. He cursed; and when the cursing didn't produce the usual soft echo in his office, since the caked paint killed the sound waves, he cursed more, louder. The cursing felt good. He was getting pissed off. What a rush!

Both the main line's phone (the sky blue one) and his private line's phone (the red one) were now red. Unnaturally red. He blinked: the one red item in the room, the *only* one, had also been covered in red paint. He grabbed his private line phone and his hand stuck to it. Murphy knew he could never bring a sticky paint-covered handset to his ear and mouth. He also knew there were extensions down in the kitchen. But no. This was *his* office. He would use *his* phones. No simple covering in red paint would defeat him, not after all the crap that'd happened this week!

He heard a dial-tone *brrr*-ing from the handset, forcing him to think quick. He let the handset loosen in his grip, until he just pinched it with a thumb and forefinger. Then he carefully set it on the very edge of the desk. He took that same soiled forefinger and punched the button three rows down and three columns over on the uniformly red-buttoned face of the phone. There was a *boop* from the handset. Murphy poked at the button in the upper left-hand corner, but no noise came—the first button he'd hit was still down, stuck. He pressed that button again to loosen it, but that didn't work. He slapped at the button again and again, cursing again and again.

The button came loose and he didn't react in time—he hit it twice more. *Boop-boop.* He'd dialed 999. He yelled, "Fuck this!" and pushed down the hang-up buttons on the cradle.

The hang-up buttons stuck also.

The hang-up buttons are covered too! he yelled at himself. *They took the fucking phone OFF the fucking hook and fucking sloshed paint there too, to completely fucking douse it!*

Fully reaching his life's pinnacle of fury, Murphy took both hands to the phone's base, lifted it up (causing a *schhhhlooop!* noise, as there was red paint under it too), and brought the thing down on the desk with a harsh bang. Paint splattered his arms and shirt; a wayward drop bounced to his nose. The hang-up buttons *schlerp!*ed up. He heard the dial-tone again and carefully hit 9, then 1, then 1.

Instantly, muffled talk buzzed from the earpiece, which (you guessed it!) was also paint-covered. Murphy wiped off the earpiece with his fingers, shouting "Don't hang up, please! This is an actual emergency but the phone is covered with something and I can't hear you!" He wiped the mouthpiece as well and knelt down so he could lean his head near the desk edge and get his message across.

His Nikes slipped on the paintball shells and he found himself deposited, face-down, in red-saturated carpet.

Chapter 42
Ejected.

"GET UP," A voice growled.

Calvin heard it, but did not obey.

"I said 'get up,' you two—*so do it!*"

Calvin's eyes sprang open: he was in a small bed with Cindy spooned against him. She was still asleep. Light came through the green curtains in the window.

Kermit stood over them, looking as if he'd been through hell. Twice even. Dark soot marks and red paint splotches sat atop the already purple bruise on his nose and ugly black eye. His clothing and hands were black, wet, sticky with paint. His Nikes were brown with pink stains: red paint thinned by water. Kermit's stance suggested weariness, defeat, loss.

"Jesus," Calvin breathed, crossing himself under the blanket. "What happened to you?"

The Camp Director's face made the usual preamble for slits. Then it halted, frozen. With blank, wide-open eyes, the man looked at Calvin, at the softly dozing Cindy, and around Cindy's tiny room. He fetched the chair from the desk in the corner, positioned it near the bed, and sat. "What happened," he said, sighing as his legs took a break, "is the worst week of my Souviens career. Perhaps the worst in my whole life."

Calvin carefully loosened himself from the mutual embrace with Cindy. They'd been facing the wall; as he was on the outer edge of the bed, he could slip the blanket aside and sit up. He tugged at the sling to give his sore, painful right arm some relief. "You and me both, sir," the lad said wearily.

"Oh really? You at least had the benefit of female attention." Kermit leveled a gaze at Calvin; not quite the slits, just a level gaze.

"And very soon you'll leave for cozy Axzubean. *I'll* remain here, in this kettle of chaos and carnage."

Calvin kept his mouth shut.

Kermit extrapolated his knotted thoughts. "This week, I lost my subordinate, Lyons; with him my full-time dishwasher—your girlfriend there. I lost my Fix-It Man to a disastrous accident which has peeled a quarter of his skin and cooked the flesh on his left thigh. I lost my beautiful desk, my beautiful office, to some mysterious flood of red paint. I lost any respect that the camp's owner, King Richard (the Third) Grant, must have silently been giving me all this time. And this morning, while you were dozing away here in Wren's arms, the latrine at your campsite exploded."

"What?" gasped Calvin. Since Kermit had said the final few words so unexpectedly, they reached Calvin's ears as news, and his reaction betrayed no foreknowledge.

"The shingles on the roof were blown hundreds of feet away, and the walls are bent out a bit," Kermit said. "The resulting fire in the cesspool wasn't any serious threat ... but it could have been much, much worse."

Calvin blinked. "I'm not sure how!"

Kermit locked eyes with him. "You could have been *shitting* in it when it went up. If you or one of your pals had died in the explosion, we would not be calmly speaking right now."

Discreetly—since he damn well knew the answer—Calvin asked, "So what made it blow up?"

Kermit slung his chin low, trying to come up with a suitable reply. "Foul play," he said. "It's safe to assume the latrine didn't blow up for any natural reason. The fire marshal will no doubt investigate; we'll know, eventually, what did it. We know, right now, who to blame."

Calvin's eyes went wide. "Me?"

"You are far from the scene of the crime, and you willingly consort with known criminals," Kermit intoned. "Do you deny how suspicious all this looks on you, Mr. Connor?"

"Well," Calvin gulped, "I admit I've conspired on others. Recently, even. But I didn't do this!"

Kermit tested that for deceit. "So be it," he uttered, making a declaration. "But someone you know—or fought against last night—*did* do it. And so you are all being blamed for it: your Devil's Troop and Troop 73. Ranger Rick is expelling you at once; whether further action will follow is not up to me."

"And if it was?"

Kermit opened his hands. "Put yourself in my shoes, kid. What would *you* do?"

Calvin thought it over. "Have the whole lot of us all locked up. Let the coppers figure it out."

"My thoughts exactly. But Tricky Dicky decided, not me."

The kid crossed himself once more. "No offense, but thank God you didn't get your way."

"*Thank* Him?" Kermit spat. "God was behind it all!"

"Was He?" Calvin bucked.

"I've no doubt. He sent the Devil's Troop to my camp. Sent Bobby White to my parked car. Sent Lyons's fist to my face."

Calvin sat stunned at the man's dark tone, his dreadful sense of defeat. "You're saying, you got punished."

Kermit nodded.

"Begging your pardon, Mr. Murphy, but that's the worst guilt trip I've ever been privy to."

"Must be nice to still be young," Kermit mused nastily, "and *not* understand the ripple effect of one's actions."

Calvin turned away. He didn't get that, and frankly, didn't want to. He glanced at his Swatch and was momentarily puzzled to also see a silly Boba Fett watch on his wrist. "Oh, right," he said, remembering. "So. Are we to go this very second?"

"Yes. Both the evil Troops await Big Prick Rick's final shouting. The Devil's Troop didn't know where you were—nor did they seem to care—but after hearing the stories of last night's events, I knew right where you'd run to."

"Well," Calvin said, "I'm glad that *you* found me, sir."

Kermit didn't understand this, so he went on the attack: "Be glad for nothing, young man. Get the hell up! Don't you even realize what's been happening while you were here sleeping with this floozy?"

"Now I do. Thank Jesus." He raised his left hand to cross himself, held it near his face, then let it fall away. He gave Kermit a couple stern slits of his own. "I need a minute alone with Cindy first."

"With who?" Kermit bugged. He looked around, clearly expecting another teenage girl to be present.

"With Wren," Calvin corrected. "Please, sir."

The Camp Director seethed. *"One* minute." He dipped his shoulders, stood, and went out to the Ranger's office.

Calvin turned to rouse Cindy, but she was already rolling over to face him, quite awake. "You heard all that?"

"I woke up the second he came in." Cindy sat up but made sure the blanket stayed glued to her breasts. "Can't wait to never see that creep again! He just fuckin' called me a 'floozy.' What an asshole!"

They sat in bed, gazing at each other.

Then Calvin spoke. "He said he 'lost' you and your da."

"My dad quit," Cindy nodded. "I'm sorry, I didn't tell you."

"Did he punch Kermit and quit, or the other way 'round?"

"Does it matter? Good for my dad!"

"Are you off to Norwich, then?"

"We're gonna split this hellhole first thing Saturday."

"How wise is that? Then there would be *two* hellholes."

It took her a while. Once she got it, she didn't really laugh.

"Anyway," Calvin rasped. "Got some paper? And a pen?"

"Sure." He moved aside, and she climbed out of bed, taking the blanket with her. In the brief moment before she could wrap it properly around herself, Calvin saw her bare ass. The cheeks snapped out before curving down to her thighs.

He exhaled sharply at the sight.

Cindy fetched a slip of scratch paper and a pencil. She jotted two phone numbers down, tore the paper in half, and handed the blank part to him. He wrote his number and they exchanged the bits of paper.

"Do you still have the Whalers hat?" she asked.

"Gave it to Crowe, and Jon was wearing it last night. I can get it back—where should I leave it?"

"No, you keep it," she said. "Find it, get it back, and keep it. When you look at it, think of me."

He laughed, then got to his feet. They stood close. He leaned down and kissed her cheek. "Bye now," he said.

"Hang on," she said, reaching up and holding his head close to hers. Her brown eyes stared at his gray ones. "You know? You were the single ray of sunshine," she whispered, "in a summer full of rain."

Calvin smiled. "I like that," he breathed.

They giggled at each other.

Kermit and Calvin left the Ranger's Office and began the long, long walk back down to camp. Most of it was uncomfortable and silent. There was none of the usual foot-traffic on the Red Trail. Calvin feared he'd have to go all the way to Campsite Quatre, just to be told to leave at once with his Troop—and then he'd have to come all the way back to the parking lot.

Kermit sensed this. "You're not getting out of the talking-to. And *I'm* sure as hell not going all the way back there alone just to say you're at the car waiting for them."

Calvin rolled his eyes. "Can I ask you something?"

"Why not," sighed Kermit.

"You won't like it."

"I don't like anything you say, Mr. Connor. Just ask it."

"Are you such a prick with *every* Troop, or just us?"

Kermit fired off a malevolent slit (#6, *"I'll tear out your tongue!"*). "You got some nerve."

Calvin gave a shrug. "It's not about insulting you. It's about why you treated us like you did. You're the Camp Director. What about loyalty and respect and being neighborly ... all that bollocks? I haven't seen you do any of that."

"I used to do that," Kermit growled. "Oh yes, I was the living embodiment of the Attributes. I was in a Troop myself, and never wanted to leave it. And, in a way, I didn't."

"So what happened?" Calvin asked—not sarcastically, but

curiously. "I believe you, but the kid who loved his Troop isn't the man I'm talking to now. You totally hate the job."

"Jesus," Kermit snapped, "so now I have to justify my attitude—my actions—my whole life's path—to *you?* Some foreign fornicator from the Devil's Troop?"

Calvin felt a bit hot about that. "I'm just going through some shite of my own now," he raged. "And life is changing against my will. This time last week, I was healthy, had brown hair, a steady girlfriend back home, and liked being in Troop 666. Now I got none of that, and what I do have, I can't stand anymore. It's not all bad, but *sooo* much has changed." He looked over at Kermit. *"Something* happened to you at some point. And obviously, you didn't deal with it right. I just, like, don't want to become a grown-up prick."

"Like me, you mean? Holy shit!" Laughing ruefully, Kermit fired a very mean look—slits #4, *"Let me at 'im!"*—that was made all the more grisly by the man's swollen and injured face. "Only the law prevents me from punching you right now, kid!"

Calvin stopped slogging and turned to face him. "We're all alone. Who would know?"

Kermit stopped as well. He flexed his stained hands, fingers to fists to fingers. "The Devil's Troop, all right," he hissed. "You tempt me."

"You're resisting," Calvin pointed out. "Maybe it's coming from that good kid you said you used to be."

"Hardly," the man said. "The good kid I used to be hadn't yet started paying lawyers to clean up his messes."

"Like the mess you made with that cop? Sergeant White?" Calvin noted Kermit's dark reaction to these words.

Kermit exhaled with heat. He almost turned to start walking again. Almost. But the guilt, the temptation from the Devil, the idea God was punishing him, the fire, the staff quitting, his office, the storm, Kevin's gross injuries ... Kermit broke under all that weight.

The man raised the hand which had the gargantuan tee-eye-tee ring on it, closed it to a fist, and wheeled it 'round towards Calvin.

The lad took a calm step back. Kermit's punch was a clean miss, and the man nearly fell over with the follow-through. Kermit stumbled back upright, hot exhaust leaving his mouth, eyes bulging at the young tempter before him.

"Do us a favor," Calvin said flatly, "I'm Irish. You think that's the first time an adult's tried to wallop me?" He turned and started walking down the Red Trail again.

Kermit seethed for a spell, then moved his Nikes to catch up. "Okay—you want to know what changed that good kid I was into the prick grown-up I am now? You want to know the secret so it won't happen to you?"

"I would love to know," Calvin said earnestly.

"Get used to disappointment. That's it. That's all. Start to finish, life is disappointment, young man. If it wasn't for that, life would be a dream."

Kermit took a sharp breath. "If it wasn't for my goddamn sterility, I would've had a legion of sons, who would've been in a Troop too. If Bobby White hadn't been such a mean little shit who took his revenge on some punks from another Troop way too far, I would never have struck him down like I did. If my wife hadn't been a frigid bitch at heart, I'd still be married."

The man gnashed his teeth. "And on. And on. *And on.* Nothing happens like you dream it will. It always 'changes against your will.' You're just along for the ride.

"So get used to it now, Mr. Connor."

Calvin said nothing for a spell. "Wow," he breathed. "I think that's actually really good advice."

"Do what you want with it," said Kermit, casually. "You're fourteen, so there's still hope for you, I guess. Not like I give a shit." He gave a couple weak slits to Calvin. "Now do an old grown-up prick a favor, and shut the fuck up for the rest of this walk. Never speak to me again. Got it?"

Calvin did not acknowledge this command verbally.

The smell of burnt wood, water vapor, and fried shit filled the air. Many voices murmured around the bend ahead in the Green Trail. Slogging closer, Calvin came on a bright red fire engine rather rudely parked in the by-way to Campsite Quatre. The truck was as wide as the trail itself, and passing by it meant getting strafed by bushes and branches. The front right tire on the truck had been torn apart. A half-dozen men, in red helmets and brown coats with reflective yellow stripes, worked to wrap up the hoses.

The hubbubbing noise came from in front of the truck—a huge crowd of teenage boys and adult leaders huddled in Campsite Quatre's fire circle. Calvin passed the firefighters, a pile of camping gear, and stopped at a heap of plastic buckets, thirty of them at least. An actual bucket brigade happened!

Near the goat-path, he spotted his lot. Troop 666 milled on one side, heads hung. Troop 73, including a snobby, stubby adult, milled to another side, heads hung. Kermit charged by Calvin and up to Mr. Grant and Satan, who were off to another side, heads hung. Satan wasn't even standing with Mr. Grant, really: he was off to one side of one side, since he'd quit and was just playing out the string.

As Kermit reported to his boss, Calvin stopped between the milling brace of Troops. He knew he'd have to go home with Troop 666, but he didn't feel right standing with them. He saw them glance his way, heard them mutter in low tones. Father, Sandy, Inky—those guys didn't give a second look. Art hardly gave a first one—he'd been humbled. Or embarrassed. His face—normally a handsome one with soft, cinereous skin and a perfect dark brown flattop—had been made grotesque by two black eyes and a rude notch in his hair. Calvin felt squirty about that.

No one from Troop 666 approached Calvin formally. At length, he moved close to Inky. The ogre's neck bore sore marks from the throttling the night before. Calvin dug into his wallet and pulled out a dollar, tossing it to the ground at Inky's feet. "You win."

Inky didn't even look at him.

Calvin sighed—can't get a man's reaction out of Inky, not even now. "Fucking cunt," he hissed, moving himself away from Troop 666 and standing by himself.

The wind changed and wafted the unreal smell of the burnt latrine their way. "Jesus Christ," gasped Calvin, crossing himself twice.

The Camp Ranger turned to face the crowd. "We finally all present and accounted for?" he asked. Troop 666's masters made low grunts.

The snobby Troop 73 man did likewise. The Ranger spoke, his voice steeped in menace: "I want all of your asses gone by the time I turn around. You will be hearing from our attorneys. Don't ever, *ever* come back." The Ranger turned to face the woods.

Mr. Maguire plopped on his "shit-nipple" campaign hat and Oldroyd pulled the brim of his cowboy hat low. Each man gave Calvin a dark look. Troop 666 gathered up its things and slogged off. Calvin let them pass him by. Only one or two even made it apparent that they'd seen him. Young Shawn Crowe took the Whalers cap from his skull and tossed it at Calvin's feet, then stood there with his hand out. Calvin held out his left arm and let the boy undo the Boba Fett watch. He was going to say "Thanks" for the boy's help last night, but Crowe immediately left. Ryan Phillips, the last to pass by, collected Calvin's hat, dollar, and rucksack, and handed them over friendly-like. Then, without a word, Ryan slogged off.

Before starting off, Calvin glared at Mr. Dixon, Mike, and the rest of Troop 73. "Mr. Murphy," Calvin called, drawing everyone's eyes. "Might be a good idea to search *their* packs."

The dead silence of the passing Troop 666 conflicted with the dull buzz of the crowd, young boys with wide expectant faces who asked over and over, "What happened?" But Troop 666 said nothing. Calvin, passing through on his own, got the same bombardment and offered the same response.

Troop 666 slogged along, eventually curling around Centre des Trois to the Red Trail. Only roly-poly Gus glanced over his shoulder at Calvin, who followed at a distance.

Lyons came jogging up after them. "Mr. Oldroyd!" he called. The Troopmaster stopped and turned. "I have a Cell key," Lyons said. "I'll let Jon out when we reach Chamberlin."

"Shit," snapped Oldroyd. "I was lookin' forward to bustin' down the dern door!" He turned and slogged on.

Lyons got as close as Calvin, then fell in with him rather than with the Troop up ahead. "Young man," he said to the lad.

"Mr. Lyons, sir," Calvin replied. "I hear you got a good right hook."

A smirk curled on the man's heart-shaped face. "I hear you got a silver tongue. My daughter says you're a real gentleman."

"She's lying, obviously," Calvin joked meekly. "I, uh, think she's cool too. She's really great. I've never met a girl quite like her. She understands things."

"I understand things too. I understand you spent the night with her."

The words—sharp and deep, rumbling out in Lyons's sepulchral voice—practically blasted Calvin out of his Reeboks. "I won't deny it, sir," the kid stammered. "You could only have heard that from Murphy."

"Yes," Lyons said, gripping Calvin's left shoulder with a squeeze that was slightly harder than friendly. "He seemed to think it would upset me. But, I'm sure you would've told me first, given the chance." He gave a small laugh. "Don't be scared. You live way too far away to worry about ol' Deputy Director 'Satan' and his shotgun!"

Calvin struggled for a reply to that. "What gauge?"

"12 gauge. I prefer buckshot." Lyons spread his left hand's fingers. "Gives a nice penetrating spread, you know?"

"I can only hope you're kidding," Calvin gulped.

"That's right, Calvin. You can only hope."

Soon Troop 666's ranks once more included young Jon, who asked questions until he was told in no uncertain terms by his dad to shut the fuck up. Lyons took his leave and the Troop trudged to the parking lot quietly.

Calvin reached Oldroyd's Silverado and Mr. Maguire's dented blue Bronco to find the others stowing their gear. All of them glared at him.

"Shotgun," he said.

The glares grew hotter.

He opened the Bronco's passenger door nonchalantly. "12 gauge.

I prefer buckshot." He couldn't stop laughing. "Gives a nice, pene-trating spread, you know?"

Troop Hall gave off a familiar, bitter musk. Calvin inhaled it, sprouting ghosts in his mind. Many an adventure had occurred or began right in this dingy room. The felt banners, dryly skulking from the ceiling, testified to the glorious Klondike Derby wins and so on, the foreign exchange with Canada and so on, the jubilees attended and so on.

Calvin gazed up at *his* banner:

The banner would outlive him. Other banners still hung here long after those immortalized had reached the end of their mortal status. Fifty years from now, Calvin mused, some kid will look up and wonder who the hell Calvin Connor III was, and why he'd been allowed to captain the Hawk Squad.

Calvin snorted. That assumed Troop 666 survived the legal action from Camp Souviens Reservation. Or, that no Squad in its future ended up *breaking* the record.

"I gotta lock up," Oldroyd said. He stomped through the barn door and dusted off his hands. "Thought you'da split the moment we parked, considerin' your reputation now."

"After that ride," said Calvin, "I needed a moment. The whole way home, I felt like I was about to be killed."

The Troopmaster's mustache bent upward. "Ya can't duck the blame for what ya done, kid."

"Bollocks. Other than ambushing Art—that was revenge, mind you—just what did *I* do?" Calvin sighed mightily. "The only one who showed me any fairness was Mr. Maguire, even though he knew I ambushed Art. And you know what he said?"

"What's that?"

"He told me to watch my back at the next meeting. 'The next meeting!' Death, where is thy sting?!" Calvin boomed a guffaw at the bannered ceiling.

"So," Oldroyd burped, "that means yer gonna quit?"

"Already did now." Calvin made for the door.

Oldroyd gripped the lad's left shoulder. "It's always about *you,* ain't it? Think the rest of us ain't been through no shit? Hell, I thought about quittin', too!"

Calvin raised an eyebrow at his ex-Troopmaster.

"But I ain't no lily-livered Irish pussy—I'll be *damned* if I'm gonna quit now!" His voice grew loud: "This may've been the worst week of my life, but quitters never win, and winners never quit! I'm stickin' with Troop 666! And ya know why?"

Calvin shook himself loose from Oldroyd's grip. As he stepped through the doorway for the final time, he said, without turning around, "I don't care."

Oldroyd stood in the empty Hall for nigh on five minutes.

"Neither do I," he said, slogging away.

... the chronicle continues in *Foul Territory* ...

"Lowest grade, but edible"

THIS NEW EDITION (2024) revises the first (2016), preserving the original text while also fixing errata and updating minor passages to align with future works. Non-English words are no longer italicized (an editor's note that the chronicler ignored the first time around). Though I respect the current attitude of capitalizing "Black" when referencing race, it seems incongruous to my eye in a tale written and published prior to that stance (and which is also set in 1987).

The temptation to add a "deleted scene"—there are many, and the one most sorely missed is a food fight in the Centre des Trois caf—was quashed by the chronicler's memories of Jabba the Hutt's pointless and shoddy reintroduction into the 1997 Special Edition of *Star Wars*. I shall eventually publish a volume entitled *The Shite! Story and Other Devilry of Troop 666,* collecting tales short and long of the Devil's Troop, covering their entire existence from WWI to 1987 ... and it is on *those* pages that you'll finally see who fought who with which foodstuffs, and meet Assistant Troopmaster Jabba.

The body text has beet reset from its original typeface with Equity (and EQUITY CAPS) with flourishes in **CONCOURSE** and ADVOCATE. These lovely fonts were designed by and licensed from Matthew Butterick. Visit https://mbtype.com.

The chronicler didn't put a "thank you" section in the 2016 edition so let's rectify that:

"Merci mille fois!" to Nèdra Bretagne, editor and consultant extraordinaire.

Hoisting a pint to Larry and Patty of Gravel Pike Inn, for hosting the release party, and to all who attended.

I've had many advocates over the decades who cheered on my writing—Duncan "Bob" Widman, Sam Lucchese, Tony Wilkes, and Kyle Seifert—but only Jimmy Pop was famous enough to ask for a pull-quote (sorry, fellas). And I didn't even use that pull-quote (sorry, Jim).

And thanks to the reader. Some authors shoot for the stars, desiring adulation and fat checks from licensing rights. I'm much happier knowing one person—i.e., you—actually read my book.

This work is dedicated to my childhood best friend.

At age 15, Rob was diagnosed with leukemia and spent the rest of his life in and out of hospitals while also maintaining a pretty successful teenage existence: he graduated high school, went to college, had a girlfriend, drove a sweet classic convertible, and made videos with yours truly.

He was not a direct inspiration to any character here but the know-it-all sycophancy of Art Maguire to Calvin Connor is basically how I behaved towards him. Rob was the center of my teenage solar system.

He passed away in late October of 1992 and would've loved to hear his entombment was on Halloween. That was his favorite holiday.

Rob read several early versions of this work (the first draft was written in 1987) and quite enjoyed the bits about the slimy dung and condom grenades.

We miss ya, man.

Christopher Morlock
February 4, 2024

About the Author

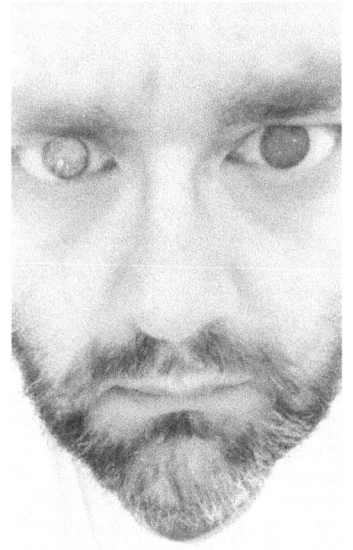

photo © 2024 CHRISTOPHER MORLOCK.

You could only dream to have a résumé as awesome as **CHRISTOPHER MORLOCK**'s. In addition to writing novels, he's run fast food joints, delivered mail, humped cable on film sets, reviewed music, sold baseball cards, edited websites, acted on television, written articles, and won poker tournaments. And at any point when he *wasn't* doing one of the above, he could be found fucking your mom.

Kindly visit www.christophermorlock.com.